Rennes-le-Chateau,

WHITE LIE

Jeanne D'Août

To Olive,
From heart to heart ♡
With love,

First Edition, August 2011
Second Edition, November 2011
Third Edition, January 2015

Rewritten and edited by Jeanne D'Août
Co-edited by Ian Campbell

All characters in this book are fictitious, with the exception of Oshu and Mariamne - who are based on the author's personal interpretation of Jesus and Mary Magdalene - and Otto Rahn, whose adventures in this book are fictional. If any of the other characters resemble real persons living, dead or fictional, it is purely coincidental. If the story line or part of the story line of this book resembles any other story lines, published or unpublished, it is purely coincidental.

This book has been printed on eco-friendly paper.

ISBN-978-2-9539396-5-1

jeannedaout.com
barincapublishing.com

*"The anxiety of mankind consists in reaching
the kingdom of the heavens..."*

Otto Rahn

-Prologue-

In ancient times, people lived their lives by omens and prophecies. Each country had its own share of prophecies. There is an ancient prophecy, for example, in Christianity, that when the end of the world is nigh, the original Ark of the Covenant must be placed in a new temple in a new Jerusalem, so that Christ can return to the earth.

Far away from ancient Egypt and Israel, the Mayan people in the Yucatan region of what we now know as Mexico, believed that the world as they knew it was going to come to an end in the year 2012 and so it was written in their calendar. In the year 2011, the world was thus divided into two groups of people: Those who believed in such prophecies and those who didn't.

Sion, Switzerland, March 2011

The large table was covered by maps, notes and dossiers. It wasn't an easy job and he knew it, but he wasn't alone. His faithful assistant and head of security, Georg Hauser, was sitting at the opposite side of the table, staring at the profile photos of two young women and their CV's.

"They check out." said Georg. "They're desperate for a job. It'll be easy."

The tall Swiss smiled, "Very good, set it up. Any news on the probe's details from Erberg?"

"It's affirmative, sir."

He was pleased. All was going according to plan. It was now time to brief Georg on their real mission. To do this, he would first have to explain an historical event that had been lost in history for over 800 years, so as soon as tea had been served, he opened a dossier with 'KT/CdC Tomar' written on the label and showed its contents to Georg.

"This is it. We were very lucky to find it. This historical account was written by a Knight Templar called Bertrand deMoye in 1201. I will tell you his story. Make yourself comfortable Georg, for it's not a bedtime story!"

The Swiss looked at Georg with serious eyes, took a deep breath and then started,

"Let me take you back to Egypt, September 1187. It had been a very bad year. Everyone in the Holy Land felt threatened by the growing power of Saladin, who managed to conquer land after land, slowly but surely surrounding the Holy Land with his armies. Then there was that dreadful battle at Hattin. Saladin had successfully defeated the crusaders and the Christian knights all knew that Jerusalem would be next. Something had to be done. The timing was also bad, especially now the Knights Templar were making such wonderful progress excavating the Temple Mount. While searching it for lost treasures, they had already found scrolls and ancient shrines, old coins, gold, silver and even relics. It had taken years to have the scrolls translated. In fact, several scrolls still had to be examined. By now, their HQ in Jerusalem had turned into a treasure house, which now created another problem: what to do with their discoveries if Jerusalem were lost? If the city were to fall into enemy hands, would Saladin destroy their heritage? For it really was *their* heritage. Many amongst the Templar knights were the sons of old noble families, who could trace their ancestry back to ancient Palestine through the heirs of Benjamin, Dan and several other lost tribes of Israel. Millennia ago, these biblical tribes had fled their homeland in search for a new home in the west. By the end of the 11th century CE, several French descendants of Benjamin would again claim the throne of Jerusalem, for it had been written in the Bible, that God had given Jerusalem to the tribe of Benjamin and that God would dwell 'between their shoulders'. Therefore, the Knights Templar, the brave warriors of the Pope, fought together with the crusader knights to conquer Jerusalem from the Saracens. They wore the red cross on their white tunics so as to distinguish the covenant with their family heritage, for the cross symbolised God's presence. The elite of the order felt it was their holy mission to conquer Jerusalem from the Saracens and to keep it until the 'End of Time'.

However, as soon as they had conquered the city, they knew they wouldn't be able to hold it forever. Their ancestors had hidden many items underneath the Temple mount and the Templars realised they had to find another safe haven for their treasure. Neither King nor Pope could force them to surrender their possessions, so their finds were kept secret. However, with Saladin now marching toward Jerusalem, the time had come to take all of their finds to a safer place."

The Swiss cleared his throat, ran his hand through his short blonde hair and continued,
"The secret mission of the Knights Templar was not an easy one. Not only did they need to find a safe place for their precious treasure - there was also the prophecy. A prophecy that spoke about the 'End of Time'. Sickness, wars and natural disasters would torment the world they lived in and they felt that this time was now upon them. It all made sense. The prophecy spoke of a battle between the white army and the black army, so they saw themselves as the white army, wearing white clothes and the army of Saladin as the black army, wearing black clothes. Furthermore, the prophecy spoke of a New Jerusalem coming from Heaven and a Grand Monarch, who would ensure peace for a thousand years. Unfortunately, the Grand Monarch of Jerusalem had been captured by the enemy, so it didn't look too good for the white army and because Jerusalem was important for the fulfilling of this prophecy, they had no choice but to symbolically build a new one elsewhere. However, there remained another problem: the prophecy didn't only speak of a New Jerusalem, it also spoke of the lost Ark of the Covenant, which had to be found and placed in a rebuilt temple. Only if this was done, would Christ return to the earth. To make this work, they all agreed that they had to find the Ark of the Covenant first and then create a new Jerusalem, so they could place the Ark in the new temple and prepare for Jesus' Second Coming."

"However, so far they had failed to find the ancient gilded chest of Moses. A Templar knight named Bertrand deMoye had searched for it deep underneath the Temple Mount in Jerusalem, only to discover that it wasn't there. However, he did find the white marble slab it had rested on. The scroll they had discovered on that spot, however, mentioned that the Ark had been taken to a realm south of Egypt, called India. We now know that this was Nubia. Obviously, Bertrand, who had been in charge of finding the Ark, had been demoralised, but then, something incredible happened. During one of the evening meals at the Royal Court in Jerusalem, Bertrand met a young King called Gebre Mesqel Lalibela, who had fled from his country. Lalibela was enjoying the hospitality at the court of the King of Jerusalem and during that particular evening meal he told Bertrand how his own kingdom was ruled by a usurper. As soon as Bertrand learnt that Lalibela had originally come from a land south of Egypt, he asked him if he had ever heard of an ancient relic called the Ark of the Covenant, a gilded chest that was once brought to a country - probably called India - many centuries before Bertrand's time. To his immense surprise, the deposed King assured him that this relic was in fact in Roha, his hometown, so Lalibela promised that if he and his men helped him regain his throne, he would show it to them. 'What coincidence!' Bertrand thought. 'This could only have been God's work!'

Lalibela had spoken the truth. His father was the man called Jan Seyum, a Priest King whom we have identified as the legendary Prester John. After Jan's death, his mother had wanted Lalibela to become the new King. After all, the priests - who were called 'the bees' for their service and work - had named him Lalibela - 'chosen by the bees'; a royal title. However, his brother, Kedus Harbey, had become jealous and had even tried to poison him. Afraid of his brother, Lalibela had therefore fled north to Jerusalem, the city of his ancestor; Solomon.

Excited about this unbelievable coincidence, Bertrand immediately explained to Lalibela their most secret and sacred mission and within minutes, both men came to an agreement. Because the Ark had to be placed inside the sacred temple in a new Jerusalem, they decided to help Lalibela re-conquer his city and recreate Jerusalem in Roha."

The Swiss got up from his chair and poured himself and Georg another cup of tea. Being in charge of a large, secret organisation is a heavy task, but it had its advantages; advantages like superb Intelligence. Clearly enchanted by the hitherto unknown story he was sharing, the Swiss continued, "A few days later, Bertrand's caravan of knights, including Lalibela, had eagerly started their journey south. There were thirty of them; some were just boys, while others were much older men. The rest of the group consisted of strong and well trained men. They had brought with them several horse drawn wagons with priceless artefacts; documents; relics; gold coins; all hidden away in sacks filled with grain. The stale sweat and dirt accumulated from weeks of travelling saturated their heavy riding clothes and the knights smelt horrible. As soon as they entered the region of the Nile's delta, they encountered a new enemy; malaria. They were plagued by swarms of mosquitoes and various other insects, so it was no surprise when one day, one of the knights fell off his horse, delirious and trembling with fever. Surrendering to his fate, he looked at Bertrand, begging his commander to kill him and get his ordeal over with, for he understood the alternative; they would not take him along with them, because he might infect the others and the thought of dying a lonely, slow death, perhaps even being killed and eaten by wild animals, made him shiver. So, after saying their goodbyes and prayers, Bertrand took out his sword and decapitated his brother knight, after which the corpse was burned."

"You know, Georg, they may have been used to being in bloody battles for years, but to kill a brother was very different. Understandably, the heavy-hearted group of knights prayed for a while and then continued their journey south, hoping no one else would get sick. It was a dangerous disease, spread by the mosquitos that seemed to thrive in the heat and the unhygienic circumstances of the knights, who slept in their clothes and hardly ever bathed. One of the members of the group suggested that they should bathe in the river to cleanse themselves of the stale sweat that attracted the mosquitoes. However, one of the rules of their order forbade them to be nude, so they decided to bathe with their clothes on. Meanwhile, also the horses refreshed themselves in the Nile river and drank their fill, but then, something horrible happened. Within minutes, strange ripples in the water at the other side of the river indicated that they had been noticed by an unwanted audience. Undetected by the bathing knights, a group of crocodiles silently approached them - their eyes and noses just above the surface of the water. The attack was sudden, relentless and without quarter. Three horses and five men were killed before the survivors got out of the water, which had turned red with blood. The injured men were shouting and screaming and were quickly carried away to a safe spot by their unscathed brothers. They had never seen such beasts before in their lives. Two knights managed to kill several of the crocodiles with their swords. Others threw rocks into the water to frighten the rest of the monsters away."

"A few hours later, when the knights had calmed down, they set up camp at a safe distance from the river. During the night, another brother died from his wounds. His belly had been perforated by the teeth of one of the monsters and the bleeding wouldn't stop. It reminded them of battle, but they were less afraid of the armies of Saladin than of these horrible beasts from hell that seemed to have just appeared out of nowhere."

"They stayed in the area for two days. Being weak and hungry, they killed and ate the wounded horses. For the owners of the fated horses, this was the final setback, as the knights all loved their mounts. A deep sadness - a feeling of loss and hopelessness - came upon them during those few days."

"After the knights had regained their strength, they continued their journey south and Lalibela showed the knights the way to the royal city of Roha. He was excited to go back to his own country and regain control. Together with the Templars, Lalibela successfully conquered the town and chased away the usurpers, after which he reclaimed his throne. The Templars had kept their word and so would Lalibela."

"In the years that followed, the Templars built a new Temple and consecrated the New Jerusalem. To celebrate this event, they created an elaborate ritual and planned to replace the Ark of the Covenant in the newly built Holy of Holies on January 17th, 1189. However, after 2500 years, the wooden parts of the ancient gilded chest were in very poor condition. Most of the wood had rotted away and only the specially made ropes were holding the container together. In fact, only the solid golden lid with the two cherubs had survived the centuries, intact."

"The young priest, who had taken care of the Ark until that moment, had carefully removed the lid, enabling the knights to take exact measurements, so they could rebuild the chest in such way, that the golden lid would fit exactly on top of the new Ark. The contents of the Ark - which were now wrapped in cloth - were kept elsewhere in the Temple during its restoration. After that, a goldsmith gently attached fresh gold layers onto the new chest. To prepare for Christ's Second Coming, the knights even put two statues to the left and right of the newly built shrine for the Ark; men-gods with the head of an ox and the head of a donkey, referring to Jesus' first manger. They carved their Templar cross - the sign of Benjamin - above the shrine, representing Jerusalem.

Now, all was ready to fetch the Ark from its old resting place and put it into the new Temple."

The Swiss opened a second file and leafed through the papers to find certain details. When he found what he was looking for, he continued with devotion,

"On January 17th, Bertrand and his team joined the people of Roha at the old Temple, where the Ark had been kept during the previous centuries. Only Lalibela, Bertrand, five other knights and the local guardian of the Ark were present inside the Temple. There it was; the Ark, almost restored to its former glory. They now only needed to restore the sacred contents to the chest and close the lid. Inside the Ark, the Spirit of God was present in the form of an amazing glowing rock. However, it was the combination of this rock with the cherubs on the lid that would prove to be dangerous. Suddenly, a blue-coloured, electric flash, which had originated from the centre of the lid, instantly killed the knight who wanted to put the sacred rock inside the chest. Unfortunately for him, he had taken no notice of the nervous waving and protesting of the guardian of the Ark. Actually, the knight had thought that the priest himself was keen on this honour and had waved in protest. The event had frightened them all into silence. When they inspected the dead body, they noticed that the blade of the knight's sword had somehow burned a deep, black wound in his thigh. The sword had probably guided the electric force that had come off the lid. Finally understanding the guardian's intentions, the knights all quickly removed from their bodies everything that was made of metal. In the commotion, the glowing rock had fallen onto the floor and had been picked up by a dog. The knights would never forget how the dog walked up to Bertrand and dropped it on the floor in front of him. Again, Bertrand felt that this had to be God's work. Unafraid and full of faith, Bertrand volunteered to place the rock inside the chest and when he closed the lid, he only felt a slight sensation going through his body.

With highest respect and solemn humility they all bowed before the Ark and prayed. Then, the chest was carried out by four knights and the guardian, who took the lead. Though covered with a thick cloth, the Ark was shown to all those who were present during its journey to the new Holy of Holies in the new Temple, where it was carefully placed. Afterward, the people blessed the water of the river and renamed it after the river Jordan. Obviously, the sacred burial of the knight who was killed by the rock - killed as if by the 'Power of God' - overshadowed the festivities that would keep the locals dancing and singing for many days and the Templars decided to give this knight - this hero - a special status and a new name to remember him by, for this knight had done many a noble deed in the past. Before he had joined the order, he had even walked from his hometown in France to Santiago de Compostela in Galicia, northern Spain. He had been the eldest son of one of the greatest men the order had ever known and deserved to be remembered as the one who had died for their sacred cause. From that moment on, they would call him the Knight of the Holy Rock, or Roch. Little did they know that this knight would not go into history as the Knight of the Holy Rock. His identity would get mixed up with a later saint and the only historical facts that would survive in some form in his legend were his name; Sir Roch; the rock inside the dog's mouth; the wound on his leg and - occasionally - his Templar identity (the red cross) and the memory of his pilgrimage to Santiago de Compostela. As he was now special to the knights, they buried him in a sarcophagus, instead of giving him the customary cremation."

Georg shook his head when his chief paused. Then, the Swiss got up from his chair and walked to the window. He gazed out through the leaded glass window and continued somewhat cynically,
"Of course they had to make up some rules. The Holy of Holies was only to be entered by the special guardian, whose

job it was to let no-one touch the Ark. Its contents were dangerous and it required great caution to safely approach the ancient chest. The knights felt that their mission was now over and they stayed in Roha - the New Jerusalem - for several years as special guests of Lalibela. However, Lalibela had broken one promise; he had not renamed the city after Jerusalem. Instead, he had renamed it after himself. On top of that, the cultural differences between the Europeans and the Ethiopians had resulted in several violent encounters, which had spoilt relations between the knights and the local people. Although several knights had married local women, others had expressed their desire to leave. Needless to say that all of them were longing to find out what had happened to the real Jerusalem in Judea - a city that was, in spite of everything, still in the hearts of these warrior monks. Perhaps a miracle had happened and Jerusalem was again in Christian hands? There was new hope, so one day, Bertrand organised a journey back to the North, but this is where it became tricky, as they didn't want to leave without the Ark, so secretly - during night time - they made a copy of the Ark and its contents. After this was done, they drugged the guardian of the Temple where the Ark was kept and sneaked away on a dark night."

He turned around again to face Georg and chuckled,
"A hundred years would pass before a guardian even noticed that the Ark in the Holy of Holies in Lalibela was not the original one. Immediately upon this discovery, the Archbishop of Ethiopia sent an official delegation of thirty men to the Pope in Avignon, requesting him to give the original Ark back to the people of Lalibela. Of course, the Pope in Avignon had no idea what they were talking about, for he didn't know that the Templars had taken the Ark. You see, Georg, this information has been kept from the Church and the Kings of Europe from the moment it arrived in France in 1199, up to the present day."

Georg was just about to comment on the story when his chief raised his hand.

"I'm not finished yet. The journey of the Knights Templar to the north with all their possessions was again a long one. They had much respect for the Holy Ark, so they took their time. Sometimes they stayed at certain places longer than necessary. Somehow, the Ark gave them a feeling of safety and power. It was as if the Ark itself represented Jerusalem. Therefore, all the places they travelled through felt like home. The group even became silent and solemn. They prayed and meditated many times and their conduct was impeccable. The knights stayed several months on an island in the Nile called Elephantine, from where they hoped to sail to Alexandria. On Elephantine they rebuilt the small sacred shrine for the Ark at the exact spot where it had once stood on its journey south, which was around 640 BCE. It was during this stay on the island that things started to go wrong. News of the Templars' presence on Elephantine had spread like wild-fire and eventually they had to leave the island in a hurry, because they were afraid for the safety of their cargo. They managed to purchase several feluccas and sailed downstream toward the coast of Egypt. When they arrived in Alexandria, they met a small group of tradesmen, preparing to sail for Cyprus. However, the news these sailors shared with the knights was far from positive. Jerusalem had again fallen into enemy hands. It was even said that the Holy City would never again be in Christian hands, because the Christian world had given it up. One of the tradesmen explained what had happened after the battle of Hattin. He spoke of the loss of Jerusalem to Saladin and how the German Teutonic Knights had now gained control over Acre. However, Pope Innocentius had shown his loyalty to the Knights Templar and not only confirmed their old privileges, he had even given them new ones. The merchant went on to explain that there had been one more, unsuccessful Crusade, but that Saladin had been killed in 1193. The good news was, that king Richard of England had sold Cyprus to the Templar

Order for 100,000 gold Byzantiums, so the Kingdom of Jerusalem - reigned over by the Lusignans - was now based on Cyprus.

Bertrand understood what had to be done. They had to sail to Cyprus. The merchant welcomed him on his ship, knowing that the knights would defend it free of charge in case of a hostile encounter during the journey. Fortunately, the journey went well and after their arrival at the port of Amathus, the knights travelled directly to Kallinikisis, the island's capital. The Templars called it Nikosia, because neither of them could pronounce - let alone write - the real name. They headed for the old palace that had been built by noblemen at the time of Alexander the Great. Because King Amalric was in Acre, the palace itself was in poor condition and the people who lived on the island had become hostile towards the knights, so when our group of knights arrived, they were greeted with anger. The locals even threw rocks at them and scared the horses. It was clear that the Templars were not very popular on this island. Bertrand decided to keep his eyes open and find a way off the island as soon as possible, preferably to France. Some of the men were hoping to go back to their families and became restless, so although Bertrand accepted the hospitality from the local lord of Nikosia, he sent an urgent message to Sir Gilbert Horal, the new Grandmaster of the Knights Templar Order, seeking his help in getting the precious cargo to safety. Within a month he received a reply from Horal, saying that he was most welcome at the Templar headquarters at Caucoliberis. Within two days, Bertrand and his knights boarded a Templar ship and sailed to France."

"When the Templar ship entered the port of Caucoliberis, they were received with honour by Sir Gilbert and his knights, who escorted them to the royal fortress. Throughout the evening, Bertrand and Horal discussed the details of the knights' adventures. Feeling comfortable, Bertrand revealed his sacred mission and the identity of their cargo, which, during the darkness of the night, was taken off the ship and put into small boats. All of the treasure, including the Ark, was brought safely into the Templar fortress through an underground passage. Bertrand felt he could trust Horal, who was an honourable man and a worthy Grandmaster, so together they made plans to seek a hiding place for the items that had come from the Holy Land and a special place to house the Ark of the Covenant. As this was a secret they could not share with anyone, neither with the King of France, nor with the King of Aragon and most certainly not with the Pope, all of the knights who had come from Outre-Mèr - the other side of the sea - were sworn to secrecy."

"Of course, there are always witnesses. Some villagers had seen the small boats moving silently in the night, secretly bringing cargo into the fortress and it wouldn't take long before the inhabitants of Caucoliberis spread the rumour that the Knights Templar had brought to France a treasure from the Holy Land. However, none of these people could possibly know that among this treasure was something so unique, so precious and so holy, that it was important to keep it hidden; for example in a church vault, a cave or a crypt. Finding a suitable hiding place for the Templar treasure had become their greatest concern, but then Horal remembered a Templar who resided deep into the country in a white, fortified tower that stood at the top of a hollow mountain in an area considered sacred already by the Celts, who had lived there before the Romans had invaded Gaul. However, in the days of our good knight Bertrand, which was around 1200 CE, count Raymond Roger of Trencavel ruled the Razès. He had been tutored by lord Bertrand of Saissac and his lands spread from Albi to Beziers and from Carcassonne to the high mountains of the Pyrenees. Raymond Roger had succeeded his father at a young age and these lands of the Razès were his responsibility. He was also a friend of the Knights Templar who lived on his lands. Therefore, Sir Gilbert Horal reached out to Lord Trencavel and together they decided to divide the treasure into thirteen lots, the thirteenth being the Ark. Carefully they wrote down its whereabouts in a secret code known only to those who were involved. Some items of the treasure weren't really hidden, but simply kept in the possession of several lords. Among these items were the scrolls the Templars had collected in the Holy Land. Some of these scrolls were genealogical family trees, while others contained the wisdom of the Kabala, the Hermetic Teachings and the words of Mani, but there were also certain scrolls that caused commotion the moment they were first translated, for these scrolls contained information that was completely different from what had always been taught by the Church. This new knowledge challenged their belief and it would lead to another mission; a mission that would result in the construction of a huge stronghold a few miles south of the ancient site of Mount Carmel in the Holy Land, where the Knights Templar started a new search: The search for a lost tomb…"

The Swiss was silent for a moment and stared hard at Georg. Then he asked in a monotone voice,
"Are you aware of the true nature of our mission, Georg?"
Georg nodded, but couldn't utter a single word. His throat had gone dry the moment it had become clear to him. Georg looked at his employer, who was clearly enjoying the moment; the beginning of a rather special mission. Then he looked at another dossier on the table; a dossier labelled 'THULE/SS/OWR'.
Then, in one smooth move, the Swiss took the file and got up from his chair.
"Alright, let's bring him in."

1

Philadelphia, USA, June 19th 2011

She was as white as a sheet when she raced to the bathroom to throw up in the toilet. "Oh God, oh no, I can't believe this!" she uttered in disbelief. Her throat was hoarse and tears begun rolling down her cheeks. She had never expected to get pregnant. Slowly she got up to turn on the shower and when the room had filled up with steam, she took off her clothes and stepped underneath the soothing waterfall, wishing feverishly that it would wash everything away. Because of the constant rush of the water, she couldn't hear the phone, which rang twice before the old-fashioned answering machine picked it up.

"This is Danielle, can't answer the phone right now, please leave a message after the bell."

Instead of the customary beep, a loud church bell chimed. On the other end of the line, Gabby held her phone an arm length away before she left her message.
"Hey Danny, it's me, Gabby. Are you there?"
After a long silence, Gabby said, "Thank God" and hung up.
Meanwhile, Danielle enjoyed her hot shower. She was home now and thought that from now on, she could pretend that life will go on like before. However, when reality hit home, she started crying uncontrollably and slowly sank down to her knees. How could she think that life would ever be the same again? Her heart was so heavy, so pain filled and now her strength had finally deserted her. After having been so strong all along, she now finally let it all out. After what seemed like hours, she got out of the shower and decided to go to bed; to sleep; to forget. She'd think of a plan when she wakes up. 'Everything will feel better in the morning,' she thought. It always does, but life has its unexpected twists.
While she was busy blow-drying her hair, she couldn't hear the front door opening and three men entering her bedroom.

When Danielle finally opened the bathroom door, the first thing she noticed was that her bag had gone from the bed. Then she saw how her bed was made up very neatly, not the way she had left it before going into the bathroom. She didn't even have time to scream when a tall, thin man suddenly put his gloved hand over her mouth and nose, while one of the others injected her with something that made her collapse into the man's arms immediately. They wrapped her in a carpet; put the room back in order as if no one had been there for some time; took away the answering machine and left the building, making sure they weren't seen.

The next day, Gabby tried to phone Danielle again, just to check one more time if her friend had really been so stupid as to go home, as she had said she would. When Gabby had called the day before, she had been so relieved to hear Danielle's answering machine, hoping that she really wasn't there, but now, the answering machine didn't pick up at all. She became worried. Third ring, fourth ring.., still no answering machine. She froze. This could only mean one thing: If Danielle had indeed gone home, then they must have taken her as well as her answering machine. Gabby knew that she too would be in great danger if they had indeed found Danielle. They would surely make her talk. She raced to her bedroom and started packing and within half an hour she was on her way to the airport, leaving behind the apartment she had only just moved into, knowing that she might never return.

It had all started four weeks earlier, on Saturday, May 21st 2011. Gabby and Danielle had met during a lecture about time travel in New York. They had responded to a personal invitation for this lecture, which included a private interview with the professor, who had two positions to offer for an exciting new project he was working on. They had found the subject so intriguing, that they simply couldn't resist going and as they hadn't been able to find solid jobs so far, they couldn't afford not to go. Although both women came from different hometowns to hear Professor William Fairfax speak, the professor had made sure that they were seated next to each other during his lecture. Within minutes, the women had been engaged in conversation and Danielle and Gabby realised how good it was to finally have someone to talk to, especially when you have special interests that only a few people share with you. However, there was one strange coincidence: Gabby and Danielle had both lost their parents and all living relatives, albeit in different circumstances. Neither of them had any family members left.

They were both alone in the world.

With her mother dying as she gave birth to her, Danielle's family had consisted of a father and one aunt. Her father had recently died of cancer and his sister had already died in a tragic car accident in Greece when Danielle had been four years old. Gabby's parents had died in a skiing accident only a few years before. An avalanche had overwhelmed them and four others in the Rocky Mountains. Having no brothers or sisters to share her grief with, Gabby had been heartbroken. Only recently had she started to venture out more.

Both women were completely alone; without a single relative and this knowledge made them feel connected. However, they didn't realise at the time that this was exactly why they had been chosen.

No one would miss them.

Danielle and Gabby were both in their late twenties; single and attractive. Philadelphia-born Danielle Parker was a stunning beauty with long blonde hair and a big fan of romantic novels and films. She had loved her years at the University, majoring in ancient languages and general science. Gabby Standford, who was born in Washington DC, North Carolina, had studied astronomy and history. Gabby was a little plump around the hips because she enjoyed cooking. She had a warm personality and was smart and attractive with her short, dark brown hair and cynical sense of humour.

Both women had enjoyed the evening. It had been a brilliant lecture on the nature of wormholes, time and space. The professor who had given the lecture was a short, young man with dark, slick-back hair and black, large-framed Burberry eyeglasses that made him look older than he was. Gabby had joked that he looked like the Leonard character from the Big Bang Theory sitcom - though a bit older - and she half-expected Sheldon to suddenly appear to 'correct' the professor on a topic. Why is it, that some people with huge brains are different looking, nerdy or a bit strange? Maybe most of the energy had gone to the head and had left no room for looks or smooth behaviour, she thought. During their meeting after the show they had noticed the professor's clumsy behaviour toward women, but he had seemed friendly and they had been very impressed by his knowledge and enthusiasm.

Then he had made them a job offer they couldn't resist.

William Fairfax, professor of quantum theory, cosmologist and specialist in wormhole theory, had discovered a revolutionary new concept, allowing objects to travel through time, backward and back to the present, completely safely and without any unwanted echoes. So far, Universities had always come up some kind of excuse to deny him the possibility to create the required machine, so he had eagerly accepted the offer from an unknown employer to materialise his invention in a secret laboratory underneath the fortified church of Valère in Sion, Switzerland. No questions had been asked and immediately, contracts had been signed to ensure secrecy. Fairfax had been impressed with his new laboratory, which was actually only a small part of a huge underground structure, consisting of several meeting rooms and private quarters for employees, who stayed at the base full-time. It was well-organised, with a large canteen and comfortable private quarters for himself as well to live in. One wing was permanently closed off. It was a forbidden zone, used only by his employer. The professor had been able to work on the project whenever he wanted and had even been given an assistant; Ms Elsa Kaiser. Then, one day, it had happened. A probe had successfully been launched through what was now called the Einstein-Rosen-Fairfax Bridge.* The professor had finally succeeded in finding a way to keep the wormhole open and stable, using a method web designers would call a *spacer.gif*. He had also successfully reversed the entrance and exit of the wormhole after programming the exact moment into the timer on the probe, which would then activate the necessary code for its return journey. To everyone's great relief, the probe had returned in one piece. The next step was to send a probe with a mouse inside. The little creature had been unconscious, but still alive on its return to the ERFAB, which was situated in the underground lab. Tests on the mouse had only showed a peak of high blood pressure during the trip, but all vital signs had gone back to normal after a few hours.

After this first success, Fairfax had been asked by his employer - with whom he only had contact by phone - to interview two carefully chosen people, who would be perfect for their first project; real people, able to return to a co-ordinate location at a specific moment in time. This was the advantage of sending people, as animals would certainly wander off.

As soon as these carefully selected women had successfully been lured to the professor's lecture in New York, Fairfax had offered them the jobs. To persuade Danielle and Gabby to accept, he had offered to treat them to a trip to his 'world famous laboratory' in Switzerland, on an 'all expenses paid' basis. Of course, Danielle and Gabby had taken the bait. However, at that time - now four weeks ago - they had no idea that they were about to get dragged into a dangerous adventure the moment they had stepped into the professor's Bordeaux-red Dodge Sprinter car, heading for the airport.

The Einstein-Rosen Bridge is the old name of a wormhole. Albert Einstein and his collaborator Nathan Rosen came up with the wormhole theory in the early 20th century.

Still unconscious and securely tied up, Danielle was sitting on the back seat of a black limousine, leaning against the shoulder of a man she knew all too well. Cardinal Antonio Sardis was 67 years old and very solemn. He didn't eat much and was therefore very thin, causing his face to be long and white with hollow cheeks. His grey hair was short and the top of his head was covered by a small, red *zucchetto*. He wore a large necklace with a heavy golden cross, which was inlaid with amethysts. His large brown eyes were staring at the pages of a diary. Danielle's diary.

2

Diary entry - Sion, Switzerland, May 23rd 2011

I never thought I'd live to see this day! It is possible! Time travel is really possible! We were invited by professor Bill Fairfax to accompany him on a trip to Switzerland. We almost couldn't go, because there had been another volcanic eruption on Iceland and a big ash cloud had formed, but the flight took off anyway. We are going to visit the laboratory to see his invention. He is looking for assistants with degrees in history, ancient languages and astronomy for a new program and he has asked us if we would be interested. Gabby said it would be an interesting experience; the chance of a life time. Tomorrow we will have lunch with the professor and afterward he will show us the time machine. I am very tempted to accept the offer.

Philadelphia, USA, June 19th 2011

Sardis stared at the woman who was just waking up. He felt her moving and heard the change in her breathing. He smiled at her; closed the diary - his thumb in between the pages and put his other arm around her.

"Don't worry, beautiful one," he said, while he touched her cheek with his cold, bony hand. "Don't be afraid, I will make sure you don't get hurt, but please don't try to escape. You'd be lost out there. I have erased your entire digital databank, you see? No one will know you have ever existed. Your life as Danielle Parker is over. Now you are mine, but I will take very good care of you."

Danielle looked at him in horror. "Erased my databank? What do you mean?" She could feel the blood draining from her head and her heart raced as she began to realise the seriousness of this matter.

As if he enjoyed sharing this news with his victim, Sardis continued, "You no longer exist. You have no passport, no social security number and your name has been erased from all computers. For example, you no longer have a bank account, not even a house. No one will be able to give you shelter, money or a job, because you simply do not exist, but not to worry, I will give you a place to live and everything you need and when your child is born, I will raise it as my own."

Sardis smiled when she stared back at him with wide eyes and open mouth, expressing utter horror and fear. How did he know she was pregnant? She had only realised it herself a few hours ago. How could he do this to her; erase her existence just like that! Now completely depending on him, she had become his possession. Danielle panicked and with her tied hands she started to bang on the car window, screaming for help. Startled by her sudden panic attack, Sardis tried to stop her from hurting herself.

"Stop it, stop it! The windows of this car are tinted; no one can see you. No one can hear you. Come now, calm down, it is for your own good that we are doing this. I was supposed to eliminate you a few hours ago. No one knows you are still alive. You're only alive because I wish it!"

Sardis spoke the truth. His partner had wanted him to get rid of the woman because she knew too much, but the Cardinal could never do such a thing. Besides, he had discovered her secret.

Danielle stared forward at the Plexiglas partition that separated her from the driver, blocking all sounds. Her vision was still blurred from the drug and she was exhausted. She hadn't had any peace since she had left Switzerland and slowly but surely she began to understand that the life she had known was permanently over. Danielle feared she'd become a zombie and be kept alive only because she was with child. It was the child they wanted, she thought. Her face turned white as another thought entered her mind.

'How did he know?'

Then she saw what the man who had abducted her was doing. He was reading her diary.

Diary entry - Sion, Switzerland, May 24th 2011

We are so excited! In about an hour, someone will pick us up with a company car and escort us to the laboratory, where Bill will show us his time machine. He calls it the ERFAB (Einstein-Rosen-Fairfax-Bridge). I have no idea what to expect. Actually, I do not understand the difficult theory he tried to explain yesterday and how he was able to get images on screen of historical events with the aid of a probe. He said he still had to work on the clarity and sharpness of the images, but he told us how thrilled he was when he first saw scenes from the past, as if he was looking at an old videotape. He said he'd show us the machine and the screen and perhaps we could even send a probe to a certain date in time and with co-ordinates to a specific location, just to see if something would show. His first try-out will be to go back in time to ancient Judea to find out if Jesus really existed and to see what he looked like! If it works, we will be very privileged. Tonight I will write in my diary. Maybe by then I will know.

Philadelphia, USA, June 19th 2011

Cardinal Sardis had a look in his eyes, that Danielle could not fathom. He looked at her and at her belly and a broad smile spread over his face. After a deep sigh he turned toward Danielle and bent over slightly, so that his face was close to hers. She breathed with short and sharp intakes, terrified of this man who had hunted her down for weeks and who had finally found her. She wondered if he would kill her after she had given birth? If he'd actually be capable of murdering someone with his own hands. A Cardinal? She couldn't believe he would actually do such a thing, but then, history was full of violent acts that were commissioned by the Church.

His hands touched her belly. Then he took her tied hands in his own and kissed them.

"I'm sure that soon, you and I will get along very well, my beautiful one. As soon as you realise your position and come to terms with it, you will know that you must accept the warm love I am offering you. Because if you displease me, you will quickly learn that I can also displease you."

Sardis turned away from her and picked up the diary again. He leafed through it and returned to the page he had been reading before.

Diary entry - Jerusalem, Judea, 32 AD

I am so glad I took along my diary and a pen, because this is unbelievable. After sending the probe, Bill had showed us several images and when we finally saw someone who could be Jesus, there was no stopping us from becoming the first people to enter the time machine and see him in the flesh! So, we've accepted the positions!

Two days later we were sent to location 31°27'55.3"N 35°08'27.6"E . We carried a small device that looks like a telephone. We were so excited. Gabby said she wanted to give Jesus a hug that would go into history! We laughed our heads off fantasising how we could end up in the gospels if we misbehaved.

When we arrived, we were absolutely shocked. It was hot and I couldn't understand a single word they were saying. Lots of people were grubby and they had the worst sets of teeth I had ever seen. Luckily we were dressed to blend in before we went through the time machine.

I must say that time travel sort of sucks your lungs out. I felt rather sick afterward and Gabby even had to vomit. It also took us about an hour to get over our fierce headaches.

So I don't think it is healthy to travel through time, but never mind that. I do hope we will be able to get back again.

We went to a bathing site near the temple of Asculapius. People go there when they are ill. It's a kind of hospital. You won't believe the state some people are in. Then we saw him. He had a warm, broad smile, his moves were slow and he looked like a guru from India. Smile and all. This had to be the man whom we know as Jesus. He's very charismatic. Gabby just melted and I almost collapsed when she suddenly said. 'Oh Christ look at that hairdo!' We just couldn't stop laughing, even if we tried. Of course we attracted attention big time. I guess we were the only ones in such a good mood. When he stared at us, we froze. He waved at us, asking us to come closer. As if hypnotised, we approached him and then, suddenly, Gabby fainted; probably still her blood pressure. Oh brother, what a time to faint.

I'm not quite sure what people called him, some called him Rabuni and others called him Oshu. I like the sound of the name Oshu. He smiled at everyone and when my eyes met his up close, it was my time to melt. He had these beautiful hazel eyes, not the blue ones we often see in art. They were green-brown and very light, as if he stared right through me, right through to my inner soul. He also had brown hair, not blonde.

Gabby was slowly getting back on her feet again when he touched her. The whole crowd went 'ahhhhh', as if he had done something really amazing. We sat at his feet while he was talking and we couldn't understand a word he was saying, but it sounded like heaven! We were glued to the spot and our eyes were glued to his appearance. The crowd suddenly reacted to something he said and then he left with his little group of six or seven people. No one was allowed close to him while he was bathing.

Well, that was the end of our incredible experience, so we returned to the exact spot where we will be teleported back to the 21st century. This is where we are now; waiting.

I will never forget this day, or his eyes. I really must learn the language and return. As requested, I have added a few items to my diary, like seeds and a few tree leaves.

3

Philadelphia, USA, June 20th 2011

Gabby had taken the first flight out of Washington DC to Philadelphia, Pennsylvania and had just arrived in Fairmount to check out Danielle's apartment. Before she rang the bell, she took a good look around to make sure no one was waiting for her. She also checked the cars to see if anyone had parked outside the building, hiding in the car, but all seemed to be safe.

She almost jumped when she heard a sound behind her. It was an old lady with her keys, ready to open up the door that gave access to the apartment block. The lady frowned at her and said, "Can I help you sweetheart?"

"No, thanks. Yes, wait! Please, have you seen my friend, Danielle Parker? She lives on the second floor in number 8."

The old lady paused and thought for a moment. Then she said with determination, "There were men going into number 8 the other day, I remember seeing them in the hallway, but I haven't seen your friend, I'm sorry…" The old lady opened the door and wanted to close it behind her when Gabby stopped her.

"Please let me in, I need to see if she is alright? She doesn't answer her doorbell."

The woman hesitated for a moment, but then let her through. However, she couldn't hide her curiosity, so she followed Gabby to number 8. The door was closed and there were no signs of a forced entry, only a small note saying: 'for rent'. Gabby was worried. If she isn't here and her answering machine is turned off, then where is she? - and who were the men in the hallway?

"Can you describe the men you saw entering this apartment, ma'am?"

"They were dressed in suits, but one of them was wearing a robe and a little red cap. I though he looked like the Pope!" she added with a chuckle.

Oh my God, the Cardinal! He has found her!

She raced out of the building and into the taxi that was still waiting for her and asked the driver to take her back to the airport. During the drive, Gabby tried not to panic and straightened her thoughts. *Where did they take her? Rome? ... and when she gets there, then what? Okay, first things first. A flight to Rome.*

Gabby evaluated the situation while she was in the taxi. It had all started out as this great big adventure that one could only dream of; an adventure which had now turned into a crazy nightmare. Where had it gone wrong? The first thing that had gone wrong was the time travelling. They had waited and waited, at the right spot and the right time; just behind the Temple of Asculapius at sunset, to be teleported back to the present, but nothing had happened and the next morning, the women had woken up in ancient Judea, instead of present day Switzerland.

Sion, Switzerland, May 25th 2011

Professor William Fairfax almost had a heart attack when he failed to teleport the women back to the present. His mysterious employer - who had been watching him through the window - was now becoming very nervous and requested an update on the situation by microphone. Fairfax fetched his note pad to see if he really hadn't forgotten anything.

Clothing – check
Medication – check
Food and drink advice – check
Hidden pouch with medication and mobile device– check

The sweat on his back had created a dark stain on his shirt. Suddenly it struck him like lightening. Time curves! The women must have created a time curve with their presence in the past! How was he going to get them back now? He'd first have to re-align the ERFAB to match their mobile devices, but how? Then, his colleague; the stern-faced Ms Kaiser,

31

made a suggestion that seemed so logical, that he wondered why he hadn't thought of it in the first place. They could send the probe! Of course, the probe had been designed to look like a rock and view most directions; all except up and down. However, it could tip over on arrival or someone might accidentally kick it. Still, it was worth a try to get the proper data.

After the probe had been sent to the same co-ordinates as Danielle and Gabby, the professor and Ms Kaiser watched the screen and saw the legs of a man, behind whom the probe had materialised. No one had spotted it and Fairfax hoped that the man wouldn't accidentally kick it. Then, suddenly, the man walked away and they could now see several men dressed in white robes. If only they could see more!

Jerusalem, ancient Judea, 32 AD
Danielle and Gabby had woken up hungry and thirsty. The sun was already heating up the day and they could hear the sounds of talking men, chickens and the lamenting of a woman in the distance. They got up, looked at one another and realised they were in serious trouble. They knew that they could well be stuck there for the rest of their lives, but first they needed food and something to drink. They were well advised on what not to eat or drink and they carried emergency medication, in case either of them fell ill or got wounded. They had also been given injections to prepare them for the known diseases of the time. However, they couldn't understand the language. When they carefully looked around the wall of the Temple of Asculapius, they noticed that a group of men in white robes had gathered in the Baths. How will they ever manage to get passed those men? They were sure it was 'women not allowed'.
It was too late; they had been spotted. One of the men shouted at them and the two women ran past the bathers, trying not to look. They ran toward the gate that gave access to the old city of Jerusalem, hoping to disappear in the

crowd, but they hadn't counted on the Roman guards standing on each side of the gate, checking every single person that wanted to get through. One of them turned toward the fast approaching women and shouted, "Desino!" Danielle understood that they had no choice but to stop running. Their hearts were pounding. This meant trouble. The Romans in ancient Judea were ruthless. Danielle jumped when suddenly, someone grabbed her arm. It was someone they had already met the day before. Danielle recognised him immediately and relaxed. Then they spotted the other men who belonged to his group. Most of them were carrying swords, so it looked as if he had come with his bodyguards instead of his disciples. He greeted the women with a warm smile and when - this time - he spoke Greek, Danielle could finally understand what he was saying. Ancient Greek had been one of the classes she had loved in her student days at the University. Unfortunately, Gabby couldn't understand a word, so Danielle became the interpreter for Gabby. Not that this was easy, as the Greek he spoke wasn't quite the same as the Greek she had learned, but at least they could have a conversation of sorts.

He turned to the Roman guards and said, "They are with me." Then he smiled at Gabby and finger pointed at Danielle. "You are not from here?"

This was tricky. Danielle now had to lie to Christ, but he wouldn't believe her if she'd say she was from Philadelphia, USA and from 2011 'Christian Era' and while thinking this, she realised the absurdity of the moment. "No", she said, forcing back a smile. She decided not to go into detail.

"My name is Danielle. You?"

She pointed at him with her index finger and his response confirmed that he was indeed who they thought he was.

"When I was born, I was given the name Immanuël. When I was a young boy, people called me Yosep, but now everyone calls me Yeshua or Oshu. I am your servant. You look hungry, come, I will feed you. Come."

They followed him and his little group of whispering followers through the gate, passing the Roman guards, until they arrived at a large house, which they all entered. He explained that he had intended to meet someone at the Baths, but that the women were now more important. He said they had come onto his Path. When they were all sitting comfortably around a huge central table, the women - who had already been present at the house - went to fetch food, as was the custom in the ancient Near East. However, Danielle and Gabby, who were treated as guests, felt somewhat uncomfortable. No matter how much they enjoyed being with him, it felt as if they were interfering; like they were uninvited guests at a party, who were politely tolerated.

Sion, Switzerland, May 25th 2011
Fairfax had spotted the two women running past the probe. It was only a flash; a second; no more. Then he lost them.
Damn!
Plan B now came into action. He had to bring the probe back. With the new data from the probe he could enter the adapted codes into the ERFAB's computer unit and match both curves. It had to work this time, because if it didn't, the two women could be stuck there forever. The professor hoped that the women would remember to return to the given co-ordinates at sunset. Pearls of sweat were dripping from his forehead. Carefully he opened the wormhole to fetch the probe, but then, suddenly, he lost the signal. Fairfax couldn't believe it and cursed out loud while running his hands through his hair. However, he didn't know that the probe had been knocked by the stick of a passing leper, who was on his way to the Temple of Asculapius.

Jerusalem, ancient Judea, 32 AD
During their breakfast at the big house in the old city of Jerusalem, Danielle had been able to ask some really interesting questions - questions people wouldn't be able to answer 2000 years later.

After hearing Oshu's story, Danielle looked at Gabby in a state of bewilderment and whispered,
"He told me that the Greek philosophers are his big heroes. He even went to Egypt a few years ago - in the footsteps of the Greek philosophers - to be initiated into the Great Egyptian Mysteries. Before that he had spent many years in India, where he studied the local religions; Buddhism and Hinduism. Isn't this amazing? No one ever knew what he was up to before. He comes from an important family and was well educated. This explains why he can speak Greek."
Gabby laughed, "… and bang goes the carpenter story!"
The women smiled and ate the bread they were offered. Gratefully, they nodded to the women who had brought the food and they both wondered if Mary Magdalene could be among these women. Danielle thought she might try to ask Oshu. However, it took a moment before he understood who Danielle meant. While chewing on a small piece of flat, unleavened bread, he suddenly yelled, "Ah, Mariamne, you mean Mariamne?"
A beautiful woman turned around and looked at Oshu. Then she smiled at the women, who smiled back in utter amazement.
Mariamne. So that is what they called her.
"Mariamne is an important woman." Oshu added. He got up, walked toward Mariamne and gave her a tender kiss, after which he said - without looking away from her - "She is my wife."
Both women gazed at them and for some reason, tears came into their eyes. So, it was true after all.

When they had finished their meals, Danielle and Gabby followed Oshu, who had invited them into an adjoining room. When the door was closed behind them, they were surprised to have him all to themselves. Oshu made himself comfortable on one of the large pillows and pointed at another place for them to sit down. Inquisitively, he asked,
"You have blue eyes, so you have come from the west, no?"

Although Gabby had brown eyes and dark hair, Danielle was blonde with blue eyes; a very unusual sight in those days in the Near East. Danielle nodded and looked around. They were sitting in a dark room with only a small window, hidden behind a beautifully handcrafted, colourful cloth that protected the room from the hot, midday sun. There were pillows and rugs on the floor. A low table stood at the centre, displaying several small clay cups and a large clay jar that contained red wine. They could smell incense and Gabby soon discovered a small, copper bowl, filled with smoking lumps of incense, hidden away in a corner. It was making them feel a bit drowsy. Gabby was just staring at Oshu, riveted to his face, but Danielle was now more interested in information, so she courageously continued her questioning.

"So what about your family? Is your family here?"

"My mother, brothers and sisters are here, yes. My father Zekaryah is not in this world, nor is my other father, Yosep. You have family here, Dani El?"

Danielle needed a little time to digest this information. Zekaryah, who could that be? She decided to ignore his question about her family and asked him about Zekaryah. However, the answer she was about to receive contained information that would go beyond her wildest imagination.

"Zekaryah was our beloved Zadok High Priest and the last of the Hasmonean kings. He had no heir and his wife, my aunt Elisheba, believed she was too old to conceive a child. However, because my mother is also an heir of Aron, Elisheba presented my mother to be his consort and she became pregnant with me. However, Elisheba gave birth to a son after all; Yohanan; my half-brother. Then it became confusing for me and my family, so my mother had to marry Yosep, an heir of David and because it had become too dangerous for us to stay here, we all had to go to Egypt for a few years. When Yohanan and I were three years old, our father Zekaryah was murdered, because he would not tell Herod's soldiers where his sons and heirs were."

"Several years later, after Herod had died, we came back to Galilee and my mother sent me to Carmel to be educated. Later I travelled to India, Persia, Assyria, Greece and Egypt. Now I have come back as a Teacher, but things have become even more complicated. These are bad times."

Oshu had a worried expression on his face and Danielle took advantage of the temporary silence to explain to Gabby what he had told her so far. With great interest, Oshu listened to the modern English language, as he had never heard that language before, so he continued to ask Danielle about her home, her family and her ancestors as if nothing else was important. Danielle decided to tell him only that she was an orphan without any relatives. She didn't have to lie about that, as this was true. Oshu stared at Danielle and smiled. Already uncomfortable about them being alone in one room with a married man - which was not customary in that culture in those days - Danielle continued with a worried frown, "Won't your wife, Mariamne, be annoyed that you are here with us, alone?"

Oshu chuckled, "No. I choose who I want to be with and today is blessed, for you, fair Dani El, have come to my house!"

Oshu patted on a big pillow to invite Danielle to come and sit next to him. Gabby looked at Danielle in fright, "Danielle, be careful, we don't actually know this man!" Naturally, Gabby was concerned, but she was also envious. Oshu didn't seem to have any interest in her; his eyes were fixed on Danielle. Suddenly, Oshu turned toward Gabby and asked her to leave. It was the most painful moment for Danielle to translate this request to Gabby, who had no choice but to obey. With tears in her eyes she left the room. Now, Danielle was alone with Oshu.

The moment Gabby closed the door behind her, the other women kindly invited her to sit with them and they tried their best to make her feel comfortable. There was nothing else that Gabby could do but wait until her friend would come back out through that door. Hopefully, Danielle wouldn't do anything foolish.

In the meantime, Oshu tried to explain to Danielle some of the knowledge he had learned while he was in India. It was not easy to follow, but she understood that he was talking about 'two snakes' that ran along the spine from the pelvis to the head and which were the big secrets of energy, balance and medicine. He also spoke of the Temple of Asculapius and slowly, Danielle began to understand why the Caduceus of Hermes had become the global sign for medicine. She realised that the origin of the Caduceus was connected to Asculapius and health and balance.

Oshu seemed very keen on explaining to her more and more of the powers of the two snakes that crawl up the human spine. He touched her back and ran with his fingers the Path of the Snake toward her head. Goose bumps appeared all over her body while he did this. Then he started to explain how the world had come into existence; how the Father impregnated the Mother with his energy, so that humans and animals and plants could live. He explained that everything was mere vibration and that the base of all health and balance of the human body, mind and spirit could be found in the balanced activity of the two snakes.

While he was explaining all this, he gently touched her on certain places to make her understand what energy does. Danielle was very impressed. Being as interested in science as she was, this lecture of the spirit of nature had her full attention. It also made her realise that she was very privileged, hearing this great knowledge from him; a Master. She surrendered to the experience and was now surrounded by the blinding light that emanated from his body. She had never felt that way before and in the end, she finally understood the power of the two snakes.

In the other room, Gabby was getting more and more concerned. At least two hours must have passed by now.

What on earth was going on in that room? She decided to go and see for herself. When the women noticed her getting up, they ran toward her to stop her from entering the room, as if it would be a crime. It was impossible to resist them, so she allowed them to take her back to her seat. Little did she know that to Oshu and Danielle, this moment of undisturbed meditation was of the utmost importance.

A little while later, Oshu came out of the room and while passing Gabby, he said goodbye to her with his hands pressed together in a wordless 'Namaste'. Immediately, Gabby jumped up and ran through the now open door toward Danielle, who seemed to be deeply asleep in the other room. Gabby had no idea what had just happened, although a disturbing thought had come into her mind. However, the serene smile on the face of the sleeping Danielle revealed that she had not been harmed at all.

Danielle awoke when Gabby touched her arm. Still in a state of bliss, she explained to Gabby everything she wanted her friend to know. As incredible as their adventure may be, they were also very aware of the fact that they were still there, trapped in time, knowing that tonight, at sunset, they had to try again to return to the present. The professor had explained that - in case of a malfunction - they should repeat the action 24 hours later and because last night hadn't worked, they were now hoping that Bill had solved the problem and that this time, the professor would succeed in teleporting them back to the present. They knew they had to go back to the Temple of Asculapius before sunset and wait, but the sun was still high in the sky. However, feeling they may have already outstayed their welcome, they just wanted to leave the house. So after Gabby had rehearsed 'thank you' in Greek, they walked toward the door to say goodbye. Suddenly, Mariamne stopped Danielle and grabbed her arm. Danielle broke into a sweat, thinking about the intimacy she had only just experienced with Mariamne's husband in the other room and the very last thing she wanted was to upset her Biblical heroine Mary Magdalene, whom she had revered since she had been a little girl. However, Mariamne smiled and instead of being angry, she spoke to Danielle with a gentle, soft voice, "Oshu wants you to stay with us; he says you are special."

Danielle blushed. She gazed into the dark eyes of this beautiful, dark-skinned woman. Then she looked at the other women who were with Mariamne and remembered what Oshu had told her only half an hour ago: "A man can be one flesh with more than one woman." - realising that the customs in the ancient Near East were very different from what she was used to in modern times and in western civilisation.

Danielle smiled at Mariamne, hugged her and before she knew it, she started to cry. Immediately, Mariamne tightened her grip and whispered words she couldn't all understand. It was wonderful that Mariamne could also speak Greek, like Oshu, but now she was mixing Greek words with words of another language; a language she couldn't understand. However, her words and kindness comforted Danielle and soon she felt all her sadness disappear.

"I will come back," Danielle whispered, "I promise!"

Mariamne nodded and kissed her on her forehead, after which she turned and left. A strange but strong bond between the two women seemed to have formed from that moment on.

Gabby looked at Danielle and they both stood there for a few seconds to digest everything they had experienced. Then they walked through the door.

Oshu and his group had already left and Danielle wondered if - before going back to the temple of Asculapius - they could perhaps spend the rest of the afternoon exploring the old city, to see what it looked like at this moment in time. Frankly, she just didn't want to be seen near the Baths if Oshu had gone back there, for she simply couldn't face him at this moment. She was so confused.

Gabby didn't really speak much to Danielle. She was still envious about the whole situation, because Gabby, too, had fallen in love with him; with his eyes and his voice, but it felt cruel that he hardly had eyes for her. She felt as if she was nothing more than Danielle's sidekick. Insignificant. Unimportant. Danielle, however, wasn't stupid or selfish; she had a hunch of what must be going through Gabby's mind, so she took her friend's arm, squeezed it gently and they walked together arm in arm through the streets of the old city of Jerusalem, on their way to places that probably no longer exist in modern times. Gabby smiled again, taking it all in with excitement, although it didn't cure the way she felt inside. She had been craving for his attention, but had to see it all go to her friend, who seemed to be only interested in facts and information and not in him as a person. However, she understood very well that Danielle hadn't caused it. It was what it was and she simply had to come to terms with it.

Sion, Switzerland, May 25th 2011

Professor Fairfax had finally succeeded in retrieving the probe. Now he had to try to get the women back to the present without making any further errors and the waiting was becoming sheer torture. All kinds of things went through his mind. He was the one who had wanted to build the time machine; he had to have human guinea pigs to see if it worked, but he had never tried it with a large animal before, simply because it wouldn't have the intelligence to come back to the same co-ordinates at a certain time. It had to be a human-being clever enough to do so. He knew and understood the risks and so did his employer, but now he was getting more and more worried about other things. What if they changed history? They had travelled back in time to an important historical moment and though the women were told to be very discrete and very careful, anything could have happened. He had given them quite a lecture on this subject, but they'd had only little time to prepare. What if they got ill or into trouble? After all, at that time in history, Judea had been occupied by the Romans, who tended to be extremely cruel toward the Jews. His mind was racing and it didn't take long before he started to panic. Had he sent two people to an untimely death? The professor looked hard at the ERFAB. He had been obsessed with his invention; obsessed with all the information the two women were supposed to collect, so he had never even wanted to think about the risks involved. If he failed to get them back tonight, would he give up? Would he admit that he had made a mistake? Then, what would his employer do to him? His increasing blood pressure gave him a throbbing headache.

Ms Kaiser - who seemed relatively calm and untouched by the whole situation - tried to support him by fetching him a glass of water and a couple of aspirins.

"Everything will be alright." she said, "You'll see."

Jerusalem, ancient Judea, 32 AD

Danielle and Gabby had an exciting time walking through the ancient streets of Jerusalem. They did, however, notice the heavy atmosphere in the city. Obviously it was the Roman rule that had made the political climate harsh for the all the people of Judea, especially for its capital; Jerusalem - the city of peace, the city of King David - filled with upper class, middle class, lower class, no class, the sick and the dead, some of whom were displayed horribly on crosses on the hill close to the road leading to the main gate. Some heads were on spikes. The brutal display of corpses made the women shiver. Gabby turned her head away from a crucifixion scene and they suddenly realised what was about to happen to the man they both loved since the moment they had met him. They were the only ones who knew... They had to warn him! However, then what about the fact that - according to Church dogma - he died to save mankind? That is the very core of Christianity. They would change history completely! Still, ever since Christianity had become the leading religion of the Roman empire, the world hadn't really become a better place, had it? On one side, the Holy Roman Church had tried to stabilise the world by creating a sort of semi-religious political state that taught people the difference between right and wrong. On the other hand, many people had been mercilessly killed when the same Holy Church tried to convert the world. Just think about the Crusades against the Cathars in the 13th century and the millions of people all over the world, who had died by fire or other forms of merciless violence, simply because they had been branded heretics, infidels, pagans or witches. Think of the so called 'Holy Inquisition' and their approval of the use of torture to make people betray each other or reveal information that might - or might not - have been the truth. Think of the stories and the lies that have been told to keep humanity dumb and the way early scientists were hunted down and killed during the Renaissance? *This* was the moment that history could be changed. It *had* to be changed.

The women looked at each other and ran back to the Baths, hoping that he would still be there.

Sion, Switzerland, May 25th 2011

Professor Fairfax cursed out loud when his first attempt to get the women back failed. He was convinced that he had made another mistake. Little did he know that this time it had been the women who had made the mistake.

Jerusalem, ancient Judea, 32 AD

It was pure luck that they discovered Oshu's group at the Baths when they arrived. They quickly walked toward them, hoping they wouldn't be chased away again. To their surprise, Oshu turned his head as if he knew they'd come. He rejoiced in seeing them again, especially Danielle, but then he saw the panic in their eyes. He asked everyone for some privacy and the three of them moved to a quieter spot, where they could not be overheard. With a soft, but anxious voice, Danielle started, "You will be betrayed soon, sometime before the next Pasha."

She could feel her heart beating inside her chest, realising she might have just altered history and thus, their own present in the future. What security do they have that the world would still be the same when they are teleported back to modern day Switzerland? The world will surely be different; there would have been different religions; different wars; different borders and consequently; different populations.

Then it struck her; what if she had never been born?

Hiding her panic, Danielle stared hard at Oshu, who first looked worried after hearing her alarming news, but a moment later he relaxed. "Do not worry Dani El, what will happen, will happen, it is written."

"No, no, no, you don't understand! You will be betrayed, caught, hurt and crucified when you let them catch you!"

Tears pricked her eyes. How could she explain that what she knew would really happen?

Concerned to see Danielle's tears, he touched her cheek and added, "Who is it? Who will betray me?"

"Yehuda Iscariot." she replied, hoping she got the name right. Oshu chuckled in disbelief, then shook his head and thought for a while. Danielle was looking at him in hope; maybe now he will listen and act. However, the answer did not reveal much. Completely confident, he simply thanked them for the information and didn't even ask how they knew. Casually, he added, "Will you come with us to the house for supper?"

Taken aback and surprised by his calmness, Danielle raised her hands. "No, thank you, we need to go somewhere, but I promise we will be back soon."

Danielle was more emotional than she had expected to be. She blushed and let her tears run free. She had never really felt that way before and was so confused. Oshu hugged both women before he walked back to his men and they doubted if the information they had just shared with Oshu would have any impact on history at all. Silently they walked to the co-ordinates. The sun had nearly set. Hopefully plan B would work.

Sion, Switzerland, May 27th 2011

The relief Bill had felt when the women had finally reappeared in the ERFAB cabin on May 25th had been indescribable. However, Gabby was not well. She had been sleeping for almost two days and was only just waking up. Immediately, she started to vomit. Danielle, who seemed to be fine, was next to her bed. She had been taking care of her friend non-stop. The base's medical assistant had discovered that Gabby was suffering from high blood pressure and an IV was now feeding her the appropriate medicine. The teleportation could have killed her, so she was not allowed to do it again. At least not while her blood pressure was high. Danielle was concerned when she saw Gabby so ill and weak, so she asked Gabby to speak a whole sentence and to lift her arms up high above her head to rule out an apoplexy.

Fortunately, Gabby could do it all without showing any signs and the whole sentence she spoke was quite clear, "What are we going to do now?"

Danielle smiled, but her eyes were sad. "I don't know, Gabby, but first I must write everything down in my diary, before I forget any details."

She gave Gabby some more water, beeped the medical assistant to take her place and left the room. On the way to her quarters, she bumped into the professor, who seemed worried and wanted her to follow him to the lab for questioning. While walking her through the seemingly endless hallways, Bill made her swear that she hadn't done anything to disturb the history line. Danielle knew there was only one simple way to find out. "Give me a Bible. Quickly!"

She browsed through the New Testament, checking every gospel, but couldn't find any change at all; Oshu had still been crucified. Danielle was completely shocked. Oshu hadn't done anything with her advice at all! Tears were rolling down her cheeks.

This sudden display of emotion startled the professor. "What did you find?" he said, nervously.

"Oh don't worry, nothing has changed!" Danielle uttered, still in disbelief. "They still crucified him!"

Ms Kaiser, who had overheard the conversation, frowned. "What do you mean, Ms Parker?"

Danielle wasn't sure she could tell them what they had done and ran out of the lab, yelling, "Never mind!"

She went to her room to write her diary; not just to write down all the details before she forgot them, but also to get it out of her system. When she had finished writing down even the most personal details, she left it on her bed and returned to Gabby's room. However, when she opened the door - half-expecting to only find Gabby, attended to by the medical assistant - she saw a stranger sitting beside Gabby's bed. She had never seen the man before. He was a tall, thin man, wearing a small, red cap on top of his grey head.

As soon as he noticed Danielle, he got up and walked toward her with his hand stretched out and a broad smile on his face. "Hello Ms Parker, my name is Cardinal Antonio Sardis. I've been informed that you had an incredible experience and I'm very interested to hear everything. *Everything! Do sit down!*" Danielle was overwhelmed.

Wow, that is fast!

Danielle wasn't a catholic, although she had had a Christian upbringing, but she had never been baptised in any specific Christian Church, so Danielle didn't feel as if she had to be loyal to the Church of Rome. She knew a little bit of both Testaments and had read the Dan Brown books, so she knew enough to fear this sudden interest and presence of a Prince of Rome. The man - who looked as if he was Peter O'Toole's twin brother - didn't even blink while he stared at her. He looked at her as if he was trying to penetrate her thoughts and mind. Unable to return his well-mannered smile, she sat down - while he himself remained standing - and started,

"So how did you learn about our adventure, your eminence?"

"Ms Kaiser was so kind as to inform us that you had gone back in time to see our Lord. I came as soon as I could, to hear all about it!"

Danielle was stunned. Ms Kaiser! She never liked that woman. "So, what would you like to know? You know that I barely saw him. I have learned nothing you may wish to learn from me. Nothing that could change anyone's view." she lied.

The Cardinal smiled and moved closer. "… and you expect me to believe that? Surely, you must have attracted his attention with your fair beauty, my dear lady. Come on, you can tell me all about it!"

She was alarmed to hear his persistence and hesitated. Perhaps she could give him a small piece of information, saying that was all. Perhaps then he would be happy and leave her alone. Gabby was still asleep and Danielle wondered if they had already spoken to each other.

"Was she already asleep when you arrived, your eminence?"

"Oh no. She was wide awake when I entered the room, so I was able to introduce myself and we had a little chat..."

Danielle went pale. "So, what did she tell you?"

The Cardinal bent over her and replied,

"What will *you* tell *me?*"

He stared hard at her, displaying a grim, confident smile, anticipating her story and Danielle was afraid that he had probably found out too much already. She decided to play along, just to keep him happy.

"Please sit down, your eminence and I will give you my full report."

Sion, Switzerland, May 27th 2011

Professor Fairfax sat in a small room waiting for Danielle to reappear. He had received new orders; his chief wants him to send Danielle back to ancient Judea - this time on her own - to find out if Jesus had really been crucified and had indeed resurrected. If not, she had to try to locate his tomb very carefully. His employer had told him that this was exactly what the time machine should be used for: to collect historical facts from the Biblical era, starting with the life and times of Jesus. However, the professor did not trust Cardinal Sardis, who had suspiciously popped up from nowhere on the very moment his chief had left the building. He also felt betrayed by Ms Kaiser, who had obviously gone behind his back to make a quick phone call to the Cardinal.

Fairfax considered his options and started to walk around the room, thinking, wondering and hesitating. Should he contact his chief to let him know about Sardis' presence, or would he already know that the Cardinal was interrogating his personnel? He simply didn't know what to do.

Although Fairfax was a very intelligent man, he lacked the charm that was usually expected of people, especially in heavily populated areas like his home town, New York. He didn't know how to handle problems or difficult situations. He had been the child that was always bullied at school, day after day. After school he used to run home as fast as he could to avoid being beaten up. As soon as he had come home, he would immediately lock himself in his room, hardly interacting with his family. Nevertheless, he had been a straight-A student throughout his school years. Apart from one or two short-term friends, his closest friend had been his chocolate brown Labrador dog called Harold. Consequently, Bill had never joined any clubs or even known how to play baseball. He had no hobbies, other than finding out as much as possible about physics; his favourite subject. His parents, who had cherished his gift, had let him be and although he had been given his share of hugs, cuddles and attention, he hadn't cared much for the touch of others as he grew up. Having been a silent student in college and University; in his professional life he had become an outcast the moment he had presented the one theory no one believed in anymore. However, he had never stopped believing in himself.

Determined to find a sponsor and a laboratory to work in, to create his time travel device, he had finally found a position in this Swiss team - albeit with an employer he had not yet met - but it was someone who seemed to have faith in him and recently he had finally succeeded in materialising his dream, doing exactly what others said he couldn't do: he had created a time machine. It had been the biggest and most important moment in his life and yet, at this moment, he could no longer celebrate it. The effects of his revolutionary invention were as frightening as they were mind-blowing. Human lives were at stake, as well as his future and everyone else's. The thrill of being successful had evaporated in the heat of the anxiety he was experiencing. He just didn't have a clue what to do next. Should he warn his employer that a Prince of Rome was here, meddling? No, his chief had to know! After all, who else could have contracted Ms Kaiser? Maybe he should simply ask his chief for an explanation. The professor returned to his seat and continued to glance at the door, waiting for Danielle. She said she'd be back.

Danielle had explained a few convenient details of their visit to the Holy Land in the first century and so far, the Cardinal seemed satisfied and congratulated her on their incredible achievement. They had been the first to have actually seen the Lord himself in the flesh with their own eyes, which proved that he had really existed. Danielle had acknowledged that he was a teacher and that he had followers - albeit ones that carried swords. She had also told him that his followers called him Oshu and that he was a healer and a very gifted speaker. Sardis was happy. For now.

"I will leave you with your friend. We will meet again in a little while, Danielle."

Danielle shivered when the Cardinal left the room and listened to his fading footsteps. While looking at Gabby she got up from her chair to sit with her on the edge of the bed. Gabby opened her eyes and smiled. "I wasn't asleep you know. I almost interrupted you when you said you'd tell him all about our journey, but then I heard that you adapted our adventure a bit, here and there."

Both women smiled at one another, but deep down they knew they had to be very, very careful.

"Gabby, I have checked the Bible and nothing has changed. Oshu was still crucified."

Gabby turned pale.

"Oh no! Perhaps he didn't believe us. Or, do you think he wanted it to happen?"

Danielle shook her head. She had brought a copy of the Bible with her, so she could leaf through it together with Gabby. Then suddenly, her eye stopped at Mark 14, verse 18, in which Jesus said:

'One of you will betray me, one who is eating with me.'

The women looked at each other in utter disbelief. "Was that our doing?" Danielle said to the room in general, wondering if they could ever be sure. Suddenly, Danielle raced out of the room when she remembered that she hadn't hidden her diary. It was still in her room, in plain sight. She hadn't thought of hiding it, because she didn't know she had to, until she had met the Cardinal. During her sprint, Danielle couldn't help wondering why she and Gabby had been separated on arrival in the first place. She ran into her room, grabbed the diary, hid it underneath her clothes and ran back to Gabby's room. However, when she arrived, see saw that Gabby had vomited all over the bed. It was obvious.

Her friend was still very sick. "Gabby! I'll get a doctor!"

Again, Danielle raced out of the room, this time in search of Professor Fairfax.

She found Bill talking to Cardinal Sardis in the lab. "Bill, Gabby has been sick again. You must get a doctor this time, I'm worried!"

Professor Fairfax immediately took his mobile phone to dial a number, but Sardis grabbed his wrist and stopped him.

What the heck?!

Sardis loosened his grip. "No need to call anyone, I happen to have an excellent doctor who always travels with me. I will fetch him for you."

Sardis went out to get his doctor, whom he had in fact taken with him in case the women came back ill, for he didn't want them to leave the building or get in contact with anyone in the outside world. He was here to guarantee that from now on, they were the property of his private office at the Vatican. The outside world no longer had any significance.

Sardis was an enigmatic person. He smiled, savouring the fact that he was now in control. He knew that his plan could only succeed because of the secrecy of this huge undertaking. The Cardinal was indeed a powerful man; he moved in the top layers of society and possessed large quantities of money, salted away in secret bank accounts all around the world. He had carte blanche for his travels; private jets; several cars with tinted glass windows and a carefully selected group of men and women, who would give their lives for 'the cause'. His cause.

The Cardinal didn't fear the Swiss - who had given the professor the secret laboratory in Sion - or his organisation. All he had to do was to stay out of his way as much as possible and take advantage of his rank as a Cardinal to gain access. Ms Kaiser had worked for him for several weeks now and she had proved to be very loyal; everything that had happened so far had been carefully brought to Sardis' attention. All the while he had been secretly collecting sensitive information and at the same time he had the power to destroy it the moment he found out that the information could shake the very foundations of the Roman Catholic Church and Christianity.

He felt it was his sacred duty to the world and to the Holy Roman Church to protect the Vatican and Christianity and to avoid the collapse of the biggest religion the western world had ever known. He knew he would get carte blanche from Rome and would willingly give his own life to protect the Holy Roman Church. Like a hawk that studies its hunting grounds, he would keep a watchful eye on the women as well as the professor. He would not let anything escape his attention and right now - having heard Danielle's obviously incomplete story - he had become suspicious.

Very suspicious.

6

Diary entry - Jerusalem, 33 AD, part 1 second trip
We're back in the Holy Land again. Sardis' physician succeeded in lowering Gabby's blood pressure and two days later we were both ready to go back. At first I hesitated, but I couldn't help seeing an opportunity here to stop Oshu from getting crucified. As I found out that my earlier warning hadn't had the desired result, I had to try again.

We wandered through the streets hoping to find him, but we didn't see him anywhere and were afraid that we were too late. Though we had been sent back to witness the crucifixion, we dreaded to do so. Nevertheless we went back to the place we had visited before, to see if he was among the ones who had been crucified. We were sick with worry when we approached what was called the Hill of the Skull because of its shape. There were only a few men fighting death and it was horrible to have to look them in the face to see if one of them was our beloved Oshu. When we were absolutely sure that he wasn't among them, we asked ourselves if we had been too late, or, too early.

According to the Gospels, Oshu was crucified the day before Sabbath - one day before Pasha (Passover) - in the month of Nissan, which is the first month of the year on the Jewish calendar. This particular Pasha celebration would fall on the full moon around the 15th Nissan in the year that the Roman emperor Tiberius was on Capri. Bill had calculated that this must have been the year 33 AD, when both the Sabbath and Pasha had occurred on a Saturday. It had been an educated guess, so we could never be completely sure. We tried to find out whether today was indeed a Friday (the day before Sabbath) and to our surprise, that much was correct.

How odd. There was a clear sky; no darkness; no Oshu and no-one even seemed to know him. We decided to go to the house we had been to before, during our first visit.

With difficulty we manoeuvred through the crowded streets, but when we reached the house, it seemed to be deserted.

Then, suddenly, a woman opened the door. This lady had also been there on our first visit and to our great relief, she recognised us. She embraced us and invited us in. We were surprised to hear her speak Greek. I thought of asking her name, but feared this might be impolite. So I got straight to the point and asked where I could find Oshu. She told us she didn't know where he was right now, but that he had plans to go to a place called 'Bethanu' sometime next month and then travel on to Carmel, a place in the north, near the coast, where he had spent part of his youth. Hearing this news, we were both struck dumb. Had we accidently entered a parallel world, where things had happened a little differently?

However, we did realise that the gospels had been written much later and that they had been based on popular stories about divine holy men and popular gods like Mithras, who - according to the myth - not only had 12 apostles, he had also been 'born of a virgin' and had resurrected 'three days' after he had died. The well-known Biblical story was full of political and mystical symbolism, written mainly by gnosists and Church-employed scribes who were much less concerned about factual history than modern day theologians would have liked.

So, the real Jesus was still alive, even planning to go to Carmel this Summer, apparently to teach small classes, like the old Greek philosophers used to do before him. As much as we wanted to go to him immediately, we couldn't possibly ignore Bill's strict order to return to the same co-ordinates within three days' time, so we can tell Cardinal Sardis what he wants to hear. However, we gratefully accepted the sweet woman's offer to stay at her house. Maybe we can find out more about Oshu from her.

Philadelphia Airport, USA, June 19th 2011

Cardinal Sardis closed the diary and stared out of the window of the car, which was now driving into a special entrance at Philadelphia airport. Here, a private jet was waiting for them and the moment they boarded, the engines started up.

It didn't take long before the jet started to taxi toward the runway, waiting for permission to take off. Danielle was still dizzy and angry about her terrifying situation and the adrenaline that was now running through her veins woke her up faster than Sardis had anticipated. She knew she had to act now, or she'd be lost. Taking advantage of the moment, she banged into Sardis, snatched the diary from his hand and ran toward the emergency exit. However, she couldn't get it to open. Calmly, Sardis approached her and smiled confidently. "I admire your courage, Danielle, but you must understand that your former life is now over. Come; sit down; relax. We will be going on a long flight and then I will show you your new home, where you will stay for the rest of your life."

Danielle, who began to realise the hopelessness of the situation, sank to her knees and started to cry. Sardis, however, was not a mean person, he was just a man on a mission, so courteously he helped her back into her seat, fastened her seatbelts and tried to comfort her.

"Danielle please, remember that I have saved you alive and that of your child and I will continue to do so as long as you allow me to."

Danielle looked up at him, still hoping she could persuade him to release her. "Please, let me go, I have done you no harm. Please, let me go home…"

Feeling lost, alone, deserted, scared and betrayed, Danielle wept as the Cardinal stayed silent. However, she didn't know was that the same airspace would soon be crossed by her dear friend Gabby, coming after her.

Gabby was determined to find her and she had a plan; if she were able to get back to the professor, she might even be able to free Danielle from under the Cardinal's nose, using the ERFAB.

Danielle knew that Gabby was her last hope, so she held on to this hope and thought of the child growing inside her. How precious was this child, but then she feared that she'd be forced to give it up after it is born.

If that would indeed be the case, she'd die of grief.

Sion, Switzerland, June 21st 2011

When Gabby booked her flight, she didn't book it to Rome. Instead, she bought a ticket to Lausanne, Switzerland and travelled by train to Sion, where she took a taxi to the underground base that housed the laboratory of Professor Fairfax. She knew she could never do this alone and was hoping Bill would still be there. It was already dark when she arrived at the house beneath the fortified church, which was the base's cover. La basilique de Valère stood proudly upon a hill, overlooking the mountains and the city of Sion. On another hill that overlooked the city were the ruins of the castle Tourbillon, built by Bishop Boniface de Challant in the late 13th century. The ruined castle was now slowly crumbling away underneath the feet of time.

Gabby knew the entrance to the laboratory well. The house, which was its front, had a secret cellar, behind which a long hallway penetrated deeply into the rock, leading to the heart of the base. Gabby nervously knocked on the door for five minutes before the door finally opened. A man, who was unfamiliar to her, asked her what she wanted.

"My name is Gabrielle Standford. I am looking for Professor Fairfax."

"One moment, please."

The young man closed the door again and came back a few minutes later, allowing her in. He anxiously looked into the street, checking whether she had come alone. Obviouosly satisfied that Gabby was indeed alone, he closed the door behind them and showed her directly into the lab.

The moment Bill spotted Gabby, he startled. "Gabby! What are you doing here? I told you to get undercover! Has something gone wrong?"

Gabby quickly explained how they had managed to get back to the States, but that she and Danielle had lost contact the moment they had separated. Danielle had told her that the last place they would come looking for her was her own home and had insisted she would be safe there.

Gabby had tried to talk her out of it, but she wouldn't listen and now she was certain that Danielle had been kidnapped by the Cardinal. The professor - who had been listening to Gabby's story without interruption - was now very upset and cursed out loud. Pacing up and down the room in total despair, he yammered, "Now he will find out that I lied!"

Gabby frowned and suddenly noticed the absence of Ms Kaiser. "Has your assistant left you?"

Bill stared hard at her and pursed his lips. It hadn't taken Gabby long to figure out that Ms Kaiser and the Cardinal were in it together. Bill gazed into Gabby's bright eyes and suddenly noticed a difference in the way she looked.

She had a plan.

The professor had already discovered that Gabby's mind was extraordinary; her intelligence had already proved her to be an excellent assistant, so when she came up with a possible solution to their problem, Bill smiled. Of course, they still had the time machine; they could go back in time! However, it would be risky and he'd have to clear it with his employer first. Naturally, this problem concerned all of them.

However, there was one snatch; the professor had never told his employer that the women had fled in the first place. Along with Sardis, his chief had been informed that Danielle and Gabby were still in ancient Judea. Bill had risked his career - perhaps even his life - to help the women escape from the base; to escape from Sardis, so the last thing he had wanted was to see either of them back in Sion. However, with Danielle having been abducted by the Cardinal, he had no choice but to tell his employer the truth.

The professor nervously dialled the number to contact his chief and Gabby felt her heart pounding in her chest. Not only was she anxious to hear the decision of Bill's employer; she was also afraid to be teleported again, as somehow, time travel seemed to disagree with her system. Behind her back she crossed her fingers, hoping there would be another way.

7

Jerusalem, ancient Judea, 33 AD
Danielle and Gabby were seated comfortably by a young woman, who presented them with some wine and nuts. Danielle was able to write a quick note in her diary. Ten minutes later, the woman who had opened the door returned, assisted by the young woman who brought more food. The lady spoke to Danielle, knowing by now that Gabby could not understand her. She said that her son had frequently asked if anyone had seen them; if anyone knew where they had gone. It was then that Danielle realised that this woman must be Oshu's mother Myriam, the one we know today as Maria or Mary.

"You, Dani El, have made a big impression on my son. Both he and Mariamne asked for you many times, but you were not here. Many bad things have happened while you were away." Mary closed her eyes in a futile attempt to stop her tears. Naturally, both Danielle and Gabby were alarmed.

"What has happened, mother?" Danielle asked.

"Oh, Oshu was so foolish. He requested to speak to the High Council and to Caiaphas in the Sanhedrin, but was denied entrance. He wanted to know why Caiaphas had made him look like a dangerous militant threat in his reports to Rome. So, one day, Oshu caused great trouble at the Temple to give them a reason to arrest him, hoping that he would then be taken to Caiaphas. He had already persuaded Yehuda of Keriot to betray him after the New Year's ritual, to make it look real and to avoid bloodshed. Oshu's twin brother, Yehuda Dydimus, was furious when Oshu proposed it. 'Remember what happened to Yohanan!' he had shouted, 'Yohanan was beheaded!' but no, Oshu was foolish."

"There were many people around my son that evening, because there was a meeting with Nicodemus, Yosep of Arimathea and several others at Gethsemane. As agreed earlier, Yehuda showed the soldiers where Oshu was, making sure they arrested Oshu and not his twin brother, Yehuda

Dydimus, who looks so much like him. Although they could take him without bloodshed, there was almost a fight when Cephas and his brother wanted to defend him. There were so many Roman soldiers, which was a big surprise to us. Oshu was thrown in prison, awaiting a trial and while I tried to persuade the council that my son was harmless and not thinking straight, Mariamne wrote to Tiberius, pleading for him and asking for his release. A fast courier immediately travelled to Capri, to the palace of the Roman emperor. Pontius Pilate - whose hand was healed by my son and whose lovely wife Claudia sympathises with us because Oshu also healed their child - tried to postpone his sentence as long as possible while we were waiting for Tiberius' reply. Oshu was held for two weeks and we were allowed to visit him. Even others could visit him. Although he was a prisoner, he just continued doing what he always did and healed people or spoke to people who asked for his advice, or wished to receive lessons from him. He stayed so calm, but we still hadn't received a reply from the Roman emperor. Mariamne had become so scared for him. We were all scared for him. Then - perhaps because of the pressure - Pilate sentenced him to many lashes, hoping it would be enough, but the council wasn't satisfied and Pilate was forced to sentence Oshu to be nailed to a wooden cross as an example to the people. We were distraught!"

Tears were flowing uncontrollably over Maria's face.

"When he was lashed, they laughed at him and mocked his Bethanu Way of Life. They even pushed a May thorn crown onto his head, forcing it deeply into his skin. Then he had to walk from the palace to the skull hill, where they nailed him and a few other men to their crosses. They stood with their feet on a narrow shelf and as we were all afraid he'd slip off, we asked a Roman soldier to tie his ankles to the wooden beam to secure him. Only a few people were allowed to be close to him and many of our family and friends stayed away, afraid to be arrested as well. My sister and I and Mariamne were with him and my sister's two sons. It was a horrible and extremely painful thing to witness, but I was also worried about Mariamne, because she is with child. When the legs of the other men were broken, Oshu passed out. He breathed very heavily, now hanging in an awkward position. Then, Yosep of Arimathea arrived with the royal pardon from Tiberius. It had finally come, so the soldiers didn't break his legs now and gave permission to take him down from the cross, for the soldiers were no longer allowed to torture him, but Oshu looked so pale. By now it was raining so hard, that we couldn't take him off immediately. I was afraid my son would die. To check whether he was still alive, one of the soldiers wounded Oshu in his left side with his lance. When his blood mixed with the rain water, we knew he was still alive. For a moment, the painful sting from the lance had woken Oshu and it was clear that he was in great pain, so when we were allowed to give him water, we mixed it with a strong painkiller. He passed out again, so he could no longer support his body, so as soon as it was possible, we took him off the cross and covered his entire body in a winding sheet."

"Poor Oshu; he seemed lifeless. They took him to Yosep's new tomb and sent us women home. We were so afraid that Oshu would die that night. Many had gone home to prepare for Sabbath and Pasha and it was not allowed to go back to the tomb until after Pasha. The waiting was horrible. Immediately after Pasha, in the early morning light, we went to the tomb, because no one could stop us from taking care of our son and husband, dead or alive. We didn't dare to hope that he was still alive, but when we arrived at the tomb, it was open and empty. Mariamne broke down, fearing Oshu had died. At first we were worried that they had taken his body away, because the Romans wouldn't want him to become a martyr. Mariamne looked around and saw a few men further away and we thought that they might be able to tell us what had happened. When Mariamne finally recognised Oshu, she became so emotional! At first she didn't recognise him, because he had been shaven and his long hair had been cut, so he was unrecognisable."

"Mariamne still had the oils, myrrh and incense in her hands to prepare his dead body. When Oshu noticed the items, he said to Mariamne with his beloved smile, that he was still alive and that there was no need for her to prepare him for death, because he had not yet gone to his Father. This was so typical of my son; after all he had gone through he still laughed. Of course he had to be moved to a safe place and it had all ended well, but ever since this horrifying ordeal, Oshu has been disappointed, so now he wants to be a Teacher of Secrets to small classes; to be Moreh HaZedec with the Essenes of Carmel. So once more, Oshu will not be here with me, or with Mariamne, when his child is born and the elders have chosen Yakobo to lead the community now! All my sacrifices have been in vain! It's agony, sheer agony! Heir of Hasmon, heir of Aron! Poor Mariamne!" she lamented.

Maria cried for some time and everyone had joined to comfort her. In the meantime, Danielle tried to explain to Gabby what had happened. Gabby was the silent one, because she could not join the conversation. However, she observed everything and it was thanks to Gabby's observations that they were able to remember almost every detail of their visit between the two of them. Danielle and Gabby both understood how horrible this must be for Maria, not to have her beloved son around. She hadn't been able to see her son much during his childhood in Carmel, nor had she been able to visit him during his travels through Asia and his final initiations in Egypt. He had only been in Judea a few years - always moving around from town to town - and now she had to let him go again. This was a tragic time for the entire family. He probably wouldn't even be around when Mariamne gives birth to his child. However, they understood that it was a frustrating time for Oshu too. He tried to change politics, reform religion and change society, which in his eyes was wrong and needed to be modernised. He had opposed the stoning of people - especially the brutal stoning of women - for even the slightest offence. He had opposed the harsh Jewish laws and system, because of which sick or poor people were considered dead already. They had no rights. People who worked for the Romans were continuously in danger and were almost always considered as outlaws by the Jewish community. Oshu had protested by meeting all of them; the sick, the poor, the outlawed and the people who worked for the Romans - even the Romans themselves. The Jewish community didn't understand this behaviour, especially because it came from their own - albeit uncrowned - king. The priests frequently tried to discuss things with him, but they always lost the debate because of his wit and his knowledge of the Scriptures. So in the end, they simply refused to talk to him, avoiding all contact. He had become a nuisance to them. Especially Caiaphas, the High Priest, hated him. The more Oshu acted in public, the more the Pharisees and the Scribes began to see him as a real threat to their system. For they knew that Oshu was the unacknowledged heir to the Hasmonean throne, as well as an heir of Aron and therefore a Zadok priest. Caiaphas considered Oshu his enemy; his competition.

Oshu personified the hope of many people. They saw in him the person who would be able to chase out the usurpers, just like his ancestor had done before him. Yehuda Maccaba, the son of Hasmon, had saved the Jews two centuries earlier by chasing out the Greek usurpers. One of the most important Jewish rituals, the Hanukah, is a strong reminder of this period in Judean history. Gabby understood that Jesus' twin Yehuda - who was now one of his disciples; the one called Thomas Didymus - had grown up in another family and probably had no rights to the title, but she couldn't help thinking of Oshu's half-brother Yohanan, who was also the son of Zekarya. If Yohanan was indeed the first born child, then wouldn't he be the uncrowned King and Zadok priest of Judea? Gabby thought of Leonardo Da Vinci's painting of John, who held up his index finger, knowing this was called the 'John Gesture'. It meant, among other things, "I was the first." Gabby decided to share her thought with Danielle, who frowned. It was indeed a question worth asking. Danielle turned to Maria and said, "Mother, may I ask you about Yohanan?"

Immediately, Maria pursed her lips and smiled sourly. "Yohanan was the son of Zekaryah, like Oshu, but he was not my son, he was the son of Elisheba, also an heir of Aron, like me. Yohanan was the firstborn and a true heir of Hasmon and Aron. He was a leader, but he also went to Egypt, like Oshu. When he returned, he had chosen the Way of the Egyptian Baptist El-Moria. He did not behave like a King's son, nor a Zadok priest. He became an Essene monk and a Holy Man, because he could not be King under Roman rule. When Yohanan was arrested and executed for his opposition to the puppet King Herod, my son Oshu became the first heir; heir of Hasmon, heir of Aron, King and Zadok. However, Oshu had also become a Holy Man, because nobody wanted to recognise him as a legal son of Zekaryah. The council preferred Yakobo as their elder, who is an important man and an heir of David, but Yakobo is not my son, Yakobo is the son of my late husband Yosep and although Yakobo is Oshu's stepbrother, he is not like Oshu. Oshu is special."

Maria just sat there and stared at Danielle and Gabby, who had forgotten that - at that time in history - John the Baptist, the one Maria called Yohanan, had already been beheaded by Herod Antipas a few years earlier.

Maria had spoken like a mother with a broken heart; a proud mother from a noble family; a family of Kings who were no longer Kings and a mother who had suffered when her son Oshu had been crucified because of his actions, his beliefs and for following his heart. The two women understood that this Holy family was actually a Royal family; important heirs of important people. The old nobility, controlled and suppressed by the Romans and the rigid representatives of the Jewish religion.

Maria folded her hands when she began to speak of her youth at the Temple, when her parents wanted her to be educated by the High Priest Zekaryah (Zachary) himself.

She had learned Greek, astronomy, medicine and history and how to behave like a royal heir to the house of Aron and Benjamin. After her first monthly cycle it was the habit that she would marry the heir of one of the most important houses in the country. Roman occupation or not, they had to remain true to their traditions. So, when she was young, she had obediently entered the Temple to become a Temple maiden.

At a certain moment she was told by Elisheba - the wife of Zekaryah - that Zekaryah was in need of an heir. While she herself was still childless, Maria - being of the right family - had been chosen to give birth to the heir of Zekaryah. Naturally, Maria obeyed. However, a few months later, Elisheba found out that she had become pregnant after all. Zekaryah, who at first couldn't believe it, was then asked by the Essenes to keep his deed with Maria quiet. Maria was then quickly married off to Yosep, an heir of David and sent to Elisheba's house in the hills above Jerusalem. She had to be kept out of sight until both his heirs were born.

After Yohanan was born, a complicated time for Maria and Yosep began, because three months later, Maria would not only give birth to an unwanted son; she gave birth to twins. One son, Yehuda, was taken from the mother immediately after birth and grew up in another family, only to be reunited with his twin brother three decades later. In spite of Zekarya's blessing, the other boy, Immanuël, was neither accepted by the Jews as a legal heir of Zekaryah, nor as a legal son of his stepfather Yosep.

The second problem was safety. As soon as the children were born, they needed to be hidden, because Herod was now King, appointed by the Romans. Herod was obsessed with power and had even killed his own children, whom he saw as competition. Zekaryah's children were therefore also in mortal danger, because Zekaryah was the Lion of Juda, the uncrowned King of Judea; the Lion who would be killed three years later 'between the altar and the Temple', because he refused to tell Herod's soldiers where his three sons - the royal princes - had been hidden.

While Yehuda was safely growing up in another family in another country, Maria and Elisheba, Yosep and the two baby boys had travelled as far away as possible. They had gone to an Essene community in Egypt.

A few years later, when Herod had died and it was safe for them to return to their homeland, they moved back north to live with the Nasurai in Galilee. In his childhood, Oshu - who was called Yosep at the time - was sent to a school in Carmel, an Essene community, to be educated. When he was 13 years old, he left for India to become a Teacher and a Healer. He also went to Egypt to be initiated into the Great Mysteries, like the Greek philosophers.

Maria had missed him very much, because she loved him and knew how special he was. However, she was able to keep in touch with her son by correspondence.

During Oshu's stay in India, his stepfather Yosep died. Although Oshu was sad to hear this news, he had replied to his heart-broken mother to be grateful that he had enjoyed such a long and prosperous life and that he was now with his Father. He refused to come home, even when she begged him.

A few years later, when Oshu finally returned home to Judea, he noticed how corrupt the social system and the entire society had become and he felt that he had to do something to try and change that. In spite of his complicated family bloodline, he still felt responsible for the people and - being a Holy Man - he also tried to teach the people a new Way of Life. Shortly after Oshu's arrival in Judea, the two half-brothers met again. Yohanan was now the uncrowned King of Judea, who had many followers and had already become a threat to the authority of King Herod Antipas, who, like his father before him, had been appointed to this function by the Romans. Yohanan was pleased to see Oshu. He told him about the way of El-Moria, initiated him into the Zadok priesthood and baptised him. In those days, Oshu became known as Ischa, Yeshua or Oshu, depending on the spoken language and dialect. It means: 'he who laughs', because he was always smiling or laughing, something he had picked up in India. The name Jesus had evolved from this nick name. Danielle was speechless and tried to digest all this new information. The silence was only broken when more food was brought in. A moment later the room began to fill with other people and Danielle and Gabby assumed they were probably members of Maria's family. Used to having guests at the table, they accepted Danielle and Gabby, but did not speak to them. The women were Maria's guests and they had to respect this, but after what had happened to Oshu, they no longer trusted anyone. The meal soon turned solemn and the atmosphere reminded them of a refectory; a monastic dining room where monks share their silent meals. Gabby couldn't help wondering why the date was wrong. Could it be that they had arrived on the wrong Friday? Danielle agreed and decided to ask.

"Mother, when was Pasha?"

"About a month ago, Myriam Dani."

This was the first time that Danielle was called Myriam Dani. It gave her goose bumps. This also meant that Fairfax's calculations were wrong*. Hopefully, he would not be wrong when they had to return home. Their survival depended on getting back to the other Sion, in Switzerland, some 2000 years later.

*When the observational form of the calendar was in use, whether or not an embolismic month was announced after the "last month" (Adar) depended on whether "the barley was ripe". It may be noted that in the Bible the name of the first month, Aviv, literally means "spring" but originally it probably meant "the ripening of barley".

Thus, if Adar was over and the barley was not yet ripe, an additional month was observed. However, according to some traditions, the announcement of the month of Aviv could also be postponed depending on the condition of the roads used by families to come to Jerusalem for the Passover. An adequate numbers of lambs to be sacrificed at the Temple

and this depended on the ripeness of the barley that was needed for the first fruits ceremony.
Under the codified rules, the Jewish calendar is based on the Metonic cycle of 19 years, of which 12 are common years (12 months) and 7 leap years (13 months). The leap years are years 3, 6, 8, 11, 14, 17, and 19 of the Metonic cycle. Year 19 (there is no year 0) of the Metonic cycle is a year exactly divisible by 19 (when the Jewish year number, when divided by 19, has no remainder). In the same manner, the remainder of the division indicates the year in the Metonic cycle (years 1 to 18) the year is in.
During leap years, Adar I (or Adar Aleph — "first Adar") is added before the regular Adar. Adar I is actually considered to be the extra month, and has 30 days. Adar II (or Adar Bet — "second Adar") is the "real" Adar, and has the usual 29 days. For this reason, holidays such as Purim are observed in Adar II, not Adar I.
– Source: Wikipedia

Note from the author:
The professor had made a miscalculation, something that could have happened very easily considering this complicated system of months and days of the year. However, he was still close enough to get the information his employer was after.

8

Sion, Switzerland, May 31ˢᵗ 2011

Danielle and Gabby were planned to return to the present from their second trip at 18.30 hours and Professor William Fairfax was getting more nervous every minute. Things were out-pacing him now. Of course, it had been quite an adventure so far and he had already received generous pay cheques from his unknown employer, so at the beginning, he couldn't have cared less who his employer was, as long as he was able to build his time machine as well as his bank account. The ERFAB was his life's work, but right now he had become concerned.

So far, his mysterious employer had always been friendly on the phone. The Swiss seemed to be particularly interested in Biblical history. Bill presumed that his chief had been present in the glass office above the lab the moment the women were brought in and he was right; through a tinted, one-way window, his employer had secretly witnessed how Danielle and Gabby were sent back in time. The women had been easy to persuade, because the probe had brought back stunning views of the most famous time in Christian history. The women had even implored the professor to be sent there and when they had signed their contracts and had disappeared through the wormhole, his employer had congratulated him on his huge achievement by means of a short text message.

Always only communicating by mobile or e-mail, Fairfax's employer had introduced himself to the professor as the director of an organisation called 'SBS-Sion', but never before had Fairfax wondered where all the money was coming from, until today. Up to this point, he had been too focused on building his time machine - his ERFAB - impatient and anxious to get it into action, so he had never asked any questions before and when Sardis had entered the laboratory - introduced by Ms Kaiser - he had initially thought that the Cardinal was working side by side with the Organisation, until the Cardinal had started asking him questions about the operation. He had insisted on seeing the ERFAB and on speaking with Danielle and Gabby the moment they had returned from their first trip. However, as Sardis seemed to know Ms Kaiser very well, Fairfax felt as if his chief had not told him everything. He had felt left out.

Ms Kaiser - who had been the professor's assistant from day one - had obviously played a double role. Now he knew that it had been Ms Kaiser who had made the phone call to the Vatican; she had betrayed the secret entrance and had opened the door as soon as the Cardinal had arrived. Obviously, the professor had expected Sardis to be part of the secret organisation that was financing his experiment and if it hadn't been for Danielle's remarks, he might have never found out in time that the Cardinal was not.

It seemed as if a race was going on; a race between his unknown employer and Sardis; a race for power. Fairfax knew that Danielle had felt threatened by this imposing character standing over Gabby's bed asking questions and she had urged Fairfax to contact his employer to check out whether Sardis was in on it, or that they should be on guard. So, as soon as the professor had found a chance to do so, he had contacted his chief, who sounded concerned on the phone, especially when he had mentioned Ms Kaiser, but the Swiss hadn't gone into it. After a meagre 'thank you', his chief had simply broken the connection.

Soon afterward, the women had been sent on their second trip that would last three days. Before he left, the Cardinal had told the professor that he would return in three days' time to hear all about their second trip. Being mistrustful, Fairfax had walked him all the way to the exit, curious as to where the Cardinal would go to and when he saw him stepping into a black, chauffeured limousine with tinted glass, it had given him the chills.

This event was followed by the mysterious disappearance of Ms Kaiser. Fairfax had no idea what had happened to her, but shortly after his latest phone call with his chief about the presence of the Cardinal, she had simply disappeared.

No one had seen her since and her personal items were also missing. After a thorough search, he had simply concluded that she had probably fled. If not, then what else could have happened to her? He refused to think about the power of the Organisation and realised that he could very well be working for people who were not only after something important, but also had bad intentions with it.

An hour spent worrying about it brought him out in a cold sweat as he finally began to fathom out the incredible adventure he had entered into, along with the two young women. It had been the Organisation that had ordered him to send the probe to ancient Jerusalem to check whether Jesus had lived or not and if it proved feasible, to send the women there to investigate. Obviously, there was an important, on-going mission here and now it was not just the Organisation, but also the Vatican looking over his shoulder. The intentions of SBS-Sion were unknown to the professor, but he could understand the interference of the Vatican. Rome had obvious reasons to become involved. They would protect the Holy Mother Church by eliminating any threats; unwanted discoveries; undesired facts or any proof that contravened Church doctrines. At all costs.

Fairfax now felt crushed by those two powers and this made him afraid for the women's safety. He felt responsible for his employees - and technically, he was. Danielle and Gabby now needed his protection and slowly, a plan was forming in his mind; as soon as the women arrived back from their second trip he would help them escape the base and get undercover. They had to get away from here; away from Sardis. Immediately he started preparations. Although his plan was well thought out, it wouldn't be easy to put it all into action before his unwanted audience reappeared. To his horror, Sardis already arrived at 18.00 hours, so he had to be extremely careful now. For the time being - and to enable his plan to succeed - the professor had to keep Sardis away from the lab, so he lied to the Cardinal that the women were expected to arrive late that evening and that he'd send for him when it was time. He then shared this same information with his employer. In fact, the women were scheduled to come back at 18.30 hours, so when both parties had withdrawn and the pressure was put off for a few hours, he nervously sneaked away to make the final preparations for the escape. Feverishly he hoped that this time, the women would arrive as scheduled.

Bill Fairfax stared at the clock. It was 18.25 hours. All things were set to open the wormhole and teleport Gabby and Danielle back to the present. He was very worried that there would be another flaw, but tried to push all negative thoughts from his mind. During the last few seconds, his heart was beating fast, but then the women appeared, covered in dust. Alarmed to see the professor's nervous behaviour, they immediately understood that something was going on.
Poor Gabby, however, suddenly got sick again, so while the professor told them of his plans, Danielle made herself busy cleaning up to make sure there was no trace that would betray their early arrival.
As soon as all traces had been wiped clean, the professor took them to another part of the underground building. He told them that they had to be as quiet as mice and Gabby, who still had a terrible headache and was feeling very sick, needed all her energy to follow them. Whenever they heard a sound, they froze and tried not to breathe too heavily. After what seemed like an hour, they reached the location of the hiding place the professor had prepared for them. He told them to keep very quiet and left them alone in the room, locking them in before he went back to the lab. The women looked around in the room, which looked like a prison cell. It probably was. In the corner was a small, open, basic metal wet room and on the beds they found their luggage, a sack with bread rolls and small cartons of apple juice.
They had no idea how long they'd have to wait.

The professor returned to the lab and arrived only a few minutes before Sardis reappeared. The Cardinal immediately noticed the wet spots on the professor's back, his arm pits and the sweat on his forehead and thought that Fairfax was just nervous. Although his gut told him otherwise, he thought no more of it.

Later that evening, Fairfax had to put up his show. He had to act as if Danielle and Gabby were going to come back from their second trip any minute now and when that moment came, Fairfax tried to open the wormhole. Of course, when nothing happened, he faked a panic attack in front of Sardis and his employer - who was following the scene as usual behind the glass window. He explained how he had again 'failed' to bring the two time travellers back. Sardis seemed to buy his act, as he became furious with the professor and demanded that he'd try again. Of course, that wasn't possible. According to the programming of the ERFAB, they'd have to wait the customary 24 hours. However, Bill's chief had seen this happen before and it wasn't as much of a surprise to him. In fact, he seemed to immediately accept that they had to wait another whole day for Bill's second attempt and there was another peculiarity; the Swiss didn't interfere or interact with Sardis at all, as if he wanted to keep the Cardinal in the dark that he was present in the lab.

Bill got confused. Did his chief accept Sardis' presence? Or was the Cardinal part of the show after all? Would Sardis even be aware of the man behind the tinted glass window? At this point, Fairfax really felt the need to confront his employer and get some solid answers this time, for it was driving him mad, but right now he had a different mission to focus on.

It wasn't until after midnight that Fairfax was able to get back to the women. Making sure no one had seen him, he turned the camera and alarm system off. Then he sneaked out, carefully avoiding being seen or heard. He held his breath at every a corner he turned and every door he opened, afraid that he would run into someone.

In the meantime, Danielle and Gabby had cleaned themselves up; changed their clothes; eaten a few rolls and had finished-off a carton of apple juice. The colour had returned to Gabby's cheeks now and she felt much better. A strange sound outside the prison door startled them. They stopped talking and didn't dare move a muscle. There was indeed heavy breathing on the other side of the door. Suddenly, the door was unlocked and they jumped, not knowing who to expect, but when the door opened, they saw a familiar face.

"Bill! Thank God it's you!" Gabby ran into the professor's arms, who now was all fingers and thumbs. He clearly felt the electric shock that went through his body, but couldn't place it. In a whisper, he started, "Shh, don't make a sound. We have to be extremely careful, as we have to go back to the main entrance and that won't be easy."

"Bill, how do we know we won't get followed?" Gabby was getting way too nervous for this kind of adventure.

"You won't, but you simply have to get away." the professor explained, "Here's some money to keep you going for at least two weeks and most importantly, don't use your credit cards! Travel through different countries; leave no trace; book into hotels under your false names and take this flight out of Paris to the States."

With this he gave them their fake passports and their airline tickets for the flight from Paris to New York. After New York they would be on their own.

"Here are the keys to a car outside; it's the only one I could get my hands on. It's a white Volvo. Drive through Germany into Holland and from Holland to Paris. I have also booked fake flights from Amsterdam to London and from London to LA under your own names. With any luck, this will confuse anyone who will try to follow you."

Fairfax had been busy on the Internet, making all the necessary arrangements. Getting the false US passports had been the most difficult to arrange, but apparently, everything is possible if you are prepared to pay the required price.

Bill was hopeful that they would escape.

Quietly, the three shadows shuffled through the corridors toward the main entrance. They hardly dared to breath. At the exit, Bill said his goodbyes and after making sure that the alarm was still off, they were able to safely open the door and get away without being seen by the cameras.
The professor had thought things through.

While Gabby and Danielle fled in the dark, Sardis felt that something was wrong and decided not to return to his hotel just yet, but to keep an eye on the professor. So, when Bill returned to the lab, he bumped into the Cardinal, who looked at him with triumphant eyes.
I knew it!
"Ah, professor, still out and about at this hour?"
"Oh, your eminence, you gave me a fright, I didn't expect anyone to wander through the corridors at this time of night."
Bill wiped the sweat from his brow.
"You must tell me exactly where Ms Parker and Ms Standford are. They are here, aren't they?"
"No, you are mistaken." replied the professor, looking at everything except into the Cardinal's eyes. "We had this problem before, not being able to get them back on the said time and then we had to wait a full day in order to try again. The machine has been programmed to create the wormhole at a certain time of day and the device they are carrying is set to these particular times. If they miss that moment, they know the wormhole won't form and they have to wait a full day."
Bill felt more confident now, for he wasn't lying about that, but the Cardinal trusted his instinct and his instinct told him that the women had flown. Slowly, a plan formed in Sardis' mind. Danielle and Gabby would depend on train stations, airports, car rentals, hotels, etc., like everybody else, so he knew he'd find them, eventually. He turned on the spot and left the building.

As soon as they reached the main road, Danielle and Gabby followed the signs to Berne, Basel, Saarbrücken and finally,

75

Liège/Maastricht. The moment the sun rose above the horizon, Danielle checked her rear-view mirror constantly to see if any particular car was following them, but by doing this, she didn't see the car in front of her moving to the left and she nearly drove into the back of a slow moving truck. Gabby screamed. Immediately Danielle hit the brakes and turned into the emergency lane. Their hearts were pounding. *Jesus Christ that was close…!*
It was obvious. After driving all night, fatigue had overwhelmed them, so the women decided to check into the nearest motel using the false names they had practiced in the car; the names which were on their false passports. Little did they know, that Sardis was already getting closer to finding them. They had underestimated his wit and power. Sardis had the means to check hotel, airline and rental car bookings. He could trace them the moment they used a credit card and even if they were using cash to pay their way and false credentials, he had put a very clever man on the job to track them down.

In the meantime, the professor's employer received a note that a white Volvo was missing from the car park. The Swiss frowned and then smiled.

Danielle and Gabby had slept well into the afternoon. After a quick snack they checked out, paying in cash. They had plenty of time, as their flight to New York would not take off before the end of the following week. It was of utmost importance to travel a lot and shake off anyone who might be following them before flying to the States. Bill had told them to stay off the main roads if possible and take crazy routes which made no sense at all. Following this advice, they now arrived in Tongerlo in Belgium and decided to act like American tourists, exploring the country. They loved the old town of Tongerlo and even discovered a Da Vinci museum in the abbey buildings. After studying several of his drawings and inventions, they were surprised to discover a large and unspoilt copy of Da Vinci's famous Last Supper. What a fantastic find! They wondered how it got there and who had painted it, so they decided to ask the woman at the ticket office. She was pleased to see their interest in the museum's most valued piece and handed over an A4 copy of the history of the painting. In English.

Allegedly, one of Da Vinci's students, Andrea Solario, had made a large copy of the Last Supper in Milan, Italy, around 1506. In 1545, this copy had been bought by the abbot of Tongerlo, Arnold Streyters, to be displayed in his abbey, which was - at that time - very prosperous. Solario probably painted the copy to safe-keep the information put on the original painting by the great Renaissance master, as soon as the latter had noticed the quick deterioration of his original mural. On the mural, Da Vinci had painted on dry plaster, not on the usual wet plaster. He had chosen this method, so he could work on the mural in stages. Naturally, this would be impossible with a fresco, which had to be painted quickly on wet plaster. Because it had been painted on dry plaster, the original Last Supper in Milan had already started to fade and crumble after only a few years' time. However, the copy - being a real painting - had remained intact. The fact that this copy had actually arrived at the abbey of Tongerlo - albeit almost half a century later - was a small miracle in itself. It had even arrived undamaged, in spite of its long journey through a Europe that was politically very unstable. The artist himself had not added his signature to the painting, which makes it even more likely that this copy was never meant to be sold, or promote the skills of the artist. Solario had painted this copy because it had been a mission, rather than a commission.

Da Vinci always told two stories in his paintings; the one to be understood by many and the one to be understood by a few. Obviously, the symbolism in this particular painting, as well as its clues and hints, were not meant to be forgotten.

With the experiences Danielle and Gabby had had during their visits to Judea in the 1st century CE, they looked upon the scene with different eyes than they had ever have done before. Of course they hadn't expected the characters on the painting to look exactly like the people they had met, but they did understand that the scene they were looking at was a special New Year ritual, held on the first day of Nissan, about two weeks before the actual crucifixion had taken place, because after the arrest, Oshu had been in prison for two weeks, waiting for the courier to return with the royal pardon from Tiberius.

Danielle and Gabby realised that this - now so famous - New Year fertility ritual with the wine and the bread to thank God and Mother Earth for the gift of food and drink, was in fact an ancient Zadok ritual; a Thanksgiving ritual that dates back to the days of Abraham and Melchizedek. The Eucharist - a Greek word meaning 'giving thanks' - would later be adopted by the Christian religion to become one of the most important rituals in the Roman Catholic Church.

Though much has changed in 2000 years, some things still exist, cleverly hidden in art, in rituals and, of course, in stories.

9

Sion, Switzerland, June 3rd 2011

Professor Bill Fairfax sensed that he was being watched carefully by his employer when he repeated his act the following evening, while faking a second attempt to get the women back from ancient Judea. Of course, neither Gabby, nor Danielle came through the wormhole, so he closed it and then turned the ERFAB off again. Sardis was standing next to him, perhaps unaware of the invisible presence of the professor's employer, who was indeed standing behind the large, tinted glass window on the office above the lab, closely following the event. Fairfax sat down and held his head in his hands, faking another, well-rehearsed panic attack.

"I'm so sorry, I cannot bring them back." he yammered, "I don't know why. Maybe they are simply unable to come to the co-ordinates. I can only try again tomorrow."

Without saying another word, Sardis turned on his heels and left the lab, obviously livid, but determined to find the women. The Cardinal was certain that they were no longer in ancient Jerusalem, but right here; in the present and he was glad he had already sent a man after them to try and locate them. He expected to hear from him anytime now and didn't want to be in the lab for the others to eavesdrop on his conversation.

The professor watched Sardis leave. He sighed and braced himself to be interrogated by his own employer: the head of SBS-Sion. He knew he had done the right thing by helping the women to escape, but how could he get out of the mess he was in now? The phone rang. It was his chief. His voice was loud and he sounded agitated. "So professor, you will agree with me that Ms Parker and Ms Standford are probably lost to us. I am expecting a full report from you - stating all the facts - on my desk tomorrow morning. Yes?"

For the first time, Fairfax felt intimidated, treated like a schoolboy.

They had apparently forgotten that it was *his* invention that had enabled the Organisation to investigate the life and times of Jesus. He got angry.

Who did they think they were?

"If this means giving up on Standford and Parker just like that, I will no longer co-operate." the professor stated. He then boldly broke the connection, fully aware of the consequences this could have for his career. Deep inside, he hoped his employer would call him back, but the telephone remained silent. His heart was pounding as he walked toward his private quarters. As soon as he arrived, he took a couple of valerian-root tablets he'd bought earlier to calm himself down. His hands were shaking and although he knew he had done the right thing, he was afraid and tired; tired of Sardis and tired of the Organisation. He wanted out, but he knew he couldn't get out. His contract with SBS-Sion was binding.

Paris, France, June 12th 2011

For over a week, the women had driven through Belgium and northern France and today, they finally arrived in one of the most romantic cities on earth; Paris. Their flights to the States were departing from Charles de Gaulle Airport in a few days' time and they wanted to be in the city on time. They were quite certain that no one had followed them. Of course they had been very careful, taking strange routes, just to see if they were being followed, but so far, nothing had happened and by the time they arrived in Paris, they were quite relaxed.

It was Gabby's Birthday and they celebrated it by treating themselves to a wonderful lunch in one of the famous restaurants in the city, but after all that travelling, the women were now very tired indeed. To get some much needed rest, they decided to look for a hotel not far from the city centre. However, the moment they checked into the hotel, they noticed someone who looked similar to the man they had seen in the motel in Limburg two weeks before. He was sitting in the lounge, trying to hide behind a newspaper.

For the first time they realised that perhaps they had been followed after all and a nervous jolt went through their bodies. Trying not to show anything, they turned and walked toward the elevators. Gabby chewed her lip when they got into the elevator and anxiously pushed through the people who were coming out, closely followed by Danielle. Their room was on the 5th floor. On a sudden brainwave, Danielle pressed the button for the 9th floor. When the elevator stopped at the 5th floor, they got out as quickly as possible and allowed the elevator to continue to the 9th floor. However, when Danielle tried to open the room with the key card, it didn't work.

"Why on earth did they stop using normal keys and replace them with these bloody key cards!" snorted Danielle.

Gabby quickly put her finger to her lips to hush her friend; someone was using the staircase. The grinding footsteps came closer and closer. If only that key card worked properly; someone was bound to turn up any second now.

Come on already!

The green light appeared and finally, the door unlocked. They jumped into the room, pulled in their luggage as quickly as possible, closed the door behind them and waited anxiously, listening to every sound their ears could pick up. When all remained quiet, Gabby opened the door slightly to check out the hallway. It was empty. There was no one there and they heard no more footsteps. If they had indeed been followed, this person could have seen them just before they had entered the room, but perhaps he had fallen for the elevator trick and had followed it to the 9th floor. Gabby closed the door again and breathed out.

Perhaps it was just their imagination working overtime.

They unpacked, fell on their beds and stared at the ceiling, unable to say a word. They realised that, from that moment on, they needed to be even more careful than they had already been.

The next day was a full day without any commitments, except for keeping out of harm's way. They didn't dare to go out of the room at all and even phoned room service for breakfast and lunch, but finally they realised that - at a certain inevitable moment - they'd have to leave the room. To avoid being followed to the airport, they had to dream up a plan to shake off anyone who might have followed them here.

It wouldn't be easy.

"What if we split up?" asked Gabby.

"Are you joking? Gabby, if we split up and something happens to either of us, then what?"

"Yes, I guess you're right."

"So what do we do?" asked Danielle.

"Why don't we go somewhere with lots of people, something like the Place du Tertre, where we can disappear into the crowd. We'll have to check out of the hotel and find another accommodation for tomorrow night though. Perhaps we should go straight to the airport and find a place there? You know; just a chair somewhere on the airport, perhaps in a lounge, far away from our gate, just in case?"

Danielle thought it through and agreed that it was the best plan they had so far, so the next morning they packed their things; left the room; took the elevator downstairs; checked out and drove off toward Montmartre. They abandoned the white Volvo a few blocks from the famous site and continued on foot. The women had to resist looking over their shoulders, so as not to attract too much attention. Then they saw the impressive, white structure of the Sacre Coeur, dominating the skyline.

"I have always wondered why there are no churches dedicated to Jesus." said Danielle. "It's always either his mother, a Saint, an Archangel or a Biblical event, but here we have this great big church, dedicated to his sacred heart! Isn't it beautiful?"

Danielle had never thought of this. The biggest and most important Roman Catholic church is dedicated to St. Peter and apart from many known and unknown Saints and Archangel Michael, there are numerous churches dedicated to his mother, Mary. Where is the church of Jesus? Which church is dedicated to The Man Himself?

"Do you know anything about the Sacred Heart Cult, Gabby?"

"Not much, but I do know it was the oldest cult of all and the last one to be accepted by the Church of Rome. Odd, isn't it?"

Danielle nodded. "You know, I've always wanted to see the churches of Paris. They say that the mysterious meridian of St. Sulpice, the 'Green Men' of the Nôtre Dame and the replica of the Ark of the Covenant in the Church of St. Roch are absolute 'musts' when in Paris. What do you think?"

Gabby agreed. She had always been intrigued by this particular replica of the Ark, wondering why it would be kept in the church of St. Roch of all places. She took out her map while they walked to the Place du Tertre and turned it to study the Metro map.

"Let's go to St. Roch and the Louvre first and then walk toward the centre from there. Look, we can take the metro from Pigalle to Madeleine. Did you know that la Madeleine church was originally designed as a monument to glorify Napoleon's army? The architect, Pierre-Alexandre Vignon, had been inspired by the Roman Maison Carré in Nimes, so it looks like a Roman temple. After the fall of Napoleon, the Catholic King Louis XVIII determined that the structure would be used as a church, dedicated to Mary Magdalene. I'd love to see it. It's not far from St. Roch, so we can do both."

That moment, a man in a hat passed them in the street. Frozen, Danielle grabbed Gabby's arm.

"Let's get out of here. I feel as if we are being shadowed right now. I'm a bit dizzy and need to sit down somewhere anyway. Perhaps we can have a coffee in one of the cafe's. I'm sure we can find a dark corner."

Danielle did look a little pale and Gabby became worried. They didn't know yet that Danielle was pregnant.

"What's the matter?" asked Gabby.

"No idea, maybe it's just the stress of the whole situation, I didn't sleep much last night."

"Well, I guess we can sit in the café over there and have a cappuccino with lots of whipped cream on top. That will bring the colour back to your cheeks!"

They decided to risk sitting in a crowded café, hidden behind one of the beautiful pillars, that had been adorned with statues of barely dressed women. It looked as if the café had once been a theatre building. They could look out from where they were sitting and ordered their cappuccino, but had to wait a long time before it arrived. However, for Danielle it was good to sit down. She took a few deep breaths and when the coffees finally arrived, she enjoyed spooning up her rich, whipped cream topped cappuccino.

When they had both rested and were ready to pay and leave, Gabby lost a heartbeat when she saw the exact same man in the hat on the opposite side of the street, looking straight at them while they waited at the cash register. It was the same man they had seen at the hotel; she was certain of it. Danielle, who had noticed the alarmed expression on her friend's face, followed her stare and when his eyes met hers, she froze. The man smiled courteously at them, touched his hat with his right hand and then casually walked away.

"Oh my God, Danielle, are we bugged or something? Quick, let's search our things; shoes; clothes; everything! We must get rid of him or we will never be safe!"

In their panic they emptied all their bags and pockets, took off their shoes and as a result, they attracted a lot of attention. However, they found nothing. Also, they didn't carry mobile phones or anything else that could possibly allow anyone to trace them.

Gabby pursed her lips. "What if it was just a coincidence? I mean, we are in Paris, this is one of the most popular sites and we did stay at a hotel, like most tourists do. Maybe he really was just a tourist."

"No Gabby, he was also at the motel in Limburg; he was in the hotel lounge yesterday the moment we arrived and now he is here. That's not a coincidence. This man is following us and he allowed us to know this, just to show us that he can find us, no matter where we go. This man is an expert and he is either from the Organisation, or he's been sent by Sardis and if you ask me, I would prefer the Organisation to Sardis. Either way, we need to shake him off and get away from here, because right now we are sitting ducks. Oh, if only I hadn't felt so dizzy!"

Danielle was angry with herself, feeling she had caused this to happen. They had to think of another way to shake off their tail. The plans for the sightseeing tour were abandoned and using the cash Bill had given them before leaving Sion, the women went into a boutique and came out - one at the time - wearing different clothes and walking off into different directions. It seemed only logical to split up after all, hoping that this would confuse the man in the hat. They had agreed to meet again at the airport and until then, they had to disappear into the streets of Paris individually.

Their plan could have worked, but the man in the hat had received specific instructions to follow Danielle in case the women split up, so he did. It wasn't all that difficult to follow a tall blond beauty around Paris and when the man in the hat arrived at the airport that evening and saw the two women meeting up, he smiled contently. He knew he was good at his job. Immediately he made a quick phone call to keep his chief informed.

Sion, Switzerland, June 16th 2011

Sardis had been in and out of the lab almost every day. He was getting nervous. The Cardinal had sent his best man to find the two women. However, as he himself was unable to contact him, Sardis had been waiting for his call for two weeks now. Gazing upon the Rue du Scex from his hotel window, he could hear the refreshing rush of fountain on the square below, but the otherwise soothing sound now failed in keeping him calm. His hands turned into fists when his last bit of patience deserted him.

What was taking him so long!

Then, the loud ringtone of his mobile startled him. He grabbed it before it rang twice. "Pronto!"

There was a long pause in which a broad smile appeared on the Cardinal's face.

"Bene!"

He hung up and triumphantly started to hum a tune from a Verdi opera. His man had finally found them, but the Cardinal decided not to let the professor know about this. The last thing he wanted was for Fairfax to contact the women to warn them off. It was better to make his own plans, so instead he played along and called Fairfax with the request to keep him in the loop about Ms Parker and Ms Standford in the event they arrived back from ancient Jerusalem. Then he packed his bags and left.

Sardis now had his own agenda to follow.

In the meantime, Fairfax had had another phone conversation with his employer, which had gone surprisingly well. Perhaps too well, but he didn't care. The professor had now been given the authority he deserved, as well as a raise in salary, which was always welcome. Apparently falling for the professor's lie about his failure to bring the women back from ancient Jerusalem, his employer told the professor that he was allowed to try and retrieve the women as many times as he desired. Furthermore, he also got permission to work on a new probe, which would be much more advanced than the first one. They were hoping to have a prototype ready in a few weeks' time. This new probe would have several new advantages that might come in handy, so over the past two weeks, Fairfax had been working hard on it and - for the first time since the day the women had fled - he was excited again about the project, though he was keeping his fingers crossed that Danielle and Gabby had safely made it to the States. Also, the Cardinal was now finally out of his hair for the time being and he felt as if a new chapter had started for him. It wasn't long before he lost himself in his work again.

At the same time, the head of the Organisation, SBS-Sion, was also pleased, but Fairfax had no idea that his employer already knew that the women were no longer in ancient Jerusalem. Everyone except the professor was aware of the fact that Danielle and Gabby had arrived in the States on June 16th. Gabby had rented a new, fully furnished flat under her false name and Danielle had been foolish enough to go back home.

Diary entry - Bethanu, 33 AD - day 1
We have travelled to a place not far from Jerusalem, which is called Bethanu. They call it the House of the Mother and it serves more than one purpose. Not only is it the home of Mariamne and her noble family, it is also a hospital for the sick and disabled; for deserted pregnant women; neglected elderly people and the extremely poor. It is also a place of initiation. In short, Bethanu is a small village with a main house and that is where we are now. We travelled with several of the men whom we've met at Maria's house, while she herself stayed in Jerusalem. These men didn't speak Greek, so the journey was very quiet. In turn we rode on a donkey, because it was a difficult walk (especially in these sandals!). After a bath and some food and drink we felt much better and now I finally have a moment to write my diary again. We have two more days before we will be 'sucked' back to the present. This means that we can stay here until the morning of the third day of our stay. We are hoping to meet Mariamne soon; they say she's here.
Unfortunately, we found out that Oshu is not. It's sad that Mariamne and Oshu aren't together. It seems wrong. Maybe she has duties here and Oshu is still in hiding? They probably want to keep it a secret that he is still alive, for his own safety. So, we decided to wait; perhaps we will see Mariamne later on. Gabby and I will now retire for the night. We're very tired and would love a lie-down. I'll write again tomorrow when I have the chance.

Diary entry - Bethanu, 33 AD - day 2
Today was interesting. We met Mariamne late this morning and spoke about Oshu. She assured us that he's alright and that we mustn't tell anyone that he's planning to go to Carmel. We are not to speak about Oshu with anybody. After we promised her this, she relaxed and gave us a tour around Bethanu. The hospital is amazing! People who need help are

treated like guests and Mariamne is clearly loved. She also showed us what looked like a temple, but we were not allowed to enter. In another building there were men engaged in conversation, some of whom we recognised as Oshu's relatives, perhaps brothers. The conversations were sometimes a bit rough, as the men seemed to disagree with one another all the time.

Mariamne asked us to stay this time and we want to so much, but we really have to travel back to Jerusalem tomorrow morning. Mariamne was sad to hear this. Obviously, she doesn't understand why we have to leave again, but how could we explain this to her?

During the evening, Gabby had attracted the attention of one of the men who ate with us. His name is Shimom. He looks a little bit like Oshu, so we thought he might be one of his brothers. Smiles were exchanged, but when he spoke to her, I couldn't understand a word he was saying. It was probably Aramaic or some local dialect, but certainly not Greek. I tried to speak Greek to him, but he just shook his head and continued in his own dialect, as if he refused to believe that we couldn't understand him. Maybe he simply refused to speak Greek. Mariamne then told us that there is a difference of opinion within the family, between those who embrace the Greek culture and those who are disgusted by it. Apparently, it reminds them of the Greek occupation a few centuries earlier, when their own Jewish culture had been repressed and the Greek culture had been forced upon them. To them - Greeks or Romans - they were all the same: usurpers. Though this difference of opinion caused friction within the royal family, they did endure one another's company at dinner and respected each other as members of the same family. Some of the family were members of the Essenes or Therapeutae; a gnostic sect, which some scholars consider to be the original Christianity. They can easily be recognised by their white robes, gentle ways and soft voices. The Essenes are very clean, bathing almost all the time. It's a sort of ritual cleansing.

We've been fortunate to meet several of them. It has become obvious to us; this family was torn apart by politics, bloodlines, differences of allegiance and differences of religion. Nevertheless, they embrace Gabby and me. They accept us as their guests and honour us with their hospitality, both here at Bethanu as well as in Jerusalem and I am grateful for that.

I feel a special connection with Mariamne; she's like a sister to me and hugs me often, but also Gabby, which pleases me so! Not being able to communicate with anyone, I can see that Gabby feels a bit lonely sometimes.

We are to set off early tomorrow morning, so we will go to sleep now. I am not looking forward to return to the present, but I do need to feel some modern comforts again.

Like socks.

Rome, Italy, June 20th 2011

Sardis laughed out loud, finding the remark about the socks very amusing. He put the diary away and prepared to leave the car. Danielle noticed they were driving into the garage of a large house, not far from the Vatican. As soon as the car was inside, the door of the garage was closed and the secure sign was given. Sardis opened the door himself, while the driver and the other man struggled with a rather lively Danielle, who refused to give in without a fight. Although her hands and feet were tied up, she made it difficult for the men to carry her upstairs and at one point she fell, hit her head against the wall and passed out. Sardis startled when he saw the bleeding wound on her head and hit the man who had dropped Danielle hard in the face with the back of his hand.

"You stupid fool, what if she's hurt, or worse?" Sardis admonished him furiously. "Come on, we better get her inside. Gently now!"

As soon as they arrived in a large room, which was furnished luxuriously with Louis XV style furniture and all the modern comforts one could ever wish for, Danielle was carried into the bedroom of the apartment. It had already been prepared for her and the adjoining luxury bathroom with free standing roll top bath with golden taps contained everything a woman would need; from towels, soaps and creams to other specific necessities for women. Sardis looked around to check whether his instructions had been carried out to his satisfaction. So far, he was pleased with what he saw, but he was worried about Danielle and refused to leave her side.

When Danielle regained consciousness, her head hurt. She felt dizzy and moaned. Immediately, Sardis' bent over her to make sure he was the first thing she saw when she opened her eyes. He wanted her to feel kindness and love for him, not disgust. Showing her kindness and love might win her for him.

"Hush, you are safe now." he said with a soft voice. "Just lie here for a while and look at your new home! Isn't it beautiful?"

Sardis smiled from ear to ear. Here she was, caught in his web, unable to escape. His mission had proved successful. His joy was so obvious, that Danielle became even more angry. He had taken everything away from her and now he expected her to be happy in this golden prison? Her head started spinning again, so she closed her eyes; she just wanted to be left alone; to sleep and forget the horrible mess she found herself in, but sleep did not come.

Sardis was a firm believer of 'The Prophecy' and in Jesus' 'Second Coming'. With Danielle and her unborn child now in his possession, he only needed one other item to be able to make Rome the New Jerusalem and Danielle would be his means of getting the artefact he was after: The Ark of the Covenant.

Ever since he was a child, he had enjoyed reading books from his father's library, which had been famous for its collection of ancient books and rare scrolls. Only a few other libraries in Italy were known to have such an extensive collection of historical books. For several centuries, his ancestors had been collecting books for this library.

Not as much for status, but to preserve and protect ancient literature and knowledge. It had happened so many times in history; famous libraries with priceless books had been burned to the ground or otherwise destroyed; sometimes accidentally, but mostly on purpose. Realising the sheer wealth of forgotten knowledge and forbidden history that was hidden in his father's library, Sardis had become a passionate student of ancient Greek, Latin and ancient handwritings, so that he could read the books that intrigued him. He had even picked up Hebrew while climbing the ladder toward the rank of Cardinal. More books were read and eventually he had learned a lot about the history of the world and the history of Christianity. Sardis had, however, also discovered an abundance of flaws, mistranslations and errors...

Throughout the ages, Church doctrines and dogmas were often based on politics or the whims of Popes, of whom several had been disastrous agents for the Catholic Faith. Sardis realised that the entire Catholic system was cracking up because of the injuries and impacts of old mistakes. The damage had been done, but was it really irreversible? Unlike many others, Sardis didn't turn against the Church of Rome. All he wanted was to put his finger on these wounds and heal them, like Christ had done during his ministry. This library had given his family power, wisdom and knowledge and Sardis felt that he had been chosen by God to become a true Pontifax Maximus, building bridges between religions and between science and mysticism. In the old days, wisdom and knowledge had been both friend and foe to the Holy Church of Rome. Although realising the myth on which the entire religion seemed to be based, the Church now had to stubbornly hold on to it, so as not to lose face, but as soon as the truth would reveal itself, either through books or new discoveries, the Church of Rome would either have to accept it, or, if necessary, destroy it. That the Church has always known the truth about the 1st century CE had become all too clear to the Cardinal.

Pope Leo X had even admitted it.
"All ages can testifie enough howe profitable that fable of Christe hath been to us and our companie."

It had made Sardis laugh out loud when he had found it in his father's library. The library of the Sardis family was a well-known secret in Italy. All over the country, books were kept behind lock and key, out of sight, but the Vatican dare not touch this one. This family was way too powerful to have as an enemy, even for the Church.

Antonio Enrico Sardis Barberini was not the first of his family to become a Prince of the Church. On his mother's side, he was linked to the Barberini, of whom one family member named Maffeo had even been elected to become Pope in the 17th century. Better known as Pope Urban VIII, he had carried a coat of arms with three bees. The bees represent a powerful symbol, going back to Visigothic times and even to the Essenes of the Near-East, who had been closely related to both John the Baptist and Jesus. The Essenes were called 'the bees' because of their industrious spiritual work, the beehive shaped houses they lived and worked in and their 'spiritual teachings that were as sweet as heavenly honey'.

Feeling closely connected with his ancestors, Sardis used this particular coat of arms and wax seal with the three bees on an azure shield, for all his correspondence. He also enjoyed visiting the Art Gallery, situated in the old palace of the Barberini's, or strolling around the Piazza Barberini with the beautiful Fontana della Api, whenever he could. The great sculptor and mystic Bernini had created many beautiful sculptures for the family.

Sardis knew that they had been lovers of art and music, but also that Pope Urban VIII had been heavily criticised by the people of Rome for taking bronze from the Pantheon to build the baldachin for St. Peter's Basilica.

Sardis smiled when he thought of the now commonly known phrase:

"Quod non fecerunt barbari, fecerunt Barberini"
What the Barbarians didn't do, the Barberini did.

Sardis promised himself and his ancestors to soon give a whole new meaning to that phrase.

The Cardinal settled himself comfortably behind his antique wooden desk in the office, not far from Danielle's bedroom and as he called for her, he began to write a letter. A letter that was addressed to Professor William Fairfax and Dr Gabrielle Standford at the Sion base. Because he had been able to trace Danielle back to her own home, he had also had someone shadowing Gabby, so he knew she was exactly where he wanted her to be: In Sion.
Danielle, who felt a little better after her lie-down, had obeyed his call and sat down in one of the sofas in Sardis' office. She stared at him, wondering why he had summoned her. While writing his letter, a sardonic smile slowly spread across Sardis' face and feeling terribly frustrated and irritated, Danielle looked away and studied the room. Then, her eyes fell on a framed, colourful print of what looked like an old fresco. The scene intrigued her. Curious to find out more about it, she got up from her sofa and walked over to take a closer look. The text, printed on a small plaque underneath the frame, explained the scene.

"Death of the Virgin Mary. Fresco by Mihail and Eutychios (1295) - St. Clement Church, Ohrid, Macedonia".

In the scene, Jesus was standing over his mother's death bed, holding a child in his arms. According to the Bible, Jesus had already gone to heaven when his mother died. Also, who would be the child in his arms? Was it the child that Mariamne had been pregnant with? Or was it another child?

Also, where was Marianne on the fresco? Danielle's gaze went from the mural back to Sardis, who had just finished writing his letter. She saw how he sealed the envelope, pressing his seal with his coat of arms deeply into the soft, red wax. Then he rang a bell to summon a servant, who entered without delay. The young man bowed his head respectfully while taking his orders and departed with the package, containing the letter and other documents. The Cardinal folded his hands and looked at Danielle with small, triumphant eyes.

"There, that's done. Now, I'm sure your friend and the professor will bring me exactly what I desire and when they get here, they will be able to see you, but so that you understand; once they arrive, I cannot permit them to leave again."

Danielle looked at him in disgust and refused to return to her sofa. Sardis, on the other hand, looked back at her with tender eyes full of love for her and for the child in her womb. The Lord had kissed her, he had made love to her and in the eyes of the Cardinal, Danielle was a saint and the mother of a new god; the son of Jesus himself.

He had it all worked out. He'd raise this child to become the Grand Monarch that the world was waiting for; the new King and the prophesised return of Christ himself in 2012, reincarnated into the body of his own son. According to the prophecy he believed in, the New Jerusalem would then come from heaven and a thousand years of peace would cover the earth. All he needed now was a new Salomon's Temple, where he could place - in its Holy of Holies - the most famous relic of them all: the Ark of the Covenant and if anyone could find this ancient artefact - which has been lost since the time of the Knights Templar - it would be Professor Fairfax and Ms Standford. Offering Danielle as a leverage, he knew that the professor would surely obey.

Sardis grinned. He knew that his plan was a cunning one.

"You know, my dearest Danielle, I have been a fan of history from the moment I could read. I have read almost every book from my father's library that was worth reading. Many secret books are kept there, you know; books that were forbidden in the Middle Ages. Because of my fascination with history I had quickly become fascinated by the idea of time travel. Professor Fairfax, however, was the only one worth following, because he claimed to have found a solution to several problems some physicists are still struggling with today. So, I became his shadow. Ms Kaiser, who is very loyal to the Vatican, successfully infiltrated the base in Sion on my orders and enabled me to access the laboratory. Already on my first visit I was delighted to discover that my greatest wish had already come true; two young ladies had been sent back in time to see Christ!"

Sardis stared at a wonderful framed image of Christ. The realistic, black and white drawing looked modern and though Danielle could see that it wasn't Oshu, the resemblance was remarkable. As if someone had drawn the image from memory.

"You see, Danielle, since the day this divine man came to earth, the entire world has changed and I think it did not all change to his liking. He'd not have wanted all the killings, executions and wars. Today he would surely disagree with many of the doctrines and dogmas of the Roman Catholic Church, but today it wouldn't be easy to change things back to the way he would have wanted it. Too many centuries have gone by and believe me, Rome now has its back against the wall."

"We can only make changes if the changes are big enough to be embraced by many and to do this, we need to convince the masses. We need to convince the entire world. So you see, I need to make an important prophecy come true. The prophecy that Jesus will return in the year 2012 and that the Ark of the Covenant will again be placed in a new Temple dedicated to God. A temple which will be built in the New Jerusalem; Rome and you, sweet lady, you were born to make this prophecy come true! You will give birth to his child in 2012 and your friends will find me the Ark of the

Covenant in France! Can't you see, all this is divinely mastered!"

Danielle was struck dumb. Finally she understood it all. The idea was almost too crazy to believe in, but the way Sardis explained it, somehow made sense to her. Her hands touched her belly. The foetus was barely a month old. Could Sardis succeed? Could all this work? Was the world as we know it going to end in 2012, because a new world order would be born? Could this indeed be the same old prophecy that had made the Templars search for the Ark in Jerusalem? She knew that the Knights Templar had tried to create a new Holy Land in southern France. Could this have been the reason? Danielle knew that Gabby had studied this during her history lessons, as they had discussed it during their European tour. Gabby was clearly fascinated by these fighting monks, who seemed to have had their own secret agenda. While protecting pilgrims on the road to Jerusalem, they had secretly searched and found relics and scrolls underneath the Temple Mount and several other places in the Holy Land. Many a secret cargo had been shipped to Cyprus and France in the late 12th century. Could the Ark have been among those items? Would there really be a chance to find it in southern France? Her cheeks glowed. How she missed Gabby. Then a thought crept into her mind which gave her goosebumps. She had to ask.

"When my child is born, will you... will you kill me?"

Silence. Sardis looked at her - his face stern and without emotion. For this was also a serious problem to him. His partner had already wanted him to make her disappear and if he found out that she was still with him, here, in Rome...

He looked away, leaving the question unanswered. Danielle shivered. She knew she had to be careful and win his trust. If Gabby found out that she had been abducted by Sardis, there was still hope and she decided to hang onto that hope.

A servant knocked on the door, announcing a visitor. Sardis seemed surprised and a little concerned. He got up and pushed Danielle toward her bedroom door.

"Go to your bedroom and lock the door, quickly now! And be quiet!"

She obeyed without hesitation. With anxious anticipation, Sardis returned to his desk. "Si?" When a strong, handsome man in a white galabya entered the room, Sardis forced a smile and suppressed the urge to get up. Technically, Izz al Din was Sardis' partner, but in reality, the Arab was his master, for it was Al Din who controlled the Cardinal. He was the one who had given Sardis the money and the power to realise his dream. However, the handsome face that betrayed both wisdom and obsession, did not smile back at Sardis.

"You have disobeyed me, my brother. The woman is here. You couldn't find it in you to get rid of her, could you?"

Sardis looked away, alarmed that Al Din had already found out that Danielle was still alive. He had hoped to keep this from him. He wanted to save Danielle's life and that of the child. However, Izz al Din didn't know that Danielle was pregnant, or at least Sardis thought he didn't.

"If I keep her away from the world, can she not live here, with me?" Sardis replied with sad eyes.

Izz al Din smiled. "Why? Do you love this woman?"

"Yes."

The Arab paused to think and then added,

"If she leaves this house, or if she has any contact with the outside world, I will personally see to it that she disappears. Until then, you can keep her, but be warned!"

He looked at Sardis' desk and noticed Danielle's diary, lying open on a certain page. Sardis quickly closed it and got up from his desk.

How much has he seen?

Sardis wanted him out as quickly as possible.

"Is there anything else I can do for you, my brother?"

"Yes. You can give me her diary."

"No! This diary has to be studied by me. I am the expert on the Gospels, not you. I will study it and give you my full report as soon as I've finished it!"

Izz al Din stared hard at Sardis, as if he suddenly understood the entire situation.

Sardis looked back without blinking, trying not to show his fear for him. The first moment that the Cardinal had started to fear Al Din, was when he had asked him to eliminate Danielle. He had no idea that Al Din would be so ruthless. He had seemed to be such a warm-hearted gentleman when they had first met in Athens, several months earlier.

The secret conference on the east-west matter had been organised by some of the richest people in the world. East and west should be brothers, but they are quickly quarrelling and this quarrelling could only damage world trade and consequently, their wealth and power. To try and solve the east-west problems and to bring peace to the world, would be beneficial for their capital. A prosperous world at peace would stimulate economic growth. In a healthy economy, purchasing-power would rise and their capital would grow with it. Sardis had represented the Vatican at the conference. After all, the Vatican was the owner of the most prosperous bank in the world. Also, being able to discuss religious topics had placed Sardis in a prior position during the conversations.

Izz al Din had approached him during lunch and they had quickly realised that both shared a dream: a Universal Temple for all religions, world peace and a Grand Global Monarch to keep that peace. Naturally, Al Din had his own agenda, but so had Sardis. Al Din wanted this Universal Temple to be in Jerusalem; Sardis in Rome. Al Din wanted to become the supreme Grand Monarch himself, while Sardis wanted Danielle's child to become the Grand Monarch, with himself as Pope. Al Din needed the support of the western world and the Christian religion to be able to execute his plans; Sardis needed the east. A coalition between the two men had started that day, at the Athens Conference. Both men had been unaware of the other's agenda, but they were nevertheless cautious with each other, always on guard.

However, after seeing the diary, Al Din's thoughts now changed to focus on Danielle.

Sardis watched him leave and realised that he had sold his soul to this man. He had united with him because he believed that Al Din was the connection he was looking for, but Al Din had quickly taken over, because he outranked Sardis with money and power. The Sardis family had always been rich, they were 'old money'. Al Din on the other hand was 'new money'. His billions were made when he had successfully invested in oil, solar power and drugs years ago. Sardis hated to be treated like his sidekick, but he had little choice at this point. There was no other way; he just had to endure being belittled by him, for the Cause.

Sardis chewed his lip and his eyes went from the closed office door to the closed door of Danielle's bedroom.

Now she knows...

Having overheard the entire conversation, Danielle was now fully aware of her precarious position. After all, the doors were not sound proof. She sat on her bed; her head in her hands in total despair.

Gabby... come on!!!

11

Sion, Switzerland, June 21ˢᵗ 2011

Dressed in all-black, as was customary at SBS-Sion, the Swiss stared down at the professor and Gabby from behind the tinted glass window. He had just got off the phone with Fairfax, who had finally told him everything; why he had helped the women to escape three weeks before and that Ms Standford had just returned with the alarming news that Danielle had been abducted by Cardinal Sardis. He knew that he had to take action fast. There was no time to lose. Anxiously, he opened the package with the red wax seal that had just been brought in. After hearing the professor's news, it hadn't been difficult for him to form an idea as to who the sender was, but he had no idea what Sardis might want from him. He frowned as he took out the files and opened the letter from the Cardinal while turning toward the men standing behind him. One was Georg, his assistant. The other was a pale, tall man who stared back hard at the others with his grey-blue eyes, whilst nervously smoking a cigarette. All of them were distressed by the news that Fairfax had just shared with them. Also, it appeared that the letter from the Cardinal was not addressed to the Organisation, but to Professor Fairfax and Dr Gabrielle Standford. The Swiss read it quickly before he would share it with the others and by the time he had finished, his concern for Danielle had become dimmed by a sudden jolt of amusement and intrigue.

To Prof. William Fairfax and Dr Gabrielle Standford,
I hope this letter finds you both in good health. I believe you may wish to negotiate with me on my terms for retrieving Danielle, who is with me, quite safe and comfortable at this very moment. I know you want her back alive and unharmed, so I must implore you to read this letter carefully, for this is not a request. It is an order.
In the hills of the Razès in southern France you will go on a hunt for me, to find a relic so rare and famous, that you must

not discuss this quest with anyone. Over the past centuries, many have searched for it, but it has been kept well hidden. When the last person who had known of its whereabouts had died, the relic got lost. Though this very fact was kept from the world, Rome didn't give up on it and continued to build churches to house the relic the moment it would be found. There are only a few obscure clues to its location and I know it still rests somewhere and to put it simply; I want it.

The deal is simple: find me the holy relic and you will get Danielle back alive and unharmed. Everything I know about the relic is in the package. It contains all my research about its history; its journeys and its destinations.

I trust you will succeed, but beware; my people will shadow you, so there is no option for escape or betrayal. I will know immediately if you find it and then you will bring it to me without delay. If the object is genuine, you will all be free to leave. One more warning: if you find it, do not touch it, take everything that is made of metal off your body, wear rubber gloves and rubber-soled shoes. Put the relic in a box made of lead and avoid being too close to the object - or the box - while bringing it to me. My trusty assistant will contact you as soon as you have set up your base in France.

Good luck! May God be with you and with our quest.

Antonio, Cardinal Sardis

After reading the letter, the Swiss opened the first file and realised that the artefact Sardis was talking about, was the Ark of the Covenant. The divine Ark that had been carried through the desert by Moses and Aaron from Egypt to the Promised Land. The Sacred Ark that had been placed in the Holy of Holies in the Temple of Solomon in Jerusalem and which had disappeared over 2500 years ago.

The Swiss understood that they had to go on an errand for Sardis if they wanted Danielle back. However, the Ark of the Covenant was one of the relics on his own wish-list, so with full attention he browsed through the hints and copies of books in the files. Still, at this stage he had no idea how they could possibly find its exact location, just by using this material. He looked at the rest of the files, studied them for a few minutes and then, suddenly, he saw something he already knew; knowledge of an historical episode that he had only recently studied. It was clear to him that the Cardinal had indeed done his homework. He leafed through several historical records that explained how the Ark had been brought to France via Cyprus and that it had been hidden somewhere in southern Occitania. He recognised the names of two Grandmasters of the Order of the Knights Templar - who had their headquarters in Occitania and the names of possible hiding places; places that the man who stood next to him smoking a cigarette may have already visited while researching 'sacred' European geometry. A smile curled around his lips.

Maybe we can kill two birds with one stone!

The Swiss pulled the cigarette straight out of the smoker's mouth and pressed it out in an ashtray. "Will you stop smoking!"

The man sighed and eyed the remains of the cigarette, knowing that it had really been the last one this time.

"Fine, whatever…"

With newfound determination, the Swiss walked out of the glass office, closely followed by Georg. The other hesitated a moment, but then followed - his hands tugged deep into the pockets of his black trousers.

To Fairfax it had been quite a shock to see Gabby back so soon and with such alarming news. After the phone conversation with his employer, he had taken Gabby to the canteen for a coffee, hoping she would tell him the details of their European tour and all about Danielle's abduction. Fairfax was surprised by how his chief had reacted, for he had half-expected the man to be angry with him. After all, the professor had no choice but to tell his mysterious employer the truth this time, but instead of being angry with him, his chief had simply asked them to wait in the canteen.

That had been two hours ago. Meanwhile, a nervous Fairfax jumped out of his skin when Gabby accidentally knocked over her coffee cup. As it was already empty, she just put the cup upright and ignored the few dark drops that had spilled onto the table. Fairfax ran both his hands through his hair and sighed, but then they heard the sound they had been waiting for. The doors of the canteen opened and a man came through the doorway - dressed in black - followed by two others wearing the same black uniforms. Immediately, Fairfax assumed that this had to be the man he was working for. Until now he had only spoken to him by telephone and his identity was unknown to the professor. They both got up from their seats, but the man quickly raised his hands and said, "Bitte, sit."

His voice was soft and gentle, but his pale face betrayed a strange mix of fatigue, sadness and excitement. Above his pointy chin were thin, red lips and when he produced a weak smile, dimples formed in his cheeks. It gave him a sympathetic look. His short, dark brown hair was combed backward and beneath his dark eyebrows, his grey-blue eyes were fixed on the professor. Without delay, the man came over to them. His body language expressed strength, discipline and calm, not unlike a soldier. He drew a chair and sat down facing the professor and Gabby, while the two other men in the black uniforms positioned themselves at both sides of the canteen door. It made Gabby feel uncomfortable. Neither she nor Bill had any idea who they were really dealing with. They could hear their own heartbeat.

The pale man gave them the letter from Sardis to read and noticed Gabby taking Bill's hand. Realising how stressful this had to be for them, he felt he needed to explain himself, so he took a deep breath and started,

"Two months ago I was brought to your era by means of the time machine and with the assistance of a person who - for the time being - wishes to remain anonymous."

Bill frowned.

What the heck...

So this man wasn't his employer?

The pale man continued, "I was brought here to help our mutual employer to find certain important and lost relics and as of today, I have been assigned to your team. My name is Otto Rahn."

Fairfax and Gabby looked at one another and then gazed at the man who had gone into history as the German writer and SS officer who had tried to find the Grail in southern France; the Nazi who had - according to the historical records - committed suicide in the Spring of 1939. Over the decades, his life's story had become an enigma, as no one really knew for sure whose side he was really on and now he was sitting right there, at the other end of the table. Rahn could see that Gabby knew who he was. Amused to see the surprised look on her face, he added,

"Over the past months I have been able to do some research on myself, to see how I had gone into history, so I know what people might think of me, but please, let me tell you my story in my own words?"

Gabby nodded with suppressed enthusiasm. Being fond of historical enigmas she couldn't wait to hear his story.

"Germany was destroyed after the Great War. When I grew up, most people I knew were poor and hungry. To escape reality, I devoured books and especially loved reading the legends, myths and history of the golden ages. Oh, how I longed for them to be revived. After college I became interested in writing; journalism; photography and film. I even played in a movie or two; just a small thing, no lines. One day I was introduced to a group of people who had some interesting ideas, so I joined this Thule Gesellschaft Society and found friends among them who enabled me to travel - albeit on a shoestring - to research ancient cultures and possible Grail sites. Inspired by Wagner and Wolfram von Eschenbach's Parsifal, I discovered the connection between the Grail and the Cathars and enjoyed doing some archaeology in southern France. I love Occitania; its many mysterious caves, castles and secret places. Fortunately, I had the time and the means to study the history of the ancient people of Occitania as well as the religion of the Cathars and found out how they were massacred during the Cathar Crusade in the early 13th century, simply because they didn't accept the doctrines and dogmas of the Holy Roman Church. These Cathars had their own version of Christianity, you see? In fact, they were more Gnostic than people think. I also found a resemblance to the heretics of Marburg, which is close to my hometown in Germany. The evil inquisitor Konrad von Marburg had burned hundreds of heretics, just like in France, so when I continued my research and read up on German religious history, a thought grew in my mind; why not link the Germans to the French and all the cultures that share a similar ancestry. Of course, at the time, everyone in the Thule Gesellschaft was very interested to hear these thoughts."

"It all took off in 1929 when I went to southern France for the first time. These 4 years of research in France were my happiest years. Most of the time I stayed with friends, but sometimes I stayed in a guest house or in a hotel. I remember those first years so well. Because I am German, the French people were very mistrustful from the start. I couldn't even buy a piece of land. Nevertheless, everyone seemed to be willing to help me with my research and I was introduced to many people in different circles, like Rosicrucians, Neo-Cathars and a group called the Polaires."

"Unfortunately, things were about to go very wrong. I already told you that I was a member of several groups like Thule, which enabled me to research the origins of Hyperborea, the capital of Ultima Thule and Aryan ancestry. Because this organisation was connected to the German government, the locals took me for a spy. They even thought I was the leader of the Polaires, an esoteric group in France, but I wasn't. I just worked with them as a researcher, but I was never their leader. My French friend Antonin Gadal tried to calm things down, but my reputation had already been badly damaged by then. Nevertheless, I will never forget the special friendships I had with these people and the excursions we made to the caves and the castles."

Rahn clearly loved this region of France with its hidden history, unsolved mysteries, stunning mountainous landscape and Occitan lore. He loved hunting for treasure, hoping to one day discover the Holy Grail itself. He got up and walked to the bar, took three glasses and came back with a bottle of carefully chosen red wine, all the while without pausing from his story.

"In 1932 I leased a hotel in Ussat-les-Bains, not far from the Lombrives Caves, which is one of the many caves that I explored with great interest. I loved each day at 'Les Marronniers'. That was the name of my hotel. However, when the hotel went bankrupt at the end of that same year, I had to leave France. That was a foul blow, because southern France and the people of Occitania had stolen my heart. I had made some good friends there, who had told me all about the old cultures and the Cathars, Gnosis and mysticism."

Otto paused and looked away for a moment, knowing that the next part would be a more difficult story to tell. When he continued, his smile had gone.

"Back in Germany I joined the German Writers Association and published a book called 'Crusade against the Grail'. This book was my ticket to Himmler's office in 1934. I wanted to write another book, this time about Konrad of Marburg, but in '33 and '34 I was asked to do some work for Alfred Rosenberg of the Nordische Gesellschaft and good old Karl Wiligut of the Ahnenerbe. You probably know him as Weisthor. I was fond of him; he was very kind to me. At the time I was also writing several novels, but these were never published. Then I travelled through Europe on my new salary and was also able to visit Occitania again on top secret missions, including a new search for Grail treasure, the Golden Fleece, Solomon's treasure and to study what is called 'Sacred Geometry'. This research involved getting hold of maps of underground tunnels that connect castles, churches and villages. However, I was getting seriously worried about the increasing violence in my country. The murder of Röhm and others in '34 had gutted me and you will understand that I would accept any job, as long as it would enable me to eat, write and be safe. Wiligut and Himmler had promised to make this possible for me, but as a consequence I had to join the Allgemeine SS."

Rahn looked away when he saw Gabby and Fairfax frown. These were the years of the rise of Adolf Hitler and his desired Third Reich; the years leading up to World War II and many gruesome things were already happening in this period. He poured himself a glass of wine and offered it to his audience, but they politely refused. After a sampling taste, he swirled the wine in his glass and continued,

"There was a big recession in Germany. Lots of people were starving and I too needed a job desperately. I was even a tutor at a school for a while. Thanks to my book, my travels and my research in '34, '35 and '36, my star was rising, but I still remember vividly how my friend Paul Ladame reacted when he saw me in Berlin for the first time, just before the Olympic Games in 1936. Paul had helped me improve my French and had even accompanied me on one of my French research trips. Anyway, here I was, all dressed up in my SS uniform with shining boots when Paul arrived. He was surprised to see me like that, even shocked to find out that I had joined the SS, but he was my friend and we spent a lot of time together. We used to go somewhere for a drink and then we'd take his Opel and drive to my house. He was a good friend."

"It wasn't until after the Olympic Games when, for the first time, I felt the real power of the people I was serving. First, the SS made me shadow Paul. Of course I told him to get out of Berlin while he still could. Then, other friends of mine were kidnapped and I discovered that my phone had been tapped. Everything went crazy and I couldn't do anything about it! It felt as if I had been sucked into a void and couldn't get out. I was caught up in it and had to save my skin, so I obeyed my superiors. My father didn't understand my situation. "You're in the SS! Do something about it!" he had shouted, but how can just one tree stop an avalanche?"

Otto looked at the table. Suppressing even more details of the argument with his father, he quickly continued,

"So you will understand that I travelled a lot, writing and researching for the Ahnenerbe, the ancestral heritage society which was a division of the Schutz-Staffel. We weren't only searching for ancient relics you know, we were also eager to find Agartha, the underground world of the Aryans. I think you call them Atlantians now. In '36 we even went to Iceland to try and find entrances and traces of sacred geometry. What a waste of time that was. I prefer high mountains and ancient woods."

"Later I found out that Hitler and Himmler were eager to possess the Spear of Destiny - you know, the lance that was used by the Roman soldier Longinus to pierce the side of Christ. They thought it would give its owner true power. As it was kept in Vienna at the time, I realise that this might well have been the real reason for the *Anschluss*, for annexing Austria in '38. They wanted to use the spear to experiment with occult power and thought that the moment they possessed the spear, Germany would become invincible. They dreamt of a new Germanic Aryan Empire and in order to create this vast empire, they had to absorb Austria, Poland, Czechoslovakia, Italy and the Vatican, France, Belgium, Holland, Luxembourg, Great-Britain, Ireland and Scandinavia into one large, Third Reich. In the footsteps of the Romans and the Hohenzollern Dynasty they wanted this Third Empire to be governed by a new religious world order, but this time it would be based on *northern* traditions. They also had the crazy idea of creating a race of pure blood Aryans to become the elites of this empire. I must admit that in the beginning, we were all obsessed with the Aryan ancestry, which is why they had created the Ahnenerbe in the first place. As if there were no tomorrow, we researched old cultures and civilisations, the origins of the Aryans and family trees and initially I had no idea that this would result in racism. I found out that if you had no Jewish blood dating back to 1750, you were fine. If not…"

Rahn took a deep breath and drank some more wine.

"Anyway, the plan was to collect all the important relics under one roof in Wewelsburg; the new Grail castle in Germany and use the occult power, drawn from these united relics, to help create this new world order; a new empire, which would last for a thousand years. However, discovering the horrors that were already taking place in my country, I lost my nerve and began to drink. Slowly I realised that I had joined the wrong party."

"One day in 1937, a friend of mine was arrested and thrown into a work camp in Dachau. To be able to keep an eye on him and to make sure he was safe, I made a scene in Bad Arolsen, acting as if I had been drinking too much. As a compensation for my improper behaviour I proposed to serve at Dachau for four months. I had stripped myself from my ranks, so I was added to the kitchen and garden staff. By doing this, I was able to make sure my friend was properly fed. It was in that particular period that I became part of one of the resistance groups. However, while at Dachau, I was automatically added to a special group called the SS-Totenkopfverband Oberbayern."

Gabby, who had also studied this recent history, knew that the notorious Totenkopfverbände used the skull and crossbones as their symbol. In WWII they had terrorised the concentration camps, so she was surprised to learn that Rahn had actually been a member. However, she also understood that he probably had no choice but to accept the 'honour'. Nevertheless she displayed her disgust. "Didn't the skull and crossbones put you off? It sort of betrayed their mission, didn't it?"

Rahn rubbed his eyes and thought about the crystal skull that he had bought as a present for Himmler in 1936. The French contact in Carcassonne had wanted no less than 1000 Reichsmark for this item. Most of these crystal skulls had come to France from Brazil during the First World War, conveniently hidden in the cargo of Paul Claudel's ship that carried food supplies to France. Rahn had collected many items for Himmler's occult collection in Wewelsburg, but he had always been intrigued by this particular artefact. Perhaps it had inspired Weisthor to design the Totenkopfring in 1937. Otto automatically touched the ring on his finger; he'd never part with it. The heavy, silver ring had been a personal gift from Weisthor and he had always been very fond of the old man, therefore, the ring had a very different significance for Rahn. He decided to let sleeping dogs lie, especially after reading on the Internet that this particular crystal skull had recently been found near Landshut in Bayern. He was sure it would eventually go to a museum - where it belonged - and hoped he'd see it again one day.

In response to Gabby's remark, Rahn felt he had to explain the symbolism of the skull and crossbones.

"The skull and bones is an old symbol going back even to the first Knights Templar. It was and still is used by Freemasons and also by many sports teams. So you will understand that - at the time - I thought nothing of it. Dachau was mainly a work and training camp in those days and it actually all seemed well organised and orderly. The military training was heavy, but I did my best to fit in, but when I found out that they were planting a wonderful herb garden, I asked to help out, trying to be there as often as I could and keeping myself well away from the rest. Of course, it was good to be on the outside again in January '38. I have..." Otto tried to swallow the lump in his throat, "I had a Swiss boyfriend, Raymond Perrier, so as soon as I left Dachau, he took me skiing to take my mind off things. Of course, the moment Himmler got a notion that I was gay, he urged me to check myself into one of the Lebensborn homes to do it with a woman until she was pregnant, 'for the record'. It was a house where pure blood Aryans were 'bred'. I was appalled and complained to Himmler about the conditions there. Not that it made any difference."

"Still, it's bizarre to think that in this present time I may have a child somewhere, who is almost 40 years older than me."

Otto chuckled and drank some more wine. His hand had started to tremble.

"My second book, Lucifer's Court, was published and I found out that some of its chapters had been edited, which I found very disturbing. I wanted to get away and travel; explore historic places and retrace myths and legends, so as the Ahnenerbe was organising all sorts of expeditions to research the history of the Germanic people, I had my heart set on the Tibet expedition. However, when the expedition left without me, I was heartbroken. They didn't think I was fit enough, because I was smoking too much and my lungs wouldn't be able to handle the high altitude. That was a big blow for me. I had climbed mountains almost all my life! Still, now I could use the doctor's note to get permission to reside at Muggenbrunn in the Schwarzwald for my health. At least this kept me away from Berlin. To buy as much time as possible, I promised Himmler I'd write a 2000 page novel called 'Sebastian' during my stay. However, my boyfriend Raymond was planning to come over in August and I didn't want Himmler to think anything of it. So when I met a woman named Asta, I thought she would make a great 'wife'. I even sent pictures to Himmler, showing us and her little boy together, lying that we were planning to get married. Of course there would be no real wedding; I just made it up to get Berlin off my back, but the pressure had already become tangible, even in Muggenbrunn. When I said goodbye to Raymond that Summer, I realised I would never see him again."

Rahn felt a lump in his throat. For him, this had only just happened the year before. He spilled some wine while refilling his glass and didn't bother to clean it up.

"The nightmare was complete when I couldn't even prove I was a pure blood Aryan, because when I researched my genealogy, as was required, I realised my mother and maternal grandfather were Jewish. There was only one thing for me to do; being a member of the ancestry department I had access to all the personal ancestry files. So I filled in my ancestry form, smuggled it into the archive and inserted the form into the system, just to be able to say that I had filed it. Of course it misses a stamp, but who cares about a stupid stamp?"

Rahn chuckled at his own cunningness, although he knew it hadn't stopped people from asking questions about it. He thought about the many times he had gotten himself into trouble.

"I must admit, I really was a trouble-maker; I got into fights a lot when I saw SS soldiers mistreat women and of course I wanted to make a career; to move further up the ladder. I was attracted by the power of my superiors, like many others and in this process I naturally gained several political enemies. My rather lively reputation must have attracted Hitler's attention, because suddenly he demanded my presence at the Berghof, his base near Bergtesgaden on the German-Austrian border. I can still remember him, sitting behind his desk, wearing his reading glasses while perusing my file. I had never seen him wearing reading glasses before. While Hitler was examining my file, I waited impatiently for his reaction. My legs nearly gave way, for he kept me standing there in complete silence for a long time. Then he looked up and gave me my new orders: I was drafted to be trained as a soldier "to make a man out of me", he said, so I took the journey to Buchenwald."

Otto started to tremble again. He could barely speak the name of the infamous KZ camp.

"Now I know it wasn't just to make a man out of me. Hitler did it to show me what they did to homosexuals and Jews. You won't believe the things I witnessed…"

Obviously distraught and no longer able to keep himself straight, he got up and walked to the back of the room, where he turned his back on the others. As it is almost impossible for a woman to ignore a person who is so upset, Gabby wanted to go to him, comfort him, but Fairfax held her back.

Otto just stood there - weeping quietly with shaking shoulders - no longer able to suppress his emotions. Then he took a deep breath and wiped his face with his handkerchief. It was clear that this was an episode in his life that he could not yet deal with. They could only imagine what he must have gone through in the concentration camps, serving there as an SS soldier and not being able to do anything about it. It had been horror for the prisoners, but also for the gentle Otto. Gabby knew that the reality of the Nazi state had driven many SS men to suicide.

One of the guards at the door automatically reached for his Glock when suddenly, Rahn started to shout,

"*All* my ideals were smashed, *everything* I had been told was a *lie!*"

Otto tried to regain his calm by regulating his breathing. Then he continued with a hoarse voice,

"I tried to get out of Buchenwald as quickly as possible, saying that I needed to work on the new edition of Lucifer's Court. I thought Himmler didn't know what went on in those camps, but when I confronted him with it, he didn't only know about it, he even tried to explain why it was necessary! As soon as I got out of Buchenwald I went back to Freiburg and Muggenbrunn and tried to hold on to the marriage act, to buy myself some more time. I also resumed my normal work and did some research on the history of St. Odilien because of its connection with the Grail stories and Parsifal. I stumbled upon a bloodline from St. Odilien to the later European elites, a bloodline that Walter Stein had called the 'Grail Race'. I was so excited and thought I had finally found the secret of the Grail!"

While speaking of the Grail, Otto's eyes had again lit up and he realised that all he had ever wanted was to research Grail lore. He felt as if he had sold his soul to the devil to be able to pursue this quest.

After a short pause, he sat down again and continued with renewed courage, "I know that my research and writings were a way to escape. I know I hid my head in the sand, but I was scared and wanted to please the powers I was serving while doing what I love most..."

Rahn took a deep breath. The next part was perhaps the hardest part of his story to tell.

"You know, in the beginning, all of us at Thule really thought that Hitler was the long awaited legendary redeemer. We were his fans and even sponsored his Nazi party. Knowing what I know now, I just can't believe I ever believed in all this shit. Like everyone else I just dreamed of a united Europe and of no more wars; no more sickness; no more poverty, but the horrors at Buchenwald and what I had learnt there had finally opened my eyes. I wanted out more than ever. Two months later I finally had the courage to send a handwritten note to Karl Wolff saying that I wanted to resign. I had told Wolff that I would explain the reasons for my resignation in person, so I travelled to Berlin. However, they were all too busy to see me. There was a car show going on and on top of that, Hitler's Bohemian tour was being organised, so Himmler's assistant gave me an invitation to join them for the Easter celebration at the Berghof, where we would discuss my future. However, as I was about to leave the building, two members of the secret state police, the Gestapo, pushed me aside and told me that I had two options to choose from: getting myself arrested and thrown into a KZ concentration camp, or commit suicide. Then they walked off. Naturally, I was so shocked that when I wanted to descend the stairway, my legs were trembling so badly that I nearly fell. That moment, I began to understand and fear the power of my political opponents. I had been too arrogant."

"After I had left Berlin I was constantly being shadowed. I felt threatened and begged my friends to help me, but they didn't. They couldn't. I even asked permission to live in southern France, but I was not allowed to leave the country. Feeling I would be safer around Himmler, I decided to hang on to the invitation for the Easter celebration at the Berghof, so I travelled to Freiburg to pack my bags. By then it seemed as if I was no longer being followed, so I relaxed, but I wanted to keep moving. I decided to take the scenic route from Munich to Söll and spend some weeks in Austria to kill some time. Easter was still several weeks away, you see? I also wanted to visit some friends and climb a few mountains. Obviously, I enjoyed my travels, knowing each day could be my last and indeed, my greatest fear was about to come true. One day I was sitting in the bus from Söll to Sankt Johann, when a car drove in front of the bus and stopped it. My heart was pounding when two men in suits, long overcoats and hats entered the bus and when I heard them call out my name it seemed to stop beating temporarily. Immediately I knew that they had been sent by the Gestapo. I was taken outside into the fresh snow. When the bus was ordered to carry on still with my luggage on board, I knew straight away that this looked very bad for me. The men - how do I say this - 'persuaded' me to sign a letter in which I would explain that I had ended my life 'to spare the SS the humiliation of my misconduct regarding paragraph 175'. I refused at first, but then they said they had evidence against me, proving my homosexuality and that my mother was Jewish. They gave me two phials of heavy sleeping pills and a bottle of French cognac, which - I must confess - looked very tempting at that moment. I had longed for a drink for almost two years, you know. Of course, I signed the damn papers because if I didn't, they would arrest my parents and naturally I was afraid for my mother. They forced me to walk into the woods and up the mountain. Feeling completely derived of any hope, my legs had turned to rubber and though my feet were cold and wet from walking through the snow, I could no longer feel them. While climbing up, I often turned and looked at the landscape, knowing that soon I'd no longer be able to enjoy the views. I walked and walked, until it was just me and my mountains."

For a moment, all three had gone silent. Then, Otto rubbed his eyes to make the memory go away and produced a smile. "But now I'm here... I'm safe."

This time Gabby got up and embraced him. She knew about Otto's suicide on March 13th, 1939. Both Gabby and Fairfax were certainly shaken by his story, but the professor couldn't help wondering how Rahn had been brought to their present without his knowledge. Someone other than himself had to know how to work the ERFAB. Someone must have studied the procedures from the other side of the tinted glass window in the early stages in February and March. Whoever had brought Otto to this present must have gone back in time, to March 1939, exactly to the right spot and at the right moment, not to be noticed by history. It also meant that Gabby and Danielle had not been at risk at all, as the time machine had already been used for human transport before. The Organisation had been confident that the ERFAB would work properly, but then the professor thought of another thing. The person who had gone back in time to fetch Rahn; *he* must have been brave!

Gabby decided to pop the question that had been in her mind from the moment Rahn had explained who he was.

"Why were you brought to our time, Otto?"

Rahn grinned mischievously.

"Because I have made many discoveries during my years of research. Also, I was introduced to circles that don't exist anymore; I have studied books, papers and maps that have now been lost for decades and I have spoken to important people who are now dead. The Organisation just wants to pick my brain."

Gabby thought about Danielle. They really needed to get a move on if they wanted to save her.

Perhaps they were already too late.

12

Sion, Switzerland, June 21st 2011

After Rahn had told them his story, both he and Fairfax had listened to Gabby's. She told them about their second trip to ancient Judea and how she and Danielle had arrived in Jerusalem a month after the crucifixion. Though they had found out that Jesus had survived the cross, they had not been able to meet him in the flesh during their second visit. They also found no proof of the story of Joseph of Arimathea, who - according to Christian mythology - had used the Grail cup to collect Jesus' blood during the crucifixion. However, Gabby believed that Joseph of Arimathea had simply come to collect the royal family; Jesus' blood relatives and pregnant wife and take *them* to a safer place. Otto was intrigued and explained that the Organisation wanted to find out where Jesus had lived after the crucifixion and where he had been buried. Now that they knew Jesus had survived the crucifixion, they wanted to find his remains. In short, the Organisation wanted both proof of the facts and of the lie.

Otto, on the other hand, would have rather gone on a Grail hunt, but he understood that with the abduction of Danielle, their mission was now a much more serious one. They couldn't just abandon her. Thinking of Danielle, Otto revealed another interesting bit of information. He let out how the Organisation had known from the beginning that the women had fled. He and his chief had witnessed everything. The professor and Gabby were struck dumb when they heard this. Otto continued to explain how they had hoped that with their disappearance of the two women, Sardis would get off their backs. They had already made plans to retrieve Danielle and Gabby as soon as they felt it was safe to do so. Meanwhile, the women had been tailed by an SBS-Sion agent all the way to their homes in the States.
Gabby and Danielle exchanged looks.
The man in the hat!

However, as they had underestimated the Cardinal, they now felt guilty because they had failed to keep Danielle safe. The Organisation had not foreseen that Sardis' aid - whom the Cardinal had sent after Danielle and Gabby - had noticed that the women were tailed by an SBS-agent; the man in the hat. The aid had found Danielle simply by following the agent to her apartment in the States. After getting rid of the man in the hat, kidnapping Danielle had been easy. Naturally, the Organisation had become very alarmed when they had suddenly lost contact with the SBS-agent and their worst nightmare had come true the moment Gabby had arrived at the base in Sion.

Rahn sighed. Even he wondered what his chief would do next. He turned his head toward the two agents posted at the door and frowned at one of them.

The canteen had been closed off for personnel for several hours now. Everyone was getting hungry, so the kitchen staff had been put to work. While the personnel were experiencing a rare treat; being served food and drinks at their quarters and stations, the professor, Gabby and Otto were served a three course meal in the canteen.

Many questions had still been unanswered. Fairfax knew certain things about the Second World War and the Nazi regime and couldn't help wondering how Rahn had managed to resign.

"So Otto, you said you resigned from the SS. Well, I know you couldn't leave the SS just like that. You must have been a special case to the Nazi's then?"

"Yes, I was Heinrich's protégé. He was a distant relation of mine, but he was also my biggest fan. I had published two books about the Cathars and the old European religions and legends and I was quite popular in Germany in my time. I was Himmler's personal researcher, so of course he gave me special favours, but that didn't mean that I could get away with everything. Like I said, I had made political enemies."

Rahn looked at Gabby and the professor. Both of them seemed to be warm-hearted people and he became more and more at ease with them, especially with Gabby. He knew he had no choice but to trust them and he felt that he could. Rahn had a way with people. His friendly smile and inviting eyes echoed an inner child in search of adventure and hungry for attention and affection. Feeling at ease with Gabby and the professor, he relaxed. His third glass of red wine loosened him up even more. After all, he hadn't touched alcohol for two years, so by the time the first course was served, Otto's stiff manners had completely disappeared.

"Unfortunately for Himmler I never found the Grail or the Ark, but I did find the Grail culture, the Grail people and the Grail Way of Life. Just read my books! However, while searching for Grail treasure I stumbled upon something else, something unbelievable!"

After hearing himself say this, he froze. He shouldn't have told them this!

I mustn't drink so much!

"What did you find, Otto?" asked Fairfax.

Scheisse...

"I'm sorry. I've already said too much."

Unseen by any of them, one of the agents at the door smiled. To avoid further questions, Rahn quickly changed the subject. "So your name, Gabby, comes from Gabrielle? I knew a Gabrielle once. She looked after Karl Wiligut."

Gabby smiled and accepted Otto's outstretched hand to confirm their new friendship. Also Fairfax offered Otto his hand and added, "Please, call me Bill."

At that moment, Sardis' files were brought in. Otto recognised them and knew it was their job to study them, investigate them and write a report on their conclusions. Within minutes, Bill, Gabby and Otto were bending their heads over an enigmatic story that has inspired archaeologists and historians for centuries. In Rahn's mind sprang a fountain of hope; that they would soon travel to the south of France, a place he was longing to see again.

He had a broad smile on his face and his heart was racing. Perhaps now he would get the chance to escape and rebuild a new life, instead of being forced to return to 1939. It had made him shiver when his chief had told him that his return to 1939 was inevitable. Knowing what he knew now about WWII - even with the promise of a fake passport - he simply couldn't face the prospect of going back. However, he had never shared these feelings with his chief.

Unable to suppress his enthusiasm and newfound hope, he looked at Bill and Gabby with a big grin.

"So, my dear friends, the game is afoot! We have a friend to rescue and a relic to find. You know, when I arrived from my time into yours, I actually thought I was being abducted by aliens!" They all laughed and the tension that had kept them all on guard was slowly being replaced by a feeling of adventure. However, Gabby was becoming more and more curious about the people in the background; the Organisation, SBS-Sion. No representative of this Organisation had ever shown himself to them and now apparently even Otto was - like Gabby, Danielle and the professor - only an employee; a puppet on a string; a chess piece, played by unknown players. She had to ask.

"Otto, who 'abducted' you?"

Rahn, who always loved to rock the boat, turned and pointed to one of the agents in black uniform who was standing at the door.

"Him!"

The Swiss, annoyed that Otto had just blown his cover, left the room immediately. It left Gabby and the professor speechless, but Otto just smirked. The head of the Organisation had been one of the guards. This way he had been able to overhear everything.

Otto took Sardis' files and followed his chief, while Gabby and Bill silently finished their meals.

The Swiss marched impatiently to his glass office above the lab. He was angry at Otto and banged the door to a close. "You fool! Why did you have to blow my cover?"

Otto impatiently shook his head. "We have to act, Fred, go out there, find the Ark, free Danielle! They will see you soon anyway."

The Swiss nodded. Of course he understood that they had to act quickly; Danielle's life depended on it. While standing at the door in the canteen, he had indeed heard everything that had been discussed, which was part of the reason why he had wanted to be there, disguised as a guard. Not only did he want to eavesdrop closely on their conversation, he also wanted to keep an eye on Otto. Though the entire lab had been bugged with cameras and microphones, the Swiss had wanted to be able to intervene. After all, Gabby and the professor had been the first 'outsiders' to meet Rahn and he had no idea what Otto might tell them. Of course, Rahn had quickly told them too much. Otto was right. Gabby and the professor were already too much involved to be kept in the dark any longer.

After having thought everything through, the Swiss turned to Rahn with renewed determination. "We must prepare for this expedition and leave a.s.a.p. Oh and Otto, you know what I want to find *too*, don't you?"

Rahn looked away. He knew what he meant, but he wasn't prepared to part from his secret that quickly. One day he might need it as his leverage.

As soon as everything was arranged, Gabby, Bill and Otto drove off in a silent, starlight-black Lexus LS600h and headed for France. Gabby remembered when she and Danielle had fled from Sion three weeks before and this new departure had given her a weird feeling of déjà vu. She stared out of the car window into a foggy horizon of dark mountains, while Fairfax drove west. Another Lexus containing their chief and his staff would travel ahead to search for a perfect place for a base camp. They quickly lost sight of the fast driving car and kept to their own pace. However, they were also being followed by another black car and half-expected them to be Sardis' men.

They remembered his letter, *"My people will shadow you, so be aware that there is no option for escape or betrayal."*

At first, Otto had felt uncomfortable going so far outside the base, for he had now entered a world that had changed much over the past 70 years. On the other hand he was also excited to be able to witness it all. He couldn't believe the car. Only now could he feel a sense of relief, knowing that the pre-war situation he had been in - which was only a short time ago for him - had disappeared into history. For now.

He leafed through Sardis' files and his eye fell on the copies of two adjoining pages from a 19th century German book. After reading it, he discovered that the unknown author had been convinced that the Grail and the Ark were connected by one particular item; a glowing stone with incredible powers. Powers to kill.

Gabby, having studied history, tried to remember what she knew about the Ark of the Covenant. As far as she knew, it was a chest, created by Moses and Aaron to carry God through the desert, like the ancient Egyptians had done with their gods. If the pharaoh had been too ill, too weak or too old to travel to a certain temple to do a particular ritual, then the god or goddess in question was 'invited' to move into a special shrine to be carried to the pharaoh, who could then perform the ritual - if necessary from his bed. These divine mobile shrines were not uncommon in ancient Egypt and Gabby understood that Moses might have designed the Ark following this example. After all, Moses had been born and raised in Egypt.*

According to the Old Testament, the Ark was covered by a golden lid and flanked by two angelic creatures called 'cherubs'. The wooden, gilded chest had been made to a certain fixed size. The identity of its contents are uncertain and soon it had become the biggest mystery of all time.

*read: 'The Eye of Ra' by Jeanne D'Août

Some people think it was a radioactive meteorite that had fallen to earth, polished by the heat of the atmosphere on entry. Perhaps this meteorite was the basis of an even older Grail story, in which one of the green stones from Lucifer's crown had fallen down from the heavens and onto the earth. This stone could be the link to the Grail stone theory.

According to Sardis' files, they had to look for a special, radioactive stone that had gone into history as the Grail stone; a leftover relic that had once been part of the contents of the Ark of the Covenant. Was it possible that this stone could eventually lead them to the whereabouts of the Ark? If so, then how on earth did this Grail stone get mixed up with the Cup of Christ? It all sounded as if the ingredients of several ancient stories had been mixed into one big meatloaf and cooked in the oven of lore. They had to study the source, to take all ingredients of the meatloaf out and then sort them, in order to make any sense of it all.

As far as Gabby knew, the Cup of Christ was not a stone, but a cup or a bowl. In ancient times, important people and priests often possessed a special cup, usually made of silver or gold. Carved into its interior were ancient words of magic or magical squares. People used these cups in special rituals, for divination and healing. The Biblical Joseph of Egypt had also possessed such a cup. Gabby knew the story well. Joseph had been sold into slavery by his jealous brothers, but he had climbed in rank to become the right hand of the pharaoh of Egypt. When later his brothers travelled to Egypt to ask for food, they hadn't recognised him. They had come to ask for food in a period of great famine and Joseph had taken this opportunity to teach his brothers a lesson. Secretly he had hidden his golden cup inside the luggage of one of his brothers, who was then accused of theft. Negotiating his punishment, Joseph demanded that the youngest brother Benjamin stayed with him. Benjamin was the only other son of his mother Rachel, Jacob's second wife and therefore

Joseph's only full brother. The tribe of Benjamin would later inherit the city of Jerusalem. Benjamin had been the first to recognise Joseph, who eventually forgave all his brothers. He welcomed his family into Egypt and this was how the tribes of Israel had come to live in Egypt, only to leave with Moses, many centuries later.

The history of the Grail cup dates back to the time of Melchizedek, who was a Zadok priest. Melchizedek used the cup in a thanksgiving ritual offering wine and bread, a ritual that paid homage to the mother goddess by giving thanks to her for their food and drink; her body and blood, which made life on earth possible. The nourishing mother symbolised the fertility of the earth. This ritual was repeated each Spring to celebrate the new year, when new life appeared. It has been kept alive in the Zadok rituals and was even performed by Jesus himself at his 'last supper'. Today, this ritual is known and performed as the Eucharist, which still means 'thanksgiving'. The Grail cup mentioned in the old stories could have been a cup just like this. Even the name of such a cup, which is called a 'Goral' in Hebrew, might have morphed into 'Graal' or 'Grail' over the ages. Gabby thought of the Jewish Passover Cup. Maybe Jesus really had possessed such a cup. However, like the Ark of the Covenant, the Holy Grail has been lost for millennia. Or has it? Perhaps it has been found and kept in a museum without being recognised for what it is. It could also be in a private collection, kept safe by someone who knows very well what it is. Gabby thought about the abbey of Tongerlo and the copy they saw of Da Vinci's Last Supper. She knew that Jesus must have performed such a Zadok ritual on the 1st Nissan, although on the Da Vinci painting there was no Grail. Strange.
She worried about Danielle. Her eyes were getting heavy and the steady sound of the tires on the road and the moving of the car finally lulled her into a much needed sleep.

Otto stared out of the car window into the night, into the black landscape in the distance. Because he had used Wolfram von Eschenbach as his guide and not Chretien de Troyes, he had always looked for a meteorite stone while searching for the Grail in the early 1930s. In Chretien de Troyes' story - which had been written toward the end of the 12th century - the Grail was still a cup or a container, not a stone. However, a few decades later in Wolfram's story, the cup had become a stone. Otto knew that around 1200, something must have happened to make Wolfram talk about a stone and not a cup in his version of the Parsifal story. He wondered what had happened. Von Eschenbach and de Troyes had both based their Parsifal stories on a certain tale, written by the Occitan troubadour: Guyot de Provence. It was common in those days for a troubadour to write a complimentary story based on his hosts and hostess in return for their hospitality. Otto believed that Guyot had written the Parsifal story as a gift for the beautiful Adelaide of Carcassonne and consequently thought that Parsifal had to be based on the young count Raymond Roger de Trencavel of Carcassonne, Adelaide's son. Otto also believed that it had been Wolfram who had told the truer version of the tale of Parsifal, so with Wolfram's book in his hand he had searched the Sabarthès region to try to find the Grail Castle of Monsalvache. However, all he could find were stories about a very special religion that was based on early, Gnostic Christianity and the tale of a stone with special qualities, called the bleeding stone or Grail stone. When rubbed and sprinkled with water, it was as if the stone 'bled'. He was certain that this 'Pyrenean Grail cup' that was used by the Cathars in Occitania must have been carved from such a stone. Maybe going back just one more time to southern France would present him some more answers.

Unquenchable, Otto researched file after file as they drove into the night toward the southwest.

Bill could hear the keyboard of Otto's laptop rattling almost all the time and smiled. That man was very determined indeed. He looked to his right and saw that Gabby had dozed off. Worried sick about Danielle, she hadn't been able to sleep since she had left the States. Perhaps she'd slept an hour on the plane. Bill was getting fond of her.

He stare returned to the almost deserted Péage - the French toll road - in front of him. What a weird adventure they had become involved in. However, they all knew the seriousness of this special mission and that failure was not an option. It would either result in the death of Danielle, or in finding one of the most famous antique relics of all time:

The Ark of the Covenant.

13

London, England, June 18th 2011

It was a typical rainy day in London; grey skies, noisy traffic and lots of people with long faces. It was the time of year when the citizens looked forward to getting away from the city, to travel - preferably to a country where the sun did shine. However, not all people wanted to sit on a beach and do nothing. Some were born for adventure.

Just behind Harrods there is a street with a small restaurant, where the food is good and inexpensive. At lunchtime it is always busy, but at the end of the afternoon, about an hour before the shops closed, it was quiet. Today, there were two people sitting in the centre of the restaurant and near the window, a tired looking old lady was slurping her tea - her plastic shopping bags taking up all the other seats at her table. She was a little irritated, for at the back was a table with four rather noisy kids - three boys and a girl - who were apparently in the heat of an important discussion. Their faces were glowing from excitement and they just talked and talked and talked. After another outburst of laughter, the elderly woman near the window had enough and demanded her bill.

"Will you be *quiet!*" The waitress was furious. What is it with kids of just under 20? Still giddy, they ordered some more drinks while she was at the table. Yanne was the only girl in the little group of four, but she was definitely the more dominant one, with her long red curls and pointy chin. She put down her drink and looked hard at Michael. "So, what I'm saying is, are you sure you can persuade your dad to have us for five whole weeks? I mean, there *are* four of us!"

Michael shook his head. "No problem; my dad said I could bring a friend and I'm sure he won't mind if I bring three. The place is big enough, it's an old farm with plenty of space. The former owner used to have cows and a few horses, but when we bought the farm, they were all gone. I do have my own horse now. I really had to beg my dad to buy me one, since I am only there during holidays and he has to take care of it for the rest of the time."

Michael was the son of a retired English movie director David S. Camford. Not that David was old, but he was just tired of the stress his work had brought. He hadn't been home a lot, had his share of adventures with other women and this has eventually led to his divorce. In search of a new lifestyle, David had travelled to southern France and had not only fallen in love with the tranquillity and stunning nature of the region, but also with its forgotten history and unsolved mysteries. The sign *á vendre* and a mysterious lane beyond the entrance gate had lured him to explore an old farm in the middle of nowhere that was for sale. Feeling that this was a sign, he had bought the farm and had lovingly turned it into a small, rural Bed & Breakfast with a gîte. There was even enough space for campers. On his royalties and the income of the B&B he could live reasonably well, though he still had to be careful. Keeping a horse meant extra expenses, but David simply hadn't been able to refuse his son anything, especially because he felt he had to make up for many years of not being around enough.

Being alone in the Languedoc - on a farm in the middle of nowhere - was not always easy for David. Ghosts from the past and feelings of guilt struck him as soon as he had a quiet moment, especially at night. He tried to escape those feelings by reading as much as possible about his one true obsession; the Knights Templar, an obsession that had also rubbed off on his son, Michael. His son meant everything to him and of course, so did his happiness. He had even bought him a horse. When Michael first saw the black and white appaloosa, his son had been the happiest kid in the world. Together they named him *Beauséant,* after the Knights Templar's black and white flag. The horse was trained and about two years old when Michael went out for his first ride. Though he already knew how to ride a horse - as he had taken lessons back home in England - the English horses had been a lot bigger than Beauséant, so for Michael, riding

Beauséant was a sheer joy. He felt just like a Templar knight when he went deep into the woods to explore. For two years now he had spent all his school holidays with his father in the Corbières and now he couldn't wait to bring his new friends to his favourite place on earth.

"So it's settled then?" Twenty year old Arthur was the oldest of the four, but also the shortest. With his short, dark curls and glasses he was the brains of the group. Arthur was into mysteries and forgotten treasures and with this in mind he had chosen his friends carefully. "From your dad's place we can explore the area to our hearts content! We will have five weeks and if we're lucky, we might find traces no one else has found yet!"

Arthur loved the forgotten history and mysteries of Occitania. Although his friends shared his interest, he was the one who had read nearly all the books on the biggest enigmas and just couldn't believe that he was now actually going there himself. As he had never been to France before, he had joined a forum to find people to travel with, or better still, spend the Summer holiday with. Out there, in Occitania.

There are several forums on the mysteries of Occitania, but there was one particular forum on which he really felt very comfortable. Using a pseudonym, he loved to share posts about his favourite subject and before he knew it, he had found himself discussing many details and theories with others. He'd almost forgotten the reason why he had joined the forum in the first place; to find a travel partner who was as obsessed with the enigmas as he was and to go to southern France. Then one day he had started chatting with Michael - who was also using a pseudonym on the forum - and it didn't take long for them to become good friends.

Michael had already planned to spend all summer in the Languedoc at his father's B&B with his friend Ben, a soft hearted, quiet Jewish boy with long, dark hair. However, Michael wasn't pleased when Ben suddenly wanted to bring his new girlfriend, Yanne. Things would not be the same now, so when Arthur posted on the forum that he was looking for a travel companion to go to the Corbières in southern France, Michael immediately agreed to meet up in the restaurant that afternoon to talk things through. Three is a crowd; four will be a better number, he thought. As they would all go in Ben's car, it also depended on Ben and Yanne whether Arthur could come or not. However, Yanne was beginning to feel more and more anxious about it all. She was in fact looking forward to some swimming and relaxing with Ben and not so much to long hikes in the middle of nowhere trying to find ancient hiding places that were probably emptied long ago anyway. Feeling she ought to have a say in it, she yelled, "So, we're not going to hunt for Grails and Arks and traces of Mary Magdalene all summer long are we?"

The group went silent. Then, Arthur responded, "Well, I have just finished this really amazing book by Jean-Luc Robin, which has been translated into English by Henry Lincoln. You have to read it. Lincoln is the 'go-to' guy you might call the daddy of Rennes-le-Château; the one who put the village on the map. They say he is often in the 'Jardin de Marie' in the village, so perhaps we can…"

"Guys, can we just NOT talk about Rennes-le-Château for a change!" protested Yanne. "All that talk about how that stupid penniless priest from that stupid hilltop village got so rich, perhaps he just received an inheritance! Occitania is also famous for its Cathar Castles, so let's talk about Cathar Castles for crying out loud!"

Ben grinned. He knew she was getting fed up with Arthur's obsession already and they had only just met. That was Yanne for you, quickly irritated, bored or angry. Ben had learned not to react when she was like that.

Michael tried to calm her down. "Alright, alright, now listen; we have five weeks, so we will have plenty of time to do both. Besides, you and Ben can stay at the farm while I take Arthur to the sites, if you don't want to come along."

"Yeah right and then you will have all the fun. No way are you leaving us behind!" Yanne commented, pulling a sour face.

Ben was still grinning. When Yanne declines something; simply take it away and she will quickly reach out and take it anyway. That was typical of Yanne and both Ben and Michael knew this. They stared at each other for a little while and then - without saying anything - all four reached out and shook hands in agreement. All of them were excited, for they knew it was going to be an amazing Summer.

Corbières, southern France, June 25th 2011

David Camford was smoking his pipe in front of the empty fire place, reading up on Templar history like he always did when he had a moment. Above the fire place was a plaque, saying:

> *"It ain't what you don't know that gets you into trouble.*
> *It's what you know for sure that just ain't so".*
> *– Mark Twain.*

The farm still had its old charm. Apart from modernising the kitchen and the bathroom, he had installed central heating using solar panels, carefully placed on the south facing side of his large roof. However, heating was not needed today. The sun was out; temperatures were rising quickly and he was only indoors to escape the strong rays of the sun. The past week he had been doing a lot of outdoor work and this had resulted in his back, shoulders and arms getting sunburnt. Next time he would wear a T-shirt, he said to himself.

The work was all done; the field had been prepared for campers; all the grass had been cut, as had the weeds along the river bank - so that his guests had access to the water - and all the woodwork had been varnished to protect it from the elements. He was pleased with himself and the only thing that was troubling him was the telephone call from his son Michael two days earlier, saying that he would bring three friends for the summer holidays. He had told his son that he could bring *one* friend, not three, but had given in after quite a bit of begging from his son, who was clearly set on bringing them. He had hung up after saying they should bring tents, because the cottage wouldn't be big enough. David smiled at the thought of seeing his son happy. He sounded so enthusiastic. So full of fire; so full of life.

A few years ago, things had been very different between him and his son. Michael had blamed his father for his mother's unhappiness and he hadn't been wrong there. Not only did his work prevent David from being home on a regular basis, he had also had several affairs with colleagues at work and one of these affairs had leaked out. David was one of those men who attracted women easily. He was handsome with his long, brown hair, his short well-cut beard and moustache and his light brown eyes. David enjoyed being seduced and he also enjoyed to be the seducer. Of course it had never been his intention to break Shannon's heart, but he had never expected his wife to ever find out. When she did, she had been furious at David and had made it very clear that she wouldn't share him with anyone. She'd had enough.

Michael was old enough to understand, but that didn't mean he had to like it. After the house in England had been sold and the farm in the Corbières had been purchased, David had sought solitude in his new home, but quickly became lonely. Hoping Michael would accept the invitation, he asked his son to come over during the summer. That first summer, now two years ago, had been very difficult for the both of them and to mend his son's heart, he had bought him a horse for his Birthday. The half-broken father-son bond, however, would not heal until one day, Michael fell off his horse and broke his arm and during the six painful weeks that had followed, David wouldn't leave his son's side. This accident had finally brought them closer together and this year, Michael seemed more excited than ever to come over with his friends and spend time with his father.

David was proud of his son. Only, he hadn't counted on having to feed two extra hungry mouths for five whole weeks.

The sound of a car pulling up the driveway woke him from his thoughts. He got up frowning, as he wasn't expecting any guests and the kids were not due until the following day. Perhaps they were just passers-by. He went outside and saw a large black SUV with tinted windows. The car also had a strange license plate. It gave him goose bumps on his sunburned skin. Three men got out of the car, wearing dark suits and sunglasses and David stepped back a few paces, not knowing what to expect. Though he had done some deep online research into secret societies, just to get some serious information on the Knights Templar, he had never been intimidated for browsing through secret web files before. He decided to wait and see what would happen, not really having a reason to hide. One of them, a tall blonde, muscular man, stepped up and shook David's hand, saying, "I noticed the sign 'Mini-camping / cottage / B&B'. We are looking for a quiet place to stay and I was wondering if you still had some vacancies.".

The Swiss took off his sunglasses and smiled as if to show David his good intentions. The cottage was still available, as David had originally reserved it for his son, but Michael was going to stay in tents now anyway, so he nodded.

"Yes, I have the cottage available for you. Please follow me." The three men followed David to the cottage, which was just around the corner. The door was wide open, but you could still smell the penetrating scent of the fresh wood varnish. David showed the men in. The cottage wasn't big, but it was comfortable enough. There was TV with a satellite-receiver, a stereo music system, several tapes, CD's, DVD's and books to keep people happy in case the weather would suddenly turn bad - which was still possible in the Corbières, even in summer. However, the men didn't seem to be interested in comfort. They checked out every corner of the cottage and every square metre of the terrain and when they agreed to stay, David noticed that they first unpacked their heavy equipment - containing auto tracking systems, laptops and other technical stuff that David had never seen - before they even unpacked their suitcases. David wasn't born yesterday; he immediately knew these men were up to something. His gut told him to keep away, so he gave them the keys to the cottage and went back into the main house. However, he was beginning to get a little worried about the safety of his son and his friends.

Within a few hours, the three men had settled in. A large tent had been erected close to the cottage and several sensors had been placed strategically on the premises. The equipment was all set up and a tiny light on the laptop screen now showed the exact location of the second car.

It was time to phone the professor.

Bill, Gabby and Otto jumped at the sound of the mobile phone going off in the car. As the professor was driving, he asked Gabby to take the call and for a second, Gabby hesitated, but after four rings she took the phone and pressed the green button with her trembling index finger. "Yes?"

"Hello Ms Standford, this is your base camp speaking. We have found a good location from where we can start our expeditions. So listen carefully while I give you directions."

Gabby took out her notepad and pencil and wrote down the exact route description to what seemed to be their destination. As soon as they got off the main road at Couiza, they realised that they were heading into the countryside. It felt as if they were being directed toward the middle of nowhere. Ten minutes later, they arrived at the woodland paradise that was David's B&B.

When David heard another car on the driveway, he almost ran to the parking to see a second black SUV of the same brand and license plate pulling up behind the first one. It was obvious that they were part of the same group. David watched the two men and a woman - who had come out of the second car - walking toward the previous arrivals.

The men and the woman exchanged what looked like formal greetings. They were not tourists; that much was certain. *What was going on?*

Bill, Gabby and Otto were very surprised to see how well everything had been organised. They had only just arrived when a third car with three others members of the Organisation drove onto the parking. Apparently, the car that had followed them all the way from Switzerland had always been part of their own group. All that time, Bill and Gabby had thought that they were being followed by Sardis' men. Counting the number of men that were part of this mission, it now became clear to them that this was bigger than they had anticipated. Obviously, Gabby and the professor were now very anxious to finally meet their employer. Although he was wearing mirror-type sunglasses, Bill and Gabby immediately recognised the Swiss as one of the guards who had eavesdropped on their entire conversation the day before. Still he did not say his name; he merely shook their hands and welcomed them to Occitania. Otto and his chief merely exchanged thin smiles. Though Otto was thrilled to be back in his beloved Occitania, he wondered why they were in the Corbières and not in the Sabarthès? He became suspicious and a little worried.

Would he know?

He decided to find out and walked over to his chief.

"So, Fred, why are we based *here*, on *this* spot?"

The Swiss knew Otto would ask him that question and smirked. "Yes, Otto, it must feel strange for you to be in this place, seventy odd years after your last visit, which for you was, when? Three years ago?"

"Yes, I was here in 1936. You *know?*"

Otto was shocked. It had been a top secret mission.

Bill, who had heard them speak, joined them and added, "So, why *are* we here, sir?"

The Swiss was prepared to share some information about their mission and started,

"As far as we know, this is the heart of the region where we may find what we are looking for according to the research information Sardis has given us. This spot is secluded and perfect for our base camp, so we won't be troubled by nosey tourists. We've brought everything you may need, including climbing gear and necessities for exploring caves. Tomorrow we will start early; the weather forecast is good. So, Otto, we will expect a briefing tonight from what you have learned so far. Anything that can get us on the right track. We have to find it!"

Their chief was now deadly serious. The smile on his face had gone and feeling somewhat intimidated, Rahn pursed his lips. He just *knew* his chief had to know more than he let on, but after seventy years, the site he had found in 1936 must be under many layers of leaf mould by now. He would play dumb. He *had to* play dumb.

During the rest of the day, Otto re-read the contents of Sardis' file and made notes in his usual, hastily scrawled handwriting. It was true that all the places of interest for them to find the Ark and/or the Ark stone were in this very area. In his mind's eye, this research took him back to his favourite years, when he had been a journalist, travelling through Europe; first on a shoestring and later on a nice monthly allowance from Berlin. Otto breathed in deeply through his nose and smelled the fresh air and fragrant scent of the pines and other forest trees that surrounded the place. He was excited.

Three agents had now set up a large tent right next to the cottage, while Bill and Gabby had put up their tent a little bit further back. Sitting outside on two white, plastic lounge chairs, fatigue almost overcame them, but they were also a little bit confused, realising that - although *they* were sent on a personal errand for Sardis to get Danielle back - the SBS-Sion Organisation was in charge of this mission and neither Sardis, nor his men, were anywhere in sight.

How strange.

It still seemed as if Sardis had no knowledge of the existence, let alone the interference, of the Swiss. Gabby studied the woods surrounding the estate and spotted the little stream that had almost dried up. It was so tranquil, so quiet. The scent of the pine trees, the blue skies and vibrant colours made her feel as if she were on holiday. Then, they noticed David - the owner of the domain - passing them with a 'complet/full' sign in his hand, ready to pin it onto the gate. David was nervous and reluctant to tell them anything about the imminent arrival of his son and friends on Sunday, but he knew that he had to at some point. David looked at Gabby and Bill. They seemed nice people. He slowed down and turned toward them. Maybe they could tell him more about what was going on. He showed them the sign and tried to start a conversation.

"Better get this hung up, it seems you guys don't want any witnesses to your holiday! Ha!"

Gabby smiled back at David. She liked him right away. He probably had no idea what the hell had hit him with these strange guests taking over his estate. She could, however, also feel his anxiety. Her smile invited David to come a bit closer. Playing the host, he started, "So is everyone comfy? Need any tips on tourist attractions, walks, nearest supermarket?"

Bill got up from his chair and introduced himself, with Gabby following his example. "Thank you Mr eh…"

"Camford, David Camford."

"Mr Camford". said Gabby politely.

"Call me David, please."

Gabby had to laugh, this was certainly a man who could play a girl. "Thank you David. I'm Gabby. Thank you for your hospitality. It must all seem a bit strange I suppose, but we are on an expedition and we need all the privacy we can get. No tourists or witnesses. I'm sure the others have already informed you that our mission is classified and that you are not allowed to speak about it with anyone?"

David frowned. *Classified? Are these guys FBI or something?*

"No," he said, "I was just told to keep things quiet and to close the rest of the accommodation, for which I will be compensated. I didn't really want to ask any questions."

"Don't worry David, you know how it can be sometimes when you are investigating something important and you are constantly disturbed. That's why we want privacy."

David nodded and sighed, but then he decided to take his chance. "Look, tomorrow my son and his three friends will arrive. They will stay in tents on my domain for five weeks. If I assure you that they won't bother you, it shouldn't be a problem, should it?"

David looked worried but hopeful. What to do if the answer was negative?

Gabby looked at the professor for a moment and knew that they really couldn't answer that question.

"David, I think that is something you will have to ask the people in the cottage. They are in charge."

David turned to look at the cottage and became nervous. He'd rather avoid the place, but he realised he had no choice. "Thanks guys. I will do that. Well, I better get this pinned on the gate first. See you later?"

Gabby nodded and they both watched him walk to the gate. *Poor David.*

That evening, David had made omelettes for everybody. Eggs were about all he had in stock, but he would do some shopping tomorrow. While inside the cottage, he had taken his time to serve everybody so he could take a good look at them all. Within seconds he saw that this looked bad, very bad. Most of the men were in black uniform; the entire cottage was filled with the most expensive hardware and software; maps had been spread out with co-ordinates already marked out and there was one man everybody called 'Sir', except for a pale man with dark hair who called him 'Fred'. Almost all of them spoke German. The other man and the woman - whom he had already met earlier - were almost always together. They were the only ones who seemed 'different'; as if they weren't part of the other group. Also, they were the only ones speaking English with an American accent. However, they didn't behave as if they were in trouble, like in 'kidnapped'. A quick eye on the letterhead of a document made David shiver;

'Non nobis, Domine, non nobis,
sed nomini Tuo da gloriam...'

David had seen these words before and knew what they meant. One could loosely translate it into 'Not for our glory, Lord, but for your glory'. Powerful words of honour that had belonged to an order he had familiarised himself with:
The Knights Templar.
The Swiss noticed how David was loitering and observing and didn't like it at all. He walked over to him and asked him to leave. As soon as David had opened the door, the Swiss pushed him outside while holding on to his arm, scaring the living daylights out of David. Shocked, David dropped the empty tray he was carrying. Hoping to make a clear impression on David, the Swiss closed the door behind them and pressed David against the cottage wall. The blonde muscular giant was a head taller than him and it had its impact. Especially while standing as close as this.
The Swiss then said, calmly, "You know that all of this is top secret, don't you? So you agree that this must be kept confidential, right?"
David, incredibly shaken by this sudden confrontation, nodded nervously. The Swiss let go of his arm and went back inside.
Jesus Christ!
His heart was pounding. This was neither the time nor the place to talk to this man about the arrival of his son and friends.

14

Rome, Italy, June 25th 2011

Danielle was beyond panic. She looked around the strange room in the large house, knowing that she had lost her identity; her independence; her friends; her house - her entire life for that matter. She was now at the mercy of a man who seemed to want to touch and kiss her all the time. She had scratched his face, thrown a lamp at him and had even hidden a knife under her pillow, just in case he would go too far one day. Sardis, on the other hand, was as calm as a mystic and enjoyed every second with her. He had no intension to harm her, he merely loved her. Danielle felt he had to be crazy. She was his prisoner and if she hadn't been pregnant, she would have jumped out of a window, or risked other more daring means of escape, but with her body aching with pains and inconveniences from her pregnancy and the idea of the child growing inside her womb, she wouldn't think of it.

Danielle had cried; screamed for help, but no one had come to her rescue and now she was exhausted and hungry. This time - she told herself - she wouldn't kick the food-tray away.

There was a noise in the hallway, which was forbidden territory for Danielle. The day before she had tried to escape by waiting behind the door and dashing through the doorway the moment it had opened, toward what had seemed to be the way out, but all doors were closed and she had quickly been escorted back to her room. Danielle had given up, Sardis had won, so now she allowed the servant to serve her breakfast and she ate it all. She even enjoyed it after refusing food for three days and with her morning sickness now gone, she dared to eat. It was as if all her strength had left her and her mind had finally come to terms with her present situation, albeit with protest. She was tired of fighting; tired of crying; tired of hating. If Sardis had been violent or abusive towards her, but no; he was always friendly toward Danielle. It was almost as if he venerated her. He probably did.

Suddenly, an idea passed through her mind. Why not try to make him believe she was on his side? Maybe then he would become less careful. This new hope renewed her strength and energy; she even smiled. All it needed was a little time and patience. So after her breakfast and a nice hot shower, Danielle decided to wear one of the dresses Sardis had bought for her, dresses she had refused to even look at until now. It fitted, but she also noticed the lower part of the dress allowing for expansion and felt really comfortable in it. When she looked at herself in the huge baroque mirror that featured in her bedroom, she saw that the dress was beautiful, but the face looking back at her was pale and her eyes looked tired and stressed. She looked around and discovered a small box on the dressing table that she hadn't noticed before. The past few days she had been so busy feeling miserable, that she hadn't taken any notice of the contents and details of her room. The little box on her dressing table indeed contained make-up, as she had expected.

After trying several items to get the effect she wanted, Danielle waited for Sardis to arrive. The Cardinal checked on her several times a day to see if she was alright, so she expected him to come over any time now. However, it wasn't until 14.30 hours that there was a knock on her door. Her heart leaped. It was the servant again, this time with coffee and slices of chocolate coated sponge cake. Where was the Cardinal? she thought. Had he gone out? Then suddenly, the very moment she poured the hot, black coffee into her colourful porcelain cup, Sardis entered the room and being as nervous as she was, it startled her and she made a mess on the lacquered coffee table. Immediately, the servant cleared it up and Sardis stared at her, noticing the dress, "Well, well, I see you are finally coming to terms with your destiny, my beautiful one."

He smiled broadly, revealing his off-white teeth. Danielle shivered, hoping he wouldn't get the wrong idea by seeing her all dressed up.

"Are you cold, my dear? These old houses have thick walls to keep out the Summer heat and I must admit, today it *is* a bit chilly for this time of year."

Immediately he clapped his hands and told the servant to make a fire in the hearth. Danielle was ashamed and angry that she had no control over her emotions - being so insecure and jumpy - but she also knew she shouldn't judge herself so harshly after all she had been through.

Both of them started on their coffee, which had been freshly made and being hungry, Danielle almost assaulted the chocolate sponge cake, which was rich and filled with strawberry jam. Sardis watched her devour slice after slice with a broad smile on his face, pleased to see she was coming to terms with her situation. It was clear to him; her resistance had been broken.

Hoping to win her heart, he started, "Danielle, listen to me. We must become friends. I will not harm you. There's a lot of money going into your well-being; look around you, you're being treated like a royal princess!" Sardis laid his hand on her arm and added, "and believe me, to me you are!"

He gazed into her blue eyes as if he were enchanted. Suddenly, a tune from Debussy's *Clair de Lune* broke the spell. It was his mobile phone. "Pronto! ... Si? Bene!"

Sardis put away his mobile and looked at Danielle with satisfaction. "Well, it looks like your friends have arrived on location, my dear lady. I am very pleased."

Danielle remembered the letter Sardis had sent them. In case Gabby and the professor find the Ark, they will bring it to Rome and then they will get caught in Sardis' web. Danielle now realised it wasn't just about her and her baby; it also involved Gabby and Bill. Quickly, she suppressed her thoughts, finished her coffee and smiled at Sardis, trying to keep up the game she was playing. "It would be wonderful to see them again. I hope they will succeed soon!" she said with faked enthusiasm. The Cardinal took out a blank sheet of paper and a pen and handed it over to Danielle.

"I hope so, too! Look, I will even allow you to write a letter to your friend Gabrielle."

Then, with a self-satisfied grin, Sardis opened a drawer and produced her diary. Like a child who had just been given a lollypop, he waved it at her, "I finished it yesterday. Remarkable! We already knew several things, but not everything and it becomes clear to me now that the man Oshu - *our* Jesus - did not die on the cross, but was healed and eventually went to Carmel, where he taught Hermetic philosophy to small classes. Christianity evolved around him, but independently of him and when the first schisms were already happening, he had made it perfectly clear that he didn't want to have anything to do with it. Isn't it cynical? Christ was the very first heretic!"

Danielle stared hard at him.

What was his point?

Sardis got up from his chair, folded his arms and turned to the window, leaving the diary on his desk. With a hint of cynicism he added, "Also, there are several details in your diary which would certainly shock the world, don't you think?"

Seeing an opportunity, Danielle jumped up, snatched her diary from the desk and held it tight. "Don't you dare take it from me. It's *my* diary!! *Mine!!*"

She was furious and ran toward her apartment, hoping to lock herself into the bathroom, but the door to her apartment had been securely locked while they had been drinking their coffee; as if somehow, Sardis had foreseen that this would happen. Sardis smiled as if he relished the scene and calmly approached her with outstretched hand. "Now, calm down. Come, give it to me. Remember; nothing is yours, not even you. Even you are mine."

With her back against the wall and nowhere to run to, Sardis now stood right in front of her and took her arms. He pulled them in front of her and casually took the diary from her hands. Then he opened it and read one of the passages to her - speaking with a clear voice - as if he was trying to confirm

144

his earlier remark. He emphasised the words, reading the text as if it were a play. "I have never felt like this before; how tender this man was. Every inch of my skin was tingling with his energy. Now I understand how one-ness can create such an explosion of energy. He taught me to draw this energy upward to my head and for a moment it was as if I could see God's infinity; oneness and eternity at the same time. Millions of stars were moving in one shapeless body that breathed in and out and when I looked at him, he glowed. His eyes were as clear as glass; his skin radiant and I could feel the power of his energy, not only inside of me, but surrounding me like a hot bath."

Sardis closed the book and stared hard at her. Danielle blushed, "You wouldn't understand…"

She felt as if he had just fouled her most intimate emotions.

"This wasn't about lust," she added, "it was about the great mystery of energy. About Kundalini! Something you could *never* understand."

She trembled. The dress she was wearing now made her feel ridiculous. For a moment - as if he could read her mind - Sardis looked at her with a serious face, but then his attention went back to the diary and his mission. "I already knew many things about our Master Jesus, Danielle. I knew he didn't die on the cross, I knew he was on earth in flesh and blood, but I also know that he was very special in every way. He was an Avatar far greater than people can imagine, but most people don't know that he was also an uncrowned King, who - in the difficult circumstances of his days - had to step in after the death of his half-brother John and step back in favour of his step-brother James, but you must understand, that although the Church knows all this, Jesus is still the Christ for all of us, our Saviour. The entire story that has evolved around his life and times may not have been fully based on the truth, but it does have a significant esoteric message that only few have discovered. That is the reason why the Church cannot just change the New Testament to fit the truth, because it isn't about truth, it is about the message. That is why I believe that the world isn't ready yet to know the contents of your diary. Yet, here you are, pregnant with our Lord's son and had that not been the case, your diary would have been reduced to ashes already. However, now it has become invaluable *because* of this, for to me it confirms the story of the Prophesy. If your son is born, I will raise him and tutor him and make him into a Grand Monarch. When he is ready, I will present him to the world along with your diary and the Ark of the Covenant, because he who possesses the true Ark, will rule the world and I am convinced that your friends will find it for me!"

Danielle stared at him; her hands resting in her lap. What would possibly drive this man to abduct a person and send others on a dangerous expedition hoping to find a relic that has been lost for millennia. She stepped up to him and asked, "Why? For world domination? Power? Greed?"

"No Danielle, no. For peace! I want this world to wake up and realise its behaviour. Your son will become the new Christ, the King of Peace!"

He closed his eyes - a tear escaped.

Danielle was aghast. "You're mad!"

"*Am* I?" Sardis snarled, jumping from one emotion to another. "Look around you! If *I* am in a state of madness, then in what state is the *world?*"

He got up and hid the diary in his soutane, stopping Danielle from reaching after it. Danielle screamed and begged him to give it back to her, but when Sardis had left the room, she could no longer fight; her legs lost their strength and she fell down on the oaken floor. It was as if her heart had been torn from her chest and she realised how important this diary had become to her. It contained her deepest feelings and emotions and all the details she had learned from the people she had spoken to. She wanted it back.

She *had* to get it back.

15

The *péage*, France, June 26th 2011

'Forever Man' was playing very loudly in the car. Yanne - who had plugged her fingers in her ears - looked hard at her boyfriend Ben, who was singing along with the others. They were having a good time while driving south through France, but after several hours of Eric Clapton songs, Yanne had become tired. She turned the music off, after which everyone protested.

"Oh, give me a break!" she yelled. "You have been listening to loud music since we left the motel this morning and I'm getting a really bad headache, so if you'll excuse me!"

Ben plucked his eyelashes - he always did that when he was a bit nervous or anxious. Not even the three boys together were a match for her. Yanne was the leader of the gang and Ben loved her for it. She was right though, he was also getting a bit tired from driving with loud music and he welcomed the silence. On the back seat, Michael and Arthur - who were still full of energy - opened their bags, took out a few books and maps and started talking about their planned expeditions. The road taking them to Toulouse was not too busy and Ben speeded up to 130 kilometres an hour, which is the speed limit in France for driving in good conditions. Yanne sat back and closed her eyes; she had no desire to listen to Arthur and Michael all the time. She and Ben had been looking forward to this trip so much and she hated the fact that Arthur had now joined them, spoiling everything for her. However, the others didn't seem to mind at all. Art was a know-it-all. Indeed, he knew more about the mysteries of Occitania than Michael and Ben combined, but Yanne felt he shouldn't brag about it so much. It irritated her. However, Yanne had no idea that Arthur had never been able to share his passion with anyone before. No longer able to suppress his enthusiasm, he started,

"I know it's possible; there were so many people either living there, or moving through the area, for many thousands of years: Phoenicians; Greeks; Romans; Visigoths; Merovingians or Franks; Moors; Templars and Cathars. There were gold mines, silver mines and spa towns - where hot mineral water attracted thousands of wealthy people throughout the ages to 'take the waters'. Some of them left their traces in the countryside. During the middle Ages, wars and plagues had killed millions of people and consequently caused many to flee to a safer place. People sometimes hid their precious possessions, hoping to one day return to collect them, but sometimes they didn't come back. The whole region is littered with legends of old treasure, hidden by those who had fled and never returned or hidden by rich locals on the eve of the French Revolution. I'm sure that some of it must have been found by people already, but there could still be plenty left if we just search in the right spot. We have five weeks and I think we really have a chance to find something!"

Arthur looked at Michael, who had been listening with interest. "Go on!" he said, encouraging Arthur, who smiled while folding the map into a manageable square. Almost bursting with excitement, Arthur continued,

"I've marked out a few co-ordinates here on the map, that could perhaps lead us to something. All we have to do is go there to see what we can find. It could just be a *menhir*, or a cave already emptied by others, but we won't know until we get there and find out and you know what?"

"What?" the others chorused.

Arthur pointed his finger at a certain spot on the map and added, "Michael, your dad's place is slap bang in the middle of it all!"

Arthur and Michael looked at each other and smiled. They couldn't wait to start their adventures.

Little did they know what danger was in store for them.

Suddenly, a horrifying scream right out of a horror movie startled everyone but Michael, who knew it was just the ringtone of his mobile.

It was a text message from his father, saying:
'We got company. When you arrive, be good. See ya soon.'
Michael frowned. What was that all about? Why do we have
to 'be good'? Something must be going on. He decided not to
alarm the others, but he suddenly got a funny feeling about
this holiday. It might not go the way they had planned it after
all.

David was very much looking forward to seeing his son
again, but it was essential that he and his friends stayed away
from his mystery guests. The large blonde man called 'Fred'
and four others had gone on an expedition early that morning
and he didn't expect them back until the evening. He knew
his son well enough to know that he and his friends would be
away most of the time exploring places, so when the car with
Michael, Ben, Yanne and Arthur finally arrived, he
welcomed them and showed them to their tent site, a position
he had chosen carefully: well away from his mysterious
guests.
Michael had been eager to see his horse, so as soon as his
tent was set up, he went to the field to call it. Arthur envied
Michael for being able to ride his very own horse, but he also
enjoyed watching the special chemistry that was clearly
visible between the horse and his friend.

At 19.00 hours, the two black SUV's returned to David's
estate. David noticed Fred looking suspiciously at the new
tents and when the Swiss angrily marched toward him,
David's blood pressure shot up. He hadn't forgotten last
night's incident and Fred's word of warning.
Oh Lord, now we're going to get it…
"What's this?" said Fred, pointing at the tents.
David decided to play the dumb, innocent father; "Hello sir,
oh, it's just my son and his friends, they are here for the
summer, but I can assure you, they won't cause any
problems."

The Swiss was livid. "Why didn't you tell me before? I can't allow it!"

David, who looked away, no longer able to hold back his fear for the man's reaction. "I thought you'd say that, but he's my boy."

Fred looked at him with folded arms, not quite sure how to handle this new situation, but then he watched the kids, who seemed to be completely occupied with their own things.

The Swiss sighed and gave in. "Okay David, but I warn you, keep them off our backs!"

David nodded. The moment Fred had gone, he breathed out. *Phew, thank God for that!*

Dinner had been served early in the main house that night and David wasn't sure how much he wanted to tell his son. He didn't want to spoil their fun, but he also wanted to make sure they stayed out of trouble, so the moment they had all settled in, David came over to the tent site to toast their safe arrival and when he had finished his welcoming speech, he asked them to listen carefully for a moment.

"You probably noticed the three black cars at the parking area, the big tents on each side of the cottage and the 'closed' sign on the gate. Like I said, we have company. These people are from some kind of institute. They go on an expedition every day and when they come back, they are all covered in dust and yellow mud. They are definitely looking for something, but their mission is kind of secret, so we aren't allowed to speak to anyone about them or what they are doing. I am not kidding, these guys are not what you call ordinary explorers or official scientists and I don't want them all over me complaining about you, so keep a low profile and do *not* go snooping around the cottage, understood?"

David was very serious and Michael could tell that his dad wasn't joking with them. Actually, he had never seen him so worried. They all agreed, but Arthur had become suspicious. He understood very well what these guys might be looking for and why they had set up their camp here.

No matter what Michael's father said, he was definitely going to keep a close eye on them.

The Corbières, southern France, June 28th 2011

Bill and Gabby didn't accompany the others when they set out on their expeditions. They stayed behind with two of the 'men in black', as they had started to call them, although now the SBS agents were no longer in suits but in polo-shirts because of the heat. The agents were always silent and in the background, though they kept a close eye on Bill and Gabby's every move.

Late that afternoon, another black car with tinted glass drove into the parking area. A woman stepped out, who seemed to be alone. Attracted by the noise of the car pulling up the driveway, Bill had come out of the tent, which he shared with Gabby. His mouth fell open at the sight of Ms Kaiser. Shocked, he called Gabby. "Look who's just arrived! What the heck is *she* doing here? Come on, let's get a little closer and see if we can find out what's going on."

Gabby nodded and as soon as Kaiser had entered the cottage, she followed to eavesdrop at the window. Then suddenly - almost immediately after Kaiser had gone inside - she reappeared and almost ran back to the car. Kaiser was clearly in a hurry and Gabby had to run and hide behind the corner of the cottage, not to be seen. After Kaiser had gone, Gabby breathed out and shook her head at Bill, who pulled a face.

That was close!

They both laughed at the situation and couldn't help feeling useless. Why did they have to come along anyway? Because the Cardinal had addressed his letter to them and not to the head of SBS? That would be silly. Perhaps the Organisation just wanted to keep Bill away from the ERFAB.

The professor sighed, "I don't know Gabby, maybe we should just behave ourselves and wait it out."

"How do you mean, behave ourselves?" queried Gabby. While asking this, Gabby touched his hand, moved closer and kissed him softly on his lips.

Still attached to her lips, he slowly put his arms around her. He couldn't believe this was happening and had no idea that Gabby had grown so fond of him. He was her boss; after all it was the professor who had employed the women, but now he was no longer wearing his long white overcoat, but stone-washed jeans and a yellow polo-shirt. Also, he was no longer wearing his usual glasses, but hip sunglasses. He was different now; playful; accessible; available. As Gabby had already noticed the chemistry between them, she had decided that Bill was just too shy to ever make a first move.

Until now, women had always frightened Bill. He would never have dared to make the first move, so if Gabby hadn't started, nothing would have ever happened between them. His fear for women had started after having been beaten up with a plastic spade at kindergarten by his first girlfriend after he had tried to give her a kiss. Bill wouldn't dream of making any first moves *ever* again, but Gabby; she was different. She was smart and warm hearted with a caring personality, a great sense of humour and what was the most unbelievable thing; apparently she was fond of him. Of *him*! Besides, Gabby didn't seem to have a plastic spade. Bill grinned. He had always felt he was such a nerd, always the one with his nose in books; working on inventions; being obsessed with time travel and wormholes and avoiding female contact at all cost, so he wouldn't be disappointed or made a fool of and yet, here he was, kissed and hugged by a women who had chosen to kiss *him*. It was as if all his molecules were vibrating in overdrive. He felt warm, his whole body was tingling and he also became aware of a certain part of his body behaving awkwardly. Quickly he moved his hips backward. Gabby noticed it and smiled. She lowered her hands, grabbed his bottom and pressed his body firmly against hers. Then she whispered softly in his ear, "There's no one here; the agents are only watching us when we're outside, so why don't we go inside our tent and see if we can both fit into one sleeping bag?"

Bill just grinned and followed her inside as if hypnotised.

The agents, who had positioned themselves on the porch with two bottles of beer, were amused. With interest they listened to the little screams, laughter and erotic sounds that came from Bill and Gabby's tent.

"Would keeping an 'ear' on them be considered the same as keeping an 'eye' on them, you think?" one of the men asked the other. "I suppose so!" the other replied, while toasting.

In the meantime, Otto and a team of four were hiking in the hills, exploring possible hiding places of the ancient relic they were searching for. The Swiss, Alfred, was one of them. He was in his mid-fifties, blonde, blue eyed and strong. He had been working out since he was 17 and it showed. His manners also betrayed his upper class status, with a fine command of the English language - Oxford style - although with Rahn he mostly spoke German, his native tongue. He was clearly in good shape, walking the hills as if they were flat. Alfred had become the head of SBS-Sion when his father had died on that tragic day in December, 2010. His family had been in this white order for many centuries, going back to the times of the Knights Templar and much like the old Knights of the Cross, this order of Sion was a defender of Christianity. Not in the same way the Roman Catholic Church was defending it, or the Protestant Church, or even the Orthodox Church for that matter, but to defend the Christianity that Christ himself might have wanted it to be: a Way of Life, rather than a religion. Alfred had in his possession many relics that had fallen into the sea of legend or oblivion; for example, the beautiful bowl or cup of gold with mystical symbols, which had been a present from an eastern mystic to a new-born prince, two thousand years ago. He grinned. If only Otto knew. He'd have loved to see the look on his face. However, for this particular mission, Alfred now focused on a Grail Stone; a stone which could lead them to the Ark of the Covenant.

Apart from finding the lost Ark and getting Danielle back, Alfred was equally desperate to discover Otto's secret.

Otto seemed to know something no other person on earth knew and Alfred already had a good idea what that might be. Therefore, Otto had become invaluable to him.

Though Alfred knew everything about everyone on his team, he himself had succeeded to remain a mystery to the others and he had decided to keep it that way as long as possible. Alfred knew that throughout history there had always been forces which had attempted to obtain world domination by controlling the masses with ancient relics. These powers were ancient themselves. The moment that Cro Magnon - our human ancestors - had first settled in one fixed place to grow food and keep cattle, the struggle for land ownership and power had begun. This had resulted in tribal wars and there had been a huge increase in violence. Soon, the ego had outgrown the heart. However, time was now running out. The danger of world domination by one super power - or rather the danger of the chaos that would proceed it - was greater than ever.

In the past few days the team had been following almost every suggestion from Sardis' notes and every location they had investigated had been carefully registered. A GPS helped them find the co-ordinates they had marked on the map. After having explored the ruins of the ancient tower of Blanchefort - known for its underground cave system and mines - they found out that the most interesting grottoes had caved in. Then they had thoroughly explored the sacred mountain called the Pêch Cardou on the opposite side of the valley, only to find out that the caves they *could* reach were empty. Apart from a few strange symbols, there was nothing there, let alone the Ark or the alleged Temple of Solomon.

The previous day, the team had set out on a hike exploring another hill called the Pêch de la Roque, only to find Celtic remains, Roman mines, a mysterious manmade rock wall and strange stone formations. Even beyond the hill in the valley of a ridge called La Pique, they didn't find anything.

On this day, the team had been exploring the other side of the valley, south of Rennes-les-Bains, with its ancient springs and many more Celtic remains. They had followed all the clues and had now finally arrived at the giant megalith ridge that had given the Serbaïrou its characteristic appearance. Named after Cerberos, the three-headed hell-hound with his bony ridgeback, who guarded the underworld in the old Greek myths, the Serbaïrou finds itself embraced by two rivers - one sweet and one salty - which meet at the north side of the hill. The whole area had been considered sacred from the moment spiritual people had discovered it. According to the ancients, this 'Exterior Temple' had been built by God for mankind - rather than the other way around. This Holy Place was magical; it was a Holy of Holies in a Sacred Valley of God. Even one of the farms in the valley was called; 'Lavaldieu', the 'Valley of God'.

Although aware of Alfred's double wish list, Otto enjoyed the hikes through the woodland, climbing the hills and rocks with newfound vigour, investigating grottoes and deserted ruins, just like he had done in the early 1930s, but now they were getting a bit too close to a certain secret location for his comfort. To lure the team away from the spot, Otto tried to make conversation by explaining to Alfred the ancient history of the region.

"Did you know that from the Provence down, we are actually walking on a giant peninsula? The ancient Greeks and Phoenicians would watch the sun set over this peninsula in winter and thought that their God Apollo went there to hibernate. So they called it Iberia; 'Winterland'. Curious to explore this peninsula, they arrived here as early as 1000 BCE and over the centuries that followed, they would bring their culture; music; legends; skills and even their language to these parts. The coastal town of Cerbère in the Roussillon is named after the hell-hound who guarded the Greek underworld, just like this hill was named after it and do you know why the mountains between Spain and France are called the Pyrenees?" Otto was unstoppable and anxiously tried to lead the team away from the location by keeping Alfred distracted with his stories.

Using his hands and arms in his passionate diction he continued,

"There were so many melting ovens in the mountains, that at night the whole mountain range seemed to be full of fires. That is why it is called the Pyrenees, from the ancient word 'pyre'; The Fire Mountains. Of course, in the ancient Greek legend it was Hercules who had built the Pyrenees. It started out as a tomb for Pyrène, the daughter of a king, who had fallen in love with Hercules. According to the story, she had followed Hercules into the forest, where she was killed by wolves. Hercules, who was heartbroken, wanted to bury her and in his grief he kept on piling up rock after rock and consequently built the entire mountain range. However, *I* believe that the name *Iberia* came from the Hyperboreans, who had colonised the Pyrenees thousands of years before the first Phoenicians even arrived."

Alfred reached out and slapped the back of Otto's head.

"You and your stupid Hyperboreans!" Alfred exclaimed, unable to suppress a smile.

Rahn was shocked and halted abruptly. "But it's true!" he protested.

Alfred laughed out loud. Otto couldn't help sharing his knowledge and wild theories, but Alfred knew all too well that in the old days, there actually *were* Atlantean colonies on this peninsula.

Otto breathed in deeply, eyeing the very spot he wanted to avoid. He had to lead them away from here. Until now, he had been able to avoid going back to the co-ordinate he had already visited three years ago - which was, ironically, 75 years ago now. At the time, he had only taken out the most important items, while leaving the rest behind. To lock it shut in an attempt to preserve the tomb, he and his companion had caused the cover stone of the dolmen to topple over. Then he used Hannibal's techniques with wood, water and vinegar to crack one of the other stones that had formed the entrance to the tomb beneath the dolmen. As a result, the large megalith had broken into two parts; one of which had slid inward and had covered the entrance completely. He was sure that 75 years of leaf mould should have covered up most traces. However, if they were to go to this particular place now, Alfred might notice that this dolmen had been man-handled and would perhaps feel the urge to investigate further. Therefore, Otto had to prevent them from discovering the dolmen, for it would definitely distract them from their mission to find the Ark; the relic they needed to save Danielle. However - in spite of Otto's attempt to lure them away from it - they were now heading straight toward it and Otto was becoming extremely nervous.

Otto ventured, "let's check out these megaliths over there, they seem to be interesting landmarks."

Rahn - knowing that neither the Grail stone nor the Ark was among the items he had seen in the tomb underneath the dolmen - quickly walked toward the huge natural standing stones that covered the hill like a dragon's spine. To his relief he noticed that the men followed him.

Oomph, that was close!

Although they checked every hole, nook and cranny, they couldn't find any niche or entrance to a cave that was big enough and by six o'clock they had given up. When the team descended the hill, Alfred was very disappointed and remained silent all the way down. Back at the spot where they had parked the cars, they noticed that both cars had one or more flat tires. A little yellow sticky note that was stuck on the window explained that this was a reprisal for parking on someone's private property. Alfred looked around and could only see a distant cottage and an old bus. He had never seen any signs that this was somebody's private land. Alfred took out his mobile phone and made a quick call to their base camp at David's B&B. Within half an hour a car arrived to bring Alfred, Otto and one agent back to the base, while three agents stayed behind to change the punctured tires. By the time they arrived at the base camp, Alfred was in a very bad mood indeed.

Little did he know that the day wasn't over yet.

As soon as Alfred arrived, Bill sprinted over to Alfred to tell him what had happened. "Sir, we had company!"

Alfred rubbed his face. "What kind of company?"

"Ms Kaiser. I saw her entering the cottage."

Alfred had expected Sardis to contact them, but this was very bold. When Alfred opened the door, he only saw the calm face of the SBS-Sion agent who had stayed behind, looking casual, as if nothing had happened. Alfred was now very irritated. "Was there a woman in here today?"

"Yes, she gave us this envelope and then left." The agent replied.

"And you let her go?!"

The agent shrugged his shoulders, "Well, yes. What else could we do?"

"You should have kept her here for questioning, you fool!"

Alfred opened the envelope and discovered a file, a letter written by Danielle that was addressed to Gabby and another letter, written by Sardis and addressed to the professor and Gabby. Alfred turned to the agent and pointed at the parking. "Didn't you notice that someone was entering the camp?"

"Yes Sir, we saw the car pulling up, but you must understand that we initially thought it was you, sir, as it was a similar car."

"Similar, or the same?"

"Similar, sir."

Alfred shook his head while he started to read Sardis' letter. The letter was printed on the now familiar stationary, featuring the coat of arms with the three bees on the letter head.

To Professor William Fairfax and Dr Gabrielle Standford,
I am pleased to learn that you have set up a base in southern France and I hope that it won't be long before you find what I want. Of course, you will understand that I have given you a limited amount of time to find it. With Danielle safely in my care, I am sure you'll realise the risk if you should fail.

As you can see, I have allowed Danielle to write a letter to her friend, Ms Standford, naturally under my supervision. Ms Kaiser will keep an eye on all of you for me. Also, it has come to my attention that the Nôtre Dame de Marceille, the ruins of the abbey of St. Martin Lys and the Church of Laval are serious contenders in the game. Research them, give attention to their history and crypts. In the enclosed file you will find my notes on the sites. Ms Kaiser will ask for your report every day. Do not disappoint me, as Danielle's life depends on it. Time is running out.
Good luck! May God be with you and with our quest.
Antonio, Cardinal Sardis

It was obvious to all of them, that they had no time to loose. Kaiser would return every day to receive their report, so each day they had to make some form of progress. On the other hand it was encouraging to find the letter from Danielle, which was handwritten and addressed to Gabby. However, the letter had been 'adapted' by Sardis, so they could only read a part of it.

Gabby's heart was beating fast. She had been anxious to hear from Danielle, so she asked to read the letter first. Alfred respected her first right to read it and noticed how her hands trembled while reading her friend's message.

"Sardis has her diary." Gabby announced.

They all realised how serious this was. It meant that Sardis now knew everything. However, Bill was just glad that Danielle was alright and that her diary had surfaced.

"At least he didn't destroy the diary." Bill remarked, but Alfred was still concerned. "Who says that he won't?"

As the contents of the letter concerned them all and were too important to be read by Gabby only, she decided to share it with the others.

Dear Gabby,
Don't worry about me, I'm fine, surrounded by luxury and comfort in Rome. Sardis is friendly to me although he has stolen my diary, which has broken my heart.
By the way, I am █████████████████

████████████████████████████████

████████████████████████████████

█████████ *so I can't wait to see you.*
Take care of yourself!
Warm hugs,
Danielle ***

They all understood that she had written more than Sardis had wanted them to read, as he had redacted her lines. There was no way to find out what was underneath the black section, no matter how they turned the letter against the light. It was driving Gabby insane. What did Danielle want her to know? Danielle is... what? Then suddenly, the thunderbolt struck her. Call it female intuition. Danielle was pregnant. Gabby decided to keep this information to herself, for now.

Everyone felt the pressure, so after a quick meal they all gathered around the table and studied the contents of Sardis' first envelope to see if they had missed anything. After several hours, Otto decided to try and find some more information on the Internet, but although there was enough on the mysteries of the Nôtre Dame de Marceille, including information about some kind of ancient secret vault he was hoping to explore, there was hardly anything about St. Martin Lys and the church of Laval, which made him even more curious. He researched the Internet all evening and at one point something was sent to the printer. However, after folding it three times, Rahn hid the printout safely in his pocket and didn't share its contents with anyone. He merely smiled to himself.

In the meantime, Bill tried to pump Alfred for more information. He wanted to know more about the plans of the Organisation; what they were after and whether they were just helping them out to get Danielle back. He chose a coffee break to speak to his chief in private.

"Sir, I really need to know more about this operation."

Alfred smiled. "Look, Bill, it hasn't been easy for me to keep you out, believe me, but it was for your own good. All information was on a 'need to know' basis, but I guess I can tell you something now. My name is Alfred Zinkler, I'm the head of the Organisation you are working for. As you know, we are called SBS-Sion, but what you don't know is that we are a worldwide organisation and that Sion is merely the name of our base in Switzerland. Our goal is world peace and to create a possibility to unite all religions under one global Way of Life. World peace is not just something that happens when war ceases to exist. It is more complicated than that."

"Today, many wars are still fought because of the differences in religious belief or culture. Throughout the ages, people have been drifting more and more apart from one another, but a long time ago we were much closer, much more related than people might think. We all remember the crusades against the Muslims in the Middle Ages. We all know that the Knights Templar fought alongside the crusaders against the Muslims. However, one enlightened Grandmaster chose to become friends with the sons of the enemy's military leader; Saladin. Several Templars even became Muslim themselves, because they found more Christianity in *their* religion than in our own. Christianity as in Way of Life, conduct and spiritual thought. It is very important that all religions seek their roots and by doing so, we will discover that we are all brothers and sisters; sons and daughters of the one Supreme Being. Though we are divided, we are circling around the same drinking trough in our religious convictions. At the heart of all religions lies the same pearl. That pearl is the Grail, the Ark, the Philosopher's Stone, the Divine Spark, Mani, the Hermetic Teachings…"

"This afternoon, Otto actually hit the nail on the head when he said that the Cathars worshipped Amor and thus endangered Roma. Get it? Roma, Amor? The Church of Love. Not lust, but love. The courtly love which was the main topic of the songs of the Troubadours; the minstrels of the Middle Ages. That divine spark that is in each and every one of us; the purest energy which connects us directly with God. This divine spark is our gate to heaven; our inner master; our consciousness; our very own Master Merlin dwelling in the deep caves of our sub-consciousness whispering magic words, waiting for us to react; to listen; to understand; to make use of that magic and I know that Rahn understands this. He is not a fool, you know."

Bill was listening closely, moved by his chief's words because they hit home, but he was curious about something. "Then what about the material objects? Are these real too?" he remarked.

"As above - so below, Bill. Mankind always wanted to put into matter what was in his mind. He used his hands to create things, paint pictures on the walls of caves thousands of years ago, to shape something that had once been an idea, a thought or a vision and then he turned it into matter. He materialised it - like God materialised thought by lowering vibration by 'speaking' at the beginning the Word that created the Big Bang - to symbolise and materialise an immaterial concept. The Egyptians did it through the Pyramids, Moses did it through the Ark, David and Solomon did it through the Temple in Jerusalem and Chretien and Wolfram did it by writing down their Parsifal stories, creating the Grail myth. They put into matter that which was first spirit and gave it an earthly existence on the material plane."

Bill took advantage of Alfred's pause and asked, "I thought the Grail was just something material, a chalice or something."

Alfred smiled. "It is first of all a concept of the divine energy, which is trapped into matter, like our divine souls are trapped inside our material bodies from the moment we were born. Hence the chalice. The cup of Christ is simply another way of putting it. The body which contains the Christ Consciousness: the awareness of the presence of the Divine Spark - the God-flame - within our being and our acting upon it. It is all about conduct; behaviour; making the right choices and being a good person."

The professor looked at his chief, sitting on a chair, stooping forward while resting his elbows on his knees. It was obvious that the man was tired, but in spite of his fatigue, Alfred continued,

"So you see, when the Grail stories were originally created to teach people this concept of the Divine Spark inside us - and actually, many stories on Jesus serve the same purpose - everyone started to look for a cup that was touchable; material; real. Cups appeared from everywhere and the Vatican finally decided to allow one special, ancient chalice to be the 'real' Grail cup. This particular cup is being kept in Valencia, Spain; not because it is the material cup that was used by Jesus, but because Rome wanted people to have something touchable to focus on."

Bill shook his head. "I don't understand why we are looking for a stone on this Grail hunt. I thought we were looking for the Ark. What is so important about this stone, anyway?"

Alfred didn't want to tell Bill that he already possessed the golden cup of Christ. He was also reluctant to tell him about his secret agenda with Rahn, so he decided to keep the professor focused on the Ark and the Grail stone instead.

"The stone we are looking for will lead us to the Ark. The Grail stone is an ancient relic in the shape of a fluorescent stone with many facets. It had been brought from Egypt about 3400 years ago and was considered sacred, much like the meteorite that is currently kept in the Ka'aba in Mecca. While the meteorite was placed inside the holy black cube in Mecca, the Grail stone was put in a special mobile shrine now known as the Ark of the Covenant. Around 900 BCE, the Ark was brought to Jerusalem, where it was put inside the

Holy of Holies in a temple, built by King David's son Solomon. However, around 650 BCE, during the reign of Manasseh, the original Ark was secretly carried away to Egypt and later to Ethiopia, while a copy remained behind in Jerusalem. The Grail stone, however, became a dangerous item when connected to a special golden lid that topped the Ark. For example, if you were wearing something made out of metal such as a sword; a knife; a belt or a suit of armour, the combination with the lid and the stone would produce a deadly electric shock. Also, according to the legend, the stone itself - when put onto a special stick - could transfer the rays of the sun into lethal laser beams. In short, it may have been used as a weapon of war and this may have been the reason why the Ark was taken to Africa; so that it wouldn't fall into enemy hands. About 800 years ago, the Ark was found again - this time by Templar knights - who had taken it to southern France to build a New Jerusalem, since the old one had been lost. The knights had chosen this area in Occitania to become the new Holy Land. Therefore I am convinced the Ark has to be here somewhere."

Alfred rubbed his face with his hands and continued,

"In 1933, Rahn wrote an interesting book about the Cathars, called 'Crusade against the Grail'. In this book he proved himself to be an expert on ancient myths, legends and religions. He had grasped the entire situation like few others had done before him, although some parts had clearly been influenced by the political views of his days. He understands the Grail, the stone that had been part of the Ark of the Covenant. You see, Rahn had studied Wolfram von Eschenbach's Parsifal and realised that Wolfram had been talking about a stone, while Chretien de Troyes - who had written the Parsifal story only two decades earlier - had written about a cup or dish. Then, by the end of the 12th century, the Knights Templar arrived in France. They had brought with them from Ethiopia the original Ark of the Covenant that still contained the Grail stone. I believe that at this moment, the 'Grail stone' took the place of the Grail cup.

From this moment on, the story about Lucifer and the stone that fell from his crown during his fall from Heaven, became popular among the people. It is this Grail stone that is connected to the Cathars, who lived alongside the Knights Templar and the troubadours in this very area of southern France. Rahn just added everything up and arrived at this conclusion. Though he had come close to finding the Holy Grail stone, he keeps on saying that he didn't find it. However, he did learn quite a lot about the Cathars and the history of the area during his search for the Grail and that is why we need him. We all want to locate the stone that was once part of the Ark of the Covenant. It is still here, somewhere, lost by its keepers and we need to keep it from Sardis, because he will use it for power. We can find the Ark and hand it over to him to save Danielle, but we can never give him the stone."

Bill began to understand it better now, but suddenly remembered to ask him about the Cardinal's position within the Organisation.

"I was going to ask you about Sardis, I first thought he was one of you guys! What can you tell me about him?"

Alfred sighed. "Not much. He most certainly isn't one of us. Apparently his partner wants to become the new world leader, while Sardis wants to become the next Pope."

Bill was alarmed. "Oh my God! ... and Danielle is in his hands. I hope the poor woman is alright."

"Yes Bill, we need to get her out of there. We are buying us some time by keeping Sardis happy, but don't worry. As we speak, special SBS agents are trying to find the exact location in Rome where she is being held. We use a special, scrambled frequency and we already managed to establish contact. They are getting close. Sardis owns a house not far from the Vatican and I can assure you, if we manage to free Danielle, we will let you know immediately."

Bill was pleased to hear this. Nevertheless, he had one more question for his chief.

"What exactly did you want to achieve through the ERFAB mission in ancient Jerusalem?"

Alfred had already feared Bill would ask this and decided to lift part of the veil.

"This concerns another item on our agenda. Of course we needed the ERFAB to collect Rahn, but to be able to investigate the origins of Christianity, we also need to understand the pearl that lies at the base of this religion, which has spread all over the world and has millions and millions of followers. We need to know the truth, even if it would prove to be a painful truth. There's only one snag; if you believe that Jesus had been crucified to save mankind from the original sin; that he rose from the dead in his original body and the ERFAB expeditions find otherwise, then how do we explain this to the world? What if, somewhere, there really are the remains of the man we know as Jesus. If these remains are found and identified, what will the Vatican do next? What if most dogmas and doctrines of the Church are based on marketing and not on divine inspiration? I believe that the Church would be in a difficult situation, because the last thing it wants, is to lose even more believers. Christianity has evolved into a large group of people who are living a life of trying to do good. Besides, many people find consolation in the words that are written in the Bible, so who are *we* to change all this? The Vatican has a dilemma, that is clear. All it can do is change slowly - accept the esoteric Christianity alongside the old exoteric Christianity - so that everyone who feels comfortable with Christianity as it is, can find comfort in their old beliefs, while a new group of people who are more spiritual will be able to study the esoteric messages of Christianity, because there are plenty of those. Our aim is to try and stimulate the Vatican to consider this evolution and change accordingly. To allow some new-found or formerly neglected truths and to alter several dogmas and doctrines which humanity has now outgrown: to embrace women as equal again; to allow birth control; to accept reincarnation and abolish obliged celibacy for their priests, so that modern followers are again comfortable with the teachings. It's the only sensible way if Christianity wants to survive. However, we believe it needs a bit of stimulation, so we hope that Rahn will direct us to the Ark, the stone *and* the bones."

"What bones?" queried Bill.

"I think that the remains of the man Jesus were either brought here by the Knights Templar - perhaps even together with the Ark of the Covenant - or by the Essenes and hidden in an old tomb underneath a dolmen exactly on the old 0° Meridian of Paris."

"What do you mean, the *old* Meridian?"

"The old 0° Meridian - used for navigation and to set the time - is today based in Greenwich, England, as you probably know, but it hasn't always been there. The old one was over Paris, but for some reason it has been renewed twice. The *true* meridian directs us to the north-south co-ordinate and it's secret is currently protected by a certain church in Paris."

"You mean, the Green Meridian from St. Sulpice?" stated Bill.

"Yes! St. Sulpice!" Alfred was surprised that Bill knew this.

"So, if I'm correct, we now only need the east-west line to have a centre?" Bill summarised.

"Exactly. We are studying clues and hints, myths, legends and symbolism to get an idea of where we must look and so far it has brought us to this place. Rahn suspects that I am also looking for the bones, but I don't think he wants to co-operate; he behaves as if he wants to avoid the subject. I need to be careful, because we still need him to help us find the Ark and the Ark stone and I don't want him to bolt. I will question him tonight."

Alfred got up, stretched his body, drank the last of his coffee and went back to the others. Bill, still trying to digest what he had just learnt, also got up and went back to his own tent and to Gabby, who seemed very upset about Danielle's letter. Being a gentleman, he first asked whether it was safe to enter and after hearing a soft 'yes', he unzipped the front 'door'.

In the first part of the tent stood some furniture and a kitchenette and Gabby had just made some tea. Bill touched her cheek. It was clear that she had been crying.

"We'll get her back. I'm sure we will…" he said softly.

However, they both realised that this was wishful thinking.

Meanwhile, the kids had enjoyed their first few days at David's B&B, but Arthur was still suspicious. From a distance, he had secretly witnessed all the activities at the cottage with his binoculars and had written down the details.

09.30 hours - Team of 5 men leave with 2 cars.
16.27 hours - Strange SUV car arrives. Woman delivers package and leaves immediately.
18.28 hours - A black SUV leaves with driver only.
19.26 hours - Return of the black SUV with driver and 3 men.
20.35 hours - Other 2 SUV's return. All gather in cottage.
Two men seem to hold guard posts outside. ??? Weird.
21.00 hours - David brings dinner to the cottage.

"What are you doing?" Michael had caught Arthur spying on his father's mystery guests, making notes of all their moves. He was worried and had decided to confront him. "My father made it quite clear that we mustn't interfere. Get back in the tent for crying out loud! What if they see you spying on them?"

"Something strange is going on, Mike, don't you want to know more about them? They are staying at your dad's place, you know? Maybe he's in danger! Maybe we're all in danger!"

However, Michael didn't want to hear it and wanted to make himself quite clear, "When my dad says to stay put and not to interfere, I stay put and I don't interfere. You hear me?"

Arthur walked off, waving one hand at his friend without looking at him. "Yeah, yeah, keep your hair on mate. I'm going to hit the sack."

16

Corbières, southern France, June 28th 2011

As the light outside was fading, the lights in the cottage and the tents were lit. Arthur, who was extremely suspicious about the men in the cottage, just couldn't stay put. He simply had to find out what they were up to and decided to sneak over to the cottage and sit quietly beneath an open window. He stayed low and tried not to step on anything that could create a noise. His heart was beating fast, but Arthur was in luck; a window at the back of the cottage was open. He risked taking a very careful look - while trying very hard not to be seen - and noticed with a jolt that the window was close to where one of the men was sitting. The pale, thin man looked familiar to Arthur, but he couldn't quite place him. Then, the tall, blonde man got up and Arthur had to duck. He could hear that the man approached the window and addressed the other in German, a language he had learned back in college and which he could follow.

"Otto, please, we know you are not co-operating and we do need your help. Do you want the woman's blood on your hands?"

Arthur froze.

Woman? Blood? Shit!

He pushed his glasses - that had slipped down from his sweaty nose - back and saw that the man he thought he recognised now got up from his chair. He seemed irritated.

"Look, I will be honest with you, Fred. Yes, I was here before; yes, I talked to the lady in the Villa Bethania and yes, she gave me a book and a map with secret codes. It led me to the area around Rennes-les-Bains, where I found clue after clue and all these clues together eventually brought me to the top of the hill we explored this afternoon. Yes, I discovered a small grotto underneath a dolmen, but you've simply got to believe me when I say that the Ark wasn't there, so let's drop it and start looking somewhere else, OK?"

Rahn stared hard at Alfred; their faces only an inch apart.

"The Ark isn't there, Fred."

Rahn walked out of the cottage and left the others in silence. Alfred sighed; he had hoped to get Otto to talk, but he had to be careful not to push him too far. After seeing Otto's reaction, Alfred understood it was a touchy subject, but he knew he had to ask him about the bones at some point. Alfred was tired. "Keep on looking for more clues on Marceille and Laval guys, I'm going to bed."

He opened the door of his bedroom and fell on his bed. Alfred rubbed his tired eyes.

Ah well, Ark first, bones later. Now, sleep.

Within seconds he was fast asleep, still with his clothes on, like a Templar.

Otto decided to take a stroll to clear his head. Right now he'd do anything for a cigarette, but understood that Alfred had made him quit smoking for a reason. Without having a goal, he sauntered around the grounds of the B&B for a while, but then he thought of something and decided to turn back to the cottage. While turning around, he suddenly noticed a strange, dark shadow just below one of the windows of the cottage. Someone was eavesdropping on them. Immediately, Otto called out to the agents.

"Everyone out, we have a spy!"

Rahn quickly ran toward the window, hoping he'd be fast enough to catch the spy.

Startled from the shock of being discovered, Arthur had fallen over backward, but got back onto his feet just in time. He ran as fast as his legs could move, with Rahn only a few seconds behind him. He could almost feel Otto's breath in his neck and Arthur wasn't sure that he could escape from him. In a moment of hopelessness, he screamed.

Then, a miracle happened; Otto stumbled over a tree root and fell hard on the rocky ground. While two men helped Rahn up, the rest of the agents continued the chase. Alfred - who had woken up from the alarm - now joined the search party. They simply *had* to catch him.

However, dusk was on Arthur's side. He disappeared into the woods and was quickly out of sight.

The commotion had alarmed Bill and Gabby - who knew they couldn't do anything but wait and hope that it wouldn't get out of hand. It had also awoken Michael, who now dashed out of his tent to see what was going on. He could just get a glimpse of Arthur, fleeing into the forest and the men from the cottage chasing after him. A jolt went through his body when he spotted that one of the men chasing Arthur was carrying a shotgun.

Arthur was almost out of breath. He thought he'd outsmart the men by taking the high path up into the woods and hide somewhere. They probably wouldn't expect him to do something like that. Then he saw an opportunity to hide behind a large protruding rock, but when he jumped behind it, his foot shot through the soil and into a cavity. A sharp pain went through his foot and ankle and Arthur could only just withhold a cry of pain. Panting from lack of breath, anxiety and pain, he closed his eyes and tried to listen. The sound of running men was disappearing into the distance. His plan had worked, but what to do now? He couldn't possibly walk with that ankle. He took a good look at the hole, knowing he could be stuck there for a while and suddenly noticed that it was the entrance to a small cave. Being short, Arthur managed to squeeze himself in completely. Being out of sight, he felt much safer, but it wouldn't be long before it was completely dark. Remembering he had brought a torch, he took it out and decided to take a better look at the small cave. It was completely empty, apart from a strange symbol, carved into the rock face. He recognised it to be the so called 'Cross of Isis', an eight pointed cross, which looked like an abstract Templar cross inside a circle. This symbol had been discussed on the forum, along with some pictures of a rock called The Devil's Chair. This particular rock was supposed to have been hewn into a chair by a member of the noble Fleury family, known for its contributions to the construction of the Sacre Coeur in Paris. It is said that he had used it as a hunting seat, while waiting for game. Arthur had never believed that story, because when you go on a hunt, you don't sit in the middle of a path for animals to see and smell you from all around. No one actually knew why it was called the Devil's Chair, though Arthur had discovered that the name was not uncommon; there were Devil's Bridges and Devil's Chairs all over Europe. He had read somewhere that ancient pagan sites were sometimes named after the devil by fearful Catholics, who detested the freethinkers and cursed all sites that had been involved in ancient ritual or worship. The Devil's Chair near Rennes-les-Bains, however, was one of the places he had hoped to visit during their vacation. He had even been thinking of bringing a compass to check its direction and alignment. He sighed, wishing he had obeyed Michael's father. Though his knowledge of the carvings on the rock chair helped him identify the Cross of Isis in this cave, he still didn't know what the Cross of Isis was all about. Still, he had a much bigger problem to solve right now. Arthur knew he would never be able to climb out of the little cave without help, so he reached for the only thing that could help him now. His mobile phone.

Meanwhile, Michael, Ben and Yanne had been rounded up by David, who was extremely upset. "I told you not to interfere!!"
"... but dad, it wasn't us, it was Art. We had no idea he would do something this stupid!"
Not waiting for his father to react, Michael sprinted over to Beauséant, jumped on his bare back and with only a rope as a reign, he took off. That very moment his mobile phone went, playing loud, evil laughter for a ring tone. Beauséant became uneasy and Michael almost dropped his phone when the horse suddenly pranced. Arthur was relieved to hear Michael's voice and tried to explain which path he had taken. He also excitedly told Michael about the small cave he had crawled into and even sent his friend a photo, showing the

Isis Cross carving. Michael couldn't believe Arthur was still so enthusiastic, in spite of his precarious situation. Trying to get his friend to understand the seriousness of his situation, he told him that one of the men who was looking for him was carrying a shotgun.

Arthur paused and then stumbled, "A.., a shotgun? Are you sure?"

"Yeah mate. You are in serious trouble. My dad is raving mad. I'm afraid our holiday is over. You ruined it for all of us, mate, but I'd better get you out of there. I may be angry with you right now, but I can't leave you there, can I?"

Arthur finally realised his blunder; how his curiosity got everyone into trouble, not just him.

"I'm sorry Mike, I really am. I just didn't trust them and I was right, wasn't I?"

"I guess so, buddy. Look, I will be there soon. Hang on, but don't hang up!"

As the horse couldn't climb the steep path Arthur had taken, Michael needed to go around the rocky crevice and reach the top from the other side. However, by doing that, he risked running straight into the search party and getting himself into danger as well. Though he understood the risk, he went for it anyway. Michael couldn't just leave his friend there. Beauséant was a young horse, so he carried him up the hill without too much trouble. Michael was careful not to make any loud noise, but his black and white horse could be visible from a distance.

Indeed, it didn't take long before Michael was spotted. He needed to act really fast now. When Michael spotted Arthur's hand sticking out of the entrance of the small cave, he jumped off his horse and pulled Arthur out. Arthur cried with pain when Michael made him climb the horse. Barely was he on Beauséant's back, or Arthur saw something slip from his pocket and fall to the ground.

Shit, my mobile!

While looking down, also his glasses slipped from his face. Arthur cursed out loud and wanted to jump off again, but

173

there was no time to loose. If they wanted to escape the now fast approaching men, they had to get moving fast. Michael quickly spurred his horse to start running. He sat behind Arthur and tried every manoeuvre he could think of to outsmart their pursuers. He couldn't see what was hidden beneath the layers of fallen leaves and knew he was taking risks when he made Beauséant jump over rocks and fallen trees. The last thing he wanted was to cripple the horse. On top of it all, it was getting seriously dark now and Michael had to descend the hill very carefully. The men behind them - shining their torches - were now faster on foot than he was on horseback and they could hear their own heartbeat. On a flatter slope, Michael decided to go for it and take his chances. If he didn't run now, all would be lost.

While running, Michael looked over his shoulder and saw that the distance between them and their pursuers was growing and realised that if he had made the decision to run only a few seconds later, they wouldn't have stood a chance. Only, the boys had forgotten that one of the men had a shotgun. "Aim for the horse! ... and you better not miss!!"

The shooter aimed and fired just as Beauséant leaped over a fallen tree. Arthur felt a sharp pain in his side and screamed. When Arthur suddenly lost consciousness and fell into Michael's arms, the boy panicked and spurred the horse to run faster. To his relief he noticed that Arthur wasn't bleeding and he hoped that the bullet had not done too much harm. Though they were now out of shooting range, Michael understood that he could no longer go back to the B&B. He had to find a safe place somewhere else.

After having followed an old Cathar path deep into the countryside, he thought he'd finally lost their pursuers. Tears were running down his cheek when a feeling of hopelessness overcame him, but then he thought of the Knights Templar, who had a reputation for never giving up - and these warriors had been in much worse situations. Michael dried his tears and decided to cross the valley to hide out on the Rennes

Plateau, so he held onto Arthur while spurring Beauséant into gallop, intending to check on him as soon as he felt safe enough.

The man with the shotgun cursed. Never had they expected their expedition to go so wrong. Then, Alfred spotted the cave Arthur had fallen into. He also noticed the Isis Cross, inside, on the rock wall and knew he had seen it before, inside the Pech Cardou. The abstract Templar cross probably meant that this place had been found and marked by someone, who had also been searching for something. Though it didn't look recent, it wasn't old either. Suddenly, the Swiss spotted Arthur's mobile phone and - a bit further down - Arthur's glasses. They were still in one piece, as the soft ground had broken their fall. He picked them up, hoping that at least one of the kids still carried his mobile.
He turned to his men. "Alright, let's head back to the camp!"
Alfred was getting worried about David. He knew that it was his boy that got himself into trouble while trying to save the other.

David saw the men returning without Arthur, Michael or Beauséant. He could just hear one of them say: "Why did you have to shoot that boy? I told you to aim for the horse!"
Then, David saw the shotgun. Not knowing what had happened - but getting a clear picture all the same - the excitement now became too much for him. Scared to death for his son's life, his legs gave way and David fell to his knees. Seeing this, Alfred immediately ran toward David to help him up. "You have a very brave boy, David, trying to save that other lad from harm. They have escaped, but you do realise that we have to get them back here, don't you? Call your son on his mobile and tell him to come back immediately. Please, for all of us."
Alfred noticed how David seemed numb, staring at the man who was carrying the shotgun.
"Oh God, you didn't..." David stuttered, in total shock.

Alfred understood David's reaction and smiled sourly, "Don't worry; tranquillizer darts."
He helped David into one of the garden chairs and although he could sense the man's panic, the Swiss remained persistent. "Get your boy on the phone. *Now.*"

A silver Vauxhall Astra hatchback drove slowly on the dark, narrow road that wound itself through the river valley. The only light on the road was shining from their own headlamps. It was getting late. Having underestimated the long drive, a young family was still on its way to their holiday destination. The mother was fast asleep, exhausted from driving most of the day and the father was now back behind the wheel. He was talking to his two young sons - aged 6 and 9 - who were sitting in the back of the car, tired but excited that they were almost there. To keep them awake, he did a quiz.
"So, how can you tell a Knight Templar from an ordinary knight?" said the father.
"He wears a white robe with a red cross and carries a black and white flag!" said Glen, who smirked at his younger brother.
"Good for you Glen! ... and what is the second clue? Scott?"
At that exact moment, a horse with two riders on its bare back crossed the road in front of them, only a few metres from their car. Immediately, the man hit the break, causing the kids to scream and mum to wake up. Then, they all gazed through the front window with open mouths and racing heartbeats, watching the horse and its mysterious riders disappear into the forest.

David had tried several times to reach Michael on his mobile phone, but only got his voicemail. David shook his head and turned to Alfred. "Maybe he just hasn't got a signal?"
Alfred rubbed his face and became worried. What if the kids went to fetch the police? He knew they had to find them quickly.

-17-

Corbières, southern France, June 29th 2011

The quiet, night sky had only been disturbed by the flights of owls and bats and the chirping of crickets. Hours had passed and when the first sunrays caressed his face, Arthur slowly regained consciousness. He protected his eyes while staring up at the ruined tower that stood on the edge of what was once the ancient citadel of Rhedae, but is now better known as Rennes-le-Château. In the distance, higher up the hill, the Tour Magdala - one of the landmarks of the area - was sunbathing in the morning sun. He had wanted to see it with his own eyes for years, but never like this.

Michael sat next to Arthur, pulling a face that betrayed mixed emotions. First of all; relief, because Arthur had only been shot with a tranquillizer dart. Secondly; worry, because he wasn't sure how to get them out of the difficult situation they were in. On top of it all, they had both lost their mobile phones somewhere on the way and Michael had no idea where he lost his. Also, why remember a phone number when it's safely stored in your mobile? So, even if he could find a phone somewhere, he neither had the money nor the phone number to contact his father.

"We're in trouble, aren't we?" Arthur's voice sounded hoarse and dry.

Michael nodded. "Yeah mate. We're in trouble, but at least they didn't use real bullets, so they aren't criminals, otherwise they'd had never hesitated to use live ammo. I am seriously thinking about heading back home. Y'know, face it, get it over with."

Beauséant shook his head up and down and neighed, as if agreeing with his master. The boys looked at each other and laughed. Michael got up. "Come on then, let's get you back on the horse and see if I can find our way home."

It wasn't easy to get Arthur on the horse; the lower part of his body was still feeble and his side was aching terribly. A red and blue coloured extravasation marked the spot where the arrow had penetrated his side and it was extremely painful for Arthur to get up at all. Nevertheless he had better be brave, for he knew he had a lot to answer for. Thinking back, he felt guilty and ashamed and when they rode off - back toward the B&B - Arthur wept silently, though loud enough for Michael to hear it. Real life adventures were very different from those in books and movies. It certainly wasn't what he had expected.

Morning had only just broken when Otto started circling through the cottage and every few rounds, he stared out of the window to see if anyone had arrived yet. Surely, the boy had overheard their conversation and he was worried about the location of the tomb and the safety of the boys. He had no idea what they would do to them, to keep them quiet. Rahn had horrible memories, which for him were only recent experiences in concentration camps, where people had been tortured in his presence and he had been unable to stop it. Though he didn't believe that the Organisation would go that far, for him it was difficult to still have faith in humanity. His soft, poetic soul had been brutally shaken up by ugly Nazi practices and he just couldn't stop his memories from haunting him, along with an ever growing fear for the two boys. He decided to confront Alfred and walked over to where the Swiss was sitting. With his arms folded, he started, "So, what are you going to do now, Fred, are you going to hurt them?"
Alfred could see that Otto was worried. Realising his background, he could understand this reaction, but still, did Otto really think that he'd hurt those kids? Alfred shook his head.
"Of course not Otto, don't worry, but I do have a favour to ask. You know they are now in too deep, so to avoid the risk of them leaking information to others, we could of course let them join our team. Besides, we could take advantage of their young brains. Ours are not too bright anymore, it seems."

The two men smiled at each other, but Otto was still somewhat reluctant.

"Perhaps, but we know nothing about these kids. What if we *do* find something? Can they be trusted then? At this moment they still don't know too much, but when we do find something..."

This had crossed Alfred's mind already.

"I hear you, Otto, but I don't think we have any choice. Let's talk to them and see what they are like. Maybe we can find out what made them spy on us and what they know already."

Otto pursed his lips. "Risky..."

"Yep." said Alfred, staring hard at Otto while offering him his hand. He could see the doubt, the fear and the hesitation just by looking at his eyes, but then, Rahn took his hand and smiled. "Alright then."

This will become interesting...

Exhausted from having been up all night, Rahn finally went to his bed to give his aching bones some rest. Within moments he was sound asleep, but the dreams he dreamed were a reflection of his anxiety. He saw Himmler's piercing eyes penetrating right through him; he heard the cries of people who were being tortured and in sharp contrast, he could see the image of his father, standing beneath a giant oak tree while speaking of God.

Suddenly, Rahn woke up with a shock when he heard the neighing of a horse. The boys were back.

Alfred - who had nodded off in one of the armchairs - had also been awakened by the sounds outside. Still slightly stiff from having slept in an awkward position, he approached the horse and steadied it to allow the boys to dismount. Alfred noticed Arthur's pain and decided not to be too hard on the boy, who was almost too afraid to look the muscular Swiss in the eye. Arthur couldn't help feeling like a lamb, being led to the slaughter.

Alfred sighed, returned his mobile phone and glasses and started,

"I know we scared the hell out of you and I understand why you ran, but you shouldn't have spied on us in the first place."

Arthur looked away, realising the seriousness of the situation. He knew he had messed with a top secret mission. This time they had used tranquilliser darts, but what would they do next time?

The others now joined them and Alfred decided to only tell the boys what they needed to know. However, it took a while before Arthur fully grasped the message. If he had understood it correctly, they were going to help a secret order find the Ark of the Covenant. He looked around at the serious faces, chuckled and then fainted.

When Arthur came to, his face was pale and he felt how he was carried toward the cottage. Yanne - who had disliked him from day one - was now very caring. To everyone's surprise she had even made him a cup of strong, hot tea to help him back on his feet. Otto had stayed out of sight for a while. Like a cat in a house full of unknown visitors he had been studying the scene from a safe distance, waiting for the right moment to show himself, so by the time Arthur had finished his tea, Rahn casually sauntered toward the boy. The moment Arthur saw him, a jolt struck him like lightening.

"You're the one who came after me last night." he remarked. Then, Arthur's eyes narrowed. Everyone was tensed; was it the right decision to let four kids into a top secret mission? Not only did they have to share the details of the mission; they realised that they also had to let them in on the existence of the ERFAB. How else could they explain what Otto was about to share?

Rahn knew he had fans, even in this era. He saw that this boy recognised him and he couldn't help but smile. All eyes were upon them now and in an attempt to break the awkward silence, Otto started,

"Hello there. I know you know who I am and no, I am not a ghost from the past. I have been teleported from my era into yours by means of a time machine designed by that professor over there." Rahn pointed at Bill.

It didn't take Arthur long to add everything up; his German accent; the ring he was wearing, the name he had overheard... Arthur had only imagined him to be taller and younger.

"You're Otto Rahn!"

Otto smiled.

Clever boy!

Arthur got up from his seat, realising that he was looking at someone he had studied for years; a man who's life had become an enigma. This was the *real* Indiana Jones!

"It's an honour to meet you, Doctor Jones!" said Arthur while shaking Otto's hand.

"Doctor Jones?" Otto queried.

"Never mind." chuckled Arthur.

Michael and Ben, who had witnessed the scene from a distance, understood the joke about Dr Jones and couldn't stop laughing.

As if talking to a celebrity, Arthur continued,

"I read 'Crusade against the Grail' and 'Lucifer's Court', your two books about the true Grail."

Otto's smile was as broad as was physically possible. Then, Arthur suddenly remembered he had heard something odd.

"A time machine?" Arthur queried.

"A time machine." Rahn confirmed.

Wicked...

Though Otto greeted the others heartily, he suddenly stopped when he arrived at a worried looking Ben, who had already realised that he was standing in front of an ex-Nazi - albeit one who hadn't been in the war himself. Nevertheless, Otto had seen more in the late nineteen thirties than he would have liked. Otto immediately saw that Ben was Jewish and said with a sour smile, "Be thankful you live in this time and not in mine, mein jungen."

Ben didn't know how to respond to Rahn and stuttered, "Would you, could you have..."

Completely shocked by being so misunderstood, Otto suddenly walked away, but then he stopped and turned - obviously very emotional - and started to shout at the boy.

"You have *no* idea what it was like for me. You weren't *there!*" Otto was trembling all over. "I was scared to *death*! I was *this* close to the fire, *constantly* followed, *every* move I made. I tried to escape into writing, I lied through my teeth that I was ill, just to be able to stay away from that hell. Oh, I've done things I regret and I saw things I couldn't live with, but I *resigned*, didn't I?"

Alfred put his hand on Otto's shoulder in an attempt to calm him down and looked at Ben.

"I know Otto better than you, Ben. He's a gentle soul, just trapped into a violent world and unable to get out. His mother and maternal grandfather were Jewish, so maybe now your questions are answered?"

Ben, who had followed it all with big eyes and had already started to pluck his eyelashes, nodded at Alfred. Then he walked up to Otto and offered his hand. After a short, somewhat awkward pause, Otto took it and looked deep into the boy's eyes. That moment, Ben could see what Alfred meant; behind those eyes was indeed a gentle soul, who had to try and come to terms with his experiences and he could only do so with the help of his friends.

Otto looked at all of them, realising that this was his team now; he had to work with them and trust them. He studied their eyes and remarked, while pointing at his own with two fingers,

"I can see that your eyes are all alive and filled with love. You know, in my time, people who had once been kind and friendly, suddenly became monsters without emotion, as if there was some kind of psychological disease going around. You could recognise this disease by looking at people's eyes. Those eyes had become cold, lifeless, filled with hate and anger, but not everyone had this disease. Sometimes people were forced to be violent and it would eat their souls. It certainly ate mine..."

Arthur looked at Otto, who was obviously troubled and visibly trying to control himself. Still, even now, Rahn had such charisma. Arthur wanted to touch his idol, but didn't have the guts to do so. He for one had never believed the strange stories going around about Rahn being some kind of evil Nazi. He thought he had read enough about him to know that his heart was in writing, not in Nazi Germany, but Arthur didn't know that he was partly mistaken. Otto had once been a firm believer in a strong, united Europe under one elite and had really believed that a 'war to end all wars' was necessary to reach that goal. However, like many other Germans, Otto had believed the misleading propaganda that had been shown to all members of the SS, an order he had once been proud to serve. Only when he had seen with his own eyes what was going on in Buchenwald in November 1938, Rahn had woken up from his dreams and delusions and had fully understood the horror of it all, but by that time, the snake pit had swallowed him whole.

However, for Arthur, who truly believed in the romantic side of Otto; the poet soul; the writer; the relic hunter, Rahn had become a celebrity and right now he just couldn't believe he was standing right in front of him. Would he dare touch him? Arthur softly placed his hand on Otto's arm, who now looked at Arthur. He noticed the boy's smile and apparent veneration.

"It's okay." said Arthur softly. "You're with *us* now."

Otto couldn't help feeling sympathy for the boy and decided not to get into things any further. Gabby walked over and gave Otto another hug. Until that moment, she and Bill had been silent witnesses to it all and finally, even Ben gave Rahn a warm smile, which Otto returned.

Alfred realised that Rahn was still emotionally unstable because of everything he had gone through. The moment he had brought Rahn to 2011, he'd first had to nurture him back to health - both physically and mentally. In the few months that had followed, Otto had gained 20 pounds and after reducing the number of cigarettes each day, he had now officially stopped smoking. Although Alfred was always careful and on guard - fearing Rahn's instability - he had also begun to see Otto's trauma and torn heart. However, Alfred failed to notice that something else was also gnawing at Otto's heart. Rahn knew that as soon as his mission here was over, he would be forced to return to 1939 and he wasn't at all happy about it.

18

Rome, Italy, July 1st 2011

It was just after midnight when Danielle woke up from violent stings in her lower belly. Being nauseous, she only just managed to reach the bathroom in time. Danielle felt so sick, so lonely and so afraid, that it was as if life had ended already. The black hole of depression - partly caused by her hormones - had almost sucked her in completely. The only thought that kept her going was Oshu and the child she was carrying. If only she knew if it was healthy. Had she been in her own town, she could have gone to a hospital to have a check-up. Now she had no idea whether the foetus was alright and growing normally. Perhaps travelling through the wormhole had harmed it. All she knew was that the sickness and pains she experienced seemed different from what was generally known as morning sickness during the early period of pregnancy. Her sickness would come at any time - even midnight - and having so much pain wasn't a good omen either. Danielle became worried and her mind searched desperately for a lifeline somewhere inside her head. Many people were praying for her child's father all over the world, but somehow she just couldn't. Instead she decided to pray to God. That wasn't something Danielle would do so easily, but now seemed like a very good time and she couldn't care less that she was in a dark bathroom, kneeling in front of the toilet.

In the meantime, Sardis was still working in his office. He had already prepared a marketing strategy. It only needed perfecting and he couldn't sleep until that was done. The phone rang; a classical ring, coming from an old model that fitted into the somewhat baroque character of his office. The Cardinal picked up with a tired voice, "Pronto?"
Suddenly, his eyes opened wide. With trembling voice he replied, "... but if these men are not ours, then who are they, what are they doing here?"

A moment later - slowly, as if in shock - he put down the phone. He stared at the door, listening for sounds and when he heard nothing, he got up and walked toward the window, hiding behind the curtain, making sure he wasn't seen. When he saw nothing, he walked toward another window. Still, nothing. The Cardinal - now in a hurry - skittered out of his office to check on Danielle. When he saw that she wasn't in her bed, a jolt stabbed his stomach and he panicked, fearing she had escaped. The Cardinal ran out into the hallway to search for her, but he couldn't find her anywhere in the building. Everywhere he went, he shouted for assistance, but as it was after midnight, only one guard responded to his calls; the same guard who had phoned earlier to warn him about the intruders. Sardis was upset to find out that the building was so badly guarded at night, but then remembered it had been he himself who had thought that one guard would be sufficient. After all, Danielle's apartment was hermetically sealed from the outside world and his office and bedroom were just one door away. Never had he expected that this location could be so easily discovered. Sardis leaned against a wall - breathless from running through the building and he closed his eyes to clear his mind. He needed to make an assessment of the situation in order to take accurate action. Knowing that he now needed all the assistance he could get to search for Danielle and defend himself against his opponents, he took out his mobile from his soutane to call the other guards, who were all asleep in their own homes. The Cardinal's mission now depended on their speed of action.

Danielle, who had no idea that Sardis thought she'd gone missing, had refreshed herself in the bathroom, the one place the Cardinal hadn't looked. After her prayer she admittedly felt a little bit better, so she had brushed her teeth and now only wanted to go back to bed. She hadn't even noticed that her front door had been left wide open, until she was already in bed. At first she thought that she had forgotten to turn off the light in the bathroom, but then it became clear that the inflowing light was coming from the hallway.

The door was open!

Making use of the adrenaline rush, she quickly got dressed, knowing she had to be very careful and quiet as a mouse.

It was now or never.

Sardis was getting more upset by the second. As he was running from one place to another, shouting orders and Danielle's name, he began to understand that he had probably lost his prize and that would be the end of everything. The end of his dream. The Cardinal almost lost his mind just thinking about it. Then suddenly, the front door was opened and Sardis had half-expected to see the extra guards he had called for, but instead, these men were dressed in black, wearing black face covers and fully armed. Sardis didn't know exactly what was going on, but he realised that the game was over and ran back upstairs in search of a hiding place. However, the 'men in black' had no idea that they had been spotted by the guards who had sped over to Sardis' house. The Cardinal's guards immediately took action. A well-aimed shot was fired and one of the men in black fell down dead. This was getting serious. The other agents - now fully realising the danger of their mission - raced through the house in search for Danielle, knowing they didn't have a minute to loose.

The gunshot had startled Danielle and she just stood there, frozen in the middle of the hallway, not knowing where to go next. The sound of the shot had clearly come from the ground floor, so she could no longer go downstairs toward the exit. Instead of running, Danielle decided to look for a place to hide. This was her only option, for she could certainly not stay where she was or go back to her room. Danielle walked further into the hallway and noticed the open door to Sardis' office. She entered the office and closed the door behind her. At the other end of the room she saw a large, wooden sliding door and wondered if there'd be enough space behind it for her to hide behind. Trying not to make a sound, she anxiously opened the large sliding door, only to find out that it was just another book case. In a state of panic, she now desperately searched for a new place to hide. Another couple of shots rang out and she could hear men shouting in Italian, running up the stairway. Quickly she jumped behind the large oaken desk and made herself as small as humanly possible, hardly daring to breath. She almost jumped when the door opened. It was Sardis. Not knowing that Danielle was hiding behind his desk, he entered the room, shut the door and stepped back. His sweaty, pale face was visible to Danielle and she could see how he, too, was anxiously looking for a place to hide. It didn't take long before their eyes met. When he saw Danielle, hiding underneath his desk, his whole face suddenly lit up. "Ha!" he shouted and ran toward her, grabbed her wrists and pulled her upright. Danielle screamed. However, the Cardinal had no intention to hurt her. He was so overjoyed that she was still there, that he hugged her, kissed her head and held her tight.

"Thank God you're safe! Bless you child. Now, come with me! Quickly!"

They ran away from the desk and had only just passed the door when several shots smashed the lock. One of the men in black entered the room. "Ms Parker!" Danielle, however, couldn't make a sound, as Sardis had put his hand over her nose and mouth. It was getting more and more difficult for her to breath, but no matter how quiet she and Sardis were, the agents quickly spotted the couple, hiding in a corner behind the long curtains. Invisible to Sardis, - who had Danielle in a firm grip so she couldn't break free - the agents approached them carefully. While holding her tight, the Cardinal's hand was pressing harder and harder on Danielle's belly. Already having breathing problems, she now also felt a sharp pain and became lightheaded. The next moment she lost all focus; everything went blurry; her head spun and then, all went dark.

The very moment Danielle collapsed - taking the curtain with her - a well-aimed bullet penetrated Sardis' forehead and left a clean, black spot. Cross-eyed he fell sideward into the corner and remained there in an awkward position, still wearing a grin on his face.

Lausanne, Switzerland, July 1st 2011

When Danielle woke up, she found herself lying in a hospital bed with clean white sheets, an IV in her arm and a worried looking nurse standing over her, trying to smile. "Hello dear, you've had quite an adventure, haven't you? Now, tell me, how do you feel?"

She took her pulse and looked at her watch. The moment Danielle tried to speak, the nurse sensed Danielle's pulse speeding up at an alarming rate and intervened. "Shhhh, don't speak, you need to rest. Everything is alright." she said as she injected a substance into the drip. Within seconds, Danielle drifted into another, deep sleep. Knowing that sleep was the best cure for the pregnant woman, the nurse checked her heartbeat and smiled to see it had now steadied again. She stationed herself at the window and re-opened the gossip magazine she had been reading earlier. A minute later, a doctor came in; a young man in his late twenties with dark hair and smooth face. The nurse turned red when she spotted him and got up from her seat. She was fond of the new Doctor, who had only introduced himself a few hours ago.

"Any change, Sally?" the Doctor asked.

"Well, no, but she no longer looks so pale."

"Is she still asleep?"

"Well, she woke up a moment ago, but then her heartbeat increased so fiercely, that I just gave her some more of the sedative. We need to keep her calm. Personally, I think she needs sleep more than anything right now."

"Perhaps, but she also has a trauma and will eventually need to let it out of her system. I will see her as soon as she wakes up. Keep me in the loop."

"Yes, Dr Days. However, with the dose I just gave her, it will take her another three or four hours to wake up."

The doctor chewed his lip. His concerned expression betrayed a deep concern for Danielle's health. Carefully, he opened one of her eyes to check the response of her pupil and the white of her eye. The presence of tiny blood vessels revealed that she must have suffered from great stress. He took her pulse and listened to her heartbeat with his stethoscope, after which he gently lifted her upper lip to check her gums. When seeing the yellowish shade of white in her eyes and the yellow colour on her gums, the doctor turned to the nurse, "Draw some blood, I need to check her liver values." He softly pressed his fingers into her belly to see if her liver was enlarged and although it felt as if it wasn't, he needed to be sure. While the nurse drew some blood, he walked over to the window and sighed,

"It's going to be a close call, Sally. We may only be able to save the mother; it will be a miracle to save them both. With Danielle being as ill as she is, the foetus might not be strong enough, but we'll have to wait and see. I need her to fight, so I want her to get over her trauma quickly and fight for her baby and for herself. She has about seven months left, so we'll see. Give me a call as soon as she wakes up?"

"Immediately, Doctor."

Dr Days walked out with Danielle's blood sample and took it to the laboratory. Then he walked over to the men's room to wash his hands and change his clothes. With great haste he then speeded toward the exit - ignoring colleagues on the way - taking the stairs instead of the elevator. The moment he was outside, in front of the main entrance, he took out his mobile phone and tried to contact Alfred about Danielle's health. However, for some reason he couldn't get through. Perhaps Alfred was in the middle of a dead spot and was unable to get a signal. Knowing he urgently needed to talk to him, Days decided to try again later. He walked over to his Rover, got into the car and drove off into the streets of Lausanne.

19

The Corbières, southern France, July 2nd 2011

Unaware of the fact that Danielle had been rescued the day before, Alfred had gathered the team together to discuss the new plans. Arthur, Michael and Otto had already compared some of their notes on hidden relics during the previous evening and Otto was impressed by the amount of information the boys had collected so far. Arthur had even discovered the existence of the secret maps of the Corbières mines and the so called 'sacred geometry' of Occitania, simply by following links to esoteric circles such as the Philadelphus Society, the Gnostic Church and the mysterious goings on around the Marquis de Fontenille and the Marquis de Chefdebien. However, Rahn didn't want to tell the boys that his visit to the area in 1936 - including a thorough search on foot to investigate this geometry - had resulted in his mysterious find; the find he tried so hard to keep from Alfred. On the other hand, the search for more Grail treasure was still high on his own personal agenda and he had high hopes to find something this time.

Suddenly, Alfred's loud voice startled them. "Alright listen up! We are all in this together now and we need to realise that this isn't just a game! This is for real and lives depend on it. Danielle is being held hostage by a man called Sardis, an influential and obsessed Prince of Rome, who has a lot of money and power. This man is dangerous and we expect him to use violence if we do not co-operate. He wants to rule the Church with the Ark at his side and if we don't find and deliver this relic quickly, he may harm her. However, as we speak, our people are tracking down his address to free Danielle, but in case they don't succeed, we cannot lose any time here. We know we are close and we need to co-operate to find the items required. Now, is all this clear? Are there any questions?"

It was silent for a few seconds, but then Arthur raised his hand.

"Look, I know I have caused a lot of trouble, but I found an interesting co-ordinate on the hill just over there and I think I know exactly where to look. Maybe we can split up into two teams, so you can go in search of the Ark and the Grail while we investigate the hill ov…"

"*Nein! I protest!*" snarled Rahn, startling everybody with his fierce and sharp reaction.

"There is *nothing* on that hill, we must concentrate on the other co-ordinates!" he added.

Arthur was puzzled. "But..."

"It's okay Art." David interrupted, using his hands to say: *quiet down!* This was obviously not a time to push anything through.

Alfred looked around the circle again. "Any other questions?"

Ben had been quiet until now, but suddenly he raised his hand. "May I propose something, sir? Michael and Arthur know quite a lot about this region, its history and mysteries. Maybe we can get our heads together and work out a plan of action?"

Alfred looked at Michael and then at Arthur; both were obviously keen to participate more actively. Realising that Arthur seemed to be the smartest of the two, he turned to him. "Okay, so where do *you* think we should look?"

Arthur became excited. Now he could finally share his knowledge with an audience that is genuinely interested. As if talking to a class, he started, "Well, first of all, Occitania has a rather complicated history. It's more like a huge, historical drama. You guys probably already know all about the Knights Templar, who brought quite a lot of secret cargo into France by the end of the 12th century. You probably also know the legend of the Visigoth treasure, which was supposedly brought to southern France after the Visigoths had sacked Rome in 410 and because the Romans had sacked Jerusalem in the 1st century - after the Jewish rebellion - historians suspect the Visigoth treasure to contain for example the menorah; the seven-branched golden candelabra that the Romans had taken from the Temple in Jerusalem. This particular scene, by the way, is shown on the Arch of Titus in Rome."

"There were several Visigoth capitals in this region: Tolosa, Carcasona and Rhedae. Rhedae by the way, is just over there, behind those hills. It is now called Rennes-le-Château. Coincidently, in the 19th century, the priest of this particular village renovated his church and suddenly got very rich; so today everyone thinks he actually found either the lost treasure of the Visigoths, or of the Knights Templar."

Alfred, who tried to play dumb, scratched his chin and could hardly suppress a smile.

"Go on…"

Arthur hastily drank some water from a small bottle and continued, "… but that is not all. This area seems to be some kind of magnet. It started with early humans like the Tautavel Man and the Neanderthals, after which the Cro Magnon arrived. Then the region was inhabited by the mysterious Ligurians and visited by the ancient traders of Minoan Crete and the island of Rhodes. In the period that followed, the Celtic Voltae lived here. They may or may not have been the people who had built the dolmen tombs, raised the standing stones and created the sacred places for worship and offerings. Personally, I believe these are older. One of the local mountain tops; the Pêch Cardou, was probably used as an astronomical observatory thousands of years ago, until the first century CE. You see; from its top, people could still observe the Southern Cross, while in Egypt it had already disappeared from the night sky. For the ancient peoples, the loss of the Southern Cross from the skies symbolised the downfall of an entire empire, so as a result, groups of people left the eastern Mediterranean and settled here in the west. Also, when there were wars in the east, many refugees fled to the west. In fact, Occitania has always been known for its mixed population. After the Celts, the Phoenicians and the Greeks came over in search for precious metals, salt and stones."

"When Rome's feared enemy Hannibal decided to march to Rome through Occitania with his army of soldiers and elephants, the Romans decided to occupy the eastern part of southern France to create a blockage. However, for the Romans, occupying southern Gaul - which was the old name of France - was only the start. Soon, the Roman Empire would try to swallow up the rest of Europe as well as the Near East. It was in this period that the most of the Jews arrived in France and with the Jews came the Essenes and other mystics. After the Roman Empire had been divided into two parts; east and west, the Gnostic Visigoths ruled most of the western empire - which was now Christian - while the Catholic Franks ruled the northern Rhineland. An alliance between the Franks and the Visigoths resulted in a new elite, the Merovingians, but in spite of this alliance, the differences between the Franks and the Merovingians would eventually result in the betrayal and murder of the last Merovingian king, Dagobert II. In the 8th century, the Muslim Moors tried to conquer France and the Frankish commander Charles Martel rounded up his Frankish army and pushed the Moors back into Spain. His victory ignited the desire to unite Europe to become one large nation that would be strong enough to withstand the threats that came from the Moors in the south and the Scandinavian Vikings in the north and so, in the year 800, Martel's successor Charlemagne was crowned emperor of a new Christian, Holy Roman Empire. The economy thrived and schools, churches and abbeys were built, promoting Christianity and its new Romanesque architecture, as well as its secret esoteric knowledge throughout Europe. Three centuries later, the Knights Templar would discover even more secret knowledge while fighting alongside the crusaders in the Holy land and the Near East and the introduction of the gothic architecture; a banking system; an organised toll road system and a new prosperous international trade industry would have an enormous and positive impact on Europe. The architecture they had introduced was called *gothic*, meaning 'secret', for the knowledge that had enabled master masons to construct all those massive buildings with their impressive domes and high windows, was kept secret. The knowledge of number, size and shape, you see, was connected to the 'heretic' teachings of the Greek philosopher Pythagoras, Moorish mysticism and science and the forbidden ancient Egyptian sacred wisdom. To keep the Church of Rome in the dark about the use of this pagan knowledge in Church architecture, it could only be shared by a few. In the Renaissance period, this knowledge and wisdom could, for instance, only be learned through underground streams such as the Rosicrucians and Freemasons."

Arthur was unstoppable and continued without pause,

"So you see, all these people together, with all those different cultures, contributed to this region. They also brought their wealth, their royalty and their nobility to Occitania. The members of these foreign, royal and noble bloodlines married into the leading elites and existing local noble families and this is where the French legend of Mary Magdalene begins. She was supposed to have been one of the people who arrived here and settled just beneath the Pêch Cardou, close to Coustaussa, at the site of a Pythagorian school near a Gnostic, Essene community. You can still see the remains of their beehive shaped houses, although many of those are now just piles of stones."

Gabby suddenly listened a bit closer when Arthur mentioned the name of Mary Magdalene. Of course, Arthur had no idea that Gabby had only just met her in the flesh.

"So, you think that there is a good chance that she actually lived in this region?" she asked Arthur, who pursed his lips. "Well, we might never be sure, but history does allow it and Mary Magdalene's legend is extremely strong here, too strong to ignore. However, there are no traces here of Jesus or any of their proposed children, so that may just be a myth. I personally don't believe he ever lived here, but let's just assume for a moment that his remains were brought here by the Knights Templar. They believed that the year 1200 would be the end of the world and that Christ's Second Coming was only possible if the Ark of the Covenant was placed in a new Temple in a New Jerusalem. We all know they wanted to create a new Holy Land here in Occitania, so what if the Templars really did find his bones in Palestine and took them to France along with the Ark of the Covenant? Perhaps they hid them together, the Ark and the bones? It makes perfect sense!"

Alfred could no longer help it. With big eyes and open mouth he had listened to the boys theory, amazed that Arthur had found out so much on his own and now had the guts to put his finger on the sore spot. The Swiss grinned from ear to ear and stared hard at Otto, who stubbornly suppressed any comment. Rahn just stood there with his arms folded and his mouth firmly shut, unwilling to share his secret. However, Arthur hadn't finished yet.

"Anyway, there's more. In the castle at Rennes-le-Château lived a noble lady, Marie de Nègre or Niort, Dame de Hautpoul-Blanchefort. These were the most important and oldest noble families here in this part of France, who had strong Cathar sympathies. They were also related to the Templars and kept their secrets well hidden. When Marie died, she confessed to her priest, sharing several family secrets. She also asked him to hide her belongings in the family tomb underneath the church. This priest, Abbé Bigou, did what she asked. In the next period, pressure from northern France and an anti-royal movement shook the area. It was the eve of the French Revolution in the late 18th century. Many a royalist made plans to flee to Spain and because they expected to return at some point, the nobility in and around Rennes-le-Château had considered it safer to give their family jewels and fragile chinaware to the priest, Abbé Bigou, instead of taking it with them; travelling with jewels and expensive china over a mountain range infamous for its gangs of bandits was not such a good idea. So Bigou stashed it all in the tomb of the lords of Rennes, walled it up and decided to leave for Spain as well. He only left a few clues bchind; clues written in Greek and Latin that could only be deciphered by another priest."

Arthur paused to ask for some more water. His audience had been glued to his lips and couldn't wait for him to continue.

"A century passed and a newly appointed priest settled in the old presbytery; Bérenger Saunière. Fond of Templar history and the legends and myths of the region, he was pleased to finally become a priest in the historic village he was dying to get his hands on. He knew it very well as he was born just across the valley in Montazels. Rennes was old; it had secrets. At a certain moment he was given money by a lady in Coursan to replace the old altar and this is how it all started. First he found this big slab that covered the entrance to the crypt. With some effort he removed the slab, that could be dated back to the 8th century CE. This could be a clue to the age of the church, which is, oddly enough, dedicated to Mary Magdalene. So, the priest found his way into the crypt and during this descent he must have discovered the other clues left behind by his predecessor, Abbé Bigou, because from that moment on he started to spend money as if it were water. He renovated the entire church, while at the same time he destroyed some of the clues. Later he was spotted digging up graves in the churchyard at night. There is speculation that he even joined a secret brotherhood. Of course, while renovating the church, he made sure to leave his own clues to what he had found by interfering with the newly added ecclesiastical art and decor. Afterward, he spent large amounts of money, building an impressive study called the 'Tour Magdala' to store his books; a large house to accommodate retired priests, that he called 'Villa Bethania'; beautiful, formal gardens; an orangery with expensive, rare plants and did I mention the peacocks? It's obvious that something funny was going on and you know, we are still debating it on forums! We still don't know exactly what it was that he had found, or what has happened to it."

Alfred realised that Rennes-le-Château was an obvious place to check out, but he knew he'd never get permission to visit the crypt of the church, let alone explore any of the caves underneath the hilltop village. Although he was certain that, one day, some kind of treasure could be found in, under or around this village, his gut told him to look elsewhere for the Ark and for the bones.

The Swiss put his hand on Arthur's shoulder. "Very interesting Arthur. Now, what if Rennes-le-Château is *not* the location of the Ark, where else would you look?"

Alfred, who was getting anxious to depart, looked at the boy through his dark sunglasses, so Arthur could only see his own reflection. He could feel the man's impatience and tried to think of locations.

"Well, apart from the places we are going to explore today, have you checked Blanchefort? Pêch Cardou?"

"Yes." replied Alfred.

"Then, I'm at a loss. I'm still researching, you know and am not quite there yet. The thing I wanted to do most of all during this trip was to check out the very hill that Otto refuses to go to."

Rahn grinned. He liked Arthur. He was a clever boy; adventurous.

Alfred got up and automatically, so did the others.

"I have made a program for today, with the following sites: Alet-les-Bains, Notre Dame de Marceille, St. Martin Lys and the church of Laval. We will split up and check each site thoroughly, after which you will all report to me."

They split up into three teams and about fifteen minutes later, everyone was standing next to their car. The first car would go to Alet-les-Bains, with an agent behind the wheel and Ben and Yanne in the back. They were bringing along a file that explained the history of Alet and the story of the magnificent abbey, that had been destroyed during the Religious Wars. As they drove off, Ben was already studying the contents of the file and became interested in the weird goings on during the Middle Ages, as if this abbey had something to hide. He liked the fact that it had Jewish origins, being Jewish himself.

Yanne was just glad she was alone with Ben on this project. At least *that* was something.

Another car drove out of the parking area, heading toward Limoux. Their goal was the Nôtre Dame de Marceille, a magnificent church on the edge of the town. Arthur, Michael and David were browsing through its history and mystery and understood that they first had to find a certain hidden vault somewhere on the grounds and afterward they would investigate the interior of the church, in search of disguised symbolism and hints.

The third and last car was off to St. Martin Lys and the church of Laval, a strange chapel on a hill in the Pyrenees. Alfred was sitting next to the driver and Otto, Bill and Gabby were sharing the backseat. For some reason, Otto was very excited to be in this team, going on a new adventure to a location he had never even heard of. Every minute was savoured by him; his eyes were wide open; his heart was beating fast and he was on a high. Nevertheless, Alfred kept a close eye on him. He had studied Otto's mental state and knew he was unstable, after all he had gone through. He had to keep him under close observation, making sure he wouldn't bolt.

Meanwhile, Alfred was talking to the other drivers on his mobile phone. They reported back that all was OK and that they were approaching their targets. When he received the call that the first car had arrived at its goal; Alet-les-Bains, even Alfred felt the rush of the adventure. He knew that the sites all fitted, as if they were parts of one big puzzle.

Alfred's team approached the Bugarach mountain and turned right toward Laval. With awe, they observed the beautiful scenery of this strangely formed, limestone mountain, which was shaped by the wind and the rain into a sculpture of divine inspiration. Neither of them could find words to describe the magical feeling they were experiencing during their drive.

The first team, consisting of Ben and Yanne, had found a parking spot opposite the picturesque spa hotel - the former bishop's palace in Alet-les-Bains. Now on foot, they followed the main road toward the ruins of the old abbey. Ben loved history, especially when there was a Jewish connection. His Jewish roots must have been the reason Alfred had chosen them to investigate this particular location. In the little tourist office - which doubled as an entrance to the ruins - they received printed information and a key to a gate at the back to see the Chapter House. However, as they didn't think it would have anything to do with any secret, they left the Chapter House for what it was.

The old abbey cathedral had almost been razed to the ground in 1577. Because Alet at that time had chosen the side of the Protestants, the Catholics had decided to destroy the entire abbey. The Wars of Religion had been very violent indeed. Ben was drawn to the apse, which had been part of an ancient temple dedicated to the goddess Diana. The sheer beauty of the building - including the sacred lamp alcoves and amazing eclectic architecture of the cathedral - had silenced them both. Suddenly, Yanne's eye fell on the glass windows of the church, that was situated next to the cathedral ruins. Each window of the church featured a huge Star of David, also known as the Seal of Solomon.

"Ben, that six pointed star over there in the church windows, is this common or unique?"

When he turned to look at the windows, Ben's mouth fell open. "Wow, the Magen David!"

He leafed through some of the material he was carrying, but couldn't find anything specific about the windows. "It could just be the makers mark, as this place was once mainly a Jewish community."

Yanne wasn't convinced. "Yes, but Ben, look at the size of them! They're huge! ... and besides, wasn't David's son Solomon the Judean King who had a Temple built in Jerusalem to house the Ark of the Covenant?"

Ben was flabbergasted. Of course! Yanne was right, but then again, what if? Where could they have put it? Underneath this church in an unknown crypt? Then, people should have found it by now, for this church had been rebuilt after the time of the Knights Templar. Ben shook his shoulders. "What if the Ark was here for a while and was then moved to a safer place during the Wars of Religion? Or, perhaps the Ark was moved just before or during the Cathar Crusades? Remember; from 1209 onward, no place in this area was safe. A huge army had come from the north to slaughter the heretics called the Cathars or Bon Chrétiens, who had a different view of Christianity. The King of France had taken advantage of the Pope's call for the Cathar Crusade and had sent his troops south to annex the lands of the feudal Lords of Occitania. If they had anything hidden here around 1209 - and according to our briefing, the Ark may have come here just before 1200 - then they had to have it moved to a safer place; away from villages, castles or churches, deep into the countryside. To a cave, perhaps?"

They looked around the ruins and decided it to be a dead end. However, the church next door was open and they wanted to check out its interior; perhaps there were more clues inside. Apart from the big windows that featured the Seal of Solomon, the church contained other interesting details. They also noticed a mural showing a pregnant woman standing at the cross. Yanne scratched her chin and remarked, "Ben, you once told me that as a Jew, you do not worship Jesus. How do the Jews see Jesus?"

"Well, according to what I have learned, he was a prophet. It is true that we do not share the vision of the Christian belief that Jesus was a Masjiach who had resurrected, or that he was literally the son of God. However, we do believe that he was a prophet, a healer and a rabbi and for being the latter he must have had a wife and - most likely - even children. I have always thought that Myriam of Magdala was his wife, so if this represents Myriam of Magdala on that wall over there, standing at the cross, I for one am not shocked to see that she is pregnant. Of course, I'm sure that the Church will have found some kind of rational explanation for this, but I'm happy that this has survived. I'll take a picture of it without a flash, because the flashlight might damage the colours of the mural."

Before going back to the car, they walked through the medieval village in search of a cold drink. However, they failed to notice several strange symbols, that were carved into the old beams of a medieval house; symbols consisting of a mysterious chest on wheels; a fish; an old Jerusalem cross and an arrow, pointing west...

In the meantime, the second team with David, Arthur and Michael had arrived in Limoux. At the roundabout, the navigation system told them to turn right, toward the Nôtre Dame de Marceille, which was well signposted. On arrival they were amazed to see a huge basilica on top of a low, conically-shaped hill just outside the town of Limoux. David was certain when he remarked, "This was definitely the site of an old temple." Arthur and Michael couldn't agree more.

They got out of the car and explored the area around the church. Following the lines on the map which was in their file, they walked downhill across the cobbled, sacred road and noticed the source on the left. "This water is supposed to cure many thousands of diseases," remarked Michael, while trying to read the Latin inscriptions. "Sources like these are usually connected to the mother goddess. The temple which once stood on this spot, was probably dedicated to Diana or Artemis."

They continued their descent toward the River Aude and turned right to cross a field right next to an olive tree orchard. Looking up to the right, they could see the Nôtre Dame de Marceille from a distance and couldn't help but notice the strange shape of the building. Eventually they arrived at an old ruin, where they discovered - under a layer of fallen leafs - an iron plate, covering what looked like the entrance to an ancient vault.

Arthur got really excited. "Come on! Help me lift this thing!" David and Arthur worked together and flipped it over. There was indeed an entrance to a space underneath; something that looked like a cellar. David didn't want to get in without the necessary gear. "Let's get our headlights and ropes and check it out!"

As soon as they had returned, they first had to crawl through a corridor filled with dirt to enter the small space underneath the ruined house. Big blocks of stone revealed that there was indeed an old structure below. There was a corridor leading into another space below, roofed with pink marble slabs. This was getting interesting. At the end of the corridor they arrived at the entrance of a small, square chamber that seemed to be part of an older building and could only be entered by a stairway leading down. The stairway, however, had crumbled over the ages; there was sand and rubble on the floor, but the iron banisters were still there. Carefully they descended into the room and discovered that there was a second passage on the opposite side. When they went through the opening, there was a third room with a vaulted ceiling. There were bits and pieces of iron stuck to the wall, but it was difficult to make out what it had been for. It looked as though something had been attached to the wall. There was more rubble on the floor and some of the rocks were actually large, hewn stones that had once been part of the construction. When they discovered another corridor that had been blocked by large stones, they had arrived at a dead end. David started to climb back toward the entrance. "Whatever was here, guys, is now somewhere else. I think this place has been investigated thoroughly already."

"Can't we move these blocks and see what's on the other side?" said Arthur, disappointed that this expedition was over so soon.

"No way, it will be dangerous and we would attract too much attention. We are not completely isolated here." The moment they re-emerged from the vault, David pointed at the farmer, checking up on his seemingly neglected olive grove.

"Besides, look how damp it is. The river is very low now, but in winter this place could be flooded. No one is crazy enough to put something of value down there. No, I think this has been used as a water storage or a pump house, or perhaps as an escape route. If the church really was a temple in the old days, then we mustn't forget that temples doubled as treasuries and in times of danger they needed an escape route to take their valuables to safety. I would date the origins of this underground structure to the 4th century, at the earliest."

Disappointed, they left the site and walked back uphill to investigate the interior of the basilica. On their way back, they decided to walk through the adjoining park. At the far end stood a white, unmarked statue of a man. It was Vincent DePaul, the founder of a generous order called the Lazarites, who cared for the poor. DePaul was known for his compassion, generosity and humility. Arthur recalled a discussion on the forum about him. It was said that DePaul had had secret business in the Languedoc around 1605. He had covered it up by telling everyone that he had been abducted, but had managed to break free in the end. Michael interrupted his friend's attempt to entertain them with conspiracy theories about DePaul's secret mission in Limoux. "No mate, the statue's here because the Lazarite order was right next to the basilica. It was never proved that the story of the abduction was indeed a lie."

"Okay, but then explain to me how he was able to enter such high circles immediately after his alleged abduction? Because before that, he had been just an insignificant country priest."

"Dunno mate. Persistence? Luck?" said Michael, shrugging his shoulders.

However, Arthur did not give up so easily. "Then what about the secretive *Compagnie du Saint-Sacrement* that DePaul was a member of? This was after all a secret order! I am positive that the Lazarists were a cover for something much bigger. Have you forgotten that Nicolas Fouquet was also a member of this order?"

David was getting confused. "Whohoho, now, slow down. Who is Nicolas Fouquet?"

Arthur explained how Nicolas Fouquet - the French superintendent of finances - had drawn the attention of King Louis XIV by writing a certain mysterious letter. Arthur pulled his little note book from his pocket, slapped the elastic band to the side and eagerly leafed through it. When he reached the right page he read out loud,

"He and I discussed certain things, which I shall with ease be able to explain to you in detail – things which will give you, through Monsieur Poussin, advantages which even kings would have great pains to draw from him, and which, according to him, it is possible that nobody else will ever discover in the centuries to come. And what is more, these are things so difficult to discover that nothing now on this earth can prove of better fortune nor be their equal."

Arthur continued, "The King was so alarmed, that he had all Fouquet's possessions searched. He also threw him in prison, where he was kept in solitary confinement until he died. Some say that Fouquet might have been the man in the iron mask, or at least that the novel Alexandre Dumas wrote about this subject, was based on him. The man who knew too much."

David was intrigued. He had never heard this story. Arthur, however, was unstoppable,

"Nicolas Poussin, of course, was the painter who painted the 'Shepherds of Arcadia'. King Louis XIV had bought it and had put it in his bedroom. It is said that he had studied it for hours each day, in an attempt to figure out what Poussin had hidden in the painting; the painting that some say is a key code in solving the enigma of Rennes-le-Château!"

Michael laughed. "What? No one has ever deciphered the painting to arrive at that conclusion. All we know is, that it has been painted with mathematical principles such as the Golden Ratio and that wasn't uncommon in Renaissance art.

Also, the phrase 'Et in Arcadia Ego', that is on the painting, has never been convincingly explained by anyone."

Arthur disagreed and was very disappointed to see his forum friend so sceptical.

"... but Michael, the painting is a map! It's the knights tour, you know; chess? The knight hops from the Horse of God onto the Pas de la Roque, then onto L'Homme Mort and then either left or right; west or east. It's the phrase 'Et in Arcadia Ego' that gives us the clue: 'And in the Ark is the Divine Spirit' or 'Et in Arca Dia Ego *Est*'. So the knight hops to the east; to the right. To *my* hill. Didn't you read my post on the forum?"

Michael shrugged his shoulders again. "Not that one dude, I thought it was a bit far off..."

David, on the other hand, thought it made a lot of sense, but then another statue in the park drew their attention. A statue of Mary standing on a snake. David walked toward it.

"Look, it's the Mary of the Immaculate Conception. In Catholicism, everyone is born with a sin that goes all the way back to Genesis. When Eve was persuaded by the snake to eat from the forbidden fruit, mankind and all its offspring was thrown out of the Garden of Eden and forever banished from Paradise. However, the Church fathers thought that this 'Original Sin', that - according to the Church dogma - has affected every human being ever since, couldn't possibly apply to Mary, the mother of Jesus and therefore it had been decided at the Council of Ephesus in 431 CE, that Mary was without sin and thus immaculate the moment she conceived the Son of God. Get it? Immaculate Conception? So what we see here, is Mary, now having become the Divine Mother of God, stepping on the snake, because she was unaffected by the Original Sin."

Michael, who had listened to his father with big eyes, had no idea he knew so much about this subject and smiled. "Wow, dad, that's fascinating! You can see how the world has turned patriarchal long ago, pushing away the rights of women and denying the female principle of God, known as the Goddess.

A few centuries ago, many artists tried to reintroduce the female principle, expressing her through their artwork. Artists like Alphonse Mucha created beautiful paintings with hidden messages and we mustn't forget the fairy tales, in which the evil witch tries to kill or abduct the princess, like in Snow-white or Rapunzel. Also - speaking of Eve's apple - it was the witch who had poisoned the apple that almost killed Snow-white. In those stories, it is always the witch who tries to keep the prince and the princess apart. Fairy tales are, in fact, clever cover ups of forbidden truths. It is so important to have the male and female principles of our world in balance. In the last 2000 years, it has been religion - with its horrible witch hunts, hatred toward women and blaming Eve for the sin of mankind and all that - that has disrupted this balance. Religion is the witch."

David smiled. Michael had grown up with a feminist mother and it showed. They stood there silently for a few minutes and then went into the church, which, as David explained, was also well known for its Black Madonna statue.

While approaching the Chapel of Mary, David explained, "The Black Madonna represents the Black Diana, the Mother Goddess, who at a certain time had been very popular here, especially during the Roman era, though its origin lies in Egypt with the Black Isis. The Romans had introduced this fertility goddess to this region when they were stationed in Gaul and Spain. During the rise of the Christian faith, the Church simply told everyone that Isis was the Virgin Mary, with the son of God on her lap. This also made it easier for people to continue their worship of the Black Mother, which eventually became the Black Madonna."

A woman, who was praying in the church, came over and explained that the original statue, which was from the 11th century, had been badly damaged by brigands a few years before and that the statue they were now looking at, was a copy. She took out her handkerchief. The recent violence and lack of respect toward church relics and statues had moved her to tears.

Then suddenly, without saying a word, David walked toward the exit of the church. Surprised by this sudden move, Arthur and Michael followed him. "I can't stand the atmosphere in this church." David remarked. However, just before they reached the porch, Michael noticed a peculiar statue of Joseph and Jesus in a small chapel to the left of the entrance. "Hey, come and check this out, this is weird!"

They gazed up at a young boy Jesus, trying to draw a map of Europe - particularly France and Italy - onto a globe with a crayon. Joseph, who seemed angry at his son for doing so, had grabbed the little boy by the arm to stop him from drawing onto the globe. Jesus pulled the sad face many children often pull when they do not get their way.

David scratched his head. "Wow, this is really strange. What would the sculptor have wanted to convey with this?"

For some reason, Arthur suddenly remembered seeing a German TV film reproduction of an old fairy tale. One lazy morning, not long ago, he had zapped through channels out of pure boredom and this film had been the only thing worth watching.

"Guys, I think I know what it means. Do you remember the story of the Princess and the Frog? The frog represents a French prince from the Provence, who had been turned into a frog by a witches' curse. He lived in a pool outside the palace of a spoilt Tuscan princess. One day the princess came out to play with her golden ball. Accidently, the ball ended up in the pool. Then, the frog appeared and comforted the young woman. He solemnly promised to bring her ball back, but only if he could sit on her table to eat and drink with her and sleep in her bed that night. She gave him her promise, so the frog dived into the pool and brought back her golden ball. However, when the frog knocked on the door that evening, she refused him entrance to the palace. Her father was very angry with her and ordered his daughter to keep her promise to him. So when the frog had eaten from her plate and had drunk from her goblet, he went to sleep in her bed and asked for a good night kiss. She refused, of course, but eventually she had to give in, hoping to finally shut him up. The moment she smashed the frog against the wall… "

"She smashed the frog against the wall!?" the others chorused.

"Yes, in the original tale, the princess smashed the frog against the wall, but then felt pity for him. In the more modern versions it was a kiss that had broken the spell and had turned the frog back into a prince. At the end of the story, the lovers drive away in the carriage of the prince, travelling from Italy all the way to France, where they were expected to live happily ever after. However, during their journey, the princess asked her prince where he was taking her to. So, in order to explain this to her, he took her golden ball and drew on it exactly what we are looking at here. Tuscany in Italy and the Provence in France."

David was intrigued. He realised that the south of France was connected to northern Italy by at least two factors; first, the Cathars. During and after the Cathar Crusade, many had fled the horrors of the inquisition and persecution in southern France and had gone to northern Italy, where they had simply continued the Cathar philosophy and way of life, right under the Pope's nose. Even Saint Francis of Assisi had been a Cathar before he decided to mix Catharism with Catholicism. Therefore, his order - the Franciscans - had originally been deeply inspired by the Cathar faith. It is thanks to him that at least some elements of the Cathar faith exist today.

Secondly, there is the mention of a bloodline, which had entered France from the Near East in the first century. In a later period, this same bloodline would be mixed with Italian nobility through multiple marriages. The French lily; the fleur-de-lis - the origins of which go back as far as the Near East and Egypt - was used on the coats of arms in France, but later it was also found on several coats of arms in Northern Italy. A famous example is the coat of arms of the Medici family and David wondered whether the sculptor of this particular group of statues here at the Nôtre Dame de

Marceille meant either the link with the Cathars, or the link with the bloodline. Then he realised it could even be both.

The third team with Alfred and Otto had finally arrived at the beautiful parking near the chapel of Laval, which was again dedicated to Nôtre Dame, Our Lady; Mary, Mother of God or simply; the Mother Goddess. Rahn was the first to leave the car and immediately ran uphill toward the chapel. Alfred had never seen Otto take off so quickly and was afraid he wanted to make a run for it. Quickly he raced after him.
Shit! You're not going anywhere just yet buddy!
Rahn slowed down, knowing that the Swiss would be on his heels no matter where he went. When they were all together at the top of the hill, they found the gates to the chapel entrance ruthlessly chained up. Hoping to find someone to open the heavy lock that was attached to the chain, they searched the grounds, but there was not a single person around.
Behind the chapel was what looked like an imitation of the garden of Gethsemane in Jerusalem. The ancient olive trees had obviously been planted there many centuries ago. The whole place had a serene, though mysterious atmosphere.
Suddenly, Rahn called out to the others. A little turret that stood on one of the outer walls had attracted his attention.
"What do you make of this?" he said to Alfred. Otto had a broad smile on his face, realising he had made an interesting discovery. In turns they studied the interior of the little turret. Behind the beautiful statue of Mary with child were several plaques with coats of arms; a pentacle; a P with a snake winding through it and a cross on a cross. Alfred was intrigued by the cross on the cross. This was a Templar sign to warn fellow Templars that something important had been hidden there. Immediately he grabbed his mobile and called team 1 and 2. Alfred felt strongly that there was something hidden here and before he could take any action, he needed all of them together.

When the second team received Alfred's message, Michael and Arthur were very disappointed. They had wanted *their* team to discover something significant. Arthur was still thinking about Otto's strange reaction that morning, when Arthur had proposed to explore the Serbaïrou hill. His persistent mind stubbornly set on discovering at least something, Arthur decided to try and persuade the others to check out the hill on their way to Laval.

"Mr Camford, there really could be something important hidden on the Serbaïrou; my calculations have pointed into this direction from the start. I have been studying the mysteries a lot longer than any of you, but no one believes me. I swear that there is something hidden on that hill and we must look for an ancient construction of some sort, something like a dolmen tomb. I know that - according to the legend - the entrance is where the sign points us to Sion, so we must find that sign. It is near the river Blanque and we will pass it anyway."

David rubbed his eyes. "How long would this take, Art?"

"Maybe 1 hour, there and back."

"Okay, but I must phone Mr Zinkler for permission first."

David reached for his mobile to call Alfred, but suddenly, Arthur snatched the phone from David's hand before he could dial.

"What the hell!" David was furious.

"Sorry David," said Arthur, "He will say no, I just know it. Please, trust me on this. Just this once?"

David looked out of the window, deeply in thought and Michael now stared hard at Arthur. He knew Arthur well enough to know that he could be right and decided to back him up. "Look dad, I know Arthur's research, he's one of the best, you know?"

"Okay, but we need to pace ourselves though. We have to do it within an hour, or Mr Zinkler will be wondering what is taking us so long and become suspicious."

David asked the driver to pull over on Arthur's call.

Although the driver was an SBS agent - answering only to his chief; Alfred Zinkler - he understood that the goal was more important now and agreed that they should give it a try. Arthur studied his map. "Alright, we need to park just around the next bend; you will see a parking space and a path leading toward the river."

The driver stopped by the road side, but had strict orders to stay with the car, so David, Michael and Arthur had to do the hike on their own. This was an unusual situation. However, the driver seemed to trust David and decided to give the team an hour before he'd call his chief.

Arthur was as excited as a schoolboy on a camp out. "Come on!" He briskly walked downhill toward the river Blanque. "We have to look for a sign; a marker of some sort, that has something to do with Sion; the Ark; the Templars; whatever. So keep your eyes open!"

When they walked down to the river, they spotted a family with kids playing in the water.

Hippies! Shit. We're not alone...

As soon as they reached the river, everyone looked for the sign. Suddenly, Michael yelled out when he found strange carvings on an old, weathered stone. "Cool, check this out! What is it?" Arthur studied the pattern and threw some water onto the stone's flat surface. Now the pattern became more visible. David studied an abstract, Jugendstil style carving of two dragonflies mating and couldn't believe the beauty of it. Arthur recognised the dragonflies and was very enthusiastic. He recalled Alfred's story about Bertrand, the Templar knight. "That's it! That's it guys! We are at the right spot!"

"So what does it mean?"

"Dragonflies is 'les libelles' in French. When the Knights Templar were in Jerusalem, a prince from Ethiopia made a deal with them. In return for helping him back on his throne, he showed them the Ark of the Covenant. His name was Lalibella! Get it? Come on, we must continue this path!"

"… but then we have to cross the river!" Michael whined, but Arthur was without mercy. "So what!"

"We'll get wet feet!" complained David.

"So what!" Unstoppable and now slightly irritated, Arthur boldly waded through the shallow waters of the Blanque. The others had no choice but to follow him up the hill. The steep climb first took them to several huge megaliths; large stones, most of them upright, which gave the landscape a somewhat prehistoric atmosphere. Michael checked his GPS and David stooped to study Arthur's map. "We need to find the old 0-Meridian and follow the GPS to that point." said Arthur, while bending over David's shoulder.

"Now, where is the old 0-Meridian compared to the new one? Because only the new one is on the map."

Then, David noticed the code *PAX 681,* written in red ink on the edge of the map. He showed it to Michael, who could only think of one possible explanation; "I guess it's about 680 meters or so to the west."

The map revealed a large number of lines, pentagrams and hexagrams. David looked at Arthur and smiled. It was obvious that the young man had done his homework.

Michael, who had set out a course on the GPS, started to follow the rocks toward the old 0-Meridian. "This way!"

Arthur tried to explain to David the importance of the 0-Meridian. "That is why St. Sulpice is so important. January 17th - a date that appears on a regular basis when researching the enigma we are investigating - is the day of St. Sulpice, the church in Paris that reveals the original Meridian, the Green Meridian. Le Rayon Vert."

Michael had overheard Arthur and smirked, remembering all the recent research they had done on the Internet on Jules Verne. They had discovered that this 19th century French writer had been an initiate and that his books were full of clues and hints. 'Le Rayon Vert', for example, was about a mysterious green ray.

Researching through a forum often gives interesting results. Not only did they find secret messages in old documents and mysterious books written by members of the underground stream - they also discovered that the Round Table legend of

Parsifal was originally based on an old, Occitan troubadour song.

Arthur showed Michael the map and pointed at the two rivers, that met at the north side of the Serbaïrou hill. One river is sweet; one is salty. Arthur elbowed his friend.

"Remember what I told you about La Colline Inspirée by Maurice Barrès, the Martinist who had written that strange book about the three brothers and the hill of Sion? Well, the Serbaïrou is the *real* hill of Sion from the book, I'm certain of it! Besides, you will remember the lady of Rennes, who had entrusted her secret to Abbé Bigou when she died in 1781? She actually owned this hill and its mines. Doesn't that strike you as an odd coincidence? The Serbaïrou belonged to the Lords of Rennes!"

Michael smiled. Arthur was right; it was all too coincidental.

David could not walk as fast as Arthur and Michael and had fallen behind. Still pondering about the mating dragonflies on the rock near the river, he realised that dragonflies symbolise change; resurrection; renewal and metamorphosis, but also that a dragonfly on its own symbolises the number four, because of the number of his wings. Two dragonflies together, therefore, symbolise the number eight. The number of eternity; the number given to Jesus in the Gematria.

David just knew that - if pointing at anything at all - this dragonfly stone could just be symbolism, referring to Christ. Nevertheless, he was certain that they were heading toward an important co-ordinate, but he was not convinced that they'd be the first to discover the spot. Would there be anything left for them to see at all? he wondered. David certainly hoped so, because if this unscheduled outing doesn't come up with anything, he would have much to answer for.

20

Lausanne, Switzerland, July 2nd 2011

When Danielle opened her eyes, she noticed that she was in a hospital and no longer in Sardis' house in Rome. Someone was standing over her and smiled. "Good morning, young lady!" Dr Days was sitting on a stool next to Danielle's bed. "How are you feeling?"

Danielle moaned. Her voice was hoarse. "Where am I? I'm thirsty…"

Dr Days put his hand behind her head and gave her some water. She drank it carefully and emptied the cup. Days took her hand. "You are safe. We have rescued you from your kidnapper. So you can now relax, it's all over."

Danielle smiled, but couldn't help wondering what had happened to Sardis. Her memory was a little bit blurry.

"I don't remember anything from the moment he discovered me in his office. What happened?"

"Your rescuers were almost overpowered by Sardis' guards, but they managed to get you out. The Cardinal, unfortunately, didn't make it."

Danielle was surprised to feel upset about this. She had seen Sardis' obsession in his urge to reach his goal, but also his care for her and his love and being as weak as she was, Danielle started to cry. It was as if a cork blew off a champagne bottle after being shaken. Her emotions; fears; worries; it all came out. The doctor let her cry, knowing it was a healing emotion and indeed, after a few minutes, Danielle felt much better. She drank some more water and tried to sit upright. "How long have I been asleep?"

"Give and take: 34 hours. We helped you sleep a bit. You were exhausted and that wasn't good for you, or for the baby."

The baby!

She remembered now. She had been worried about her being sick so much and alarmed by the frequent pain attacks.

Her heart pounded when she asked, "How is the baby, doctor? Is it okay?"

Days didn't want to alarm her, so he decided not to tell her everything. "Your baby's fine! It is *you* we are worried about. You're very weak, so you need to get stronger as quickly as possible. However, this is a very fine hospital and you are safe here."

Danielle thought about her secret missions and her diary. Where would it be now? Had the professor been involved in her rescue?

"Who are my rescuers?" she asked.

"You will be briefed later, as soon as you are stronger and then you also will be reunited with your friends."

"Yes, where are they? ... and where's my diary?"

Danielle breathed heavily now and looked around for the precious notebook.

"They will be back soon and your diary is safe, so don't worry, all is well. Now, get some sleep..."

Days injected the drip with a mild sedative and walked out of the room. Within a few seconds, Danielle dozed off and Sally returned to her seat. She stared at the sleeping Danielle for a while before she opened up a romantic novel, knowing she'd be there for a while.

Laval, southern France, July 2nd 2011

Alfred was getting impatient. He was very eager to start investigating the interior of the chapel, but needed his team to be together. So far, everyone had arrived but David, Michael and Arthur and he realised that he needed them most, especially Arthur. Getting more impatient by the minute, he decided to give the chauffeur a call. Naturally, the chauffeur explained how his passengers had wanted to explore an interesting co-ordinate first and that he was expecting them to return any minute now. Alfred appreciated that they wanted to investigate everything, just in case, but he also knew that he couldn't afford to lose much time here either. He decided to have one agent posted as a look-out on the parking, another at the other exit to the main road and to find a way to get inside the chapel while waiting for the team to arrive. Prepared to handle multiple situations, they had brought climbing gear and several tools to open locks, so within a minute they were able to unlock the chain and open the iron gate. Now they had to find a way to open the old, wooden door without doing any damage. Also here it only took a few minutes before the lock turned and the door opened. The interior was amazing, but the damage that had been done to the old rectal behind the altar was unforgivable. Who could possibly have done this? Now Alfred understood why the church was closed and locked. He took a look at the file again and noticed a date that seemed to be important; 1781 - the year when the chapel's new altar had been placed into its present position. It was as if he had heard that date before. Then he noticed the strange medallion on the front of the altar and wondered why the arms of the angelic creature that was depicted on the medallion seemed to warn people not to come too close? He definitely needed Arthur and knew that the boy would be able to give him the information he needed. Arthur may know something about this date. The Cardinal had written 1781 down for a reason, so it had to be important.

Suddenly, Alfred's mobile rang. "Yes?"

There was a long silence. Alfred walked away from the others to be more private and bowed his head.

"I see. Thank you..."

Alfred - now pale and trembling - had to sit down. That was the worst possible news. Their entire mission had suddenly lost its significance. Still, he knew that he had to remain strong and inform the others that they had failed.

So close, and yet...

"Please, everyone, sit down, I have some bad news." he started. Alarmed by the sudden emotion in Alfred's voice, everyone sat down, even Otto. For a moment it was totally silent. Then, a nightingale started to sing his song so loud, that they could even hear it inside the church, echoing off the walls and the ceiling. Alfred swallowed away the lump in his throat and continued, "Danielle has just passed away. Our agents had been able to free her, but because she was so weak, they had brought her to a hospital in Lausanne. The doctors tried to save her, but..."

He started to cry; he had been strong for too long. Never before had he failed - his job or anyone - until now. The search for the Ark, Jesus' remains; it all seemed so meaningless now, but he realised that there was a greater cause and for Danielle he had to be strong and continue, or her death would be in vain. Still in tears, he looked at the others, who were all shocked and struck dumb. Also Gabby cried; she was so frustrated and angry, that she banged the wooden seat with her fist and yelled, "It isn't fair! She was pregnant! I know it for sure! It's so unfair!"

Everyone was shocked. Gabby had only figured out that Danielle was pregnant after reading her friend's last letter and she hadn't shared those thoughts with anyone, until that moment. Even now she carried that letter with her. Bill held her in his arms, knowing how close the women had become over these last few weeks through what they had both experienced.

A moment of silence followed when the complete tragedy sunk in. For all the members of the group, the entire atmosphere of excitement, enthusiasm and adventure had now disappeared completely. The loss of Danielle and her unborn child was a foul and extremely painful blow.

As soon as Alfred had regained his calm, he started to walk around to shake off his emotions, which rapidly changed from sorrow into anger. He eyed the door to see if team 2 had returned yet. They needed to get on with it.

Alfred turned and shouted, "For Danielle we must continue! This is about world peace! Let's make sure she didn't die in vain. Now, where the fuck is David!!"

21

Corbières, southern France, July 2nd 2011

"This is unbelievable!" Arthur had taken the others to the exact co-ordinate of his research and angrily kicked one of the large, upright stones of a dolmen; a prehistoric tomb that had collapsed. Part of the stones that had once been part of the tomb had blocked what seemed to have been the entrance to an underground chamber. Now it was impossible to enter the tomb or dig a new entrance.

So this was it; they had found the tomb, but what could they do with it? Nothing. Arthur was livid. "Look! Look! This was done on purpose. You see the crack? It's not older than what; 60, 70 odd years? See how neat the crack is? … and this cover stone has been tipped over. It was sealed alright! Someone's been here before us!"

Again he kicked the stone. Michael and David were just as disappointed as he was, but David knew that this might well have been the place where, long ago, certain unknown people had reburied the mortal remains of Jesus. He figured that - perhaps sometime around World War II - the remains had been either locked in or taken out, after which the entrance had been sealed. However, if there was no longer anything of value inside, then why bother cracking the megalith to block the entrance? … but then, David thought of Rahn and his mysterious resentment of this hill and how conveniently he could have been here just before WWII. Maybe it had been Rahn who had blocked the tomb?

David decided to share some of his thoughts. "Suppose that someone discovered the site and realised that whatever was buried here was not supposed to see the world?"

While Arthur's mind immediately went to the mysterious behaviour of Abbé Saunière, the priest of Rennes-le-Château, Michael turned around to take another look at the broken tomb. Then he spotted something behind the dolmen. "Hey, check this out!"

They walked over to what looked like two *menhirs;* standing stones from prehistoric times that stood on what could be the roof of the tomb for which the dolmen itself had merely been an entrance. The ground below them sounded hollow. Michael ran his hand through his half long, light brown hair. Perhaps there was another way in, somewhere else? However, before they could explore the site properly, David's mobile phone rang. It was the chauffeur, saying, "Something has come up, you need to get here a.s.a.p."

David turned to the boys, who were already exploring the cliff's edge for another entrance. "Guys, we need to go, something has happened!"

Immediately, David started to walk back to the large megaliths and down toward the river, expecting Michael and Arthur to follow, but the boys were very reluctant to abandon this site so soon. Then, Michael noticed that his father had almost disappeared in the distance and smiled compassionately at his friend. "We can always come back later, Art."

Arthur nodded sourly and made sure the exact co-ordinates were securely programmed in his own GPS. By the time they had crossed the river, the black car had already stationed itself at the road side - engines running - ready to drive off to Laval. The hot sun had made them thirsty and the water bottles were handed out as soon as the car drove off.

David turned to the chauffeur, "So, what's happened?"

"The chief called." said the chauffeur. "Danielle has been rescued from her kidnapper."

"… but that is brilliant news!" said David. All cheered, but the chauffeur hadn't quite finished yet. "I'm afraid she was very weak, she just passed away in the hospital in Lausanne." Now gaping at the chauffeur and in a state of shock, David stammered, "Oh no, that can't be!" Lost for words, he stared out of his window. He didn't know the woman personally, but this was awful. It felt as if it was unreal; not part of the Cosmic Plan. The boys were equally upset and there was an unusual silence in the back of the car.

"So, what's going to happen now with the mission?" David queried. The chauffeur couldn't take his eyes off the winding road, so he replied without looking at David. "We are being called back to regroup and take new orders. I also believe they found something important."

Arthur and Michael, who had overheard, looked at one another, wondering what this could be.

The car drove toward Bugarach, the highest mountain of the Corbières and then took a right turn. Everyone had been silent until Arthur recognised the Bugarach mountain and its characteristic shape from photos.

"Hey guys, look, it's the UFO mountain. You know? 2012?"

He hummed the famous tune from 'Close Encounters of the Third Kind', knowing that the story for this movie was probably inspired by the tales of aliens and UFO's that surround this mountain and the prediction that it would be the only safe place to be in December 2012, when the world was going to end...

"Oh shut up, Art!" said Michael, who was still in a melancholy mood.

When they arrived at Laval, everyone decided to take five minutes of silence to honour Danielle's memory. The silence was only broken by the wind touching the leaves, a few crickets and the singing nightingale. Gabby cried non-stop; she didn't even bother to dry her tears. With Sardis now dead, she just wanted to go home. She leaned against Bill - who was very upset himself - and realised that he probably felt partly responsible for the entire situation, though he had done his very best to make things right. Then, all of a sudden, she remembered the time machine. When the thought made its full impact, she squeezed Bill's hand so hard, that he looked up from his silent prayer. When Bill looked into Gabby's eyes, he noticed a mischievous smile and that very moment - as if through ESP - it also dawned on Bill.

As soon as the five minutes were over, Alfred turned to Arthur. The Swiss desperately needed the boy's help. "Can you tell me the significance of the date 1781?"

Arthur smiled; enjoying being treated as if he were an expert on the Rennes-le-Château enigma, but then again, perhaps he was. He cleared his throat and started,

"Has anybody ever thought about why the entire enigma of Rennes-le-Château is not all about Rennes-le-Château? Okay, so I already explained that one of the keepers of the alleged secret used to live there in the 18th century; Marie de Nègre d'Ables, Dame de Hautpoul-Blanchefort. Once upon a time, several treasures of the Knights Templar were brought to France, after which these treasures were divided and carefully hidden. There were two items of great importance among these treasures. One item may have first been hidden underneath the Templar chapel of Bézu, while the other item was probably hidden in a cave underneath a castle called Blanchefort. The item underneath the Templar chapel of Bézu must have been moved to a natural site in the immediate area before October 13th 1307, when most Templars were arrested, although Bézu had been spared for some reason. The item that had been stored underneath Blanchefort must have been moved to Alet-les-Bains just before 1209, when the Cathar Crusade started. Of course, when Alet-les-Bains was no longer safe, other places were found and used; perhaps they brought it to the Nôtre Dame de Marceille, which is probably why you sent us to investigate the basilica this morning. However, every time they were forced to move these items to safer locations and to safe keep the new co-ordinates, new maps were created and new clues were left behind in art and writings. Now - centuries later - we look at the map and see all kinds of different co-ordinates, layer upon layer, old upon new and we can no longer distinguish the old from the new. So this brings us to the following question: which of all the hints and clues we have discovered so far could possibly point us toward the right co-ordinates? We may never know. Unless we stumble upon a new clue..."

Arthur smiled mysteriously and took from his bag an old and weathered book. He remembered well how he had found it.

Someone in France collected old diaries to sell on E-bay and this particular diary had been found at a *brocante* in the French port town of Collioure. Arthur had been lucky enough to spot the item on E-bay and recognise it for what it was.

"This diary once belonged to the priest Abbé Bigou of Rennes-le-Château." Arthur proudly announced, lifting the diary up for all to see. "We know that he had been entrusted with the entire secret of Marie de Nègre d'Ables of Rennes-le-Château when she passed away in the 18th century. In this diary he gave us hints to where he had stored her belongings, without betraying the locations right away. Unfortunately, some pages have been badly damaged and not every clue he wrote down is still legible, but after careful study, I have been able to make this translation:"

He put the diary back in his bag and took out a notepad.

"It speaks of a fleur-de-lis carved in stone and her sister, whose house is on a hill in the valley of... and then something with bread and water. It all sounds like a poem, but I can't put my finger on it. Any ideas?"

"Tell us about 1781." Alfred reminded Arthur.

"Aha, 1781. Yes, well, that was the year in which Marie de Nègre d'Ables of Rennes-le-Château died. Naturally, coming from an old noble lineage, her inheritance must have been considerable. As promised, Bigou had taken all her belongings, as well as her family secrets, to safety. Perhaps these secrets included the true co-ordinates to some of the Templar treasures."

"So, what could the Cardinal have meant when he wrote down this specific date?" Queried Alfred.

When Arthur shrugged his shoulders, Rahn, who had been quiet all that time, checked the French notes he had made so far and turned to Arthur.

"In these notes about the Laval church, the author writes that they changed the altar in 1781. Perhaps Marie de Nègre left something to this church in her will? What if there is more to the altar than we can see on the surface? I know that an altar is often put right above a saint's tomb, but sometimes it is also used to semi-permanently shut the entrance to a crypt. In the era of the Knights Templar, crypts were also used as treasuries and as far as we know, this chapel once belonged to the Knights Templar order. We already saw the symbol of the cross on the cross outside in the turret; perhaps this is a pointer, telling us that the Knights Templar had once kept a precious item in this crypt."

All stared at Otto now, for suddenly, the penny dropped; the entrance to the crypt must be underneath the altar. Perhaps someone had taken advantage of the space underneath this church to hide something and had then sealed its entrance with a brand new, heavy marble altar. However, the altar wasn't large enough to hide the entrance to the crypt. What else was done in 1781? The floor tiles around the altar? Otto was deep in thought; he knew for sure that the Ark was not underneath the dolmen on the hill, as he had been inside the tomb in 1936, so perhaps it was here. Perhaps they really did find the actual resting place of the Ark of the Covenant. He reread his recent notes and became more and more certain that this had to be the right place. The church had architectural resemblances to the Nôtre Dame de Marceille from the mid-15th century and certain things had been changed and renovated in 1675, during the administration of Pavillon, the then Bishop of Alet-les-Bains. It was certain that this church had been part of the mighty bishopric of Alet-les-Bains. Then he saw in his notes that there should be a small chapel on the pilgrim path that leads up to the church. This chapel is called: the Nôtre Dame de 'Donne-Pain' (giver of bread). His frown betrayed his excitement.

"Hello, hello, guys, this must be it! This really is the 'house on the hill' from Bigou's diary! The so called 'sister' of this chapel was St. Martin Lys in the gorge called La Pierre Lys. The stone fleur-de-lis! Both churches were possessions of the bishopric of Alet-les-Bains! It's all coming together! Here's what I think; the Ark must have been taken to Blanchefort first around 1200. Then, just before the Cathar Crusade in 1209, it was moved to Alet-les-Bains and in 1209, when the crusade started, it was moved deep into the mountains to the abbey of St. Martin-Lys. Eventually it was moved here, to this place, which has, after all, been fortified for a reason. This information must have been known to some of the old elites, so, after the death of Marie de Nègre d'Ables in 1781, only Bigou must have known the location of the Ark of the Covenant."

Alfred was hopeful. "We'd better find a way to get into the crypt without leaving any traces. Any ideas?"

22

Lausanne, Switzerland, July 2nd 2011

Dr Days felt horrible; he had just told Alfred the terrible news of Danielle's untimely death. The poor woman. He had only been out for an hour on a lunch break and when he got back, she had already been moved to the morgue. He shook his head, knowing she couldn't have died from the sedative and her liver condition hadn't been all that bad either. He was puzzled and decided to try to pull some strings to do an autopsy. Days walked toward the private car park of the hospital in Lausanne, took out his car keys and unlocked his car from a distance. His hand was trembling and he thought he'd better get himself a drink somewhere to calm himself down and think of a plan. He got into his car and sat there for a while, staring at the hospital's main entrance, at all the people coming and going; all of them burdened by their own troubles. Now, where was the nearest bar? He turned the key and instantly the car exploded with great violence, shaking everyone in the immediate environment and setting off the alarms of dozens of other cars. Within minutes, ambulances and police were present and soon after that, the first News cameras were taking shots of the crime scene for a live broadcast.

"Half an hour ago, a car exploded in the private car park of the University Hospital here in Lausanne. We heard that there was only one person in the car when the bomb went off and we are waiting for information about the identity of the..."

Izz al Din turned off the TV, rubbed his face and sighed. He knew that Days would have talked, but he so hated violence. He looked into the adjoining room and saw that Danielle was still fast asleep. She had no idea that she had been taken from the hospital to another location. The drug had done its job, all had gone well, so he should feel happy.

His sidekick Sardis was dead, so now he could finally focus on fulfilling destiny himself. Al Din had found out about Danielle's pregnancy and had quickly figured out who the father was. It had been a wise move to put Ms Kaiser inside Sardis' household. Immediately he had thought of all the possibilities; if he had Danielle's baby; Jesus' own son, he could raise him to become a true Muslim. With Jesus' son promoting Islam, the west could finally embrace the Muslim faith; its beauty; its wisdom; its order. World peace would be so much closer.

A knock on the door shook him out of his thoughts. "Come in!"

Ms Kaiser stepped into the room with a broad, self-satisfied smile. "Well, with Sardis and Days out of the way, we only have one witness left. We are safe for now, as Danielle has been reported dead and the nurse is not asking any questions. Days, however, was one of them; an SBS agent. He was getting suspicious, so he needed to be eliminated."

Al Din raised his arms, "Yes, but a car bomb?!" It attracted a lot of attention too!"

"Call it drama. I like bombs." she responded with a proud but stern face.

Al Din stared hard at her. "Obviously, but I must admit it was smart of you to fake Danielle's death, which means that SBS-Sion won't cause any further trouble. Surely, they will now continue with their own business. Hah! To think that the Cardinal had wanted to have the Ark for himself! .. but he didn't have the faintest clue that I was already onto him. You did a good job, Elsa, it was good of you not to trust him! … but now we are back in control. All we have to do now is let SBS-Sion find what they are looking for; follow them and take it from them. Perhaps they really do find the Ark. Besides, I don't think they will stop looking for it now, they are so close! I am sure their agenda is similar to mine…"

Sounds of moaning and groaning from the other room showed that Danielle was waking up. Because she had been kept asleep for so long, she had a major headache and an empty stomach. When she opened her eyes, she saw Ms Kaiser and an unfamiliar, dark-skinned man wearing a white galabya, staring back at her. Utter horror came over her, paralysing her entire body.

This can't be true. This just can't be true!

She started to scream so loud, that Kaiser hurriedly closed all open doors and windows. Al Din slapped her face and the mere shock of it made her stop screaming, but then, Danielle began to hyperventilate. Al Din was getting impatient. "Now listen young lady, no dramatics! I am serious! You co-operate with us, or you won't get through this alive. Think of your baby, he needs you. So live for him!"

Danielle hugged herself and moved into a foetus position. She feared this strange man more than she had ever feared Sardis. The man's voice sounded familiar; she had heard it before, at the Cardinal's house in Rome. If this was really him, the man who had wanted her dead, then...

"Who are you? What do you want of me?" she asked.

"My name is Izz al Din. I know all about you, your baby and the time travelling, so don't play dumb. Talking about travel, we will be doing a little bit of travelling ourselves. Tomorrow we will fly to Israel where you will live in my house and as soon as your son is born, I will raise him to become a faithful Muslim and then I will show him to the world along with your diary. I know that your friends are currently still on their errand for the late Cardinal, searching for the Ark of the Covenant in southern France, but the Cardinal no longer needs it now. I do! Therefore, if your friends succeed in getting me the Ark, it will be even easier for me to be elected as the new Religious World Leader!"

"Sardis had been very useful in the beginning, but lately he had become a nuisance. I had already suspected that the Organisation would try to rescue you from Sardis at some point and when they did, they saved me a lot of trouble, but it was tricky to get you out of that hospital and make people believe you were dead. Of course we had to put a look-alike in your cold cell in the morgue to fool them, but the woman who took your place was mortally ill and felt no pain."

Danielle looked at him in disgust. These men would stop at nothing to get what they wanted; world domination. She closed her eyes. Maybe she had to terminate her pregnancy, to stop this insane man from getting what he wanted. What would become of her son in the life they had planned for him? She thought of Gabby and Bill. Perhaps they would be able to help her out of this mess. At least *they* were still alive. For a moment this thought gave her hope, but then a harsh truth suddenly hit her.

Oh God, they must have been told that I'm dead...

The thought struck her like lightening and all hope now seeped out of her body. Feeling powerless and miserable, she simply crawled back under the sheets. All she wanted now is sleep. Al Din left the room and closed the door. He knew she hated him, but she'd soon see him for what he really is.

All in good time.

The next day Danielle was again injected with a sedative and taken to a helipad, where the journey to Israel started. Within six hours they were at the airport in Tel-Aviv, where a stretched, white limousine was waiting for them. It didn't take long before they arrived at a superb villa with lush, heavenly fragrant gardens, that were filled with colourful plants and flowers. This was Al Din's private and well-guarded paradise on the outskirts of Jerusalem. Immediately after Danielle woke up, she was given more drugs and over the next few days she would only eat, sleep and bathe - without speaking, without thinking - living in a dream world of her own, while her child grew inside her womb.

Laval, southern France, July 2nd 2011

Inside the church at Laval, Alfred and Otto were studying the floor, hoping to find a way into the crypt. They noticed that several tiles had already been lifted some time ago. Whoever had done this, hadn't bothered to put them back neatly.

They also noticed a large, white marble slab on the floor in front of the altar and Alfred thought he recognised it from the descriptions in the old Templar accounts. Directly above them, attached to the domed roof, was the eight-pointed sun of the Templars. Alfred was pleased; the eight-pointed sun was an important sign. However, it appeared as if this particular sun had once been part of the old chapel and for some reason, the builder in charge had found it important enough to put it back after the chapel's renovation. Their hearts pounded when they tried to lift the tiles and the marble slab, but all they could find was dirt on top of rubble. The more they kept on digging, the more they realised that this chapel was probably built on the site of an older chapel that had once stood on the same spot before the present church had been built; an old chapel that had been completely destroyed. The task seemed impossible. If the Ark was here, it rested underneath tons of rubble, perfectly hidden in a deep and dark crypt. The one who had moved the tiles before them, must have probably been on the same quest. They wondered who this could have been? The only logical explanation was, that Marie de Nègre d'Ables had told her priest, Antoine Bigou, that the Ark was resting safely underneath the chapel in Laval and that it was in her will to pay for a new altar to honour the sacred site anonymously. Naturally, Bigou had done what she had asked on her deathbed, but perhaps he couldn't resist the urge to lift a few tiles himself, to see if he could get to the Ark. Obviously, he had found the same rubble pile that the team had just discovered and had given up. Even Alfred had given up.

David - who had done most of the work - was covered in sweat and dirt and stared compassionately at Alfred, who was visibly at a loss. The Ark, unreachable; the Shepherd's Tomb, inaccessible. If only Rahn would tell them more.

Seeing the Swiss so desperate, Arthur decided to explain their afternoon side trip to the 'forbidden' hill. When he heard where they had been to, Rahn became furious - an anger that emanated from fear - but then he realised that everything had now changed anyway; Danielle was dead and he knew that Arthur will never give up; the boy will return and find a way inside that tomb with or without his help and because he knew he had already taken out the most important items in 1936, Rahn decided to finally give in.

"OK, I will tell you, but I have one condition."

Alfred looked at Rahn, smiling broadly.

"About time, Otto! What's the condition?"

"I want to stay here, in 2011." said Otto adamantly.

Alfred knew that this was virtually impossible, but also realised that he had to give him at least something.

"I will see what I can do."

Rahn smiled distrustfully, walked toward Arthur and whispered, "Do you want to know how I found it?"

Arthur's eyes grew big. "Are you kidding me? Tell me!"

Otto, who now had everyone's full attention, folded his arms, stared at the floor and started,

"You know, I was fortunate to be able to study several maps and documents that revealed a strange, secret geometry, covering most of Occitania's subterranean world and consisting of caves, mines, underground tunnels, etc.. Its main centre lies at Rennes-les-Bains. The clues that came with these maps revealed that Point X was in fact an ancient Celtic or pre-Celtic tomb or *dolmen,* to be found on the old 0-Meridian. That, of course, was only the north-south line, but then I was able to find the exact co-ordinates of this tomb when I managed to decipher the codes in a strange book, written by a man called Henry Boudet, who was the priest of Rennes-les-Bains in the 1880s. His book is called; 'Le Vraie Langue Celtique et le Cromleck de Rennes-les-Bains'. In it was a map, drawn by the priest's brother. There were also several drawings by the same brother, one of which was of a dolmen. Immediately I showed it to my superior, who filed it in my report, but it turned out that it wasn't the right one, as this one was at the northern slope. You see, my gut told me that it was on the southern slope, so I followed the line of the megaliths on that map, until I reached the old 0-Meridian."

Michael and Arthur understood that Otto was indeed talking about the same hill they had just visited.

"By doing so, I indeed found the right dolmen and I can take you there." said Otto, "but you won't be able to get in."

Arthur was curious, "How did you find Boudet's book?"

"Well, between 1930 and 1933 I used to stay in a hotel in Montségur and the proprietors had a sister who ran a café in Quillan; a town not far from the Rennes valley. She advised me to go up to Rennes-le-Château via Couiza and talk to a woman called Marie Denarnaud, who kindly lent me the book. Regrettably, I never returned it to her."

Arthur and Michael boxed; it all made complete sense to them now. Madame Denarnaud had been the housekeeper of the rich priest; Abbé Béranger Saunière.

Alfred decided that they should still try to get into the tomb, so half an hour later, the three SUV's drove toward the Rennes valley. They parked close to the stone with the dragonflies, crossed the river and marched up the hill, following the huge stone megaliths all the way to the site of the broken tomb. Otto and Arthur were talking all the time, exchanging details of their research, realising that there were indeed many clues and hints - all leading to this exact spot; hints of long ago and hints of not so long ago; hints that wove the web, which for some was a trap and for others a clear path to certain success, but then - when you were on the right co-ordinate - you'd simply reach a dead end, over and over again.

Rahn recalled how he used to explore the woods, caves and castles of the Sabarthès. He had tried to find the Grail cup or whatever Grail treasure there might be, but he had never found anything. Otto chuckled.

"Talking about pressure; I needed to please my superiors and prove that the Grail was indeed hidden there, or I would lose the fee that sustained me. At the time I was still exploring the caves around Tarascon-sur-Ariège, so I thought I'd create a few interesting drawings on a cave wall, take some photographs and send them to Berlin, just to buy some more time, you know? No harm intended, but my friend Joseph was so shocked when he saw me draw on the cave wall that he knocked me out! I even had to go to the hospital!"

Arthur stopped and stared at him in sheer disbelief.

"You made drawings in the caves?!"

Otto smiled sheepishly, amused to see Arthur so shocked.

"Do you know how many people actually believe that they were made by the Cathars?" said Arthur, "They even have initiations and meditations there now!"

Otto laughed. "Oh dear! Well, I'm sure these caves were very important to the Cathars, who used them as hide outs. Besides, I only did it once..."

Then suddenly, Arthur remembered something he had wanted to show Otto. He reached for his bag and took out his map. After folding it into a convenient format, he pointed his finger to a particular location on the map; a site far away from where they were right now.

"Otto, you said that you were trying to find the Grail castle called Mont Salvaesch from the Parsifal story. You see this place? It's called Terre Salvaesch and there is a peculiar table mountain in the middle of it, with ancient remnants of a Celtic-Roman oppidum and ruins from early medieval times. I thought you might find it interesting."

Otto snatched the map from Arthur's hands and stared at it. Then he took out his notepad and wrote 'Opoul-Perillos' on a new blank page and underlined it twice. He returned the map to Arthur and without saying another word, he continued his climb, leaving Arthur completely puzzled; as if Arthur had insulted him. Arthur decided to leave the subject alone.

For now...

In the meantime, Gabby and Bill had stayed behind a bit, so they could talk without being overheard. "What if we get back to the lab in Sion and use the ERFAB to get Danielle back?" Gabby said with a hopeful smile, but Bill pulled a sour face. "If we do that, we may cause a ripple. We mustn't forget that everything is part of a large chain of action and reaction, from extremely small to very big. Also, to pull this off, we will need to know exactly when the original rescue operation took place; the exact co-ordinates; the exact time; I'd need a full report. Of course, I will only be able to get this report from Mr Zinkler. So you see, only if he authorises our plan, we can use the ERFAB to rescue Danielle. However, there will be a change in some of the events that took place *after* the moment we teleport Danielle to the lab in Sion, so I have to think about the risks involved. Be patient; I'll try to talk to Mr Zinkler in private as soon as I get the chance."

Gabby nodded and sighed. Being untrained, she halted for a second and noticed that also Bill was panting. Both of them weren't used to talking and climbing a hill at the same time. However, their slow climb created a growing gap between them and the others and at a certain moment, they had lost sight of the others completely. Gabby stood still. "Shhhh, listen. Where are they?"

There wasn't a sound. Bill sat down on a large, flat rock and moaned. "No idea. Let's wait here until they come back. I'm going no further."

Gabby sat down beside him. It had been a sleepless night and a long day.

The rest of the group had now arrived at the site and Arthur pointed at the cracked stone while looking at Otto with anticipation. Rahn looked at the boy and then at Alfred, who stood next to Arthur with his arms folded, waiting impatiently for Otto to share his story. Alfred hadn't promised him anything solid in return for his information and Otto felt that he was now being pushed into talking; forced to give up the only leverage he had left. He became edgy, but realised he had to give them something.

"Alright, alright, I did it. I cracked the stone. It's an ancient method; Hannibal used it in the Alps when he had to break some rocks to clear a path for his elephants."

"What was inside the tomb?" David asked, almost certain of the answer.

Otto picked his nose. By now, Alfred had nearly lost his patience. "Go on! Tell us!"

Otto cleared his throat and started casually, "Well, I could only just squeeze inside; there was white chalk all over my clothes when I crawled through the passage. I entered a small, low chamber where I could hardly stand up straight. I hacked through what looked like an entrance and discovered another, larger chamber that smelled ghastly; the air was mouldy and humid. Being now almost in the dark, I lit a lamp and then I saw it; a small, stone coffin, like an ossuary, with strange inscriptions carved into the side. I looked inside and discovered a Templar scroll with the seal still intact and a strange object, that I later identified as being a Skandala seal, on which the name and other details - such as the date of birth and passing of the deceased - are inscribed. This is how I could identify the remains."

There was a short pause. Alfred stared angrily at him. "And?"

"Well, guess who? Although on the Skandala seal he is named Amanil bar Zekaryah, we - of course - know him by his Greek name; Jesus. He was the son of the High Priest Zachary. Now we know for sure that Jesus wasn't of the royal house of David, but of the royal house of Hasmon. That sort of shakes things up a bit, doesn't it?"

Otto smiled broadly when he noticed their mute bewilderment. Then, Arthur touched Otto's arm. "Why are you telling this only now? Why did you wait so long? Didn't you trust us?"

Otto pulled his arm back, "No, I didn't trust any of you! I have to be careful with whom I work; what I do; what I say; what I share... You can't blame me for being careful!"

Otto was right. After all it was a good thing that he had kept it quiet. He had already been in Sion, Switzerland the moment the Cardinal had come into the picture. Alfred understood and appreciated his loyalty, but he was getting more nervous by the minute, so he put his hand on Rahn's shoulder and asked the inevitable question.

"... and what did you do *then*?"

Otto cleared his throat. "I took the Templar scroll, the skull, two lower arm bones - with the injuries from the crucifixion still visible - and the Skandola seal, put them in my bag, took it to Germany and gave it to Himmler."

Everyone was shocked and Alfred now lost it completely. "You did what!!!!!"

Alfred turned and ran his hands through his hair in total despair. "... and what did Himmler do with it!?" he queried, fearing the worst.

Otto pursed his lips. "Sorry, I can't tell you. Don't ask me. Please."

Rahn refused to give up all of his leverage. Only when he could stay in 2011, he'd tell Alfred what he wanted to know. Tired and upset about the dramatic turn of a day that started so well, Alfred shook his head and started his descent toward the river. He had to clear his head. Michael and David followed Alfred, but Arthur turned to Rahn with another smart question. "So, the rest is still down there? I mean, the other bones?"

Otto looked at the boy. "Yes, like I said, I only took the skull, some bones, the Templar scroll and the Skandola seal. That's all. The other stuff should still be down there."

"What other stuff, just the rest of the bones, or was there more?" queried Arthur.

"Just… stuff…"

The Swiss was very angry with Otto. To think that Rahn had actually travelled to Germany with the holiest relics of Christianity in his luggage was beyond his comprehension. He had to control himself, but remembered just in time that Otto was, after all, a heretic. Rahn simply saw the mortal remains of Jesus as ordinary human bones.

Arthur followed Rahn closely and when he saw the opportunity for it, he asked him another question. "Otto, did you examine the bones and the skull? Were the remains indeed of a man who had died before the age of 40?"

Otto looked at Arthur and admired his intelligence.

He decided to tease him a little.

"Well, the skull was indeed examined by specialists."

"Well, how old was he when he died?"

Rahn was amused to see the boy so excited and chuckled when Arthur stepped in front of him.

"Tell me, Otto *please!*"

Rahn looked around and saw that they were quite alone. Knowing he could not be overheard, he decided to share it with Arthur. With a solemn smile, he said softly,

"The remains tell us that he was about 70 years old when he died."

23

The Corbières, July 2nd 2011

While walking downhill, Alfred and the team ran into Gabby and Bill, who were still sitting on the large, stone slab. Alfred hadn't even noticed that they weren't at the tomb site and realised how self-focussed he had become. So when Bill asked to sit next to Alfred in the car, he agreed immediately. During the drive back to David's B&B, Bill explained to his chief how he and Gabby had been thinking about retrieving Danielle from underneath Sardis' nose on the exact moment she was rescued, by using the ERFAB. If Alfred could get his hands on the exact time, date and co-ordinate and would give him a small team, he might be able to fetch her back without too many ripples to their present time and future, because it had happened so recently. Alfred listened to Bill silently while nodding and sighing. All the while, Bill could only hope that his chief would grant his request. He himself would risk his life to get Danielle back, because he felt partly responsible for what had happened. However, he didn't realise that his chief felt much worse, because Alfred had been the one who had set the mission up. Therefore, Alfred approved of the plan, relieved to hear that there was still hope for Danielle. Bill was over the moon and wanted to text Gabby, who was in one of the other cars, but Alfred stopped him. "No signals, just in case."

In spite of the fact that they had most likely found the location of the tomb of Jesus and the probable resting place of the Ark of the Covenant, the mission had failed completely. As far as they knew, Danielle was dead, her diary lost and they were unable to get to the desired relics. They knew that they were facing a dangerous enemy and although Sardis was no longer alive, they knew he had a partner and Alfred feared him more than anything.

It was only a short drive back to the B&B. Everyone had turned silent, pondering all they had experienced. David shared a car with Michael and Arthur, while Gabby shared a car with Ben and Yanne. They all needed to write up their reports and download their photos as soon as they got back to the B&B. That evening they took turns on two lap tops and a computer and together they created a new file on their finds. The information and photographs of the locations of Alet-les-Bains, Nôtre Dame de Marceille and the church of Laval were stored and studied and even during the simple dinner that David had cooked, all remained silent. Much depended on their next action, for the next day, they would go back to Switzerland and take a chance with the ERFAB to try and save Danielle from her untimely death.

Jerusalem, Israel, July 4th 2011

Danielle looked out of her bedroom window. The Dome of the Rock was visible from Al Din's villa and unconsciously she compared it to the city she had seen in the 1st century CE. How it had changed. However, the colours were still similar and she could recognise the lay out of the old town; the Temple Mount; the old quarters; the Mount of Olives and far away in the distance, only barely visible, Bethanu.

Her heart longed to go back. It was as if she didn't belong in this time anymore. It surprised her that she was more homesick for ancient Jerusalem than for her own home in the States. In the past few days, Danielle had become stronger, although the soft drugs had erased most of her short term memory. It confused her, as it prevented her from thinking clearly. Once more she was treated like a princess, but this time the oriental way. The beautiful quarters where Danielle was staying were decorated in Arabian style, with many, soft pillows and long, draping curtains, made of the most luxurious and colourful fabrics. The food was delicious; there were nuts, fruit and dates; unleavened flat bread; hot rice dishes and meat, cooked with medium hot spices. The soft, warm air of the Judean summer felt agreeable on her skin when it moved her long, blonde hair, that had been washed, trimmed and curled. Lovely perfumes and soft clothing massaged her senses. Al Din was spoiling her with gifts, jewels and gold and small, carved images of animals. The day before, he had brought her a very beautifully adorned Quran. It being an authorised English translation, she had actually leafed through it, which pleased Izz al Din, for he wanted her to get acquainted with it. He had been the most wonderful; generous; soft and gentle host to her in comparison to his earlier behaviour toward her. As Danielle had given up all hope of ever being rescued, she desperately wanted her son to see life more than anything in the world. Danielle had broken. The thought of one day holding her child in her arms, knowing it had been a gift from the man she had fallen in love with, a man so powerful; so soft; so enigmatic, now gave her a renewed joy of life.

Al Din was both religious and possessive. He had told her that he would take care of her and her son, but he had made no threats. So far, he had never given her the idea that she would be of no more use to him after the birth of her child, like Sardis had done by remaining silent after her question. Aware that she was responding well to his drugs and brainwashing, Al Din started to feel more confident with her now. He noticed how peaceful and relaxed she had become. It seemed as if she had finally accepted her fate and at that very moment, while she looked out of the window over the old town of Jerusalem, she smiled again. It was true; she had found peace.

Danielle had started to call him Aladdin, a nick name that she thought suited him, not just because it sounded like his real name, but also because one lucky day - several years ago - he had suddenly become rich, just like Aladdin in the tales. The man was obviously loaded; the jewellery that he had given her must have cost him a fortune. He had servants who treated Danielle with the utmost respect and he possessed cars; private jets; helicopters and - above all - power. Though he was surrounded by many beautiful women, he now worshipped only Danielle. He had fallen in love with her blonde beauty and uniqueness.

That evening, when Danielle was just about to try one of the specially prepared snacks that had been presented to her on a silver tray, he came to her room. "Is everything to your pleasure, my sweet Dani?"

She smiled at him while he kissed her hand. Danielle found his manners attractive and discovered that she was falling for his charm and posture; after all he was a handsome man. He noticed her smile, the peace inside her mind and the complete surrender to the situation she was in. The drugs she had been given these last few days had worked their magic. Al Din was pleased and decided it was time to make his move.

"I would like to honour you with some music and a light supper. Please, sit; make yourself comfortable."

He clapped his hands twice and without delay, two people arrived with a small harp and a flute, as if they had been waiting outside the door. They probably had. While enjoying the dreamy music and the sweet surprises of their supper, they talked about the world; their lives; their interests; their fascinations and Danielle even told him things she had promised herself never to tell anyone. It aroused him, although it also made him jealous. The thought that he would never be her first lover, annoyed him. Nevertheless, she was so beautiful and pure, especially now, in these wonderful, soft clothes, wearing such a sweet perfume. He touched her arm with his fingers and made her look at him. When Danielle looked deeply in his eyes, he took his chance and kissed her softly on her lips. She didn't resist him and - unaware of who she was actually dealing with - she kissed him back. Al Din reminded himself to reward the magus who had composed the drugs to get these results. She wasn't drowsy, but keen and willing, just like the magus had said she would become. He took advantage of her willingness and went even further. He caressed her soft breasts and then covered her body with his own, slowly spreading her legs with his knees. He penetrated her carefully, not to injure the foetus and decided to be soft and slow. Al Din usually preferred it a lot harder with his other girls and was even

241

feared in his harem for his sometimes violent cravings, but this time he could control himself, for he actually loved Danielle and enjoyed the prolonging of his climax. Also Danielle enjoyed the soft, erotic massage; she did not want him to stop and didn't struggle when he turned her over. Al Din started to kiss her from her shoulders down to her legs before grabbing her hips and penetrating her again, this time a little deeper and increasingly faster when coming close to his climax. Danielle was breathing heavily when he reached the short, rapid thrusts and her arms started to tremble. Then he grabbed her breasts and gently squeezed each nipple between his fingers and thumbs to make her come. It was important for them to come at the same moment; to create the energy flash to which he aspired; the energy that had now come from his toes into his hips, through his spine, stomach and chest, up through his neck and into his head. When he felt his ejaculation, he made an uncontrollable, deep, low groaning sound; like a predator eating his prey. Danielle moaned; also she had reached her climax at the exact same moment. Exhausted they fell into the pillows, deeply satisfied. The bond between them had become stronger.

Until this moment, his plans to introduce Islam to the Christian world and persuade millions to join his religious convictions had been his obsession, but now, his heart was devoted to Danielle. He stared at her for a while, but knowing she needed her rest, he left her, deeply asleep.

The next day, Al Din enjoyed his conversations with Danielle when he tried to explain the teachings of the Holy Quran; teachings that give order to the society and strengthen the bond between men and Allah. He spoke about Abraham being the Patriarch of the Jews, Christians and Muslims; how the Quran also speaks of Jesus, or Isa - describing him as an important prophet and how these three religions have so much in common. The Prophet Mohammed - peace be upon him - had come centuries later as the last prophet to bring one more time the Divine Message to the people.

All three religions announce the existence of only one God and several religious verses were even similar, just different in their wording. Besides, God responds to needs, not names. With great enthusiasm, Al Din spoke about uniting the pearls of these religions in order to create wholeness, tolerance and world peace. He told her that it was necessary to discourage extremism, because extremism caused hatred, intolerance and violence and Allah doesn't want us to hate, but to love each other.

"You see, each of us has his or her own path to follow on the ladder of the evolution of the soul. The more love you possess, the closer you are to Allah. The more hate you possess, the further away you are from Allah."

Danielle smiled in agreement. She sat at his feet and listened to his words like she had listened to Oshu; always eager to learn.

"In all societies it is the conduct of the people that determines the happiness of a community. It isn't about the choice of religion, but about conduct; the way of life and the union with Allah, in order to do what Allah wants us to do: evolve and live according to his Divine Plan."

"Is there a way to discover the roots of our religions, to be able to make some sense of it, for all believers?" Danielle asked.

Al Din smiled. Danielle had a gift for true understanding.

"Of course this goes a lot deeper than the religions that were formed during these past millennia. Religions are man-made vehicles to support a thought; a philosophy; a divine message, but unfortunately it has also become mixed with politics. Although both religion and politics deal with conduct and behaviour, only religion deals with philosophy and we can only thank all the prophets and avatars for sharing their visions and philosophies with us. Depending on the level of our own individual soul growth, we can either choose to follow one religion, or choose the pearls from *more* than just one religion. When the path of your soul does not match the philosophy of the religion you were born into, we must have the freedom to unbind ourselves. God gave us freedom of choice to grow and evolve and it was never meant for us to impose a certain religion onto others, like the Christians and Muslims have done during the Middle Ages."

It had always been Al Din's conviction that people should invited to embrace Islam, not forced and he hoped that one day, Islam would be modernised into a powerful philosophy and way of life, becoming global through the choice of the world, rather than a religion that forces itself upon it.

"Force disturbs peace and balance and as the world is turning on a fragile Cosmic Balance, chaos, violence and hatred must be avoided at all cost."

Again, Danielle agreed with what he said. She didn't know, however, that it was all self-preservation that had made him search for a solution in the east-west matter, so that he could sleep again, not lying awake worrying about losing money in world trade disruptions caused by the pressures between the super powers; pressures caused by religious differences and conflicts, which had alarmingly increased after the 9-11 disaster.

Danielle, who had leafed through the Quran, had also noticed some harsh words in the Holy Book and queried, "There is something I need to ask you, Aladdin. I am disturbed by the beating of women and the way Muslims treat their wives, sisters, daughters and mothers. I have read some things in the Quran that I cannot agree with, for I believe that man and women were created equal."

Al Din pursed his lips. "Sweet Dani, in your Bible it is said that women have to be stoned to death when they commit adultery."

Danielle raised her voice, "In the New Testament of that same Bible, Jesus protested against those old values by protecting women from unfair penalties and by treating them as equals. We've grown since the Exodus, you know!"

Al Din smiled. "Of course! All this was written down millennia ago, in another world, another era. Most Christians and Jews behave differently today because they have learned to pick from their Holy Book what they need for inspiration; that which is fitting for *this* era of mankind. These people are smart enough to realise that these ancient laws no longer apply to our modern world and so must we, Muslims, also learn to separate ancient laws from the laws and needs of this century and recognise the equality of men and women."

"Perhaps it's more about the difference between cultures, rather than the difference between religions?" Danielle suggested.

Al Din smiled. Again she had hit the nail on the head.

"Of course, the cultures of the desert - of the orient - are different from the cultures of the west and as a consequence, religious laws are also different. Perhaps now the time is right to introduce an esoteric, global, holistic religion, rather than the one culture-and-society based exoteric religion and that, sweet Dani, has been my plan all along."

Danielle sat back and watched this man, who had become increasingly important in her life. In a certain way he reminded her of Oshu, but Danielle had a gut feeling that she should keep her wits about her. Unlike Al Din, Oshu was a freethinker. He had taught her the Hermetic Teachings that rise above religion, society, law and culture.

It concentrates on the way of life.

It concentrates on the bonding with the God of your heart.

It concentrates on seeking a way through life spreading light, love and wisdom.

It concentrates on the evolution of the human soul.

To blossom like the lotus through mud and water into the light.

To blossom like the lily through mud and water into the light.

To blossom like a rose on the crossing point of spirit and matter.

To give inspiration to others who are on that Path.

To study nature and yourself, because it was written;

> *'Know thyself and thou shalt know*
> *the Universe and the Gods'.*

It had been the language of the Greek philosophers who had inspired Jesus, but also the pearls from both Hindu and Buddhist teachings that Jesus had studied in India, as well as the Egyptian Mysteries he had studied while he was in Egypt. Jesus had taken the pearls from all of these oysters and had developed one new Way of Life according to his philosophies. He had considered it his mission to introduce this Way of Life to the people of Palestine who had been subdued by ancient rigid laws and he had kept on walking his Path of Love and Forgiveness, even after he had been captured and tortured.

How Danielle longed to see him again and how she longed to see the Magdalen again, but she knew that this would never be possible now. Her friends will believe that she is dead and they will have given up on her by now.

Then, suddenly, she remembered the ERFAB.

Would they...

Her heart leaped. Al Din noticed the sudden change in her face and eyes. "What is it, Dani? What are you thinking of?"

Danielle shook her head and smiled. "Nothing, sweet Aladdin, nothing. These discussions we are having are so refreshing. It helps me understand many things. Thank you! For your kindness, your time and your care."

Al Din kissed her on the forehead and said his goodbyes. His helicopter was standing by to take him to distant shores that very evening. He had to get back to his usual business; making as much money as possible - and at all cost. Al Din was, above all, a man with two faces. How strange are the dual interests and split personalities of certain people; how narrow-minded the individual, selfish ways of mankind.

24

The Corbières, southern France, July 3rd 2011

It had been a windy and sleepless night, but at 07.00 hours, Bill, Gabby and Alfred were already packing in a hurry. Though it was hard for the team to break up the camp after their failed mission, they needed to get back to Sion as soon as possible to start the ERFAB rescue mission. The night before, Alfred had already asked his SBS rescue team for a detailed report on July 1st; the day his agents had rescued Danielle from the Cardinal, so now he knew the exact time and co-ordinates and could set up a plan together with the professor. He hoped that they could do it without causing any more disturbances to their present than absolutely necessary, all in all it would be a dangerous operation. One couldn't possibly know what a single ripple could cause in their space-time continuum. One error in their calculations and the rescue team could arrive in the middle of the shooting. Bill knew he had to make his calculations with the utmost care and felt the heavy weight of this responsibility almost physically, but along with Alfred, also Gabby showed complete confidence in him. Gabby had become a close friend over the past few days and this friendship had given them both new energy.

Otto, on the other hand, had a good reason for *not* wanting to go back to the lab in Switzerland, because he didn't know how much longer Alfred would need him now. If Alfred still sends him back to 1939 - which Alfred had told him was inevitable - he would be in the same hopeless situation as before, even if he had the promised false passport. He wanted to stay in this era, but he had no identity; no passport; no social security number. According to the outside world, Rahn didn't exist in 2011. He walked around in a world that he wasn't supposed to see; a world that wasn't supposed to see *him*, but then he had come across something on the Internet; information that had given him new hope. All he had to do was to tag along and wait for the right time to escape.

The kids had decided to stay with David and enjoy their summer vacation in the Corbières, as planned, but first, Alfred insisted they signed a contract of silence. They were not to talk to anyone about what they had learnt, or share anything about these past few days with anyone, ever. Knowing that it would be difficult for Arthur to keep quiet, Alfred looked deep into the boy's eyes before they parted. "Don't mess things up! Keep your head clear and your mouth shut, you understand?"

Arthur nodded, realising that Alfred was dead serious and respectfully confirmed, "I promise!"

It was strange to wave at the tinted windows of the three black SUV's driving off, unable to see if anyone waved back. David had followed the cars to the gate and took the *complet/full* sign off; life could now return to normal. However, life itself would never be the same again. On his way back from the gate, David passed Ben and Yanne, who were going for a walk to clear their heads. They told David that Arthur had gone back to his tent. The boy was exhausted, for he hadn't slept for several nights, but he was also very melancholic, for he knew he'd probably never see his hero ever again.

David looked around and noticed the sudden silence on his estate. Then he spotted Michael, waiting patiently for him at the parking and somehow, words had become unimportant. They both knew that they had been part of an adventure that could have gone very wrong. David hopped inside for a moment to fetch his pipe and over the next hour, father and son both sat on the veranda, staring at the hills; the trees; the butterflies and the birds, while David smoked his pipe.

It was quiet. Deliciously quiet.

Sion, Switzerland, July 4th 2011

In the morning of July 4th, the SBS-Sion team, consisting of Alfred, Otto, Gabby, Bill and their agents, arrived in Sion. They unpacked and headed straight for their quarters to get some rest. Otto had niddle-noddled during the entire trip, but was very awake now and decided to do some more exploring on the Internet, accompanied by a hot cup of tea, a pen and a paper notepad. His head was spinning. Coming from the 1930s, Rahn had left a very complicated world. On one side it had been full of tough discipline; order; obedience; fear and terror, while on the other hand it had been the world of Grail expeditions; journeys into the unknown; exploring myths and legends and going on beautiful hikes through glorious, mountainous landscapes. Still, it had been the world in which he had felt the depressing reality of seeing his own country turn into a Nazi horror state - run by powers he could no longer accept - as well as his inability to escape from that world. After seeing web page after web page on the Internet about the horrors of WWII, he began to think about the ERFAB. Why couldn't they use the time machine to undo this part of history? Send a sniper in, kill Hitler and get back. The world would be a different place, indeed.

However, in what way would it be different?

Would other powerful men have tried instead?

Would something worse have taken its place?

He understood that it wasn't that simple. It wouldn't be a light decision to change something that huge, as this would surely cause billions and billions of ripples. Perhaps the entire frame of the world would collapse in the attempt alone. He chuckled. Perhaps not, but he simply *had* to discuss his future with Alfred as soon as he could. If there was one particular thing Otto desperately wanted to prevent, it would be his return to 1939, to the place where Alfred had picked him up. They owed him a new life. It's true, Otto had done some deeds he regretted; it ate his conscience and his soul. After all, he had had no choice but to follow orders in the concentration camps of Dachau and Buchenwald; he had been forced to shadow friends and to share his research, material that - as he had now discovered - would later inspire racist thoughts. He had joined the SS, had to have sex with a woman to keep up his appearance as a hetero and had worked for the Ahnenerbe and Himmler with complete loyalty.

The memories made him shiver. He could still hear Himmler's hoarse, high voice; see his small, piercing eyes behind his round, frameless glasses and hear him laughing at everyone and everything. Even at death. Power seemed to have that effect on people...

The only moments he had truly felt alive was during his travels abroad. It had allowed him to escape the reality of the Nazi world. Otto rubbed his face. There *must* be a way to live *somewhere*, but not there, not then. Suddenly, a thought entered his mind. Carefully he typed several keywords into his Google search engine and when he saw the links appearing on the screen, a smile formed on one side of his face. There really *was* a way...

Gabby and Bill had met up with Alfred after lunchtime and were now making preparations for the rescue mission. Bill had just set his time machine and the portal control to a well calculated code. The next moment, three men in black clothes and with black face covers entered the lab, fully armed. It was an impressive sight and Gabby had high hopes that they would return soon with Danielle. She kept her fingers crossed while saying countless short prayers. While Alfred briefed the armed men - making sure they knew their orders well - Bill made the final checks on the computer. All was set and everyone was ready, but the sweat on their brows betrayed their anxiety. Everything could go wrong, but they had to have faith in themselves.

Alfred nodded. It was now or never.

First, a note to 'stand down' was sent back in time to the original rescue team that had gone to Sardis' house on July 1st. As soon as this was done, the new rescue team was taken to the ERFAB cabin where the wormhole would establish. Bill stood behind the control panel of the computer and pressed the main key to engage. Seeing the wormhole suck up the men was a strange sight to witness and Gabby now understood why she had been so sick. The image of the three men became distorted - as if morphed in Photoshop - when they were literally sucked into a void. Bill seemed calm enough; after all, he had seen this before when she and Danielle had gone through. Gabby looked at the clock; it was now only a matter of time. In exactly 10 minutes, at 14.20 hrs., the men would be sucked back into the present with Danielle. That is, if all goes well on the other end of the wormhole.

Rome, Italy, July 1st 2011

Sardis was still working in his office. He had already prepared a marketing strategy. It only needed perfecting and he couldn't sleep until that was done. The phone rang; a classical ring, coming from an old model that fitted into the somewhat baroque character of his office. The Cardinal picked up with a tired voice, "Pronto?"

Suddenly, his eyes opened wide. With trembling voice he replied, "… but if these men are not ours, then who are they, what are they doing here?"

A moment later - slowly, as if in shock - he put down the phone. He stared at the door, listening for sounds and when he heard nothing, he got up and walked toward the window, hiding behind the curtain, making sure he wasn't seen. When he saw nothing, he walked toward another window. Still, nothing. The Cardinal - now in a hurry - briskly walked out of his office to check on Danielle. When he saw that she wasn't in her bed, a jolt stabbed his stomach and he panicked, fearing she had escaped. The Cardinal ran out and into the hallway to search for her, but he couldn't find her anywhere in the building. Everywhere he went he shouted for assistance, but as it was after midnight, only one guard responded to his calls; the same guard who had phoned earlier to warn him about the intruders. Sardis was upset to find out that the building was so badly guarded at night, but then remembered it had been he himself who had thought that one guard would be sufficient. After all, Danielle's apartment was hermetically sealed from the outside world and his office and bedroom were just one door away.

Never had he expected that this location could so easily be discovered. Sardis leaned against a wall - breathless from running through the building - and closed his eyes to clear his mind. He needed to make an assessment of the situation in order to take accurate action. Knowing that he now needed all the assistance he could get to search for Danielle and defend himself against his opponents, he took out his mobile from his soutane to call the other guards, who were all asleep in their own homes. The Cardinal's mission now depended on their speed of action.

Danielle, who had no idea that Sardis thought she'd gone missing, had refreshed herself in the bathroom, the one place the Cardinal hadn't looked. After her prayer she admittedly felt a little bit better, so she had brushed her teeth and now only wanted to go back to bed. She hadn't even noticed that her front door had been left wide open, until she was already in bed. At first she thought that she had forgotten to turn off the light in the bathroom, but then it became clear that the inflowing light was coming from the hallway.

The door was open!

Making use of the adrenaline rush, she quickly got dressed, knowing she had to be very careful and quiet as a mouse.

It was now or never.

Sardis was getting more upset by the second. As he was running from one place to another, shouting orders and Danielle's name, he began to understand that he had probably lost his prize and that would be the end of everything. The end of his dream. The Cardinal almost lost his mind just thinking about it. Then suddenly, the front door opened. Sardis had half-expected to see the extra guards he had called for, but instead, these men were dressed in black, wearing black face covers and fully armed. Sardis didn't know exactly what was going on, but he realised that the game was over and ran back upstairs in search of a hiding place. However, the 'men in black' had no idea that they had been spotted by the guards who had sped over to Sardis' house. The Cardinal's guards immediately took action.

A well-aimed shot was fired and one of the men in black fell down dead. This was getting serious. The other agents - now fully realising the danger of their mission - raced through the house in search for Danielle, knowing they didn't have a minute to loose.

The gunshot had startled Danielle and she just stood there, frozen in the middle of the hallway, not knowing where to go next. The sound of the shot had clearly come from the ground floor, so she could no longer go downstairs toward the exit. Instead of running, Danielle decided to look for a place to hide. This was her only option, for she could certainly not stay where she was or go back to her room. Danielle walked further into the hallway and noticed the open door to Sardis' office. She entered the room and closed the door behind her. At the other end of the room she saw a large, wooden sliding door and wondered if there'd be enough space behind it for her to hide behind. Trying not to make a sound, she anxiously opened the large sliding door, only to find out that it was just another book case. In a state of panic, she now desperately searched for a new place to hide. Another couple of shots rang out and she could hear men shouting in Italian, running up the stairway. Quickly she jumped behind the large oaken desk and made herself as small as humanly possible, hardly daring to breath. She saw how Sardis was running through the corridor. One of the men in black grabbed Sardis and hit him hard on the head. Another agent ran into the office and found Danielle hiding behind the desk. He pulled her out and shouted, "Move! Move! We have little time!" However, Danielle broke free from his grip and yelled, "My diary! I'm not leaving without my diary!" She looked around the room, but when she couldn't find it, she panicked. Then suddenly she saw it on a chest near the fireplace. While running toward the fireplace she could hear the 'beep - beep - beep' warning signal she recognised as the ERFAB mobile signal to get back into position.

They were using the time machine!

There were only seconds left now.

The two men from the rescue team ran back to the hallway, shouting at Danielle to run after them. Danielle grabbed the diary and ran as fast as she could, but when she came into the hallway, she was just in time to see the anomaly of the morphed men in black, teleporting out.

She was too late.

In one final attempt to catch up with them, she jumped into the morphed vision shouting 'Geronimo!'

Sion, Switzerland, July 4th 2011

Everyone at the lab was alarmed when they noticed how only two agents materialised in the ERFAB cabin, but they froze in utter horror when - a moment later - they heard an awful, eerie scream and witnessed a strange image morphing into a human shape. A few seconds later, Danielle banged hard against the cabin wall while screaming her lungs out.

"Jesus!" she said with a hoarse voice. "Remind me to *never, ever* scream again when I am time travelling!"

The moment Danielle had appeared, everyone had felt a strange, electric shock and suddenly they had no idea why they were there or how they had been able to retrieve her, because the entire rescue mission had now seized to exist. Nevertheless, the reaction ruled the action and Danielle's return was celebrated by all. As if skipping places on a game board, Danielle had just jumped ahead four days in time; a bizarre experience, knowing that the past few days had never happened - at least for Danielle they hadn't. The ripple caused by the interference had changed the present; Sardis was now still alive; there had been no abduction by Izz al Din in Lausanne; Dr Days never died in a car bomb explosion and also; the time Danielle had spent at Al Din's villa in Jerusalem had never happened either. On her Birthday, Danielle would be four days younger now - physically - which resulted in a strange, hollow sensation. These four days of her life had evaporated into thin air in the physical memory of her brains. However, Danielle's soul - which didn't depend on time, space or matter - had stored each second and each detail in a subconscious *akashan* memory that goes far beyond any physical memory.

Because Danielle had never heard of Otto Rahn before, he had much to tell her, but conveniently left out some less 'interesting' facts, like Dachau and Buchenwald. However, during this conversation, she suddenly became very pale. Immediately, Alfred jumped to her side. Danielle explained how she had been sick a lot and told them of the pains in her lower belly. As Alfred didn't want to risk anything, he called the clinic and asked for a physician to come over as soon as possible. Everyone was afraid for Danielle and her unborn child; a child that - one day - could change the world.

After dinner - when Gabby and Danielle were sitting side by side on Danielle's bed, waiting for the doctor to arrive - Gabby put her arm around Danielle. How they had missed each other. Gabby had already told her everything about their adventures in southern France; how they had found the possible hiding place of the Ark of the Covenant; how Otto had brought them to the dolmen tomb where Oshu's remains had been hidden and how they had failed to retrieve the relics. It was strange for Danielle to hear Gabby say, 'Oshu's remains'. He had, indeed, been dead for almost 2000 years, a harsh fact that both women could barely comprehend, but Danielle's heart felt as if he was *so* close; as if he was still with her. It made her determined. "Gabby, I want to go back. I want to see Oshu and stay with him."

Gabby smiled. This was exactly what she, too, wanted more than anything. Gabby didn't care about the fact that Oshu only had eyes for Danielle; just being in his company would be enough for her. "I have no idea what Alfred's plans are, Danielle, but know that you are safe here now and that the Organisation; Alfred, Bill and I, will always protect you."

That moment, the physician arrived and Gabby left to give her friend some privacy with the Doctor, but a moment later she wished she hadn't, although Gabby could have never known that the doctor wasn't what he pretended to be.

However, Danielle - or rather; her soul - recognised him immediately. Al Din was all dressed up like a Doctor - complete with bag; equipment; a brilliantly faked pass and identification. Before she could make a move, Al Din put his hand over her mouth and injected her with a sedative. Immediately she fell into his arms, fully unconscious and while acting like an alarmed doctor, he carried her out. "Make way, I need to get her to a hospital. Quickly, let me through!"

Al Din thought it would work perfectly; he would be able to carry her out and into his 'borrowed' medical car, straight to a nearby airfield, where his helicopter was already waiting. However, the syringe he had used was still sticking out of his chest pocket.

Gabby, who was shocked to see that Danielle had fainted, spotted the syringe sticking out of the doctor's pocket and became suspicious. She immediately blocked the doorway, which irritated the already uptight Al Din. "Get out of the way woman, can't you see this is a matter of life and death?"

Gabby didn't move and cried out for assistance, which quickly arrived. Gabby turned to the agent, "Take us to Alfred, Danielle is not leaving my side ever again!"

Having no choice but to accept the escort, Al Din carried Danielle to the lab. Alfred was shocked to see Danielle in the arms of the doctor, who now started to shout at him, still acting like a worried doctor. "I demand that you take me to my car, she needs to go to a hospital immediately!"

In his anger, Al Din betrayed his Arabic accent.

Alfred became suspicious. "Who are you?"

"I am doctor Zeiger, haven't you just checked me out, man?"

Having observed the situation, Otto volunteered to take Danielle from him, but Al Din took a step back. He lowered Danielle until he could hold her in one arm and quickly produced the hypodermic syringe from his chest pocket. When he pointed the needle at the artery at the left side of her neck, all froze, but at this point, Obersturmführer Rahn was about to prove his worth.

Trained to react quickly at Buchenwald, he shot his arm around Al Din's neck, pushed his knee in his back and squeezed so hard that it took the Arab's breath away. Within seconds, Al Din dropped everything, collapsed and fell to the floor. However, Danielle fell too. Now completely lame from the injected drug, she fell hard on the concrete floor. While three agents scotched Al Din, Alfred carried Danielle to her quarters, with Gabby immediately behind him. Alfred suspected that this might very well be Sardis' partner and before he left the lab, he turned to his men and commanded, "Lock him up! ... and have every room checked for bugs!"

Alfred understood that it was now becoming too dangerous to get help from the outside world. He felt he was being watched. Immediately, all phones, machines and rooms were checked on bugs; little microphones and cameras that were installed by either Sardis or his partner to keep an eye on the goings on in the lab.

Indeed they were found. All over the building.

Alfred realised that it could have only been Ms Kaiser who had had the opportunity to plant them everywhere while working in the lab as Bill's assistant. Clever Gabby; if it hadn't been for her gut feeling and sharp eyes, Danielle could have been lost to them forever.

Poor Danielle was out cold and they all knew it would be better to let the drug work its way, rather than to wake her up too quickly, especially because she had fallen on the floor and had hit her head. However, waiting for her to gain consciousness was a stressful time. Alfred regularly checked the reaction of her pupils to a flashlight, but the response was normal. Also, her breathing was steady and her blood pressure was normal. He was sure that it was only a matter of time before she would wake up. He wished he could get her to the hospital, but he knew that they were trapped; the risk of being followed and caught while driving to the hospital was too great. For now, they were prisoners inside their own building.

They didn't even dare call the hospital, not knowing whether that phone call would cause more problems, so Alfred decided to search the Internet to find more information on difficult 1st trimester pregnancies. All he could find was 'rest' and 'create a healthy sleep and food pattern'. So they let her sleep. In the meantime, they were on high alert and everyone was screened, over and over again, until Alfred was finally satisfied that all his personnel checked out.

Now picking up where they had left, Alfred asked the professor to perfect the probe and consider starting new missions to ancient Judea to continue their research and collect material evidence from the 1st century CE.

Accompanied by Georg and a fresh pot of coffee, Alfred sat down in his office where they began studying Danielle's diary thoroughly, for they all understood that there was much to discover, still.

In the meantime, 500 meters away from the lab, in a dark, underground containment cell, Al Din was still shaking from his encounter with Rahn. He had never seen anyone react so quickly. Why hadn't he broken his neck? Or his back? He could have! Easily! Al Din was furious that his attempt to kidnap Danielle had failed. When Danielle had disappeared from Sardis' house in Rome four days earlier, he had already expected the Organisation to be behind it and that she'd be back in Switzerland, so already the next day he had taken up position in Sion, waiting for the right opportunity to arise. As Ms Kaiser had already planted cameras and microphones all over the lab in Sion in the early stages - even in their mobile phones - he knew that Danielle had safely returned to the lab that afternoon. The moment Alfred had made his phone call to the clinic, the outgoing call had been rerouted to Al Din's phone. Together with his team, he had created the false ID to enter the base undetected, acting as if he were the physician Alfred had called for. Everything had been planned in such detail. He cursed in Arabic.

It could have worked!

However, he was fascinated with Rahn.

The discipline, incredible! He should be on my side!

Still, first he had to find a way to escape. He knew he had a strong team waiting for him outside, so he took a good look at his cell. It was all solid concrete and steel. The door was locked; there were no windows; there was no daylight and apart from the hard bed he sat on, there was only a small stainless steel basin and a toilet. He rubbed his face and moaned. It was impossible to break out of there. He sat down and felt how his back still ached from the impact of Otto's knee. He had come so close.

Rome, Italy, July 1st 2011

Sardis woke up with a fierce headache, noticing he was still lying on the floor in the hallway. He had been hit on the head during the attack and had lost his zucchetto somewhere in the building. Sardis was all alone, except for five dead bodies further down the hallway - four of whom were his own guards. While trying to get up, he tried to remember what had happened. Dizzy, he hobbled into his office, where his fears were quickly confirmed; the diary was gone and so was Danielle. Then he felt something warm trickling down his face. It was blood, flowing from his head wound. Sardis walked over to the nearest bathroom to clean himself up. Carefully dabbing the wound with a paper towel, he looked into the mirror and saw a pale face staring back at him. How he had underestimated the Organisation. Cursing his arrogance, he realised that they could have easily killed him, but they hadn't. Still, he felt terribly weak and his hand automatically went to another strange, painful spot in the middle of his forehead, right above his eyes. He half-expected to see another wound, but when he looked in the mirror there was nothing to see.

How strange...

The Cardinal sat down behind his desk. He had to think of a new plan now; how to get Danielle back and how to retrieve her diary.

Would he behave himself like a true hunter, waiting for his prey to come out by itself? Why not? He thought of Al Din. The Arab would be very displeased with the current situation, but he decided to contact him anyway. The very least Al Din could do for him was to get rid of the dead bodies in the hallway and replace his guards. After all, he himself had to act as if nothing had happened and continue his ecclesiastic duties. Although the Vatican had no idea what the Cardinal had been up to, he was still a Prince of Rome and until he came up with a new plan, he'd better act like one.

25

Sion, Switzerland, July 4th 2011

Alfred felt as if he was back at square one. He had set up the entire operation several months ago, only to find out that the Ark was impossible to retrieve from underneath tons of rubble; that Otto clearly didn't want to co-operate in retrieving the remains of Jesus and that the expeditions to ancient Judea had come to a temporary halt, with Danielle still recovering from her trauma; the injuries of her fall and the unstable pregnancy. Gabby, naturally, wouldn't leave her side. Although their biggest enemy, Al Din, had been captured and imprisoned below in the basement containment cell, Sardis was still out there and they had to be careful. So when the crew reported to Alfred that the building was now safe and that there were no more bugs, he breathed out. He could now concentrate on sending the probe to the 1st century CE, for he didn't want to give up. Alfred wanted to collect more evidence of specific historical happenings, to slowly lead the world into a new age; the age of tolerance; understanding; oneness and peace.

That evening, Alfred had arranged a meeting with Bill and Otto; maybe together they could come up with a plan to continue their investigations into the mysteries of the first century. Perhaps he could finally persuade Rahn to share with him what Himmler had done with the bones, that were so important to his mission.

During this meeting, the professor tried to explain the limitations of the probe, "So you see, a probe doesn't move; it stays at one spot and collects the image from that co-ordinate. It can't be put into a house, because it will attract attention; it cannot follow a person on the street; it cannot converse in ancient Greek, like Danielle."

"I will go…"

All turned. A pale Danielle stood leaning in the doorway, eavesdropping on the meeting with Gabby right behind her.

"No Danielle," said Alfred resolutely, "you must rest and heal before you can even think about this!"

Danielle smiled. "Don't you see? If anyone can heal… it is him…"

They all understood what she meant. Hit by a sudden brainwave, Otto got up from his seat. "Is there any chance I can come with them, to protect them?"

Alfred shook his head. "No Otto, we need you here, I'm sorry."

He wouldn't think of letting Otto loose in such a fragile situation. Besides, he needed to talk him into sharing his knowledge on the whereabouts of Jesus' remains. Alfred needed Otto here, at his side, but Otto walked over to him and looked at his chief; his rescuer, with eyes that betrayed his fears. "Please, Fred?" he begged, holding up his folded hands. However, Alfred was relentless. "No Otto, I cannot do that. Trust me, I cannot."

Otto lowered his arms, turned and walked away. He could understand Alfred, but he felt a deep disappointment, missing out on meeting the one person he believed capable of absolving him for what he had done; for the deed that was eating his soul. Rahn now needed some time alone and refused to respond when Alfred called him back.

"Let him go, Alfred." sighed Bill. "You don't know what is eating him up. He needs some time alone. I will try to talk to him later."

Alfred stood upright and raised his voice. "*I* don't know what is eating him up? Please Bill… who do you think I am?"

Bill stared at Alfred, realising that neither of them really knew their chief at all. "I don't know, sir. You tell us: *who* are you?"

Alfred looked at Bill and then at Danielle and Gabby. They were not just his employees anymore; they had become friends and he had to be frank with them. If he couldn't trust them now, then when could he? Perhaps it was time for him to tell them everything.

He walked to the door and ordered one of the guards to bring Rahn back to the meeting table. It was time for a *real* meeting; open and honest.

Rome, Italy, July 4th 2011

Several days had passed since the rescue mission and the Cardinal was still fast asleep when a visitor was announced, who wouldn't wait. The Cardinal had been suffering from a severe headache ever since the attack, so he needed his time to get dressed in his soutane. When he finally entered his office, he saw Ms Kaiser behind his desk, snooping through his things.

"Excuse me?" he said, completely overwhelmed by the sight.

"Antonio, we are in trouble. They have Danielle, the diary *and* Al Din!"

Kaiser was furious. Having lost her true master, Al Din, she now had no other choice but to seek out the help from his 'partner', the man she was now beginning to find irritably soft. Knowing that also Sardis feared Al Din, she hoped that the Cardinal would still help her. After all, Al Din had followed his own agenda and Sardis had found out soon enough that he had become his puppet rather than his partner in this great mission. The Cardinal had become distrustful and now seemed extremely weak. Ms Kaiser looked at him and noticed to her horror the relief on the Cardinal's face when her message hit home.

Al Din is a prisoner of SBS-Sion!

"Oh, is he now? … but what can I do about it?" Sardis asked, suppressing a smile. Kaiser couldn't believe his cowardice.

"You have to go back for him! Use your power, your status!" she shouted, but the Cardinal shook his head. He turned toward the window. "I can't go back there. They will take me too!"

Kaiser spit when she snapped at him, "Of course not! You are an untouchable! They cannot just arrest or abduct a Cardinal!"

"Yes they can, Elsa. I have kept my mission a secret from the Vatican, they know nothing of my actions and I have to continue my normal duties or they will become suspicious. I'll have to wait for the right moment, the right opportunity, but right now, I need to rest and think."

Kaiser was disappointed in him. "Then I shall have to find someone else to free my master!" she declared.

Sardis frowned. *Her master...?* It finally dawned on the Cardinal where Kaiser's allegiance really lies. Kaiser walked out and angrily banged the door shut.

For a while, Sardis just sat there, staring at the closed door. Then he picked up the phone and dialled a number. Inside the dossier that Ms Kaiser had left on his desk, he found her reports on the SBS-Sion expeditions in the south of France. From their base camp in the Corbières, the teams had explored the entire area and all the sites that Sardis had asked them to visit. Although they had found an important co-ordinate, they hadn't been able to recover the Ark. They seemed to have given up and gone back to Sion, Switzerland.

Sardis assessed the situation; Danielle was back in Sion and Al Din was now no longer a concern. Slowly, a smile formed on his pale face. A voice on the other end of the line startled him. "What can I do for you, your eminence?"

Sardis now knew exactly what to do. "I am going on a trip. Prepare a car; my jet; my luggage and arrange an accommodation. I want to leave in two hours."

"Yes, your eminence. What is the destination?"

"Sion, Switzerland."

Sion, Switzerland, July 4th 2011

There was a deafening silence in the meeting room at Sion base. It was getting late and they were all tired. Gabby, Danielle, Otto and Bill were sitting around the table, looking at their chief and none of them felt very comfortable.

What was Alfred's secret? Who was this man, really?

Suddenly, as if he wanted to get it over with, Alfred got up, took a deep breath and started,

"First, I would like to apologise. My personal agenda has risked the safety and even the lives of each of you, but there is much at stake, so please, hear me out."

Alfred sat down again. He rested his lower arms on the table and folded his hands as if in silent prayer. His face betrayed sorrow and regret, but also determination.

"I am the grandmaster of a grand, mystical order and the heir of Hugues de Payens, the first grandmaster of the Knights Templar. I am also clairvoyant, but that doesn't mean I can see everything. When I was younger, I had many visions of the future. I saw horrible disasters; chaos; hatred; wars; violence… It was disturbing. I called it 'The Wave'. Somehow I knew I had to do my part to find a way to keep this next Wave from destroying mankind."

Gabby and Danielle looked at each other.

What on earth was he talking about?

"I knew that there was only one way to stop this and this is exactly what I have been trying to achieve with this mission from the very start. I want to create a lasting peace by setting straight the lies that have made humanity so stubborn. The entire world is eaten up by religious and cultural differences, creating racism, hatred and intolerance."

He sighed as if he could sense the negative energies of the world and continued with a soft voice,

"I must admit that I was lured by the thought to use the ERFAB to change history, to take out the elements that had made each Wave so destructive, but when I meditated on this, I knew this could never work. I don't expect you to understand this, but there is a certain force pattern attached to the past which doesn't *want* to be changed. It is connected to things we cannot possibly comprehend. There are regular Waves, which create good times and bad times; chaos and order; ups and downs. If I were to take out one bad historical tragedy, another one would happen to take its place. This is a result of a more or less magnetic, Cosmic balance. It has always been our free will to respond to it either correctly, or incorrectly. Every tragic historic moment has had its reasons, its response and its healing. It would not be wise to try and change it, because it would simply be replaced by another tragedy, or, it would erase the good Wave that had automatically followed the bad Wave; for if you take away the action, you also take away the reaction. Therefore, I started to focus on the future; on playing the Wave that has not yet come to pass. However, I found out that even *that* would be impossible, simply because the irreversible Divine Order demands that there can only be an physical reaction to a metaphysical action. As above, so below."

"Then I had an inspiration: as below, so above! To anticipate and change the reaction before the action; to avoid future human tragedy by learning how to respond properly to the next Wave. The biggest reason for human suffering at this moment is the threat of violence from intolerant behaviour, such as extremism. However, extremists are themselves victims, because they misunderstand the Divine Message; God does not crave violence; destruction; hatred; slaughter or war. These brainwashed people - who do their merciless deeds in the name of a God they do not understand - bring shame upon God's high expectations of mankind."

Rahn looked at Alfred; they have had these discussions before, but never had Alfred been so clear about something that had gone through his own mind so many times. He seemed to run into people like Alfred all the time. Unconsciously his mind went to another person who had claimed to be a descendent of Hugues de Payens; his dear friend, the countess Pujol-Murat, with whom he had spent many hours when he was doing research in southern France. He regretted losing her as a friend when he became absorbed by Hitler's Germany in 1933. He shivered while thinking about it, knowing that this had been one giant Wave indeed and he was glad to be in this present time, with a United Europe and United Nations, something he had always thought would never happen. However, Alfred's speech did not only inspire him, it also worried him. Suddenly, he grabbed his friend's arm and asked, "So, Fred, if I understand it well, we are now at the eve of a new Wave, which will again test the response of mankind. Does this mean that you helped me escape one Wave, only to experience another!?"

Alfred looked at Rahn with a sad smile. "Yes, Otto."

Gabby, who had been quiet so far, queried, "So, what do you have in mind? Where can we help?" She was determined to do something. If they were on a mission to help humanity get through a new Wave properly, she wanted to do everything possible to help turn this mission into a success. However, Gabby also had another reason; more than anything she wanted to take Danielle back to Oshu, so she could get her health back and give birth to a healthy baby. Gabby didn't care about the dangers that lie ahead; if necessary, she would give up everything for this.

Realising that his speech had hit home and as an answer to Gabby's question, Alfred looked at each person individually, to make them realise that what he was going to say next was of the utmost importance.

"We know that Jesus survived the cross, but to prove it we need to find his remains. Why do I want to prove this? Not to attack the Christian faith. I want him to have a proper memorial tomb to honour him and for people to visit. To give them a sacred place for inspiration, comfort and prayer, to experience a sense of closeness, but especially because I want this tomb to become a Universal, Hermetic Temple, to be erected and dedicated to his memory and his universal teachings. To awaken in each Christian - and in anyone who is attracted to his teachings - the true Christ within ourselves; the Christ Consciousness. This new Temple needs to function as a philosophical centre, unattached to any religion, for it will stand above rules, dogmas and doctrines; a Universal Temple for the study of philosophy and Hermetic teachings, which are, after all, also *his* teachings."

Alfred's eyes were big. His vision of a Universal Temple for all humanity - detached from any religion or culture, but focused on the evolution and growth of the soul of mankind as a whole - was obviously a deep desire.

With fire, he continued, "This Temple, which will form the centre *not* of a religion, but of a Way of Life, is *everything* Jesus would have wanted to achieve; for all humanity everywhere to have a platform where mysticism and science, physics and metaphysics will be bridged by joined efforts! Just imagine children all over the world learning Hermetic principles; meditation; the powers of mind and balance and above all; that love is God! That in accepting love within themselves, they accept God within themselves and that only by loving, being loved and giving love, one can be one with God's true essence!"

Alfred looked at Rahn, knowing this was a vision they both shared. It now also began to dawn on the others; Alfred was indeed a visionary, with the very best intensions, but with plans so immense, that they were afraid he wanted to achieve too much in too short a time. However, history was full of proof that big things *can* be achieved if people work together.

Alfred turned to the women, "Gabby and Danielle, you have already made contact with some of the main characters of our Gospel story. They know you and have accepted you. I need you to go back, to become his students and to find out as much as you can about his philosophy. Infiltrate; become one of them, but stay on the background, so you don't attract too much attention or accidently alter history, as it needs to continue on the path it has chosen. Dear all, we don't have a moment to lose. At this moment, the political and religious pressure is enormous and being so close to the great Wave that is coming, we need to alter the state of mind of mankind *before* the wave hits our space and time. No matter how long you will be staying in ancient Judea, we will get you back to this present within 24 hours. So in our experience, you won't have been gone much longer than one day."

Alfred turned to Bill. "I asked you earlier, professor, to create a program in which they are in ancient Judea for a month, while I need to be able to retrieve them to our present within the same day. Did you succeed?"

Danielle and Gabby looked at each other. A whole month! That sounded very scary. What if something goes wrong? They could lose their mobile ERFAB device or their sense of time. However, Bill was way ahead of them. "Yes, I did, sir. I have designed a new device, which Danielle and Gabby can carry inside a pendant on a necklace. It will automatically activate one month later, no matter where they are, together or separate and they will arrive at a set time in this present. However, I need to make sure that the ERFAB matches the signal *exactly*, so I would like to do some tests before we send them."

Alfred agreed with a quick nod and now turned to Otto with a serious frown and a burning question. "Otto, I need to speak with you in private. Please everyone, would you leave us?"

Immediately, everyone but Rahn left the room. All of them were overcome by what Alfred had told them and it had left them quiet, plunged in thought.

Their absence in the meeting room created a deafening silence. Otto was still sitting at the table, studying his thumbs. He knew what Alfred wanted to know, but it wasn't easy for him to explain. He was considering lying to Alfred, feeling he had no other choice. He couldn't help Alfred, even if he wanted to and as soon as Alfred found out that Otto had no more use for him, he would simply send him back to 1939. The thought had driven him almost to panic; he had even thought of escaping from the base, but had no idea how. He just had to come up with a story and maybe, just maybe, Alfred would buy it.

When Alfred had taken a seat at the opposite side of the table, Rahn decided to give it a try and before Alfred could say a word, Otto started, "I know what you want me to tell you Alfred, so hear me out. You know that I didn't find the Grail, but something much more important. I know where Himmler hid it and I can bring you to this place, but for this, we need to go back to southern France and this time we need to go to the Sabarthès. I will only take you there on my terms and… we must go alone."

Alfred stared hard at Otto, trying to digest what he had just told him. He clenched his fists; they had only just returned from southern France! What a waste of precious time! Suddenly, Alfred lost his patience and nearly punched Otto, but instead he grabbed a chair and threw it across the room against the wall, where it broke into two pieces. It had made such a noise, that two agents came running into the room while pointing their guns at Otto. Obviously, they had been given orders to stand-by and protect Alfred. Slowly, Rahn raised his hands to show them he was not armed and chuckled. Betrayal was so much easier when it came from both sides.

He will never trust me anyway.

Alfred intervened. "Weapons down, it's OK, but Otto, why the Sabarthès? Why not Germany? Why would Himmler hide it in southern France?"

Otto shrugged his shoulders, "I discovered that Himmler had been to Montségur in 1944. So, why do you think he went there? I know him well and will give you a clue. I once wrote several chapters for a book that was never published; a book that would have been called 'Mont Salvaesch und Golgota.' Now, you know that Mont Salvaesch was the Grail castle in Wolfram's story of Parzifal and that I believe Montségur was this castle. I also think I know exactly where he has buried the skull and bones."

Alfred realised the logic now. The skull and bones could have been buried there by Himmler himself, but he didn't realise that Otto had only made this story up as a reason to go back to France.

"Alright, we will go." said Alfred, "I will ask Bill to retrieve the women from ancient Judea *after* we have returned from France. Oh, and Otto… no tricks. It's you and me now. Just you and me."

Alfred looked deeply into Otto's eyes, hoping to make him realise that this was his last chance. Rahn watched Alfred walking out of the room and smiled contently. Alfred bought it. His Internet research had also paid off.

He took out a piece of paper that he had kept in his pocket and looked at the address of a place in Montségur that he knew like the back of his hand. He was certain that he could hide there for a while and then disappear altogether in the mountainous land he had come to know so well. He couldn't help Alfred and he was *never* going back to 1939. Otto needed to get back to France and he needed a lift. All he had to do when they got there, was to escape.

26

Sion, Switzerland, July 5th 2011

After the smooth flight from Rome to Sion early that morning, the Cardinal was now enjoying a pleasant, short drive from the airport to the SBS-Sion base. Ever since he had found out that Al Din was now no longer a threat to him, he had felt such a relief; as if God had given him a second chance. His love for Danielle had driven him into taking this new action, alone, without any partner and he had decided that joining SBS-Sion would be his best chance of getting closer to her. Besides, he really wanted to be on *their* side. The Cardinal had thought a lot about this over the past few days. Because Ms Kaiser had planted countless bugs all over Sion base, he had been able to eavesdrop on all of the conversations between Alfred and Otto - even before Danielle and Gabby had entered the scene - and Sardis realised that both he and Alfred shared the same goal, so he was sure that Alfred would hear him out. Perhaps he could become an ambassador for SBS-Sion to help Alfred build a relationship with the Roman Catholic Church and with any luck, this would also bring him closer to Danielle. It was his biggest wish to be there throughout her pregnancy and to hold this child into his arms; to touch the son of Christ! He did not want to be the enemy in their eyes any longer. The Cardinal had high hopes that Alfred would hear him out; that he could see his point of view and accept him in their midst. He knew Alfred was not a bad man, because if he was, he'd have had him killed on July 1st, when his agents freed Danielle. He thought it through one more time and became more confident by the minute that Alfred would accept his hand in friendship, if only they let him explain himself.

Again, Sardis had to cancel some of his ecclesiastic duties, but he was old and could explain his absence by telling his office that he had gone to Switzerland for his health. He had already explained that he was feeling poorly and had suffered from a fall, which was not exactly a lie and he had to admit that the pleasant fresh, mountain air - in comparison to the pollution in Rome - was invigorating. He hummed a tune and casually pushed the button to lower his window even further, while his chauffeur drove him to the Sion base.

"What a beautiful morning!" Sardis exclaimed. Little did he know that it wouldn't go as smoothly as he had expected.

Alfred, who was in the midst of preparing the short trip to southern France, was not at all pleased to see Sardis arriving just as he was putting his luggage in the car.

"Blast!" snarled Alfred. "The last thing we need... Georg!"

The broad-chested agent, who was never far from Alfred's side, quickly ran toward his chief to get his orders. "Sir!"

Alfred had to keep his voice down, not to be overheard by the Cardinal, "Check him for weapons and bugs and escort him to my office... and don't let him out of your sight!"

"Yes, sir!" Georg immediately walked over to Sardis' limousine.

Alfred frowned; the Cardinal seemed so relaxed. He even waved at Alfred with a big smile on his face, as if nothing had happened.

The nerve of the man...

A moment later, after he had finished putting the luggage in the car, Alfred walked back to his office and offered Sardis a seat. "Your eminence, I cannot say it is a pleasure to see you, I'm sure you understand what I mean. What on earth brings you here of all places?"

Sardis smiled sourly and with piously folded hands, he started, "My dear sir, please let me explain; I came to apologise. I can see now how my actions were wrong and I would like to join you, help you on your quest. As a Cardinal I could be your ambassador; for Rome. What can I do to help you? What can I do to help Danielle?"

His eyes looked sincere, that much was clear to Alfred. He also noticed the black rings beneath his elderly eyes, the paleness of his skin and his trembling lips. It looked as if this man really came to offer his friendship.

However, Alfred was still afraid that it might be a trap. He also found the timing very disturbing; with Sardis' partner Izz al Din a prisoner in one of his containment cells at the base; Bill preparing the ERFAB for the women's next mission to ancient Judea and with himself in a rush to get ready for a quick visit to southern France with Otto.

For this new trip to France, everything had been planned to the detail in record time; a small jet would fly them to Pamiers-Les Pujols airport and after that, Alfred only had to follow Rahn to Montségur castle. They needed to find the skull and bones as quickly as possible and get back to the lab. Then, Danielle and Gabby could be retrieved from ancient Judea, hopefully with new information about the original teachings of Jesus. Alfred's mind had already been working at top speed, so Sardis couldn't have arrived at a more inconvenient moment. However, he decided not to tell the Cardinal that Al Din was imprisoned at the base, but of course, he had no idea that Sardis already knew this. Instead, Alfred needed to focus on his priorities and right now, the Cardinal was everything but a priority.

"Come back in a few days, your eminence and you will be welcomed by my entire team for discussions and debates, but this is a bad moment, so if you will excuse me."

Alfred got up, shook Sardis' hand and left the room; a clear signal that the meeting was over. As soon as Alfred was out of hearing range, he ordered Georg to escort the Cardinal out of the building and to keep him out until further notice. Obviously, Sardis was not pleased to be dismissed like this, in spite of all his good intentions. How he had longed to see Danielle again, to be able to apologise to her personally for what he had done; a deed he sincerely regretted. He wanted to let her know that he was now on *their* side. He had come all the way from Rome for this and this dismissal was a hard pill to swallow, even though he knew that he was allowed to come back in a few days' time. So, when the Cardinal's limousine drove him to his hotel in Sion, his smile had gone.

Bill was impatiently waiting for Alfred, who wanted to be present when the women were sent back to ancient Jerusalem. Danielle and Gabby had been very quiet this morning, nervous to return. Knowing that Alfred and Otto would leave for France immediately after, also Bill was more nervous than usual. He dreaded the idea of being left alone with just a handful of agents and Al Din locked up below, so the moment Alfred and Otto arrived at the lab, he decided to talk to Alfred about it. "Sir, can't we postpone this until you and Otto are back?"

Alfred sighed, understanding Bill's anxiety. "No, Bill, we have no time to lose. Until further orders you can set the timer to tomorrow evening, 23.00 hours. If all goes well, Otto and I should be back by then."

Rahn enviously stared at the women. He felt uneasy about lying to Alfred and would rather have gone to ancient Judea with Danielle and Gabby. There was no certainty that the two young women would be safe. After all, they were expected to spend an entire month there. Not only thinking about himself this time, Otto decided to give it another shot. "I still wish I could go with them, to protect them."

Alfred looked at Otto and saw his worry. He too was worried about them, but he couldn't risk setting Rahn loose in ancient Judea and besides, he and Otto were about to leave for southern France. As a response to Otto's last request, Alfred merely shook his head without even looking at him. However, before he allowed this cold response to affect him, Otto read the stress from Alfred's face. Obviously, the Swiss was under a lot of pressure and Otto decided to leave the subject alone. Alfred's order to activate the ERFAB was disguised as a quick nod at Bill. Everything was ready; the devices to ensure the women's safe return had been cunningly processed inside a pendant on a necklace, which they wore discretely underneath their clothes; they each carried medical emergency kits and solar watches, hidden in special pockets and they had been carefully briefed.

Their clothing was again adapted to the time period and when they had all said their goodbyes, Gabby and Danielle walked into the cabin. Bill opened the wormhole and started the countdown. First, a distortion blurred their images and within seconds they disappeared into the void. That very moment, seeing the women disappear into the wormhole, Otto felt a violent sting stabbing his heart.

Ooff, what was that?

It surprised him. It was almost a year ago when he had last experienced love or even fondness for another person. Perhaps it had been Gabby's hug that had rekindled this emotion. He found her to be the sweetest woman and he so wished for her and Danielle to be alright, to be safe. Until now he had simply stopped caring for others to save his mind from going mad, having seen too many horrors in his time; too many loved ones hurt...

Rahn turned on the spot and walked out of the lab. He needed to focus on his own plans now.

Bethanu, ancient Judea, 33 AD

This time, Danielle and Gabby had been given the assignment to return to Bethanu. It had been about a month since their last visit. Bill had chosen the Mount of Olives as their co-ordinates, as this spot hadn't changed much in the past 2000 years. It had just grown bigger. Besides, Bethanu was only a short walk from the Mount of Olives. The professor had hoped that his timing would now be correct, so the women could meet Oshu in Bethanu and travel with him to Carmel to become his students.

It didn't take long before Danielle and Gabby reached the small village and found the house of Mariamne, who was very pleased to see them again, but also shocked to see how Danielle had changed. She noticed how pale she was and it was clear that she had lost some weight, too. "Myriam Dani, what has happened? Are you ill?"

Danielle smiled sourly and allowed her to tears to flow. Now very worried, Mariamne asked them to follow her into the main house. As soon as they entered, she clapped her hands to order some food, after which she took Danielle's hands. "Did something happen to you?"

"No Mariamne, I am pregnant."

Danielle realised that - to Mariamne - her encounter with Oshu was now many months ago, while in her own time and present she had only been pregnant for just over a month. She hoped that - because of this - Mariamne would not suspect that Oshu was the father. Mariamne put her hand on her belly and smiled sisterly at her, with joyous eyes. It was true, both women were pregnant, although Mariamne was a lot further than Danielle. She hugged them both. "Be welcome as my sister, Myriam Dani and you, Myriam Chabi. Come, eat, drink, get your strength back!"

They followed Mariamne deeper into the house and into a room where they could relax and eat. It was at this moment that the women realised how tired they really were. After eating the food they had been offered, Mariamne prepared a room for them so that they could rest. It was during these hours of rest that Danielle and Gabby could finally fathom the seriousness of the situation they were in. First of all, they had been fortunate to find Mariamne so quickly, which probably meant that this time, Bill had sent them back to the right place and the right moment. Gabby's thoughts, however, were of her beloved Bill. He had to wait just a day for her to come back, while she had to wait for an entire month. It almost broke her heart. She realised that she had really fallen for the professor, an emotion that had made it much easier for her to accept Danielle's special bond with Oshu.

Later that day, Mariamne came to their room to talk. It clear that there was something on her mind.

"I need to know, will you stay?" she queried nervously.

Danielle smiled sourly at her. "We can only stay for a month, but we would like very much to become Oshu's students."

This surprised Mariamne and she stared at them with open mouth, as if offended.

"You prefer Oshu over me?" she exclaimed.

Danielle was alarmed and confused. "What do you mean, Mariamne?"

"Oshu will soon go to Carmel, but I am a teacher too. You don't have to go to Carmel, you must stay here. I will teach you the mysteries."

Danielle was silent for a moment, experiencing mixed feelings of surprise and disappointment, but then she realised why Mariamne might not want them to follow Oshu. She explained to Gabby that Mariamne was a teacher too, like Oshu and that they were welcome to stay in Bethanu and be taught by her. Of course, Gabby was terribly disappointed.

"Danielle, remember the mission Alfred gave us; we have to follow Jesus' teachings!"

Mariamne understood that the women preferred Oshu and was hurt and disappointed, but she tried not to show it. "Oshu will come here, to Bethanu." she announced with a broad smile. "He is still in Yerushaláyim, because there was much to talk about with the others and with the family, but he will come here first to say goodbye, before he travels to Carmel. Although I can ask him, it will be *his* decision whether you study under him, or under me." She kissed them on the brow and left the room. However, already in the doorway she hesitated for a moment and turned. "I will ask Oshu to have a special class while he is here."

Gabby's heart leapt when Danielle explained it to her, but Mariamne wasn't yet finished.

"Myriam Dani, you are very weak. Travelling to Carmel is a long, difficult journey, especially for you. Therefore you must consider staying here, with me. I am sure Oshu will agree to teach you while he is here and then, after he has left for Carmel, I will take over from him and teach you."

Danielle nodded. This was a hard decision to make, but she knew Mariamne was right; she had to think of her own health as well as the baby's.

The next day, everyone was waiting impatiently for Oshu's arrival. Especially Gabby and Danielle were nervous; their hearts were pounding and they simply couldn't eat. Mariamne had noticed their anxiety and decided to talk to them, to keep their minds off the waiting.

"Oshu told me that you, Myriam Dani, are special. I wonder; when he talked to you, did he mention the balance of male and female energies? or did he talk about other things?"

Danielle remembered those precious moments with Oshu, which had resulted in her pregnancy. He had spoken to her about the kundalini energies and had proved to her that these energies actually exist; that they are the basis of balance, health and union with the Divine. She tried to remember the Greek words and replied, "Male and female energies."

Mariamne smiled. "Then perhaps my husband will have to explain other matters to you now, but first we will have to find out how much you know about the Mysteries."

Suddenly there was a commotion outside and Mariamne got up from the floor to look through the window. It was a warm, humid day and Mariamne slid open the colourful curtain. They could see the red blossom of the old pomegranate tree against the grey, clouded sky.

"He's here!" Mariamne exclaimed. She raced out of the room, followed closely by Danielle and Gabby. It started to drizzle and after the hot day, the scent of ozone was intense. In the courtyard there were indeed several unknown men, but Danielle couldn't see Oshu anywhere. Still, Mariamne dashed toward a tall man with short hair and a smooth face and kissed him passionately on his full lips. Gabby suddenly recognised him. "Dani, that's him! Didn't Maria say that they had shaved him and had cut his hair?"

Danielle smiled, took Gabby's hand and both bashfully sauntered over to them. When Mariamne saw them approach, she clapped her hands. "Oshu, I have a surprise for you!"

Oshu looked at Danielle for a moment and then at Gabby. Against all expectations, he walked over to Gabby first and hugged her for a moment. Gabby was overjoyed, but also very surprised and reluctant to let him go. Then, Oshu looked at Danielle with sad eyes. When he spoke, his high, soft voice betrayed a deep concern. "Come. Come!" He took Danielle by the hand and refrained from the usual, customary greeting. The moment they entered the main house, he closed the door behind him, making it clear to everyone that he needed privacy. "Sit! Sit, Myriam Dani."

Slightly alarmed, Danielle obeyed. Why had Oshu not hugged her like he had Gabby? Had she done something wrong? Was he upset with her? Tears were pricking her eyes, but then she realised what Oshu's intentions were.

"Dani El, lay down and close your eyes. Think of the sun and imagine yourself crawling into it. Feel its warmth, see the light…" Then, Oshu started to hum a word that sounded like 'kay'. The sound soothed Danielle, bringing her in a state of trance. Oshu kneeled next to her; his left hand on her lower belly; his right hand on her head. Gabby, who - along with Mariamne and several others - was looking at the scene through the window, smiled. Of course he would know of her condition. How could she think that anyone needed to explain anything to him and indeed; he was healing Danielle that very moment.

When he was certain that Danielle was in a deep sleep, Oshu put his finger to his lips and signalled everyone to be quiet. Then, he asked Mariamne to enter. "She needs to rest now, Mariamne, but stay and guide her spirit on its journey until she wakes up."

Mariamne sat down beside Danielle's low bed and when she began her meditation, Oshu left the room. When Gabby saw Mariamne watching over her friend from the window, she realised how fortunate she was to witness this. Then she looked around and couldn't help feeling a bit lonely, unable to communicate with anyone. The drizzle had stopped already and even the sun was coming out again.

Suddenly, a moment of courage came over her and she walked over to Oshu. Not knowing what to say, she remained silent and simply reached out to hold his hand.

Oshu looked at her just a second before her hand touched his, as if he knew she would reach for it. He accepted her hand with a warm smile and could feel her love; her need to be with him, just *be* with him, so although he was having conversations with some of the other people of Bethanu, he allowed her to sit with him, quietly, even during his meal. She so wished she could understand what he was saying as the people were glued to his lips, but then, his eyes spoke to her. Eyes that said: 'Do not worry, Myriam Chabi, all will be well.'

Sion, Switzerland, July 5th 2011

It hadn't been easy for Bill to say goodbye to Gabby that morning. They had grown close. Naturally, he was afraid for her safety; being alone with Danielle in an exotic city during a turbulent period that knew different values and he felt an almost uncontrollable urge to send the probe after them to see if they were alright, but he didn't have a single clue as to where they were, *exactly*. Bill had decided to set the co-ordinates for their journey to a certain point on the slopes of the Mount of Olives, because he had found out that the Biblical Bethanu was close to the Mount of Olives; just outside Jerusalem on the road to Jericho. Bethanu was now called El Azarryeh after Lazarus, who had lived there with his sisters, Martha and Mary Magdalene. It had been the place where Jesus had raised Lazarus from the dead. Although Bill knew that he only had to wait until the next day, he realised that this would be an entire month for Gabby and Danielle and he was worried for them. Bill also felt uncomfortable being alone with a total of four agents and some staff, knowing that Al Din was locked up less than 500 meters away in an underground containment cell.

He remembered Alfred's last comment; as soon as Alfred and Otto arrived in southern France, Alfred would contact him by mobile phone to keep him posted on his mission. Also, Bill knew he could always phone Alfred, just in case something came up at his end. Nevertheless, he felt terribly uneasy, so he decided to lock himself into the lab and to sit it out with the doors locked.

The professor had been there all day now and didn't like hearing the rumbles of an approaching thunderstorm. Though the lab was built deep underneath the fortified church of Valère, he could hear and feel the tremble of the thunder. He had only just sat down on his temporary bed when a loud bang scared him witless. Lightning seemed to have struck the fortified church. Immediately, all the lights went out. Bill froze. If the electricity fails and it doesn't get repaired before tomorrow night, he wouldn't be able to get Gabby and Danielle back. His heart sank. Carefully he walked toward the door in the dark; maybe he could still open it, but the door was shut by an electronic lock, so with the electricity now gone, it couldn't be opened. Bill panicked. Another thunderclap trembled the building. Then, suddenly, the emergency power went on and Bill breathed out in relief. The lab was now bathing in green light, giving it a rather eerie atmosphere. Bill had never been brave in these kinds of situations, so he tried the door again. He held his breath when he dialled the locking code and this time the door opened. Without giving it any other thought, he ran out to check on the agents and on Al Din. Accompanied by two agents he nervously entered the basement of the building, where Al Din was imprisoned. However, when they reached the cell, the door was open. Obviously, Al Din had taken advantage of the situation and had escaped from his cell, but he couldn't possibly be far. Bill wondered where he could hide. Maybe they had already passed him, hiding in a dark corner when they were on their way down. Immediately the agents ran toward the exit, but when they couldn't find him there either, the two other agents were brought in and questioned. No one had seen Al Din. Another thunderclap. Lights were flickering on and off and Bill desperately wanted to phone Alfred, but there was no signal. Lightening must have struck the antenna. *Damn!*

Unable to find Georg, Bill had to make a quick decision and ordered the agents to search the entire building. The men spread out - each into his own direction - guns at the ready and the moment Bill realised that he himself was now completely deserted and unguarded, he decided to run back to his lab and lock himself in again. He could already see the door to the lab and the moment he dashed through the doorway, he quickly slammed the button to close the door behind him and dialled the locking code. When he heard the click of the lock, he breathed out.

Bill looked around; his spooky, green laboratory gave him the creeps. Nervously, he tried his mobile phone again to see if he could now reach Alfred, but there was still no signal. It was driving him mad. In his fear he became angry; angry at Alfred for leaving him alone like this, alone with Al Din, who was now loose somewhere in the building. Bill noticed he was sweating heavily and felt a sudden jolt in his chest, as if something was trying to pull out his most important organ.

Oh God, my heart...

The professor stumbled toward his temporary bed, sat down and loosened his striped, silken tie.

"You are not getting a heart attack, are you, professor?"

Bill jumped. He stared up at the tanned face of Izz al Din, who pointed a gun at him and smiled. "Calm down professor, everything is now as it should be. You will help me get Danielle, you will give me the keys to a car and you will help me leave this base."

"That's impossible!" yelled Bill. "Danielle and Gabby are not here. They are... not here."

"Then bring me to her! Now!" shouted Al Din angrily.

"... but I cannot! They are out there, in ancient Judea. Please, don't shoot!"

Bill's plea, however, didn't help. Al Din was furious and impatient, realising that Danielle had slipped away from him again. He considered his chances; "When will she be back?" he queried. "I don't know!" yelled Bill, hoping he sounded convincing.

In an unexpected move, Al Din hit him hard in the face with the back of his hand. Immediately, Bill collapsed on the bed; blood began to seep from his nose. In an attempt to buy time, Bill decided to act as if he had passed out. Al Din, on the other hand, was no fool. He could recognise the difference between a man who was out and a bad actor who was scared to death. Al Din knew he couldn't use his gun; the agents would surely hear it, so instead he decided to find a more ancient method to make Bill talk. He put his gun in his pocket and searched the lab for an item or an instrument that he could use to loosen Bill's tongue. Not knowing that Al Din wasn't buying his act, Bill kept his eyes firmly closed and could only guess at Al Din's next move. The professor didn't dare move a muscle. The fierce nosebleed was making him dizzier every minute, but that wasn't his biggest worry. As he laid flat on his back, streams of blood were now also running into his throat and at a certain moment he almost choked. Bill coughed. Immediately, Al Din turned around like a predator. Bill sat up, his shirt covered in blood.

"Give me a fucking Kleenex man!" he yammered.

Al Din just smiled at him. He had found his instrument of torture. "Not used to anything, are you, professor?"

Suddenly, Bill saw what Al Din was holding in his hand. The Arab approached him with a malicious grin, but before he could do anything, Bill could no longer sustain himself and fainted. For real, this time.

27

Ariège, southern France, July 5th 2011

It had been a quick flight to the small airport at Pamiers-Les Pujols in the Ariège region of southern France. They now had the entire afternoon to get what Alfred was after: the remains of the man we know as Jesus. Alfred believed Rahn's story and had no idea that he was just being used as a quick ride to freedom. He thought that Rahn was on his side, because they shared the same ideals. Actually, he was very excited to follow Rahn into the country that the relic hunter knew so well; the country he loved and had promoted in his books on the Grail Legends.

As soon as they got off the plane, they stepped into the white Audi that was already waiting for them at the airport. Alfred was alone with Otto now; Rahn had insisted on this. He had told Alfred it would be a top secret mission, with - on their return - a top secret cargo and if any other person finds out what they were here for, their mission could be easily compromised. Nevertheless, Alfred missed having Georg around; his special agent had never left his side before.

It was a beautiful day, cloudless and not too hot yet. Alfred drove the car south toward a town called Tarascon-sur-Ariège. In the distance they could make out the dreamy silhouette of the Pyrenees and somehow, Alfred found the space in his mind to enjoy the moment. Rahn, however, had mixed feelings. On one hand, he was enjoying the smooth drive - recognising the landscape he loved so much and marvelling at the modern roads - but on the other hand he realised that he was now in too deep to come clean about his deceit. Though it gnawed at him, he had no choice but to hold on to his escape plan. Then he saw a familiar signpost. "Turn off there, in the direction of Lavelanet."

Trusting that Otto knew the way, Alfred slowed down so as not to miss the junction. They drove over the viaduct that hadn't been there yet in the 1930s and followed the signs toward Lavelanet. A little further on they passed a tour bus with a sign on the side, saying: 'Sacred France Tour 2011'. Otto smiled.

Sacred indeed...

Then, they spotted the exit to Montségur and Alfred turned right. He had never visited this part of Occitania before, though he had read about it; about the Cathar Christians, who had been hunted down by representatives of the Catholic Church because they refused to accept the dogmatic visions of the Roman Catholic Faith. However, it wasn't only the religious conflict that had caused the massacres; this was also about possession. The feudal south had been governed by Occitan lords ever since Charlemagne had given them feudal rights, but by the year 1200 - 400 years since Charlemagne's Holy Roman Empire - Europe had once more become divided and full of war lust and the French king desperately wanted to annex the independent south to strengthen his French kingdom. However, as Spain was closer than Paris, the counts of Occitania had preferred to be loyal to the counts of Barcelona and the royal house of Aragon - not to the king of France. The Cathar Crusade had been organised by both King and Pope - not only to get rid of the Cathars to make the Pope happy, but also to conquer Occitania, to make the French King happy. The 'Occitan Quest', however, would go into history merely as the 'uprising of the southern lords' against the French crown, which was quickly dealt with by King Louis. Alas, the true history was much more complicated than that. This crusade against the Cathars and other 'heretics' that had started in 1209, had soon turned into a holocaust, involving many more people than only Cathars and the 'uprising of the southern Lords' was simply the response of the Occitan counts to protect themselves; their castles; their cities and their people - Cathar, Jew and Catholic alike - against the truculent crusaders. Within two centuries, close to a million innocent people - even babies - had been brutally murdered and while they were at it, the soldiers stripped the entire south of its riches; its culture; its dignity and its independence. Alfred remembered how the late Pope John Paul II had apologised for this horrific crusade in the name of the Church, ashamed that this had ever happened. The Pope had called it a 'black page in the history of the Church', but Alfred wasn't sure that these apologies had ever been accepted. Today, this Ecclesiastical Ship has almost run aground because of its many, often unbelievable choices and actions in the past, which are still reflecting in the present. One day, the Church will have no other choice but to admit the white lie, instead of covering it up, but for now, the least it can do is to change their attitude by explaining the self-inflicted wounds on their flagship and embracing the truth and the original teachings of Jesus. If only they could accept the equality of people and allow their followers to give their children the freedom to make their own religious choices. If only they could accept birth control and lift the ban on abortion, especially in cases when the mother had been raped. If only they could embrace the concept of reincarnation, abolish celibacy and accept women as equal to men, as Jesus himself had done during his life. Perhaps then people could respect the Church again as a religious rule instead of a means to rule.

Alfred and Otto were nearly at their destination and could already see the castle of Montségur from a distance. At a certain point, the view was so impressive that Alfred stopped the car at the side of the road and got out. At the top of a steep mountain stood the ruined castle of Montségur. It looked like a stone ship that had stranded on a high cliff during a legendary flood. In awe, Alfred gazed at the battlements. If a castle could stand so proud even in ruin, it must have been magnificent in the 13th century. Rahn grinned; he knew it would impress Alfred. Otto, however, stayed in the car; he was far too impatient to get out, knowing that the parking was only a few bends away and being on edge, he pressed the horn. Alfred jumped and realised that he had just left Otto alone in the car with the engine still running. What was he thinking? He quickly got back in the car.

Otto smiled at Alfred. "Mont Salvaesch; the Occitan Golgota. Impressive, isn't it?"

Alfred pursed his lips. "Very impressive. It must have been a difficult castle to take!"

"Yes it was. More than 10.000 soldiers besieged the castle for about 10 months before it surrendered. More than 200 people chose immolation in the pyre built at the bottom of the hill over recanting their faith, while the others - who were not part of the Cathar community - could walk free. It has always been a big mystery to me, how people could choose death over life, because they wanted to be true to their faith and I have often asked myself; would I have been brave enough to actually throw myself onto the pyre; or, would I have been a Cathar at heart and then lie about it, so I could walk free? I mean, what would you do?"

Without answering his question, Alfred studied Otto, who clearly had several issues with himself. Perhaps if Otto had been with the Cathars up on that mountain for almost a year, he wouldn't have wanted to betray them by lying about his faith in front of the people who were on the pyre. Alfred didn't think of Otto as a coward, but apparently, Otto himself wasn't so sure.

Rahn asked Alfred to drive on and park the car on the parking area, but upon seeing several other cars there, both realised they weren't alone and Alfred knew that they could only get to the skull and bones after dusk. Even though it was a warm day, Otto took his jacket from the car and put it on. He didn't want to leave it behind in case he succeeded in getting away from Alfred. They passed the field with the old laurel tree, where over 200 human beings; men and women; young and old, had been burned alive. After a silent, respectful pause they continued their ascend. It was a short, but steep climb to the monument; an extraordinary place with a breath-taking view to a stunning, mountainous landscape. A landscape that was now so silent, so peaceful, so tranquil.

The monument itself wasn't old. It had been erected by the Société du Souvenir et des Etudes Cathares in 1960. It said: 'In this place on March 16th 1244, more than 200 people were burned alive. They chose not to abjure their faith'.

Many people from all over the world come to southern France to visit this site - some of whom inspired by Rahn's first book - to honour the Cathars and their quest to protect the origins of Christianity. Someone had left a handful of rose petals at the monument. Of course, to know that this historic event had happened on that exact spot in 1244 was an experience for any visitor, but for Alfred, time had just become a more controllable dimension, so it made a huge impression on him to be there. Seeing Alfred in a state of reverence, Otto felt that it was now or never. Piously he turned to Alfred and said in a soft voice,

"Maybe we should meditate here for 10 minutes to honour these brave people?"

To Otto's surprise, Alfred immediately agreed. He sat down at the base of the monument and closed his eyes, ignoring the sound of visitors who were coming down the mountain. Otto took advantage of this and tiptoed as quietly as possible toward the steps. He tried not to make a sound until he was further up the slope. Then he disappeared between the trees, following a secret trail. On the way up, he suddenly noticed the wooden cabin where visitors now had to buy their tickets and Rahn made sure he wasn't seen. He had climbed this mountain countless times and didn't have to keep to the path. Knowing exactly where to go, he criss-crossed the slope to reach the higher parts. When he reached the tree line, he returned to the regular path. Carefully, he looked down. By now, Alfred must have noticed that he was alone. Otto smiled. Alfred couldn't possibly catch him now. Rahn was a well-trained climber, faster and younger than Alfred and more importantly; he knew the trail down the other side of the mountain. Looking up, he could already see the entrance to the castle. As soon as he was inside, he trotted across the empty courtyard toward the northern gate.

In the 13th century, this courtyard had been much smaller; the buildings and workshops that had been built against the outer walls had now completely disappeared. Otto walked through the northern gate and found himself on the other side of the castle. For a moment, he stared at the ruins of the old Cathar houses, that had been built on the rocky edges of the mountain. Then he ran down toward the ruins of barbican and further down to reach the rocky outcrops on the far end of the *Rock de la Tour*. Otto remembered the story of how the castle was taken. The French troops knew that this impregnable castle could only be conquered by wit and betrayal so they persuaded a Basque mountain guide to betray the secret path that was used to provide the castle. This path also gave access to the tower that had once stood at the far end of the barbican and as soon as the soldiers had taken the tower, they destroyed the building and constructed on the same spot a huge catapult called a 'trebuchet'. For two months, the rocks and stones that bombarded the castle almost destroyed the entire stronghold and the surrounding cottages. Otto shook his head, remembering his own betrayal to Alfred. Though it felt wrong, there was no way back now. He spottd the start of the secret trail that leads to the village; to safety; to life.

However, he hadn't anticipated running into an old friend.

Or a young friend, for that matter.

Enjoying the view, David, Michael, Ben, Yanne and Arthur were standing on the edge of the rock, taking pictures and pointing at sites. Arthur pointed at Rennes-le-Château and Mount Bugarach and the binoculars were passed from one to another. Suddenly, as if touched by an invisible hand, Arthur turned around and spotted Rahn. "Hey look! It's Otto!"

Rahn jumped.

Oh nein!

Of course, Arthur had no idea why Otto was there and as he was expecting a hearty hello, the boy was alarmed and confused when Rahn suddenly bolted. He realised something was wrong and decided to run after him.

It didn't take long before Alfred too came out of the castle, shouting Otto's name. He was panting heavily, so he had to sit and rest. He couldn't walk another step. Ascending the mountain is already a heavy exercise, let alone running up all the way. When David spotted the Swiss, he quickly came to his aid. It was clear to him that Alfred was in trouble. "What's happened, sir? How can we help?"

"It's Otto, he lured me into taking him here. I should have known, I shouldn't have trusted him! *Damn!*" Alfred was panting too much to talk and David gave him his water bottle.

In the meantime, Arthur, Michael and Ben had followed Otto, who was now taking the dangerously steep, secret path that leads to the village below. Suddenly, Ben slipped. The fright gave him an adrenaline rush and he quickly grabbed a bush. Holding onto the branches he managed to pull himself up and when he got a foothold on solid ground again, he exclaimed, "He's out of his mind! The man's mad!"

Yanne had been watching him from the top of the path and it was clear that she was angry at him, but relieved to see him unharmed. However, Michael and Arthur were still in pursuit, but it was now a slow chase, as every miscalculated step would result in a deadly fall. Otto became concerned. He didn't want the boys to risk their lives for him. "Go back! You don't know what you are doing! Go back!"

However, Michael and Arthur ignored Otto's shouting. Something was wrong. "Otto come back, please, let us help you!" yelled Arthur, but Otto refused to listen. "You cannot help me! Leave me alone! *Waahhh!*" Otto slipped and could only just grab the course surface of a cliff. Suspended over the chasm, he nervously gazed into the depth below him and knew he needed to act fast. When he saw a ridge over to the left, he decided to risk it. He pushed himself up and with amazing skill he climbed sideways, slid down the rocky slope and landed on the ridge. From there, he managed to climb toward a more convenient descend. The boys had to give up at this point. They were not that tired of life.

Everyone realised that Otto was now lost to them. Alfred cursed. "He knows all the paths and the entire area like the back of his hand. I can only hope that he won't do anything stupid! We need to find him, at all cost. He has to go to the village at some point. After all, he is human, he needs food, shelter…"

Alfred looked at David. He realised how fortunate he was to have encountered them here, at this critical moment, knowing he couldn't possibly do this alone.

"Please, will you help me find him?"

David nodded, but he couldn't help feeling sympathy for Otto. "Sir, I understand that you told him that he had to go back to 1939. If I were him, I think I would have run for it, too."

Alfred rubbed his face. He couldn't help feeling misunderstood. "I also told him that I'd get him a false passport. I have always been honest with him. He knew he would have to go back and I know that this would be difficult for him, but perhaps I didn't realise it had become *impossible* for him, knowing what he knows now from his Internet research on World War II. If only he had talked to me more openly. The sad thing is, I believed him. I thought we were really going to collect what I am looking for. He just used me to get away to a place he knew well and if we don't catch him, I don't know how he will survive. He has no ID, no money…"

David got up. "Come on, we haven't a minute to lose."

As soon as they arrived back at the parking area, they returned to their cars and drove to the village of Montségur, which was only a few bends further down the road. However, by now, Otto was way ahead of them. Having climbed down the rocky, steep part, the slopes were now more gentle and he could run and slide most of the way down. The moment he reached the village, he slowed down and walked casually through the streets, trying not to pant too heavily. It was an amazing, though bizarre feeling to be in a place he had been to not so long ago in his experience, but which had changed during the almost 80 years that separate the moments in time. Feeling edgy, he skittered through the quiet village streets and alleys, passed the church and then turned left to get to a small courtyard, that was at the rear end of one of his old accommodations; the hotel Couquet. Otto smiled. It still existed. His Internet research had paid off.

First, he had to get off the street and out of sight, so he risked going inside the hotel, using the small, wooden back door. He was lucky to find it unlocked. It was dark inside and he almost stumbled and fell over the objects sitting on the bottom steps of the stairs; steps he must have walked up and down hundreds of times. However, he couldn't know that this staircase was no longer in use and that the clients of the hotel now used another staircase, that was hidden out of sight at the back of the breakfast room.

From the top of the stairs it only took him three steps to reach his old room. Again he was in luck to find the door unlocked; the room probably needed to be cleaned. When he entered the room, he found it practically unchanged and couldn't help becoming emotional. He touched everything; the beautiful wooden knobs on the bed frame; the chair; his old writing table, where he had spent many hours writing his Crusade Against the Grail book… Tears ran down his cheeks. He sat down on the bed, allowing his memories to come flooding back.

He remembered going out for long walks with his stick and backpack and when he returned - his clothes wet and dirty from his hike through the mountains - he could always borrow a pair of pants from Monsieur Couquet. He remembered the gentle landlord smoking his pipe, the dinners with the family and little Memée, their daughter, sitting on his knee, playing rocking horse. Compared to the present, these were his golden days, when the only stress had been the absence of money. Most days he even had to wear the black clothes that had been sent to him by his order, because he simply couldn't afford to buy his own.

Sponsored by the Thule Society, he had been able to travel, albeit on a shoestring and had been able to indulge himself wholeheartedly into his favourite past time; researching Grail legends and the origins of religion, myth and legend. It was this research that had brought him to Montségur, believing that this was Mont Salvaesch, the Grail castle from the Parsifal story of Wolfram von Eschenbach. Here he had explored every cave and every castle and had enjoyed discussing historical topics with people like the countess de Pujol-Murat, Antonin Gadal, several archaeologists, writers, neo-Cathars, Rosicrucians, farmers and shepherds. These were the days when he still did not know what his superiors had in store for the world.

He awoke from his thoughts and looked at the room. He couldn't believe that the sink and the central heating were the only big alterations to the room since 80 years. Otto threw some water into his face and washed away the tears; he had to control himself.

Because his old pension was now called hotel Couquet, he thought that perhaps little Memée Couquet had taken over from her parents. This could also be the reason that it hadn't changed so much. How old would she be now? In her eighties, for sure.

A noise startled him. He got up, looked through the window onto the street and watched Alfred, David and the kids walking through the main street. Then he saw Arthur pointing at the hotel, after which the boy looked up at the exact room he was in.

Of course he'd know, der Dreckskerl!

Quickly he hid himself from view and hoped that he hadn't been seen. Entering from the main street, David, Alfred and the kids now climbed the stairway to the first floor, where they found the breakfast room just off the landing to the left. As soon as they arrived, a woman - who seemed to be the old landlady - greeted them and asked how she could be of service.

David tried his best French. "Did you see a man here, medium height, a bit thin, dark hair combed backwards, German accent?"

The woman shook her head. "No monsieur, no one."

They didn't understand. Arthur was so sure that he had seen Otto at the window. How could Otto have got past her without being noticed? Impossible! They looked into the room, but couldn't see a stairway leading up from where they were, so they looked into the breakfast room; the dining room; the kitchen... Nothing. No one. How strange.

28

Sion, Switzerland, July 5th 2011

A *defibrillator* is a device that is used when someone goes into cardiac arrest. It reactivates the heart muscle by giving off a strong, electric pulse, which stops the heart for a moment, allowing it to go back to its normal rhythm. The defibrillator saves many lives each year and nowadays there are automated external defibrillators or *AEDs* in most public buildings. Naturally, there also was a mobile AED in the lab.

It didn't take long before had Bill regained his consciousness. When he opened his eyes, the first thing he saw was the defibrillator and he wished himself away. Whatever Al Din had in mind, it was definitely not a healthy idea.

Al Din smiled sourly at Bill. "So, now do you remember when Danielle is coming back?"

Bill was feeling sick. Never in his entire life had he been so scared. He screamed his lungs out for help in the hope that someone would hear him, but now, Al Din became even more impatient and pushed the button to activate the defibrillator. When Bill heard the rising tone, he froze. Then, in a quick move, Al Din pushed the two electric paddles against the inside and outside of Bill's upper leg and activated the pulse. Bill's muscles jolted so intensely that it felt as if he had violent spasms. He screamed, but Al Din merely grinned. "I wonder what happens if I try it on your soft parts..." Al Din recharged and went for his lower belly. Bill panted heavily; he had no idea how his intestines would react to this pulse and knew that spasm could actually be deadly - maybe not instantly, but slowly and very painfully. "No, please, they're due to come back tomorrow. Tomorrow you son of a b..."

Al Din smiled broadly and deactivated the defibrillator. He hated violence, but he simply had a mission to achieve. "Thank you. Now, was that really so difficult? Professor, let me make myself clear. You *will* enable me to get out of here unharmed together with Danielle. Please, don't underestimate me, for I will eliminate anyone who blocks my path. Do you understand?"

Bill nodded, still feeling very sick and trembling all over. The nosebleed had stopped, but he was covered in blood. It felt as though he had lost a few pints. Pretending to feel dizzy, he lay down on the bed, trying to buy some time while thinking of a plan, but neither of them knew that they were being watched from Alfred's glass office.

Bethanu, ancient Judea, 33 AD

When Oshu had finished his meal, he looked for a short stick and turned to Gabby. He pointed at his eyes and then at the floor, as if he was saying; I will draw something for you in the sand. Although he wasn't talking - for he knew she wouldn't understand him anyway - he giggled almost constantly, like a guru from India. It was perhaps also his way of making her feel at ease. Gabby was surprised, but over the moon that he was trying to communicate with her. This was going to be interesting. What would he draw that she could possibly understand? Oshu flattened the wet sand with his hand and started to draw a circle. Then he drew a square inside the circle, a triangle inside the square with the point up, a triangle with the point down and a dot in the centre. Finally, he made a circle around himself using his arms and said: "Abwoon."

Gabby understood that Oshu probably showed her the symbol of the entire creation. Abwoon probably meant God; the All. She had once read a book on symbolism and knew that the circle meant 'the All' while the square meant 'the earth'. The double triangle, which she immediately recognised as the Star of David, pointed at the means of communication between the All and the world, between God and people, but she wasn't sure about the dot in the centre. Gabby pointed at the dot and shook her head as if saying, 'I don't understand.' Then, Oshu merely pointed at her heart. She couldn't help speaking out loud. "Oh, the soul!"

"Abwoon." he added.

Gabby was confused; she had never actually thought of the idea that through her soul, the All was part of her, like she was a part of the All. It made sense, though.

Oshu then drew a Greek letter in the sand, which looked like an abstract letter E. Gabby recognised it as an elongated 'Sigma'. Next to it, he drew what looked like an abstract number 3. Patiently he waited for her to grab the idea and smiled at her while she was in deep thought. Gabby knew it had something to do with 'understanding' and 'vision' and that the symbol was generally connected to Aquarius, but what about the abstract number 3? Then, all of a sudden, the penny dropped; it was the mirror image of the sigma sign, meaning 'reflection'. It was the first lesson of the Hermetic Teachings of the Gnosis. She remembered what her history professor at the University had told his class over and over again; a sentence that was even permanently on his blackboard:

Know thyself and thou shalt know
the Universe and the Gods

This text was written above the entrance at Delphi in Greece, one of the major centres of Hermetic studies in antiquity. This ancient knowledge wasn't new to her; she had read a few books on the topic for a university project. The Hermetic teachings - the knowledge of the ancients - had come from the Indus Valley to Egypt, where it became known as the knowledge of Thoth or Tehuti. People from all over the ancient world travelled to Egypt to study the 'Mysteries'; even the Greek philosophers, who had taken this knowledge back to ancient Greece, where they had renamed it 'Hermetica', after Hermes Trismegistos, the Thrice Great. Hermes was the Greek version of the Egyptian God, Thoth. Through the Hermetica, the basic principles of nature; physics and metaphysics, were explored and studied. The great philosophers then introduced this wisdom to the west and right now, Gabby felt honoured to be taught by the greatest of them all. She wanted to tell Oshu that she had figured out what he had tried to explain with the double sigma, so she pointed at her eyes and looked at the palm of her hand, making it look as if her hand was a mirror. Oshu contently clapped his hands; she had understood. As above, so below; as it is in the heavens, so it is on the earth.

The Mirror of God.

When Oshu kissed her on the head and walked off to get some rest, Gabby decided to keep Danielle company. When she arrived at her room, Danielle was fast asleep and Mariamne was still watching over her, like Oshu had requested. When Mariamne noticed Gabby's presence, she smiled at her and invited her to sit down on the other low bed that stood in the room. Gabby absorbed everything around her as if in a dream. She missed Bill and remembered with fondness the holiday-like outing to southern France, which had been exciting and wonderful, in spite of the worrying about Danielle's safety. It is strange how the mind tends to wonder off when the stress gets too big. She had fallen in love with Bill and missed him terribly, but at the same time it was both sweet and strange to be with these historical people. To Gabby, they were 2000 year old celebrities, with a much deeper fame than any other, modern day celebrity. She also sensed that there was something bigger going on; something she couldn't yet put her finger on, much like the sensation the archaeologist Schliemann must have felt when he had finally found the mythical city of Troy, proving it had indeed existed. It was true, Gabby felt insignificant amongst these amazing people - a fly amongst elephants - and regretted not having studied ancient languages. Her history professor had begged her to at least study Greek and Latin, but she was already too busy studying astrophysics. She just couldn't find the time. However, thinking back, she was glad she had chosen astrophysics after all, because this is how she had met Danielle. Otherwise she might have missed out on all the adventures, although some of the adventures were a bit crazy. Come to think of it; all were a bit crazy.

The sound of yawning and stretching woke Gabby from her thoughts. Danielle had woken up. Immediately, she speeded over to her friend. "Hey you, how are you feeling?"

As if she had slept for days, Danielle blinked slumberously at the two gentle, smiling faces. Mariamne took her hand. "You have slept deeply being on one side, Myriam Dani and now you have come back to another."

Danielle was puzzled. "What do you mean, Mariamne?"

"Oshu and I have lead your spirit, so you can heal faster."

Danielle had to admit that she felt so much better now; stronger. The pain in her lower belly had gone; her dizziness had gone and she was no longer pale, but blushing. Slowly she got up and looked at Gabby, who seemed changed; positively changed. Spotting the special chemistry that was clearly present between the two women, Mariamne left the room, so they could talk.

"So what time is it? How long have I been asleep?" asked Danielle.

"For hours, I don't know. I'm not wearing a watch, you know. I had lunch with Oshu and the others and he taught me the basic principles of the Hermetic Teachings."

Danielle thought she was joking and laughed. "Yeah, yeah, sure…"

"No really. When you were asleep, Oshu and I left you and he allowed me to stay and sit with him while he was having his meal. Afterward, Oshu drew me some symbols in the sand. He didn't talk, but I actually understood what he was trying to teach me."

Danielle clapped her hands. "Oh, I am so pleased! The one thing I was afraid of, was to see you struggling here."

"Why?" Gabby queried.

"Because you're like a tourist in a strange country where no one speaks English…"

Gabby laughed out loud. "I know! … but don't worry about me. These people are obviously used to having strangers around who speak dialects or other languages. They just did a lot of body talk, hands and feet, you know? Showing me some bread and asking something could easily be translated into: Oye! Want some bread?"

Both laughed.

Mariamne came back with a water jar and three cups. Immediately behind her was Oshu, who closed the curtain that separated the big room from the room they were in. When Oshu asked Mariamne to fetch something, she obeyed without delay. He invited them to join him and drink some water to purify themselves. Then he sat down in a cross-legged position. "Myriam Dani, Myriam Chabi, welcome to Bethanu, the Place of the Mother. This is our Grand lodge near Yerushaláyim. Here we study; we heal; we initiate; we educate. We are the Essenes, in all ranks and professions. We never talk loud; we are modest in our ways; we avoid our ego and we do humanitarian work. We would like you to learn our ways."

Danielle nodded and translated his words to Gabby, who became excited. "Tell him we want him to teach us the mysteries, Danielle!"

Oshu turned his head toward Gabby and chuckled. "Oooh... Myriam Chabi wants me to teach you very much." Then, Oshu laughed out loud. It seemed as if he was laughing constantly. It was amazing to see how this incredibly wise and honourable man - a king! - was obviously cherishing his inner child. They laughed along with him until they spotted the wounds on his wrists where the nails had been hammered through only two months ago. The wounds had healed surprisingly well. When he continued, the first part of his sentences were always in a somewhat high pitched voice and all the while, all of his actions and words were loaded with love, warmth and a fair amount of humour. However, it did surprise them that he had understood exactly what Gabby had said to Danielle, who replied, "You are right, Oshu, we would like you to teach us very much."

Still grinning, he got up, kissed both women on the brow and placed his left hand on his right shoulder and his right hand on his left shoulder.

"This is the way we greet others, how we show our respect as well as the willingness to serve and learn."

He made the women copy this gesture and Gabby laughed when Danielle - being an American at heart - did it the wrong way around. "No Dani no, the *left* hand on the right shoulder, then the right hand on the left shoulder."

Oshu nodded in approval.

He bowed his head and quietly walked a full circle through the room, as if in thought. Then he started his first lesson.

"The one who knows and sees that all beings are in the Soul and that the Soul is in all beings, shall no longer know fear. The Soul does not contain flesh. It cannot feel pain; it cannot bleed; it cannot be killed. The Soul is both the seer of all things and the controller of all things."

After hearing the translation, Gabby told Danielle about the dot at the centre of the symbol that Oshu had drawn for her and drew a copy of it in the air. Oshu was impressed that she had remembered it so well and hugged her before continuing his teachings.

"Suppose two are resting on a bed. One will die, but the other shall live. Explain this to me."

Danielle didn't even translate his question and answered straight away, "The body dies, but the soul will depart and live." Gabby thumped Danielle's arm, making Oshu laugh even louder, but then he turned and became serious again.

"It is the miracle of Abwoon, who is mother and father - matter and spirit - in One. Everything we need is provided by Abwoon; food; clothing; beauty; inspiration and the breath of life itself. Abwoon also gives us each a Path that we need to follow; a Path that - in the darkness of this world - can only be illuminated by the stars of our heart; sparks of heavenly light that help us navigate life itself. From the materials given to us by Abwoon we make our clothes, we go into the field and get the food we need; we can create from clay our cups and jars and from stones and metals we make our tools, tents or houses. Abwoon provides for us. We are only the hands between the product and the material. This is the same with our spiritual food, which can only be harvested if we are willing to do the work on the field. Also, we do not have possessions here, in this house. All things are shared, for when you have nothing, you cannot lose anything. Also, you are blessed to be poor, for the poor can enter the Kingdom of Heaven without any desire to return to the material world. We have no earthly treasures, because we are focusing on Heavenly treasures."

He pointed at their necklaces.

"Take these off; you cannot wear these when you are part of our community. When you want to be my student, you will not attach yourself to earthly things. You will wear only the clothes we provide for you and these shall be white, to symbolise your willingness to become pure."

Danielle froze. Oshu would never understand that they must not part from their necklaces. These were their tickets home! … but Oshu was holding out his hand as a token that this was not debatable. Gabby looked at Danielle with big eyes while reluctantly taking off her necklace and handing it over to Oshu. When Danielle had done the same, he put both necklaces in a bowl in the corner of the room and clapped his hands. As if she had been waiting outside, Mariamne entered the room with a package of clothes, which she handed out to Danielle and Gabby.

"Change into these clothes to become his students." instructed Mariamne. "You are very lucky that he has decided to teach you. Oshu will stay here until he believes you are ready."

Mariamne smiled gratefully. Her heart had been broken, seeing Oshu suffer so during his crucifixion, but her heart had also healed while treating his wounds and helping him to heal himself. However, she realised that Oshu would not stay put and she was right; the moment he was fit enough to travel, he made plans to go to Carmel and to make preparations for this journey, he had gone to Cephas' house, the one called Simon Peter, to meet with the others. Mariamne had missed him so much, but now, thanks to

Danielle and Gabby, he would stay in Bethanu much longer than originally planned.

Although it was clear that Oshu knew Danielle was pregnant - his actions earlier that day had said it all - she wasn't sure whether he knew it was *his*. She also wasn't sure if she could ever tell him this. It just wouldn't make any sense to him.

Without being able to protest, Danielle and Gabby changed into their new, white clothes, which were not as comfortable as the ones they had worn so far, but they could still secretly hide underneath, the other small items they couldn't afford to lose. However, they had to leave the necklaces in the bowl where Oshu had put them and could only hope no one would take them. It was very scary to leave these precious items there, but they really had no choice.

When the women returned to the main room in their new clothes, they were disappointed to see that Oshu had already gone. Mariamne asked them to follow her. The sun had set and again they were given the opportunity to wash and bathe, whether they were dirty or not. After their cleaning ritual, they were taken into a large room where everyone was gathering. When Oshu entered the room - being the last person to arrive - everyone became quiet. After a short silence, he started to sing a prayer in Aramaic.

Abwoon d'bwasmaja, nitkadesj sjmach. Abwoon d'bwasmaja, nitkadesj sjmach. Teetee malkoetach, neghwee tsevjanach. Ajkana d'bwasjmaja af b'arhah.

After he had finished his prayer song, everyone joined in to repeat the last word; '*Ameen*'. Danielle had recognised the one Aramaic word she knew: 'malkoetach'; Kingdom. She had goose bumps all over.

This was the original Lord's Prayer!

Oshu opened his eyes and spread his arms. "Come, sit, eat!"

Gabby observed the room; all the people were dressed in white and all of them were quiet, except for Oshu, who was giggling, as usual. His people seemed to be used to it; some of them even started to join in. It was as if everyone had heard a joke. Gabby looked at Mariamne, who acted as if everything was just as it should be and she didn't dare ask her why Oshu almost always giggled. Gabby had once seen a guru from India, doing exactly the same thing and even the Dalai Lama seemed to be in an everlasting good mood, but why? She elbowed Danielle. "You know, I think I read somewhere that guru's from India always laugh because they have understood the Great Cosmic Joke." Danielle nickered at Gabby's remark and almost choked on her bread, so now, all eyes were fixed on her. The attention was overwhelming for poor Danielle, who blushed and studied her food, causing everyone to laugh out loud. Mariamne, who had been quiet until now, understood and turned to them, trying to outvoice the commotion. "Laughter is healthy, it is a very powerful medicine!"

Now, they understood.

All went quiet when Oshu started to speak, this time in Aramaic, so Danielle couldn't understand it. Everyone now looked at them; it felt as if they were being introduced. Then, Oshu turned to Danielle and changed to Greek. Everyone listened in. However, his smile had gone.

"I have witnessed much sorrow in this world. People could not even see in what I said and what I did, that I am a bringer of truth, peace and light. They have even asked me to judge over matters and to divide properties or belongings, but I am not a divider. I am the way to the truth, which is being obscured by those who say they are the keepers of it, but I am just one man. Abwoon has provided us with big fertile fields, but there are only a few workers to harvest it and this saddens me. The world is a bridge; go over it, but do not build your house on it, because not the Heavens, nor His children, but only Abwoon knows when this bridge will collapse."

Mariamne, who sat at Oshu's right hand side, suddenly kissed his hand. "… but you have many who know you, understand you and love you, my darling."

Oshu looked at her and kissed her on her lips. Then he looked around at everyone present and smiled. "When this bridge collapses, none of *you* will taste death."

They continued their supper in silence, but then, a moment later, Oshu started to giggle again and the warm atmosphere had returned to the room. How magical laughter is and how powerful.

That evening, Danielle and Gabby were very pleased to see him enter their room, although it was already late. There was no sign of Mariamne; she had probably retired. Oshu hugged Gabby and pointed toward the door. Her heart sank; he wanted her to leave the room, but when he saw her sad face, he hugged her again and whispered something in her ear. "Parakalo…"

Although she couldn't understand the word, she understood what he meant; he probably wanted to talk to Danielle alone. Gabby left with a heavy heart and sat down beneath the pomegranate tree. She had no desire to look for Mariamne, because she couldn't talk to her anyway. It was chilly and she hugged herself. The thought of having to stay here for a whole month frightened her. Tears rolled down her cheeks, for she didn't know if she had the stamina to carry on for long. She rested her head on her folded arms and started to weep. Suddenly, a hand touched her shoulder and she looked up at Mariamne, who took her to another part of the house. There were other women here as well. Mariamne spoke softly to her, trying to sooth her and showed her to a bed where she could spend the night. Now, Gabby realised that Oshu was going to stay with Danielle and she was very disappointed, but then she looked at Mariamne, Oshu's wife, who seemed to support all her husband's actions - not questioning anything - as if in total acceptance. It was true; Oshu wasn't just a man, he was special and so were his actions and choices. Somehow, all of this had created a bond between the women. Exhausted from the day, Gabby closed her eyes and nodded off.

Back in the other part of the house, Oshu confronted Danielle with something that was troubling him. "Who has done this to you?" he asked, while pointing at her belly. Although it was a difficult question to answer, Danielle smiled and whispered, "You…"

Oshu shook his head. "That is not possible. We were together many moons ago. You are only with child one moon."

His eyes pierced right through hers, but he could not find a lie. Danielle just smiled. She had absolutely no idea what to say next. Suddenly, Oshu's eyes grew big. "Are you a Master?" he queried, suddenly filled with joy.

Danielle frowned. "A master of what?"

Oshu tried to explain. "I have seen people appear and disappear before, but I could not touch them, for these people had mastered the skills of apparition, but you, you are very real. Please, I want to know, how do you do it?" Oshu clapped his hands and laughed, obviously intrigued, but Danielle still couldn't think of a way to explain this to him. "I don't know." Unknowingly, Danielle stared at the necklaces in the bowl. Oshu followed her eyes. "Crystals?" he asked inquisitively. Danielle nodded; that was actually a great way to describe them. Oshu got up and wanted to touch them, but Danielle stopped him. "No, no, no, please don't touch them, they are important. Keep them there, please?" Immediately, Oshu understood and hummed. He had travelled through many countries when he was younger and had talked to many Masters and Magi, so he knew that not everyone was willing to share their knowledge with him. Oshu was impressed. As if everything suddenly made sense, he concluded, "So, this is *my* child?"

29

Montségur, southern France, July 5th 2011

Arthur was very disappointed. He knew that Rahn had stayed at the Hotel Couquet in the early 1930s; Arthur had researched Rahn's life well enough to be sure of this. "Sir, I just know he's here, I saw him at the window. He must have gone upstairs without being seen by the landlady."

The Swiss nodded. "We'll keep a close eye on the hotel and spread out, away from the door and windows. We will allow him to see us leave. David, you stay here with Ben and Yanne to keep an eye on the place. I will take the higher road. Arthur, you go around the back."

David was afraid that Rahn might use violence at some point and touched Alfred's arm.

"Is this wise? What if he hurts one of the kids?"

Alfred shook his head. "I don't think he will. It's true; the Hessian is a survivor and obviously desperate to get away, but I have discovered that Rahn is also a gentleman and I can't imagine him using violence to gain his freedom. Besides, he is unarmed. Don't worry David, I won't let any of the kids out of my sight."

Only half convinced, David took Ben and Yanne to a convenient spot to keep an eye on the building without being seen and watched with anxiety how his son Michael left with Alfred and Arthur to take up their positions.

Otto, however, wasn't born yesterday. All he had to do was wait until they gave up. He thought he was safe in his old room and that time was on his side, but it didn't feel right. Here he was - as if time had stood still - sitting on the same bed at the same hotel as before and again he felt trapped; he was all alone, without freedom, without money. He chuckled. *What's new.*

He had always been in debt, always been poor. All the money that had been promised to him by the publisher of his first book had all been a lie. Eventually it had been poverty that had driven him into the Allgemeine SS.

Of course, himself being a gentle person, he had been torn between his superiors in Berlin - with their increasingly brutal ways - and his own personal Grail quest. However, the very moment that he had joined the SS, he realised that there was no way out, except feet first. He had simply been sucked into a dark pool and found out far too late that he was actually swimming with sharks.

When he had met Himmler for the first time, Rahn was both intimidated and intrigued. Himmler and Hitler were both - like Rahn - big fans of myth and legend, eager to find the truth behind the stories. Of course, Himmler had wanted both the Grail *and* the Ark. Enthusiastic about Rahn's first book, 'Crusade against the Grail', he had asked him to write a sequel for a handsome salary. Of course, Otto couldn't refuse. He had been too poor to refuse. Going bankrupt with his hotel business in Ussat-les-Bains had already resulted in his eviction from France in 1932. Naturally, it had upset his French friends. By 1933, his reputation in the Sabarthès had been smashed by bad media, calling him a sect leader and a Nazi spy. He had attempted to go back to southern France to continue his Grail search, but something had blocked his way and it wouldn't be until the Autumn of 1934 that he finally managed to return to France, where he would start a European tour that would bring him to Italy, Austria and Germany. In 1936 - while researching Sacred Geometry for Weisthor and Himmler - he had been given the opportunity to visit the Corbières region in southern France on a special mission. Unfortunately, he had also had to go back to Berlin afterward. Rahn had tried to escape from an increasingly violent Germany by faking ill health and had settled himself in Muggenbrunn in the Black Forest, where he had begun writing a 2000 page novel under great pressure from Himmler. He had even felt obliged to fake an engagement to a Swiss woman named Asta, only to get Himmler off his back about paragraph 175. Being a homosexual was - after all - life-threatening in Nazi-Germany. Of course, his being gay would soon be used against him by his political enemies.

Like many other Nazi's, he had thought about the option to escape to Switzerland along the Vatican's escape route, but his friends had been too afraid to help him out. So, in 1939, Rahn had - quite literally - arrived at a dead end the very moment Alfred had collected him on that Austrian Alp.

It was difficult to think of the fact that all the friends he had made here back in the 1930s were all dead now. Antonin Gadal would have helped him for sure, if he had still been alive. This Rosicrucian friend and mentor, who had helped Otto with his research in the early 1930s, had, however, stopped replying to Otto's letters from Germany since 1935. This had worried him sick. Had he been angry with him for joining the SS? He could only guess. Of course, Nazi Germany and Rosicrucianism didn't mix well. Also his friend, the countess Pujol-Murat, had passed away already in the mid-1930s. Then there had been his best friend and lover, Raymond Perrier, who was also dead now. All these thoughts made him feel miserably lonely. He felt trapped and when he became hungry, he realised he couldn't stay there forever.

He had seen his pursuers leave at least fifteen minutes ago. Should he chance his luck? Gingerly he looked through the window. There was no one in the street. He tiptoed out of his room and down the old stairs. Carefully he opened the back door and stuck his head around the door to see if anyone was there.

"Leaving your safe haven, Otto?" said Arthur - arms folded and with a broad grin on his face.

Scheisse!

Rahn raced out through the alley, but found the exit blocked by Alfred's broad posture and outstretched arms. However, Otto was quick like a serpent and managed to duck and slide through Alfred's grip, who only just missed grabbing his arm. "Get him!" he yelled at Arthur, who ran after Otto as fast as he could. Arthur knew that Otto could run fast - he had experienced this not so long ago, though then it had been the other way around. With so much at stake right now, Rahn was very fast indeed, but running uphill slowed him down.

In an attempt to shake the boy loose, Otto quickly turned to cross the terrace of the *café/artisanat L'Auselou*, a building he remembered very well, as it had once belonged to the countess Pujol-Murat. He threw several plastic chairs in Arthur's direction, hoping to slow him down and indeed, Arthur quickly turned his back toward the large ammunition. Taking advantage of this, Otto raced across the pétanque field next to the tourist office, where two men wearing berets were having a go at the famous French ballgame. Two old dogs started barking at him, but Rahn quickly outran them and speeded toward the road, taking the steps up. Arthur was scared to death of dogs, so he decided to take the road on the other side of the block. When he arrived at the roadside, he saw that Rahn was way ahead of him now. Running downhill, Otto could run at top speed, but so could Arthur, who tried to ignore the pain in his right ankle; his old injury was playing up.

Otto turned to look.

Verdammt! That boy runs fast!

He quickly turned left at the lower parking and ran into a field, passing a statue. The distance between him and Arthur was getting shorter and he increased his speed even more. Already breathing heavily, Rahn now started to wheeze; after having been a heavy smoker, his lungs were unable to extract enough oxygen from the air. Then he saw that the field he had run into was fenced off and turned to see if there was another way out, but Arthur was almost upon him and his heart sank. In one giant leap, Arthur threw himself upon Rahn and both were now struggling in the high grass.

"Don't make me hurt you boy!" he shouted. Otto was fond of Arthur, but right now he could drink his blood. He punched him in the face and tried to get up again. Arthur's glasses had fallen into the grass and his nose was bleeding, but he had to stop Otto and grabbed his jacket. Otto raised his fist to punch him again. In an attempt to stop Rahn from beating him up, Arthur yelled, "*No Otto, please!* Alfred just wants to talk to you. You must come with me. *Please!*"

Otto's fist froze in mid-air. "I don't want to go back! *Nie!*"

"You don't *have* to! Shit man, you don't *have* to!" Tears were rolling over Arthur's face; fighting his hero was not what he had in mind. Rahn looked at the boy's face; his tears mixing with the blood from his nosebleed and it was clear that Arthur was upset about the situation. All the boy wanted was to prevent Otto from doing something stupid; to try and survive in a world he didn't belong to - without a passport, without any money - and Otto realised that it could only have been love that had made Arthur come after him. He took out his handkerchief and wiped the blood from Art's face. Arthur just stared at him while he was doing this; at his gentle, bright anthracite eyes and his famous frown. Nazi or not, SS-Totenkopf member or not, he couldn't believe that Otto would ever really harm him. Still in tears, he reached out to touch Otto's face. This gentle gesture startled Rahn and for a moment, neither of them were paying any attention to their surroundings.

At the edge of the village, Alfred, David and the kids had now lost sight of Otto and Arthur completely. David looked at Alfred. He was seriously worried and had become angry at Alfred. "So what did you say again, I won't let any of the kids out of my sight?"

The Swiss took out a small device from his pocket, checked it and cursed. Just before they had left Sion, he had given Rahn a friendship ring with a big onyx, hoping it would replace that horrible Totenkopfring. Otto had accepted this gift with gratitude and had put it on a finger on his left hand, after which he had simply moved the Totenkopfring to a finger on his right hand. The friendship ring, however, also served another purpose, for it had a tracking device. Should Rahn escape during their trip, Alfred would always be able to find him, but he hadn't counted on the unusual electro-magnetic field that surrounds places like Montségur, so the device didn't work properly. He had seen the moving dot on the screen for a moment and then it had totally disappeared.

They had no choice but to trust their ears, eyes and guts. Alfred had seen Otto and Arthur running down the road after passing the tourist office, each taking another side of the building that used to be the old village school. Alfred cursed. "Where the fuck did they go?"
David had forgotten to bring his binoculars and started to run down the road while trying to find tracks. Then he saw the trail through the grass. "Sir, I think they went into the field!"

Rahn looked at Arthur, moved by the love that he showed him. He casually supported himself on his elbow and exhausted from the sprint, they just lay there, side by side, not noticing the others approaching them from a distance. Otto ran his hand through the boys short curls, looked into his azure eyes and smirked. "You know, without your glasses you are actually very cute…"
Arthur smiled through his tears. He knew Otto was gay, but that didn't bother him; he had no idea what he was feeling himself. Arthur had never really been interested in girls, but he had never even thought that perhaps this meant he'd be more interested in boys. He had never felt any attraction to either a boy or a girl before, until now. The sound of the approaching group attracted Arthur's attention and he wanted to get up. "C'mon, we'd better…"
Suddenly, Rahn grabbed Arthur's arm to stop him from getting up. To find out whether the boy was also gay, he wanted to see if this would scare the boy, or that it would arouse him. "Do you know that I had boys like you for breakfast?" he said teasingly.
Arthur chuckled. "No you didn't."
Rahn pushed Arthur into the grass and while he brought his lips close to Arthur's, he insisted, "Yes I did!"
They could feel the chemistry and the sweet stings going through their bodies.
Both froze when they heard the gunshot.
Alfred had only seen something that looked like a fight and was afraid that Rahn would harm Arthur.

When they both got up, Otto with arms up in the air, Alfred relaxed. "Step away from the boy, Otto, slowly!"

Otto moved aside and Arthur, who was confused about the situation, trotted toward Alfred to beg him not to hurt Otto. "It's okay, sir, I told him he didn't have to go back to 1939. He *can* stay, can't he?"

Shit.

Alfred now understood that he no longer had any choice. He had to make preparations to let Otto integrate in the present, somehow, but for the moment he was just glad he had him and that Arthur was okay.

David walked over to Arthur. "So, what were you doing Art, were you fighting him?" Arthur looked at David and then at his friend Michael, who frowned.

"No, really, it's nothing." explained Arthur, but Michael was not blind. Not only did he notice the traces of Arthur's nosebleed, he also saw that Arthur had been crying and became concerned. "Did he hurt you? What did he do to you?" That very moment, Alfred and Otto passed them and for a second time, Alfred had to give Arthur his glasses back, but this time they were broken. Rahn winked mysteriously at Arthur and raised one eyebrow, as if he wanted to say; 'welcome to the club'. Arthur blushfully smiled back, feeling confounded; as if he had just come out of the closet, without having said anything.

Sion, Switzerland, July 5th 2011

Georg, Alfred's special agent, had seen everything from the glass office, but how could he reach Bill with the door closed from the inside? He noticed how Bill was suffering from the electric shock to his leg and had immediately contacted the other agents. They were now in code red; this was a hostage situation. Georg desperately needed to contact Alfred and decided to use the satellite Internet connection to send a direct message to Alfred's mobile phone:

Code red. Al Din broke out. Taken Prof hostage. Awaiting your orders.

All he could do now was wait for a reply from his chief, while he had to watch Al Din putting more and more pressure on the poor professor. "Is there any chance you can get Danielle back *now*?" Al Din queried, but Bill shook his head. "The devices that Parker and Standford are carrying are programmed to activate at a certain date and time; I cannot change it from here, so we have no choice but to wait."

Bill kept his fingers crossed that Alfred and Otto would return to the base before that and tried to buy some time, hoping Al Din wouldn't get too impatient. However, he quickly found out that Al Din was not a patient man. "I want them back *now*. I don't care how you do it. Just get them back *now*. Or at least Danielle. I am serious, professor."

Bill looked into Al Din's wild eyes, without moving a muscle. Suddenly, the Arab lashed out with the back of his hand, hitting Bill full in the face. *"Do it!!"*

Bill felt his nose and sat down behind his computer. He realised that he was no match for Al Din, who was at least a head taller than him. He wouldn't stand a chance.

Unless…

Pamiers, southern France, July 5th 2011

Alfred cursed when he received Georg's message on his mobile. They needed to get back to Sion immediately, so as soon as he and Otto had taken leave of David and the kids, they drove toward the airfield. On the way, Alfred felt he had to share the situation with Otto, who had been very silent since their departure from Montségur. "We have a situation at the base; Al Din has broken out and is now keeping the professor hostage in the lab."

Otto pursed his lips. "We'll have to get him out of there then. Just keep me away from that damn time machine, will you?"

Alfred understood Otto's cynical pun and called the airport to prepare the jet for an emergency take off. The airspace was clear at that time of night so they could take off the moment they arrived at the airport. As it wasn't a long flight, they should be able to touch down at Sion airport within the hour and Alfred could only hope that nothing would go tragically wrong in that precious hour.

Sion, Switzerland, July 5th 2011

Bill knew that he could easily outsmart the Arab, but Al Din didn't give him a minute to come up with a plan, as he was breathing down his neck all the time. The pain in his leg was killing him and he became irritated. "I need to make very careful calculations now, so if you don't mind, could you get out of my hair for a moment and just let me do my work?"

Al Din stepped back a few paces. "Just get on with it!"

Trying to keep his cool, Bill faked all kinds of formulas on the screen, which looked real enough to Al Din. He had to find a way to unlock the door and get out of here. Desperate for help, he looked up at the glass window, hoping someone was up there.

The thunderstorm was still roaring over Sion and Al Din nervously circled the green-lit room like a tiger in a cage. "How long before you finish your calculations, professor?"

Bill rubbed his face. "This is careful calculus you know, one mistake and they are lost to us forever! Is that what you want?"

Al Din couldn't believe that the professor would need such a long time to reprogram the codes and felt he was up to something. He had watched the screen constantly to make sure that he wasn't sending out any e-mail messages, but so far he had seen only formulae. Al Din looked up at the clock. "You have 30 minutes, professor. If you haven't brought Danielle back by then, I will become your worst nightmare."

Bill sighed.

You already are...

Another loud thunderclap made the lights go on and off again, but this time, Bill's computer crashed completely. Even when the green emergency lights went on, the machine refused to start up.

Shit! Oh, God no...

316

Bill held his head in his hands. That was it. It was as if all his body functions had suddenly come to a full stop. A weird feeling of numbness came over him when the horrible truth dawned on him; Al Din or no Al Din, Danielle and Gabby were now stuck in ancient Judea for the rest of their lives.

30

European airspace, July 5ᵗʰ 2011

During the flight back to Sion, Otto thought about his short, intimate moment with Arthur and wondered if he'd ever see the curly-haired, blue-eyed, twenty year old English boy again. Arthur reminded him of Raymond, his lover and best friend in the 1930's and couldn't help feeling lonely. He wondered if Arthur would miss him, too. Otto thought about many things, but he also noticed that something inside him had changed when he found himself focusing on the future and no longer on the past.

In the meantime, Alfred had been busy communicating with the base in Sion. He frowned at Otto. "I'm afraid we'll be heading into a thunderstorm. Georg said that the electricity has gone off and that Bill's computer has crashed. This is an alarming situation Otto. If Bill's computer has crashed beyond repair, it means we cannot get Danielle and Gabby back."

After hearing this, Rahn woke up from his thoughts and stared hard at Alfred, who seemed worried sick. He also noticed how tired the Swiss was and felt even more guilty. "Has the computer crashed beyond repair?" queried Otto.

Alfred sighed. "We'll know soon enough. That thunderstorm doesn't sound good though. It means we may have to fly to another airport and then it will take even longer to get back to the base."

Otto rubbed his face, aware of the seriousness of the situation. "How long till we get there?"

"At least another 20 minutes. If we go to Sion, that is." said Alfred sourly, while looking out of the window. They already felt the increasing turbulence. Immediately they put their seat belts back on and braced themselves.

It was going to be a bumpy ride.

Bethanu, ancient Judea, 33 AD

Danielle's heart was aching for Gabby. Where had she been taken? Over the past hour, Oshu had done some more healing on her and afterward he had told her all about his plans. It had been a special time; private, but then Mariamne arrived with aloe, allowing Danielle to witness something she would never forget. Oshu carefully took off his garment, so for the first time she saw the damage that the infamous 39 lashes had caused on his back and legs. Though this had happened over two months ago, the deep wounds mercilessly betrayed the violence with which poor Oshu had been tortured before his crucifixion. With the love and care of a devoted wife, Mariamne carefully rubbed the aloe onto the wounds and scars on his skin, while both of them were intonating a word; the same word Oshu had also intonated when he was working on Danielle; the elongated 'kay'. When she had finished, Mariamne helped her husband into his bed and before she left, she kissed both Oshu and Danielle on the forehead, as if they were children she had just tucked in. "Kalinichta…" she whispered.

Like most men, Oshu was fast asleep within minutes. Danielle smiled when she heard his soft, rhythmic snore, but couldn't help wondering why on earth he'd want to stay with her if he only wanted to sleep? Danielle, on the other hand, simply couldn't sleep and an hour later she got out of bed, tiptoed into the courtyard and softly called out for Gabby. Only a few seconds later, Gabby came out of the other building. She couldn't sleep much either.

"Is something wrong?" she queried.

"No," said Danielle softly, "I just can't sleep. Oshu told me that they are going to leave Bethanu the day after tomorrow; it's too dangerous for him to stay here any longer. His mother has already left for Ephesus with one of his brothers, Mariamne's brother has left for Cyprus and Oshu will go to the Essenes in Carmel, where he plans to teach small classes and write down his teachings, while Cephas will stay in Jerusalem with Ya'akov to run the community together.

However, Mariamne will be going to Egypt with the rest of the family and we are welcome to accompany her. Mariamne wants to have her baby there before she journeys on to Gallia, which is France. Gabby, we mustn't forget to take our necklaces. Oshu thinks they are crystals, but he knows that we need to keep them with us, so I'm sure we are allowed to wear them again at some point. He said he would talk to Mariamne about it."

Gabby stared at Danielle with open mouth. "… but are you fit enough to travel that far?"

"As most of the journey to Egypt is by boat, Oshu feels it would be best for us to go with Mariamne. Unfortunately, this also means that it will be Mariamne who will teach us from now on, not Oshu."

Gabby shook her shoulders. "I believe we were already fortunate and besides, now we know that Mariamne probably did come to France!"

Danielle's eyes grew big. "You are right! It's just a pity that we will be going back to our present before we get there."

They both stared at the sky. Somehow, the firmament made an incredible impression on them and they were looking forward to Mariamne's lessons on astronomy and astrology; her speciality. During their briefing in Sion they were told only to listen and take notes. It was of the utmost importance that they didn't share their modern knowledge with anybody.

Unnoticed by the women, Mariamne, too, had come out and her voice startled them. "Myriam Dani, Myriam Chabi, come…" She was annoyed with them. Feeling a bit embarrassed - being caught out of bed and out of their rooms - they followed Mariamne into a small room where she lectured them. "Myriam Dani, you really must go back to your bed! Oshu wants to speak to you as soon as he wakes up. It will be the last moment you will have with him and after that, he will stay with me. Myriam Chabi, you must stay with me. Tomorrow you will be reunited with Myriam Dani, but tonight you must give them some privacy."

Gabby went back inside and also Danielle slowly walked back to her room, not realising that she had hurt Mariamne's feelings by leaving Oshu's side. It didn't matter whether Oshu was asleep or not; the aura that surrounded the avatar was a healing aura that Danielle needed to heal herself and her child. The time that Mariamne had generously donated to Danielle was precious and it was painful for her to see how Danielle was wasting it. Realising that perhaps Danielle didn't know about this, Mariamne decided to explain this to her. Naturally, Danielle felt ashamed when she understood and quickly returned to her bed, where she quietly remained during the rest of the night, bathing in Oshu's presence.

When the light grew stronger, she realised that she had been awake all night, listening to the regular, gentle breathing of Oshu and thinking about everything both she and Gabby were caught up in. The first birds started whistling their tunes and slowly, Oshu woke up. Danielle watched him stretch and move his head toward her and when their eyes met, all she could do was smile. He got into her bed and held her close, but Danielle was afraid to touch his back in her embrace, so she put her arms around his neck instead. Their noses touched and Oshu kissed her softly on the lips.
"Kalimera, sweet Dani El."
The embrace filled her up with new energy and she quickly forgot the fatigue she had suffered from the sleepless night. When she felt his warm body lying against hers, she never wanted to let go. It was a heart-breaking thought that this was going to be their last intimate moment; that as soon as he'd leave her room, she could never be alone with him, ever again. She tightened her embrace and Oshu understood her emotions. "You are so special, Dani El and Mariamne knows this. You have a special task of which we can only understand the essence. That is why she approved of you being here with us; with me. I must go very soon, but I will carry both you and Mariamne in my heart, always."

He kissed the palm of her hand. "I give you this kiss; it will last forever. Separation is only tangible to earthly matter, for in spirit there exists no space; no time; no separation. Our souls will always stay connected. Eternally. It is a fact."
Danielle savoured his words and wept softly during the hour that came and went; their last hour.

That afternoon, Oshu called a meeting. It was clear that this was an emotional moment: this was the eve of the separation of a group of people who had formed such a strong community for several years; a community that had gone through so much together, but now it was of the essence that all of them went into different directions to spread the Hermetic Teachings and the Good News that no one is truly mortal, for the soul is eternal; the soul is the Kingdom where the Father is and therefore, Paradise is within each of us.
The moment all had gathered in the large room, Oshu started to speak. His face was serious, but his eyes were bright.
"At this day before our parting we find ourselves together in this room one more time and you will feel sadness in your hearts, but I can only tell you that in this material world, mankind has always been divided; from the moment we were born. I have only been here with you to undo this division, which had started at the beginning of time. How can we experience union? It is important to know and understand, that it takes two to become One and when two become One, miracles happen. The unification of the female and male principle of Abwoon inside each and every one of us, will lead to great deeds and will make us all Sons of Men. Alone we cannot achieve miracles, so I command you to always work side by side, teacher and apprentice. Know that when we work, not all seeds we sow fall on the field; some also fall on the roadside. The seeds we sow will partly be devoured by birds and worms. Some of the small plants that had already started to grow will be suffocated by thorns and weeds, but the rest that has fallen on the fertile earth will ripen to become the best grain the world has ever seen! Alas, this

world is not a safe place. Like the farmer who stays awake to guard his possessions, so will the world treat us. Therefore you must surround yourself with the orb of protection, allowing you to be safe from both farmers and robbers alike. As soon as the grain ripens, you must trust the moment and harvest it, no matter where you are. Your rewards will be great; you will see what the eye would never see; you will hear words the ear will never hear and you will experience what a human heart couldn't possibly imagine. Abwoon has prepared great treasure for you in the Heavens, so work fast. Be safe. My thoughts and my heart go with you."

Oshu touched his brow, his lips and his heart with his right hand and closed his eyes, leading everyone into a meditation.

As expected, Oshu spent the rest of the day with Mariamne and all meals were taken in silence. All meals but one, for that evening, a big party was thrown with food, music and dance. All had come; even the sick and the old had been brought in to be part of it and for those precious hours, it felt as if everything was alright. They ate until they were full and danced to the music until all were exhausted.

The next morning was an emotional and painful one; a historical happening that would be described in Danielle's diary as 'The Great Separation'. Both Danielle and Gabby had a very short, private moment with Oshu just before he left with his small group of people; a group that undoubtedly consisted of several future saints. The very moment he was out of sight, the pain lashed their hearts, tearing them apart and it was heart-breaking to see Mariamne's deep grief. Knowing that she would never see her husband - her soul mate - again in this life, had made her clamour and lament until she could cry no more.

That afternoon, Mariamne's heartbroken, silent group left Bethanu for the port of Jaffa. This was the harbour from where they would board a ship to Egypt and their focus had now changed toward the future, not the past. Although it had started out as a silent journey - travelling through the Judean mountains to the coast - the prospect of the sea voyage seemed to cheer them all up the moment they spotted the blue sea. Standing on the deck of the ship, Gabby noticed how the mainsail was swooping in the wind and she felt the rush of the new adventure. She grabbed Danielle's arm. "Danielle, what does 'pepromeno' mean?"

Danielle looked at her friend. "Destiny. Why?"

"Oh, no reason." Gabby smiled secretively at the sea and caressed a hidden item underneath her clothes. When they both reached their destiny, Gabby would give it to her. Danielle frowned at her friend, but as Gabby changed the subject, she quickly forgot about it and thought of it no more.

It was on that same evening, when the stars seemed brighter than ever, that Mariamne started her first class. They weren't the only students; there were several others clinging to her every word and they realised that the astronomy Mariamne was teaching them was incomparable to the one-sided teachings that Gabby had studied at the university, for this was meta-astrophysics. It wasn't just about the laws of the stars and their movement in the galaxy; it was permeated with mysticism, astrology and religion. The impact this force has on literally everything, became all too clear. This ancient knowledge was not only used for navigation, agriculture and the study of the seasons, it was also a window into future events. It was even a window into the state of health and destiny of certain individuals by drawing up detailed birth charts. For Gabby, this particular point of view was difficult to accept, because her university professor had always mocked astrology. However, Mariamne seemed to emphasise the strong relations between religion; mathematics; the knowledge of the heavenly bodies; health; architecture; sacred geometry; agriculture and the future in a very convincing manner. While Danielle did her very best to give an accurate translation, Gabby took notes using Danielle's diary and combined her own knowledge with Mariamne's. These notes were important to understand nature in all its qualities; to understand the knot that unites the above and the below and to preserve this holistic knowledge for future generations. Gabby thought about the + and the – polarities of a battery. The battery needs both sides, or it just wouldn't work and she finally understood that this also applied to science and mysticism.

When they had safely landed on Egyptian soil and the month had almost passed, Danielle and Gabby were allowed to wear their necklaces again in anticipation of the moment for them to go back to the 21st century. Although Marianne's teachings were immensely precious and their stay in Egypt an experience beyond words, time seemed to pass quickly and they became more nervous every day, hoping that nothing had happened and that the devices would work on the programmed moment. Gabby was amazed that - though separated literally by time and space - she still felt the special bond between herself and Bill and she couldn't wait to go back. Nevertheless, she had a strange feeling in her underbelly. It was as if she knew something had gone wrong…

Sion, Switzerland, July 5th 2011

The thunderstorm wasn't over yet and Bill was getting more and more upset with the whole situation. He desperately wanted to get to that door. Then, suddenly, both he and Al Din froze when on the other side of the door, hell seemed to be breaking loose. It sounded like midnight on New Year's Eve; shots were fired from at least ten guns. Bill looked at Al Din, who was getting pale. The following moment, the lights flickered and the normal lights turned back on again. They could also hear the door lock click.
The sliding doors are working again!
Bill raced toward the door as fast as his painful leg allowed, but immediately Al Din sprinted after him and the moment Bill opened the sliding doors, Al Din got to him and threw his right arm around Bills neck, squeezing tightly.
"You are not going anywhere, professor."

Both men were now facing the hallway and they could see dead bodies everywhere. Then Bill spotted Ms Kaiser, who - assisted by a team of armed men - had successfully entered and secured Sion Base. Apparently she was the only survivor. Kaiser pointed a gun at Bill and smirked when she saw the hopelessness in his eyes. The taste of victory had always been relished by her. Bill knew that all was lost now, but then, two new shots were fired. No longer smiling, Elsa Kaiser collapsed; one of the shots had killed her instantly. Bill, who was now struggling to free himself from Al Din's grip, spotted Georg at the back of the hallway, still holding up his gun. He had a pale face, as if in shock. Instead of feeling victorious, Alfred's special agent seemed alarmed. Though Georg had fired only one shot, he distinctively remembered hearing two. Then he saw where the second shot had been fired from. The impact of the shot that had killed Kaiser must have triggered her finger. Bill suddenly felt a burning pain and noticed the fresh blood on his shirt. Then, his legs gave way and the last thing he heard - a split second before he hit the floor - was a third shot; the shot that took down Al Din. After that, everything turned black.

Clinique de Valère, Sion, Switzerland, July 7th 2011

Bill woke up and saw the blurry image of a TV news flash.

"... resulted in the capture of drug lord and oil magnate Izz al Din, who had been reported missing on July 4th..."

He also felt someone squeezing his right hand.
"Hi sweetie, how are you feeling?"
Bill's eyes grew big when he saw Gabby sitting next to his bed. "How on earth did you get here?" queried Bill, completely confused. Gabby smiled. "Georg saved the day and Alfred got us back safely. Fortunately, the computer itself was undamaged."
Bill smiled from ear to ear. That was fantastic news.
"So, what date is it?"

"It's July 7th; you have been here for over a day now. Thank God it was just your shoulder, although the operation took a bit longer than expected. The bullet had penetrated deep into your shoulder, so they had to be really careful taking it out. You lost a bit of blood though!"

Bill was aware of that. On top of his nosebleed he had been shot, but then he noticed the bag of blood dangling above him and knew he would soon be fine. Nevertheless he was in a lot of pain. "How is Danielle?" he asked.

"She's fine, we've all heard the baby's heartbeat for the first time with a Doppler machine!"

Bill smiled at her, but still felt a little dizzy. He rested his head on his pillow and within seconds he slipped back into a deep sleep.

That same moment, Alfred entered the room.

"You're too late, sir, he just fell asleep again." said Gabby.

Alfred was visibly exhausted, but refused to go home to get some sleep. "How is he doing?"

"I think he's still in a lot of pain, but he gets his fair share of morphine. How's Al Din?"

"He's in a coma. It was a complicated surgery, but he'll live. However, the doctors don't know when or if he will ever wake up. As soon as he is stable, he will be taken to the Zürich Airport Prison medical ward for the time being. I just think it's sad that someone like him - who has such understanding and intelligence - falls for the dark side. People get obsessed and then choose to use violence to reach their goals, even when those goals are primarily good. I know what some people in the West think about Muslims and Islam, but actually, extremism is the real enemy."

He looked at Gabby, staring at her sleeping soul mate while cradling his cheek in her hand. Without looking up from him, she said to Alfred in a soft voice, "All I want is for the hurting to stop. Really, sir, I just want the hurting to stop."

31

Vatican City, July 29th 2011

The summer vacation was almost over at David's B&B in the Corbières and the kids had become a little sulky, not wanting to go back to England. Little did they know that their vacation would suddenly get an extra twist. It all started when a few days earlier, David had received a mysterious text message on his mobile, saying:

friday july 29 at 10 am on st peters square rome no excuses!

Intrigued, David had agreed to the extra outing, so the day before, they had all boarded the Ryanair evening flight from Girona to Rome Ciampino. David had booked a package with a rental car and a nice hotel close to the famous square, so he and the kids had arrived at the basilica on time that Friday morning. Anxiously they browsed the famous square to see why they had been summoned there and by whom. Never having been to Rome before, they were all impressed by the sheer size of St. Peter's Square and the Basilica. David looked around, but didn't recognise anyone yet. Suddenly he heard someone shouting his name. Then he saw Bill, Gabby and Danielle waving at them. They quickly walked over to each other, relieved to see familiar faces.

"Were you texted too?" asked Gabby.

"Yeah! So, do you have any idea who's behind this?" queried David.

Gabby shook her head and took the opportunity to introduce Danielle. David was glad to see that their planned rescue mission had been successful. Of course, he had already heard a lot about her, but he had never thought that Danielle was so beautiful. David couldn't utter a word; he just stood there and stared at her.

Oh my God, she's absolutely fabulous!

Danielle, who was still a bit affected by her experiences in ancient Judea, noticed David's gaze and smiled.

She had seen men looking at her like that before and unintentionally wondered if he were single. She looked at his hazel eyes, his handsome, tanned face and his lips. Then she looked away.

He's gorgeous, but it's too early...

Then, David saw that Bill's arm was resting in a sling and was concerned, "What happened to you, professor?"

Bill pursed his lips. "I got shot, but I'm fine now."

Gabby casually held onto his other arm. "These last three weeks we have been in Switzerland to get our breath back, but we haven't seen much of Alfred. We have come in his jet though, so he should be around somewhere..." Gabby looked around the square and wondered where he'd gone off to.

"Let's have a coffee somewhere and catch up!" proposed David, suddenly forgetting that he hadn't come alone. Meanwhile, Arthur had been casting his eyes around the square all the time; searching; hoping. Then he spotted Alfred. How could they have missed this broad shouldered Swiss giant? Alfred, on the other hand, tried to hide his surprise when he saw David and the kids and forced a smile. "So, you were texted too, huh? I wonder where the agitator could be."

Then suddenly, as if drawn by a magnetic pull, Arthur turned and spotted him. Rahn leaned casually against one of the columns - his hands in his pockets - wearing a broad, nonchalant smile. He had been watching them from this location ever since they had arrived at the square, enjoying how they had failed to notice him. Perhaps it was because he was wearing a hat and a nicely trimmed beard. Overjoyed at the sight of him, Arthur sprinted over and stopped about a meter away from his hero to admire him and his new, slick style. "Cool, very Italian!"

Rahn smirked. "No glasses?"

Arthur shook his head. "Don't need them anymore. I had a laser treatment in the hospital in Carcassonne."

Otto tenderly ran his hand through the boy's curly hair. Although the others had now also joined, Otto's eyes were still fixed on Arthur, who seemed frozen. Rahn chuckled, not really knowing what to do next. This beautiful boy seemed to like him - perhaps he even loved him - and he realised that he had to make a decision sooner or later. Finally, Rahn turned to greet the others. It was now clear to all of them that it had been Otto who had sent the mysterious text message; he obviously had something important to share with all of them. Indeed, a moment later he raised his arms like a ringmaster and started, "Now, follow me, ladies and gentlemen, on my magical mystery tour. Prepare to be amazed!"

The moment Otto walked off to lead them toward the transept of St. Peter's Basilica, Alfred winked at Georg to follow without being seen.

During the walk, Rahn showed Arthur his new ID.

"Otto Adler?" said Arthur, slightly amused.

Otto grinned. "Yeah, like it? Fred gave me a new passport and a handsome bank account, so I decided to explore the world. I get itchy feet, you know, can't stay put for too long. I never could."

Arthur was pleased for him; he had been given a new life, but he hadn't failed to notice the cold manner in which Alfred was treating him at the moment. Arthur reached for his hand; he desperately wanted to stay with him, but didn't know if Otto would allow him into his life. Arthur had fallen in love with him, with his eyes; his smile and the dimples in his cheeks; with his romantic side; his adventurous side; his cheeky side, but the moment their hands touched, Otto startled and he withdrew impulsively. He looked at the boy and frowned. "I'm almost twice your age, boy. You know that, don't you?"

"Does that bother you?" asked Arthur, somewhat taken aback.

Rahn smirked and looked away. "Nope."

Otto had never had any problems with younger boyfriends. Raymond had only been 19 when they had first met.

Otto put his arm around Arthur and laughed. "So you want to stay with me, huh?"

Arthur felt relieved. "Oh yeah, absolutely!"

Unaware of it, both skipped a heartbeat at the same time. How wonderful life is at the meeting of the waters; when one finds his love answered by his true soul mate. The soul has no gender, which makes love so complicated sometimes.

The heart wants what the heart wants…

When they reached the entrance to the Vatican Grottoes, Alfred became suspicious. Where was Otto taking them to and why? He thought the German would be cruising the world by now. Within days after Alfred had given Otto his new life, Rahn had bolted and Alfred was surprised to see him back so soon and in Rome of all places.

Would Rahn be loyal after all?

Earlier that month, Alfred had received a written note from Rahn, requesting permission to do some research in the Roussillon near Perpignan in southern France, so he had initially thought that Otto had gone there. The written note, however, had made Alfred chuckle. Why hadn't he just asked him? There had been no need for him to put the request into writing, but then, Alfred remembered that this had been the drill that Rahn had become used to; requests to visit and investigate particular places had to be neatly typed out and addressed to the Reichsführer SS. Although Alfred was now Otto's chief, he wasn't Himmler and he certainly didn't want Otto to compare him to that fellow.

Alfred paced himself to catch up with Otto; he needed some answers and he needed them now. He grabbed Rahn's shoulder and said in a soft, but serious tone, "I got your message, I'm here and apparently all the others are too. Now what the hell is this all about?"

Otto smiled at his chief. "I owe *all* of you the truth, Fred, not just you. Just trust me for once?"

In silence they walked the entire length of the Vatican Grottoes until - at the far end - they reached a beautiful, serene tomb that was placed on a travertine base.

It was the tomb of Pope Pius XII.

Otto turned to face the others and started, "You know, I hated the Roman Catholic Church for what it had done to the Cathars and to all the people who didn't agree with Church doctrines and dogmas, but when I met Archbishop Pacelli in Germany, I could sense he was different. I was impressed with his humanitarian work and found him a gentleman and a Cathar at heart. I just knew he could change the course of the church, if only he had the chance and actually, I thought he'd make a great Pope, but then of course I found out through that wonderful modern medium of yours called the Internet, that he actually did become the next Pope! While I was reading up on Pacelli's role as Pope Pius XII and the terrible accusations made against him of either staying too silent or even being on the side of the Nazi's, I discovered that this had been a KGB plot; to undermine the reputation of the Pope. There is, however, solid proof that Pacelli was far from silent. Though being in a fragile position, he still tried over and over again to persuade Hitler to stop the war and in secret, he helped close to one million Jews to escape from Germany and Austria. The Berliner Morgenpost stated how Pacelli's election to become the new Pope on March 3rd 1939 was not accepted with favour in Germany. Why? Because he openly opposed the Nazi state politics. In December 1942, the New York Times wrote that Pacelli was the only ruler left on the Continent of Europe who dared to raise his voice at all. Pacelli even recited a very strong Christmas message, in which he bravely spoke out against Hitler, being the only one who dared to do this at the time."

Rahn took out a piece of paper from his pocket, unfolded it and started to read from it.

"The Church stood squarely across the path of Hitler's campaign for suppressing the truth. I never had any special interest in the Church before, but now I feel great affection and admiration and am forced thus to confess that what I once despised, I now praise unreservedly. – Albert Einstein."

"Hah, silent Pope indeed. Pacelli was terribly misunderstood. You know, I loved my meetings with Pacelli when he was in Germany. We both shared an interest in hiking; nature; archaeology and I even sent him a copy of my book 'Crusade against the Grail' in 1933. I was also the one who had persuaded Himmler to give him Jesus' remains."

Alfred felt how all the muscles in his body suddenly blocked his breath and motion. The others were also speechless. Noticing their shock, Rahn continued, "When I researched the history of the sacred geometry around the two Rennes in the Corbières in the Autumn of 1936, I did not just stumble upon the stories about the rich priest, I also found the tomb of the Nazarene. Like I told you, I took the skull and lower arm bones, the seal and the Templar scroll to Himmler. Heinrich thought it would be a big joke to give Jesus' mortal remains to the Church and laughed his head off when I proposed it. In fact, I think they really did it, too. In January 1937, I received a handsome promotion and a few months after that, Weisthor gave me one of the first Totenkopf rings."

Rahn showed them the ring he was still wearing and it began to dawn on them where Weisthor might have gotten his inspiration from. This thought filled everyone with horror. Otto noticed how his audience had gone pale and feeling obliged to explain, he continued without delay,

"Now, here's my theory. Pacelli, who was shocked to suddenly possess the holiest relics of Christianity, must have shared his secret with Josefine Lehnert - a.k.a. Sister Mary Pascalina - who was Eugenio's shadow; his secretary; his best friend. Both must have been dead set to keep this from the world. After all, according to Christian dogma, those remains shouldn't exist at all, so what to do with the remains? Of course, I had to research the Internet from this point onward and I believe that in 1939, Pacelli had found the ultimate hiding place for the skull and bones of Christ. The cover up was brilliant; a secret, archaeological dig for the remains of St. Peter, to be carried out in secret, underneath the basilica."

"The plans were already made in 1939, immediately after Pacelli had been elected Pope, but the first excavations wouldn't start until 1941. At first, Pacelli refused to dig underneath the high altar, which would have been the obvious place to start. He probably had no intention or whatsoever to disturb the real tomb of St. Peter in his fabulous plan, but when they started to unearth several tombs and graves of historical interest, the excavations soon became real eye-openers for Pacelli and his archaeological team. You must realise that this was still a top secret mission; while WWII was ravishing Europe, the secret diggings of whom no-one involved was allowed to speak, continued deep underneath the St. Peter's and they were now slowly moving closer to the space underneath the High Altar. When the diggers discovered a place of pilgrim veneration dating from 2nd century, they thought they had come close to the actual tomb of St. Peter. However, when they finally found the body that had been venerated as St. Peter by the early Christians, tests showed that the dating didn't fit; the bones were too old, so it couldn't have been the fisherman after all. Not giving up hope, the enthusiastic team now started to focus on possible other graves in the surrounding area, but no one seems to know if they had actually found anything solid, as there are no photos or records available. However, in 1950, the Pope suddenly announced in his Christmas Message that they had found the tomb of St. Peter, but he was less specific about what had been found *inside* the tomb. Pacelli more or less left it in the middle. It is known that all the bones that had been excavated so far had been in the Pope's possession, safely tucked away in his private apartment and if you ask me, he had probably hid them next to the skull and bones that he had received from Himmler before the war. Because the Pope had unlimited access to the crypt and the dig site, he could have easily sneaked in and out of the crypt at night without asking anyone for permission, so theoretically, Pacelli had the opportunity to bury the skull and bones in the soil underneath the altar."

"I also believe that he could have only achieved this with the aid of sister Mary Pascalina, his faithful assistant. You know, history has never proved that St. Peter ever came to Rome; the scholar Eusebius even denied the apostles' presence in Rome in his writings and Pacelli and his successor Paul VI never produced solid proof that any of the bones they had found were those of the apostle. So, how do we know that Pacelli had indeed secretly buried Jesus' remains underneath St. Peter's basilica? Well, first of all I think it was not a coincidence that he had already started to plan this archaeological dig the very moment he had been elected to the Papacy in March 1939. Secondly; in 1949, Pacelli decreed that the Order of the Holy Sepulchre - which had always been seated in Jerusalem - should also be seated here, in Rome. Their main building stood just off St. Peter's Square. As you may know; this order - which dates back to the first Crusade - had originally been created to protect the tomb of Christ."

Everyone stared at him with open mouth. David suddenly thought of a coat of arms he had seen in his hotel and wanted to ask a question, but Rahn was unstoppable.

"In 1958, Pacelli must have felt the urge to leave a clue to the whereabouts of the holiest relics on earth, or to confide in someone; to make sure at least someone else knew about the skull and bones. After all, he was the sole keeper of the biggest secret of the western world and should anything happen to him... I think only sister Mary Pascalina knew about the secret. Then suddenly, one day after his regular check-up by his personal physician, professor Riccardo Galeazzi-Lisi, the Pope died mysteriously. The physician stated that Pacelli had been in excellent health the day before he died and that he was shocked and surprised by his sudden death. Later study revealed that Pacelli had been poisoned. Though she had been a suspect, sister Mary Pascalina was not pursued, but had to leave the Vatican immediately after the Pope's burial. I believe she had wanted to shut him up; to stop him from sharing The Secret."

"However, there's more. While still alive, Pacelli had mentioned in one of his speeches that St. Peter's Basilica was actually the Church of Christ, not of St. Peter. So all in all, I believe that *this* is the Universal Temple Tomb you wanted to create, Fred. No one will ever be able to dig up Jesus' bones now anymore; for I believe the holiest relics of Christianity are already underneath the holiest church on earth."

Alfred was paralysed, feeling lost. Suddenly, an outbreak of laughter behind them made them all jump. They turned around and gazed at the victorious face of Cardinal Antonio Sardis, dressed in a scarlet red choir vestment. "Forgive me my friends, the irony; I couldn't help it!"

"How on earth did you know we were here?" queried David.

"Forgot to check your mobile phone for bugs, Mr Camford?"

Shit! He must have seen Rahn's text message!

"You forget that you are on my turf now. Would you be so kind as to follow me, please?"

There was no way out. Sardis had come with four Swiss guards, who were dressed in the typical, prescribed costume that Michelangelo had designed for The Vatican half a millennium ago. Alfred despised the Cardinal's love of drama, but he was curious to what he had in store for them. He also realised that he now had the opportunity to start serious negotiations with Cardinal Sardis about the future role of the Holy Mother Church. However, their visit to the private parts of the building also meant that Alfred's trusty agent Georg could no longer follow him.

Sardis led them through the Sacristy into an adjoining building and after walking down another hallway, they arrived at a beautifully furnished room that looked like an office. He courteously showed Danielle and Alfred in, while the others were escorted to a separate waiting room. Otto, excited about their current whereabouts and eager have a moment alone with his new boyfriend, just couldn't stay put and as soon as the Swiss guards had left to station themselves at the exit of the building, Otto sneaked out, closely followed by Arthur. They skittered down the hallway, leaving David and the others alone in the waiting room. When Otto found an alcove, he stopped and playfully pushed Arthur against the wall. Both chuckled. Realising that they were inside the Vatican, they couldn't help enjoying the mischief, but Arthur also became a little nervous. He knew that his love for Otto blinded him. After all, how well did he really know the man? He noticed how Otto started to lean and stared shyly at his cheeky smile.

"S.. so, what are you up to?" stuttered Arthur, "We're inside a Vatican building you know; there may be camera's here and…"

"Shh, halt die Klappe." whispered Rahn teasingly, while putting on an overconfident grin. For a short moment they were face to face and their noses touched. Rahn imprisoned his new boyfriend in-between his arms and felt so much tenderness for Arthur. The chemistry between the two was overwhelming, especially for Arthur, who couldn't help enjoying the rush he got out of the intimate, somewhat tight moment. Otto realised that Arthur had only found out recently that he was gay and could not only see excitement in the boy's eyes; he also saw hesitation and fear. Was he going too fast? He stared at his eyes and then at his lips.

"*Oy*, what the hell are you doing!"

Both froze, but they relaxed when they saw it was David, who was in fact furious at the two. Quickly he made them march back to the waiting room, but the moment they took their seats, they started to chuckle, after which everyone started to laugh. Somehow, their mischievous, somewhat childish behaviour reminded them all of their school years and even David couldn't be angry for much longer.

In the meantime, eight metres away in Sardis' office, the atmosphere was a lot more serious.

"Now, Danielle, tell me child, are you alright?" Sardis asked.

"Yes, your eminence. Me and my baby are very well. Thank you."

"You must be how many weeks now?"

"Just over three months, your eminence."

She didn't forget to count the month she had been in ancient Judea, though it had only lasted a day here in the present. Sardis folded his hands. "Only a short while ago I had come to Sion because I wanted to join you, collaborate with SBS-Sion and become an ambassador between you and the Holy Mother Church. Again I reach out to you with this same offer. Now, will you accept it?" The Cardinal looked from Alfred to Danielle.

"… and what is your price, your eminence?" queried Danielle with a cynical undertone.

Sardis shook his head. "I am not like Izz al Din. I found out about his second agenda too late and I *am* sorry. I abducted you to protect you from him and yes, I must admit, I was in love and yes, I also had my own personal agenda to follow, but unlike him I have no need for money, nor a desire to dominate the world. All I want is world peace and if I can do my part in it, then I will gladly do so. My only personal ambition is to become the next Pope and to proclaim your baby to the world as the Son of Christ. Alas, we now have to do this without the Ark of the Covenant, but if I do become Pope, I can assure you, Mr Zinkler, that I will help you create your Universal Temple here, in Rome."

Sardis' eyes penetrated deep into Alfred's, trying to fathom his thoughts. Alfred realised that he needed an alliance between his ideals and the Church of Rome and here was a man who had obviously been misled by Al Din in the past and who was now willing to become a powerful ally, but naturally he had to consult Danielle first. He looked at her, but didn't need to say anything.

"It's alright, sir," said Danielle. "I have thought a lot about this over the last few weeks."

She turned to face the Cardinal. "Your eminence, I would rather keep my diary and my child for myself, but when I give birth to my baby and the world is really ready for this, I will consider working with you."

Sardis hadn't anticipated this answer and was overjoyed. "Young lady, will you stay with me during these six months?"

Danielle shook her head. "No, your eminence, I wish to be left in peace. I want you to let me come to you by my own choice and when the time is right, not before. In this you will just have to trust me."

Alfred was proud of her, standing up to a man who had, after all, been obsessed with his mission and had abducted her only a few months ago. He got up from his chair and offered her his arm, showing the Cardinal that they had finished talking. Sardis knew he had to let them go, but on his way out, Sardis touched Alfred's other arm. He looked at him with begging eyes and whispered, "Take care of her for me?" Alfred stared at the floor for a few seconds and then understood what he meant; the Cardinal had wiped Danielle's records and she now needed a new ID and a new home. The Swiss looked at him and nodded, after which they were all safely escorted out.

When finally he saw his chief and the rest of the group walking out of the building and into the square, Georg relaxed, but remained out of sight. For a moment, the silent group just stood there, staring at each other and at the basilica, allowing the past hour to sink in properly. Suddenly, David broke the silence and said, while rubbing his hands together, "Come on, let's get that cup of coffee!"

-32-

Rome, July 29ᵗʰ 2011

While Otto tried to explain that in Italy there are different prices for a cup of coffee - depending on *where* you plan to consume it - the little group entered one of the cafés that are situated just off St. Peter's Square. Otto frowned when they all took a seat and ordered their hot drinks, knowing that this would be the most expensive choice, but he convinced himself that he was invited anyway; another old habit that proved to die hard.

So far, this had been a fascinating summer for all of them, especially for Michael and Arthur, who had experienced the adventure of a lifetime. Although Gabby and Danielle weren't allowed to tell them all the details about their trips to ancient Judea, they could share some and forum mates Ben, Michael and Arthur were thrilled to find out that Mary Magdalene had at least planned to come to southern France. However, they had already suspected long ago that Jesus hadn't died on the cross. After all, clues to that suspicion could be seen in paintings and churches throughout Europe; even clues that Jesus had been the son of Zachary, that he had a twin brother and that Mary Magdalene had been pregnant.

Next to that, they had made some amazing discoveries themselves; the tomb of Jesus on a hilltop in southern France - with part of his mortal remains resting underneath the St. Peter's - and the probable location of the Ark of the Covenant underneath tons of rubble in an old crypt which once belonged to an old Templar chapel; a chapel that no longer existed and had been replaced by a new chapel centuries ago. The kids agreed to return there the next summer and spend an afternoon in the olive grove, just to be on the very spot. They also intended go back to the dolmen on the hill, as for them it had now become a sacred place.

They were all discussing future plans and exchanging details, when suddenly, Bill asked to speak with Alfred in private.

He had an intriguing question for him; a question that had been on his mind since the moment he had first met Rahn. Apparently, his chief had already successfully tried out the ERFAB behind his back, way before they had sent Danielle and Gabby to ancient Judea. However, he also knew that the very existence of Rahn in *this* present, leaves one problem…

"Sir, if Otto is not going back to 1939, then who's body did they find in the woods near Söll?"

Alfred smiled at Bill and understood his curiosity. According to history, Otto's decayed body had been found in the melting snow on a mountain slope in May 1939, two months after his death. If Otto were to stay in this present, there would be no dead body and Rahn's historical account should have changed. However, Alfred had found a clever way to solve that problem.

"I knew you would ask me that, Bill. I'd have been disappointed if you hadn't. You will remember the moment that Otto and I arrived back at the base after the short trip to southern France? You were being held hostage by Al Din, my agents had tried and failed to free you, but Georg had managed to take out both Kaiser and Al Din. When I arrived at the spot, the hallway was full of dead bodies. Half of them were illegals, hired by Kaiser and one of them actually looked a bit like Otto, so we moved him to the lab, removed the bullet and 'repaired' the wound. Then we dressed him in the same clothes Otto had been wearing the day I collected him; I put his passport in his pocket and then I took the body back to the exact same site where I had found Otto in 1939. I parked the corpse underneath a fir tree near the river - along with the two almost empty bottles of sleeping tablets and his half-empty bottle of French cognac that Otto had with him - and covered up my tracks. The rest has now become history."

Bill chuckled. Of course, Otto didn't know this and having overheard most of their conversation, Rahn looked at Alfred with genuine gratitude.

"Thank you Fred, for saving my life and thank you also for returning to me my *dietrich*."

Alfred understood what he meant by this. Rahn's 'dietrich', his skeleton key, was his personal talisman. This talisman helped him pass through periods of change more easily, because with this 'key' he found the strength to face the future and unlock its secrets. It had also formed Otto's source of inspiration for his Grail philosophy. This talisman was in fact a small hematite-like pebble that he had found in one of the Sabarthès caves; a pebble that had been sacred in pre-historic times because it could 'bleed'.

This, he felt, was *his* Grail...

It was time for everyone to go home, wherever that would be. For Arthur it had all been quite an experience. First of all he had accidently run into his old hero and now he couldn't live without him anymore. His friend Michael didn't know what to think of Arthur's relationship with Rahn, but they both knew they'd always remain friends, no matter what. Michael stared at his friend, who was conversing with Rahn and seemed happier than ever. Otto seemed to be a nice person and he hoped Arthur would be happy with him. Michael eavesdropped on the conversation for a while to see if he could find out what they were up to next, but Otto was talking German to Arthur and Michael could barely follow.

"So, shall we go to my hotel and pick up my bags then?" asked Arthur, hoping that Otto would still want him to stay with him.

"Fine by me. You just won't believe where I'm staying!" said Otto triumphantly. Arthur was curious to what he meant. Would he be staying in a fancy hotel? He knew that Otto had travelled through Europe in the 1930's, visiting many cities, also Rome, so he probably knew his way around.

Otto got up, finished his coffee while he stood and said his goodbyes to everybody. Closely followed by Arthur, he walked toward the exit without offering to pay, or thanking anyone for the treat. Alfred smiled.

He will never change.

Michael watched them both leave the café and it was obvious to him that Arthur wouldn't be going home. Knowing his parents would not understand, Arthur had made the decision to follow his heart, giving up not only his family by doing so, but also his education; all that for a man he hardly knew at all. Michael couldn't help being worried, but Alfred - who had noticed the boy's concern - touched his arm. "I know what you are thinking, Mike, but I believe they need each other. Art would be an amazing assistant to Otto and besides, I will keep a close eye on them."

Alfred gave him a wink and they all watched the happy ex-Nazi leaving the café with Arthur immediately behind him. Everyone waved. Still not convinced, Michael turned to Alfred. "Sir, are you sure Arthur will be okay? I mean, can Otto really be trusted?"

The Swiss smiled. "Don't worry son; Rahn's a survivor, but he's loyal to me and I trust him now. After all, he owes me his life. You know, two weeks ago he played a piece of Händel for me on my grand piano in Sion. It was incredible! He is very gifted. I will let him run around for a few weeks to enjoy his new life. Art will help him get acquainted with this modern world, but then I will call him back. I'm still his employer and there is a new mission waiting for him, which will be successful."

Michael looked at Alfred and frowned. "How do you know it will be successful?"

Alfred smiled and looked at a ring he was wearing. "Because it is already written."

They could still hear Otto and Arthur laughing and talking when they passed the window of the café. "Do you like Blues music? Armstrong; Johnson?" queried Otto.

Arthur took out his iPod. "Yeah sure, but wait till you check this out!"

The last thing they could see from behind the window of the café was Otto's face when he heard the first tunes of Eric Clapton's 'Layla'.

Alfred looked at David; his knowledge of the Knights Templar and of history in general had come in handy during their research this summer and Alfred felt that David would be a great asset to SBS-Sion. He explained to David that he was a descendant of Hugues de Payens, the first Grandmaster of the Knights Templar, who had lived in the early 12th century and hoped that this would persuade David to accept a position on the research team in Switzerland. Naturally, David was honoured by Alfred's offer and accepted it without hesitation, but then he thought about his B&B in France. He thought about Michael. Taking the job meant that he'd have to move to Switzerland and he realised that he'd then have to put their French paradise on the market. It was true; they both loved it out there, but the offer was simply impossible to refuse, especially when Alfred offered to collect Michael's horse Beauséant to be stabled with his own thoroughbreds in Sion. Still, it won't be the same. Perhaps it was better to keep it from Michael for now, he thought.

After saying goodbye, David and Michael left the café and walked back to the hotel Columbus where they were staying. The bond between father and son had never been stronger, but when Michael enthusiastically told his father about their new plans for the next summer in France, David shamefacedly looked away and unbuttoned the top of his shirt.

He would tell him, soon…

Ben and Yanne were the third couple to leave. They wanted to see the rest of Rome that weekend and then return to Girona with David and Michael. After all, Ben's car was still in the Corbières.

Bill and Gabby - who had become inseparable - also decided to stay in Rome to do a bit of sight-seeing and spend some quality time together. They would return to Sion at a later date. Not only had they fallen in love with each other, but also with the Swiss Valais district, so they had decided to make Sion their home.

Danielle's future, however, had come to a screeching halt. She had been the biggest victim throughout the entire operation. She had been abducted, her very existence had been erased by Sardis and on top of all that, she had fallen in love with the father of her child - a man who had now been dead for two thousand years; someone whose remains - or at least part of them - were buried a few hundred meters from where they were now. Deep in thought, Danielle stared out the window; feeling confused and lonely, but then, Alfred suggested something she had never expected from him. He had already played with this idea, but after meeting the Cardinal that morning, he was now dead certain that it was the right thing to do. Alfred offered to officially adopt her as his daughter and heir. The Swiss was very tactful when he brought up the subject and took her hands in his. After all, what if she said no? Perhaps Danielle was angry with him for allowing all this to happen. However, she said yes, wholeheartedly. A tearful Gabby, who had witnessed the moment, jumped up and cheered. "This is fantastic! That means we will all be together in Sion! We must celebrate!"

Gabby had been worried from the start about Danielle's future and spontaneously kissed Alfred on his cheek while he shook hands with Bill. Relieved and grateful to see their positive reactions, Alfred ordered some champagne and winked at Georg, who had followed everything from his seat, discretely huddled in a dark corner of the café.

After lunch, Gabby and Bill left to start their tour of Rome and Georg took Alfred and Danielle to the airport, where the Learjet was already waiting to take them back to Sion. This was the first time that Danielle was alone with Alfred and he realised that he now had to allow her into his private life. He had never done this with anyone before, as his private life was a complicated, secretive one.

"Danny, I would like you to know a few things about me, but you must promise to keep it confidential, even to Bill and Gabby."

"My full name is Alfred Johannis Zinkler. I was born in Geneva in Switzerland. My father had already initiated me into his secret order when I was at a young age, so I grew up, not only learning history, but also forgotten history and I quickly realised that many myths and legends have their roots in true events, or conceal a higher knowledge. In the footsteps of my father I became involved in the SBS, but in a private cell called Sion. I cannot go into detail about the SBS because then I would break my oath of silence, but I have created something new now; I have founded a Universal Temple, just like I said I would. Let me show you."

Alfred opened his laptop and went online to a web page called www.sionuniversaltemple.org. Danielle stared hard at the website. She knew that Alfred had been busy, but she also knew how much Otto's conclusions on the whereabouts of the bones of Oshu were affecting him, but when she saw his new website, she became immensely proud of her future father, because this was what it was all about: The evolution of the soul; the Great Work. Alfred watched her while she was reading and looked at her big, blue eyes and her beautiful smile. More than ever he realised who she was and what she was about to become.

"It's all about conduct you know," he continued, "conquering negative emotions like egoism; hatred; intolerance; anger; jealousy and replacing them by positive emotions such as love; understanding; compassion; tolerance; peace; service and soul growth through study and conduct."

Danielle nodded in agreement, but she wondered what was so special about the name 'Sion'. "I see that you have named the Universal Temple after Sion. Why would you do that? It's just a city in Switzerland."

"Not really. Of course, it is where I live; it's my base, but the name mainly refers to Mount Zion in Jerusalem and to my ancestor; Hugues de Payens; the founder of the Order of Our Lady of Sion. The word 'Sion' is derived from the ancient word 'Cyon', which means 'centre' and the centre is where the soul is. Where God is. It is the true content of the Grail;

the dot inside the circle and the square. The Lady of Sion is the Lady of the Grail."

Danielle became excited now that the penny dropped. She remembered Oshu's lessons about the square being the earth, the circle being the All and the dot in the centre. He had called the circle 'Abwoon', but the dot as well. Abwoon was the name he had given to God. It represented the plural; the female and male principle in One - Father and Mother.

Danielle pointed at the screen. "You have also used a dot, here, in the logo of the Universal Temple. Can you explain what you mean with this logo?"

"Yes of course. You see how the U forms the cup; the Grail? The left arm of the U ends in a snake, representing the Kundalini energy and the mother goddess reaching for the sun. The snake also protects the Grail, like the cobra symbol protected the pharaohs of ancient Egypt. The T is the Tau cross, representing the male energies and esoteric teachings. The four lines which are added to the T create a Djed pillar, an Egyptian symbol that stands for soul growth. The dot underneath represents the soul that lies at its base as a servant to Creation. The colours represent the Beauséant; the Knights Templar flag, which was a reminder to all knights to be gentlemen; to be fair. No matter how fierce the battle might be, one should always behave like a true knight. My Universal Temple is against violence and force, so in this case, the colours represent Boaz and Jachin; the black and white pillars of the Temple of Solomon, symbolising the balance of the female and male principles of God, without which there would be no earth. Now you may also understand why the female principle is sometimes represented by the black Isis or the Black Madonna, as this black goddess refers to the black, female pillar of the Temple; Boaz."

Danielle sighed. It was a lot to take in, but she was impressed with the purity of the new concept, which she hoped would inspire many people.

"How can one become a member?" she queried.

"If you follow the lines of conduct, you already are a member, because then you belong to the invisible society of kindred spirits. There is no membership; no membership fee; just good conduct. These guidelines are created to elevate humanity and enable us to react differently this time when the Great Wave comes. It is also of the utmost importance that we take good care of God's Bride; our planet; it's elements and its flora and fauna, as we are responsible for her wellbeing."

Gabby had told Danielle that Alfred had spoken about a Great Wave. The first signs were already there; with so much commotion in the world and increasingly violent natural disasters. It's now up to humanity to change the outcome for the united human soul. Danielle put her arms around Alfred's broad neck and rested her cheek against his.

"I am so proud of you and so grateful that you will have me as your daughter. My baby will have the best of all grandfathers."

He smiled and cherished this tender moment. Alfred had a lot to show her and was looking forward to bringing her home.

Sion, Switzerland, September 18th 2011

The months had passed quickly. Alfred possessed a beautiful estate in the hills just outside Sion and because Gabby and Bill had been able to buy a house in the city centre, they visited each other often. The experiences in ancient Judea had changed the women; the way they dressed; what they ate and how they behaved. They frequently burned incense, myrrh and candles and enjoyed dancing on Skarazula's Kürdilihicazkar Longa, a specific song from a CD that Arthur had sent them. This song reminded them of that last night in Bethanu, when they all danced, even Oshu.

During their last visit to ancient Judea, Danielle had adorned the cover of her diary, using all natural materials from the area. It had become their most treasured souvenir.

Then, on a beautiful, hot day in August, David had arrived from France, bringing with him all his belongings. Alfred had already sent for Michael's horse Beauséant, which had arrived a few days in advance. Danielle had watched David settle into the gate house and was overjoyed to see him again. Alfred secretly hoped that they would find each other. It is important for people - especially when they are expected to carry out heavy duties - to be with a twin soul; to experience the power and the magic of the Two who become One. After all, Deus and Dio - both names for God - is merely Latin and Greek for the number 2; the male *and* female principles of God, *within* the one deity. Alfred himself had always been alone, without a partner at his side and he always felt painfully lonely. However, while David and Alfred had soon become good friends, it was still difficult for Danielle to allow David into her heart and Alfred knew it just needed time. Of course, David had not yet been told anything about the father of the child; all he saw was the beautiful woman he had fallen in love with in Rome. Being realistic, he didn't think he'd ever be able to win her heart or understand her deep secrets, or even whether she would ever share these with him; he just knew she was special and so he kept a respectful distance. Hoping, dreaming…

Alfred loved showing Danielle around his house, which was full of memorabilia from many centuries of history and mystery. He didn't show it to her all at once, but in stages and this morning he had shown her the golden Goral - an ancient heirloom once given to a Judean Prince - that had been in his family for many generations.

This afternoon, Alfred showed her into a special room that was entirely dedicated to the Templars. With wide eyes she looked at the old paintings and the Templar flags and swords. There was a beautiful ring that had once belonged to Hugues de Payens himself and a mural, showing his original coat of arms with the three Moorish heads. Danielle studied the coat of arms and frowned. "Why are there three Moorish heads on the coat of arms of Hugues de Payens?"

Alfred was surprised she recognised the Moorish heads. "Well, although there is a connection with Corsica, my ancestor Hugues had black hair and a dark complexion, like Allesandro de Medici, who was nicknamed *Il Moro*. This became Hugues' original coat of arms."

Danielle stared at the blonde Swiss. "Hmm... there isn't much of his dark complexion in you!"

Both laughed. "No, after 900 years of mixing blood and a blonde, blue eyed mother..."

They continued their tour around the room and studied the ancient coins; hats; clothes; medals; books; scrolls and robes that were on display. It was like walking through a museum. Then, Danielle spotted an ancient book, bound with wood and iron, with rusted locks and hinges and she could just make out an engraved symbol of two pyramids connected by their base to form an abstract diamond. She pointed at it. "Isn't that the symbol of the Illuminati?"

Again, Alfred was surprised she knew this and smiled proudly at her. However, growing up in the States, Danielle realised how this old name, that had once belonged to a peaceful, enlightened order of mystics, had now been misused to name the elite that seemed to rule the world with their vast amounts of money and power. This misuse of the old name had now irreversibly polluted the worldly reputation of the original Illuminati.

She became sad. "It's a pity that the old order no longer exists."

"Oh, but we are very much alive today…"

"We?" queried Danielle, slightly surprised.

Alfred winked at her. He would tell her soon enough that the true, original Illuminati have always been in the background, trying with love and tenderness to spread the Hermetic Teachings throughout the world and help create world peace. The *real* Illuminati have never been violent and never will be, as they represent peace, love and soul-growth.

However, there was no time to get into it now, as Alfred had something important to show her. He led her toward one of the walls of the large, somewhat dark room and showed her a copy of the altarpiece of the Adoration of the Lamb by Van Eyck, of which the original can be seen in Ghent, Belgium.

"Look; what do you see in 'The Hermits'? and then I mean *this* bit, next to the painting of the lamb." Alfred pointed at a detail and although Danielle had to look really carefully, she startled when she saw her; a blonde woman standing next to Mariamne, while they were watching a group of men passing by from behind a rock. She couldn't believe it; that woman could have been her twin sister! "This is very weird, Alfred, how could anyone know?"

"Maybe you did go into history after all." said Alfred, who had already noticed the woman appearing on the painting months ago, right after their second journey to ancient Judea and even in books she was already there, as if she had always been in this painted scene. Danielle stared at the painting and touched her belly. A disturbing thought entered her mind. "Do you really think the world will end in 2012?"

Alfred sighed. "The world is nothing more than a bridge between spiritual planes, Danielle. Only God knows if it will stand the force of the Great Wave, but if it does, then it means that there will be a new Covenant between God and mankind and new hope, but I happen to know of at least *one* person who had high hopes!"

Alfred carefully unrolled a small piece of parchment that had been written in ancient Greek.

Danielle froze. "Is this from Oshu?"

Alfred nodded. "He had actually asked Gabby to give it to you when you had both reached your destiny."

Danielle remembered the sea voyage to Egypt, when Gabby had asked her what 'pepromeno' meant. Destiny…

With pounding heart she tried to read the text, but she started to tremble and tears were beginning to prick her eyes, so it became impossible for her to read the words. Danielle gave it to Alfred. "Read it for me, please… what does it say?"

Alfred took a deep breath; he too was now getting emotional. He reached for his pocket, took out another piece of paper with the text already translated into English and read it out to her. It wasn't easy for him to keep a straight voice.

> *"Dearest one, my Myriam Dani El,*
> *blessings to you and our unborn child.*
> *You must call her Deborah,*
> *in honour of our most honourable order,*
> *and raise her in our teachings and ways.*
> *Peace unto you both.*
> *I will be forever with you.*
> *Oshu* ▲ ▼ "

She tenderly kissed the palm of her hand where Oshu had planted his kiss and laughed through her tears. Then she hugged Alfred and exclaimed, "It's a *girl*…!"

Acknowledgements

This book would not have been possible without the research and/or assistance of the following people:

Henry Lincoln, Jean-Luc Robin, Theo Patocka, Andy Andrews, Jean-Bob Ildanach, Graham Hancock, Klaas van Urk, Kevin Thaelemans, Crichton Miller, Erik van Leenders, Anne Mie Pigelet Tacq, Jack Lawson, Ms. E. Couquet, Mr. M. Mounié, Nigel Graddon, Richard Stanley, Tim Wallace-Murphy, Chev. Simon de Saint-Claire (OSMTH*), Ankie Nolen, Ian Campbell, Rosicrucian Order AMORC**, Ms Baiden, Peter van Deursen and others who have expressed their wish to remain anonymous. You know who you are.

Last but not least I would like to thank my muses for their inspiration and insight. It was an honour to be your 'hands'.

*The OSMTH is an active and modern ecumenical Confraternal Order that seeks to address the very real needs of today's world. Such work is often carried out in partnership with and for the benefit of other faiths, creeds and ethnic backgrounds.
Their mission consists of humanitarian aid, human rights, interfaith dialogue, peace-building and sustainable development. More: osmth.org

**The Rosicrucian Order AMORC is a community of Seekers who study and practice the metaphysical laws governing the universe. More: Rosicrucian.org

Also from this author:

www.jeannedaout.com

For over 35 years I have been researching the hidden history of mankind and its religious and cultural path through the past. I have visited many countries including Italy, Greece, Turkey, Israel and Egypt, just to be able to sense its soul.

However, it wasn't until we settled on Occitan soil that I truly understood the deeper secrets of mankind. I discovered how rich this area is, how important its role was throughout history and still is. Sometimes I would find clues to major enigmas without even looking; all I had to do was to follow the breadcrumbs.

How mysterious are the ways in which we are led to discoveries, truths and the path we need to set foot on.

With this book I would like to share my findings - as well as some of the teachings that I have found illuminating - with as many people as possible and help heal a few wrongly damaged reputations while I am at it.

Naturally, the story is my brain child and entirely fictional.

… Or is it? ;-)

Jeanne D'Août

A pregnant Mary Magdalene standing at the cross in Alet-les-Bains and an aging Jesus above the main entrance of the Villa Bethania in Rennes-le-Château, France.

14th century fresco by Lorenzo and Jacopo Salimbeni. Elizabeth gives Mary to Zacharias to produce his heir. Note the squares around the heads of Zacharias and Elizabeth. These squares tell us that they were married. Also note the pregnant woman behind Mary. She makes a gesture which in art symbolises holy union or sexual intercourse.

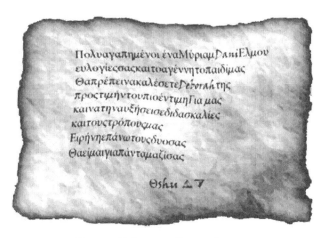

Copy of the small parchment

The drawing by Edmund Boudet of one of the *dolmens,*
with the German SS stamp in the bottom left corner.

"The Hermits' is one of the 24 parts of the altarpiece called 'The Adoration of the Mystic Lamb', which was completed by Jan van Eyck in 1432. This masterpiece was painted for Jodocus Vijdts and his wife Elisabeth Borluut and can be seen in the Cathedral of St. Bavo in Ghent, Belgium.

Jan van Eyck was the leading painter of his time and became famous for his attention to detail. It also has a history of theft. First in 1934, when two fragments were stolen and second during WWII when the entire piece was stolen by the Nazi's. It is a small miracle that the painting returned to Ghent in one piece.

Otto Wilhelm Rahn, author of 'Crusade Against the Grail' and 'Lucifer's Court', was born in Michelstadt, Germany in 1904. Being a researcher of myth and legend he was interested in the origins of European religion. He fell in love with Occitania and the Cathars of the Middle Ages.

As a member of the SS he worked for Himmler as a relic hunter and researcher of Arian origins. However, he had been terribly shocked when he discovered the violence of Hitler's Nazi Germany. In the Spring of 1939, his body was found, frozen in the snow in the mountains near Söll, Austria.

He had taken his own life.

ABWOON
Abwoon d'bwasmaja. Nitkadesj sjmach.
Abwoon d'bwasmaja. Nitkadesj sjmach.
Teetee malkoetach, Neghwee tsevjanach
Ajkana d'bwasjmaja af b'arhah

Habwlan lachma d'soenkanan jaomana
Wasjbooklan cha-oebween ajkanna daf chnan
sj-bwokan l'chajabeen Wela taghlan-l'nesjoena

Ela patsan min biesja. Metol dillachie malkoeta
waghajla watesjboechta l'oghlam
Almien, Ameen

All-Father-Mother
All-Father-Mother,
All One of the All and in the All
Holy and secret are Your names
You live in activity and Light
Let Your desire be with mine, here now and in the All
Touch me, feed me with your astonishment
To fulfil Your desire
My surrender to You, the other and the All.
Accept me, that I am not yet whole,
Not yet connected to You
Forgive me my hesitant effort to connect myself with You
As I accept my fellow-man
His being un-whole, his being un-healed.
Lead me away from show and ignorance
And free me of what keeps me from the Light
Because in You and from You
Is the Light, the power and the Life
Here, now and for ever
Amen

The Cathar Creed

It has no membership, save those who know they belong.
It has no rivals because it is non-competitive.
It has no ambition - it seeks only to serve.
It knows no boundaries, for nationalisms are unloving.
It is not of itself because it seeks to enrich all groups and religions.
It acknowledges all great teachers of all the ages who have shown the truth of love.
Those who participate, practice the truth of love in all their being.

There is no walk of life or nationality that is a barrier.
Those who are, know.
It seeks not to teach, but to be, and by being, enriched.
It recognizes that the way we are may be the way of those around us because we are that way.
It recognizes the whole planet as a being of which we are a part.
It recognizes that the time has come for the supreme transmutation, the ultimate alchemical act of conscious change of the ego in to a voluntary return to the whole.
It does not proclaim itself with a loud voice, but in the subtle realms of loving.

It salutes all those in the past who have blazoned the path, but have paid the price.
It admits no hierarchy or structure, for no one is greater than another.
Its members shall know each other by their deeds and being, and by their eyes and by no other outward sign, save the fraternal embrace.
Each one will dedicate their life to the silent loving of their neighbour and environment, and the planet, will carry out their task, however exalted or humble.

It recognizes the supremacy of the great idea, which may only be accomplished if the human race practices the supremacy of love.

It has no reward to offer, either here or in the hereafter, save that of the ineffable joy of being and loving.

Each shall seek to advance the cause of understanding, doing good by stealth and teaching only by example.

They shall heal their neighbour, their community, our planet and living beings in whatever form they take.

They shall know no fear and feel no shame and their witness shall prevail over all odds.

It has no secret, no Arcanum, no initiation, save that of true understanding of the power of love and that, if we want it to be so, the world will change, but only if we change.

All who belong, belong; they belong to the Church of Love.

Source unknown

42059591R00205

Made in the USA
Charleston, SC
18 May 2015